The Cooks.

RENEGADE SKYFARER

STONES OF TERRENE CHRONICLES

BOOK ONE

May you always
remember who you are
& where you've been.

R.J. METCALF

Proverbs 16:9

To Mike, the one who first daydreamed this amazing world.
Thank you for sharing it with me and making this entire series a dream
come true for both of us.

ACKNOWLEDGMENTS

This book and series is truly a labor of love, and like all labors of love, there's a host of people supporting the production and the insanity behind it all.

I have to give a huge thank you to my mom and dad for all the sleepovers they've had with my boys. Keeping those two energetic monkeys content can be quite the challenge, and I appreciate your sacrifice of sanity for me to have a quiet house to write in.

This would never have happened if God hadn't arranged for me to meet Jamie Foley through a chance online encounter. Through that, a friendship blossomed between Fire Nation West and Fire Nation South that rocked all semblance of sanity. Jamie, if you hadn't pushed for us to start writing, I doubt Mike and I would've considered this endeavor for at least another decade. Thank you for being stubborn.

Thank you to my paladin "framily," who let me bounce ideas at random times (oftentimes interrupting other nerdiness going on), and who kept me encouraged and excited about this project even on days where I was feeling at my wits' end. Never forget: *One must die.*

Huge shout-out to my beta team for all their help with pointing out rough patches and letting me know when I was getting too gross in my bloody descriptions: Karen, Lizzy, Scott, Abbey, Janine, Kathy, Amy Grace, Josh, and Hannah, y'all rock. *Renegade Skyfarer* would not be what it is today without your insights!

And my amazing, patient, bloody-brilliant production team: Jamie Foley, C. W. Briar, Bryan Wark, Eric Sasina, S. D. Grimm, LoriAnn Weldon, Janeen Ippolito, H. A. Titus, Sara White, and Julia Busko.

You took this rock of a book and noob of an author and worked us into a polished gem. Thank you.

And all glory to God in the Highest, the Ultimate Author of All.

PROLOGUE

Chilly predawn wind cut through Blade's patched coat. His toes ached from the numbing cold that seeped through his worn boots, but he couldn't leave the observation deck of the airship. Not even if he wanted to.

Master stood in front of Blade, deliberating with the first mate, Lupin. Shadows added depth to Lupin's scowl as he shoved his hands under his arms.

"I'm leaving." Crystal lamps illuminated Master's angular face, showcasing inky hair that rippled in the winter breeze. "I have a mission of utmost importance." He settled a black bowler hat on his head and snugged it down, trapping flyaway strands.

Lupin nodded, the leather straps on his air-cap swinging with the motion. "Yessir." His gaze darted past Master to rest on Blade. Caution and a hint of hatred reflected in Lupin's pupils. "Are you taking him with you?"

Blade tightened his eyes and stared back at Lupin. *Like you care.*

"No, I'll be going alone." Master half-turned to regard Blade with a slanted eyebrow. Then Master pulled something small from his white coat pocket with a detached flourish and pivoted back to

Lupin. A finely wrought silver bracelet of woven metals with an inlaid red gem rested in Master's open palm. He held it out to Lupin. "It'll give you the same type of control over Blade that I have, but my controller overrides yours. Don't get any ideas."

No. Get ideas.

"Thank you, sir." Lupin slipped the thin band over his wrist and inspected the gem with a critical eye. "And it will work? Even with you wearing yours?"

"Try it and find out."

Lupin grinned and gestured at Blade with a lazy flick of his wrist. "Polish my boots with your shirt."

Blade barely had time to relish the resentment that warmed his gut before a familiar haze rose from the edges of his mind and pushed his emotions aside. It moved him forward without conscious thought to kneel before Lupin. He shrugged off his jacket and his shirt, shivering when the icy air bit into his skin. He scrubbed his last clean shirt against Lupin's mud-caked boots while his teeth chattered.

Lupin chuckled as he pushed his boot toward Blade's face. "I could get used to this. How long do you expect your mission to take, sir?"

"A few months, at least." The deck vibrated underfoot as Master paced. He pivoted, and his heel squeaked on the worn wood of the airship deck. "I need you to keep searching for that bloodstone–it's the centerpiece of my plans for the barrier."

Memories of blood, wavering curtains of light, and pain, so much pain, flashed through Blade's mind at the mention of the bloodstone. He hunched over Lupin's boots for a long heartbeat before the weight of the command bracelet faded the flashback. He shuffled sideways on the ground to better reach the heel of Lupin's boot.

"I'm hoping this mission will provide some clues or a lead," Master continued, "but I expect you men to keep at your jobs."

"Beggin' your pardon, sir, but if you aren't here, on board, sir, what do you want us to be doing?" Lupin asked. His hand slipped down to his sword hilt. "Perhaps we get to have some honest thieving?"

Boots finally clean, Blade settled on his haunches and waited as the haze of compulsion faded away like mist in the sunlight. He grimaced at his filthy shirt and shook it out before slipping it back on. *Because thieving is honest?*

Master shrugged. "Continue moving cargo and search for anything that may interest me. If you decide to pirate, don't get caught. I'll be in contact, in case you find anything useful."

Lupin gripped his sword belt and offered a half bow. "Yessir."

"And don't use Blade recklessly," Master added in a firm tone.

Blade looked over his shoulder into Master's dark eyes. It was like looking into the depths of the Aerugan Hollows—deep, dark, and deadly.

"He's my masterpiece, and more important than you will ever know."

CHAPTER ONE

BEN

Pain woke Ben. The disembodied screaming surrounding him ensured he'd stay awake.

His head throbbed like waves crashing against rocks on a shoreline, and his heart pounded as if he'd been swimming against the current for hours. Even through his closed eyelids, the light was too bright, amplifying the agony throbbing in his limbs. He groaned and twisted his face away, moaning as nausea swept over him. He lay on a firm, yet soft, surface. The whole bed vibrated lightly, and he could barely make out the distant whine of machinery over the sounds of yelling, clanking, and roaring.

Where am I?

After a few deep breaths, he slitted his eyes open and widened them while they adjusted. Sunlight streamed in through a closed glass pane window. He was in a medical room, as evidenced by the skull on the shelf, an oddly colored diagram of the nervous system, and a tray of wicked-looking metal instruments. Pine walls held a variety of other charts—skeletal, muscular, and something full of colors and stones that he'd never seen before. Darker wood shelves displayed different colored rocks of various sizes.

A plunking sound startled him, and he realized he wasn't alone. A black-haired man in a calf-length white coat stood with his back to Ben. He opened drawers and dropped medical tools on the counter with a smooth haste.

A tingle wormed its way up Ben's spine. *How did I get here?*

The unfamiliar man glanced over his shoulder, and his dark eyes widened. "You're up."

Ben swallowed hard and cleared his throat of what felt like gravel. "I...yes."

The man strode closer and leaned over Ben. "Is your name Dubray?" He tapped against Ben's chest, pointing out the neatly stitched name on his thick jacket.

"I think so." Ben sat up, wincing. Something under his shirt jingled with the movement, and he fished out a silver chain. Fastened to it was a delicate silver ring with three diamonds in a row, and a rectangular plate with smoothed edges. Small gaps ran lengthwise through the metal, as though it was designed to be snapped into two pieces. He angled it in the light and read aloud, "Dubray, Benjamin. Twenty fifteen." He frowned. "I go by Ben, I think." Why was his own name fuzzy?

"Mmhmm." The doctor nodded as he pulled down on Ben's bottom eyelid, looking first in one eye, then the next. "I'm Jaxton, the doctor here on board the *Sapphire*. Do you know where you are?" He held up a yellow-toned finger before Ben could reply and continued, "Focus on this, please. You seem to be fairly healthy, aside from all your cuts and scrapes and that metal blob I removed from your leg."

Ben blinked away the dizziness from following Jaxton's finger and looked down to see a bandage wrapping his calf and his bloody pant leg neatly rolled up above his knee. The bizarre situation seemed to be spiraling beyond any semblance of control, and his head throbbed with confusion. Should he admit to how little he was following this conversation, or should he pretend he knew what Jaxton was talking about? He chose the former. "A metal what?"

Jaxton nodded toward a second tray on the counter. A bloody metallic ball sat in the shallow dish. "I pulled it out and performed a light healing to reduce the swelling. I did add stitches to give it more support. Take it easy for a few days." Jaxton folded his arms and cocked his head. "Where are you from? How did you get that in you? Why were you so close to a dragon nest in the Wyld Woods, and unarmed?"

Something about the shiny lump itched at Ben's mind with a distant air of familiarity. But trying to conjure answers made his head hurt even more. A yell from beyond the door brought a fresh cascade of pain over his tired brain. "I-I don't know. What's going on out there? What's the *Sapphire*?"

Jaxton leaned against the counter and crossed his ankles as he surveyed Ben. "You don't have a concussion. I can tell you that much. The *Sapphire* is an airship that covers a wide range of jobs—import, export, dragon hunting, and the random odd job here or there." Jaxton shrugged and twirled a pen across his fingers. "We're near the Perennian border currently. Do you know where that is?"

Dragon hunting? The *what* border? "No. I don't think I've ever heard of it." Ben squeezed his eyes shut before opening them again in an attempt to better focus on the clean white countertop closest to him. The sharpness of the headache began to fade. If only the commotion outside would die down, too.

The door banged open behind Ben, and he jumped. Colors

kaleidoscoped, and he scrambled to grab the lip of the bed to brace himself while the room spun.

"What happened?" Jaxton hustled around the bed. "Are there terrors out there, too?"

"Of course there are terrors," a female voice snapped. "When are there not terrors during a dragon attack? This is the kind of day where everything goes wrong!"

Ben turned slowly, trying not to aggravate the resurgent throbbing in his head. Jaxton snorted and helped settle an attractive, chocolate-skinned young woman onto the table by Ben. Something about her clothing—a burgundy blouse, ebony half-bodice, and thick brown pants—struck him as unusual, though he couldn't say why. She hissed through her teeth as she sank down and clutched her arm to her chest. Her blood-soaked jacket slid off her arm to reveal horrid gashes surrounded by burned flesh that wept blood and clear fluid.

A second woman hovered nearby, her blue eyes wide. She wiped a streak of blood onto her grease-stained khaki pants and gestured at her injured friend. "Do something!"

Jaxton muttered under his breath as he pulled out a basket overflowing with gauze and bandages from the cabinet. He glanced back at Ben, set the basket on the counter, and then reached for a tray of gleaming tools. "Memory loss. It'll likely return within a few hours or weeks. You're free to go when you want. But don't wander by a dragon nest. I'm not fixing you up again just because you don't remember anything."

Ben dipped his chin in a slow nod. "Yessir. Thank you." The room no longer curved around him as he turned his head, but he wasn't about to test his legs. Not with the two newcomers watching. Besides, it wasn't like he remembered anything yet or had anywhere to go.

Black braids framed the injured woman's face while she grimaced and held her flayed arm. The other woman stood against the wall, her bearing as regal as an avenging angel. No, falling in front of these two beauties was *not* an option. He slid down on the bench, away from the injured woman, in an effort to show consideration for her privacy.

The other woman paced to stand in front of Ben, and she dipped her head forward, her milk-white face inches from his. Freckles lightly dotted a galaxy across her cheeks and nose, and strands of red hair waved in the air from her sudden movement. "So, you're awake." She shook her head and straightened, crossing her arms while raising an elegant eyebrow. "Lucky you. You missed all the excitement."

"Be nice," the woman next to Ben said, her voice pinched in pain as Jaxton cut the sleeve away from her arm. She shot Ben a small grimace, her large brown eyes glimmering with unshed tears. "Jade's a she-dragon when worried. Ignore her."

"Am not!" Jade protested. "And I'm allowed to be worried. You got slashed *and* burned!"

Ben stared in horrified fascination as blood welled up in her broken flesh. Jaxton wiped it away with a clean cloth. The skin around the gashes was charred into crispy, black flakes. He chewed on his tongue to regain some moisture in his mouth. "What happened?"

The injured woman bit back a shriek, and Jade's voice cracked. "A terror."

The doctor held a basin under the woman's arm and poured water over the injury as if deaf to her whimpers.

Jade swallowed hard, and her eyelids fluttered shut. She clenched her fists. "I stabbed it, but not before it shocked Krista."

Krista sucked in a sharp breath, tears pouring down her cheeks as Jaxton blotted away the excess water. He frowned and replaced the metal pitcher and basin on the counter, then pulled a light pink stone from his white coat and held it over Krista's arm. His brow furrowed as he half closed his eyes. He exhaled deeply and splayed his fingers, stroking the air just above her injuries. Her swollen flesh sank down to match the smooth skin of the rest of her arm. She shook and shuddered, taking deep, calming breaths.

Ben pulled back from the two, slack-jawed. His skin crawled and the hairs on the back of his neck rose as Jaxton continued his silent ministrations. What was happening? Ben subtly pinched his arm and winced. *Not dreaming.*

"We'll stitch it together after the burns have healed a bit more," Jaxton said as he straightened. "Too much at once isn't a good idea for this type of injury." He turned to the door, and only then did Ben notice the lack of chaotic noise outside. Jaxton's lips quirked. "Enough time has passed. I expect it should be safe to go out now." He looked to Jade. "Poke your head out and see if they're done."

Jade pushed away from the wall she'd settled against and nodded toward Krista. "I'll let your boyfriend know you'll be fine."

"No. I'm not fine," Krista muttered. Her eyes gleamed. "Tell him that I'm in horrible agony and only his cinnamon spice cookies will soothe my pain."

Jade snorted. "As long as you'll share whatever he makes."

"You know it."

Ben's head and stomach settled. Listening to their banter lightened the oppressive feeling in his chest. But he couldn't help his jittering nerves after witnessing the strange magic that Jaxton had performed on Krista's arm. *I gotta get out of here.* He cautiously slid off the medical bed and gestured at Jade. "I'll go with you."

Maybe I'll remember something. Anything.

Ben stepped out of the medical room and into an enclosed hallway that stretched to his right, where a frigid breeze flowed from a tiny open window. He shivered. To his left, just beyond the dim hallway and Jade, an open deck and blue sky beckoned. His leg ached, but not as much as he'd expected. Still, he walked cautiously behind Jade. Overdoing it and falling while she was watching was not going to happen. He wouldn't let it happen.

He touched the wood slats of the wall and rubbed his fingers together, brow furrowed. *Why can't I remember anything? Should everything feel as foreign as it does?*

Though weak, the sunshine blinded him as Jade led him out from under the covered hall. Ben shielded his eyes and waited for them to adjust. Once they did, he took in the stairs on his side of the deck, the metal hand rail that ran along the edges, the other set of stairs on the other side—were those *trees* that brushed the far side of the deck from *below?*

Then he saw the beast.

It looked like what might happen if a lizard and a bat mated. A terrifyingly huge scaled lizard and equally large bat. Large, leathery wings met in a body covered by tiny, chitinous plates. Oversized metallic talons larger than Ben's open hand adorned small paws. The claws shone in the sunlight. He dimly registered Jade's voice as he gaped at the corpse. The sensation of drowning in the unknown crashed over him.

A bald man in pin-striped pants and a short-collared shirt with a matching pin-striped vest knelt by the scaled thing and set a wooden chest by his knee. He held a clear vial to the creature's neck and slowly filled it with black blood.

Ben swallowed and tore his gaze away, searching for Jade. She stood by the outdoor staircase, her back to him.

"Jade, what is he—" Ben's words died in his throat when he noticed a dark-haired man behind her.

Ben's neck tingled as the stranger glared at him. The man said something too low for Ben to hear and pressed a hand against Jade's shoulder, pushing her aside—all without breaking eye contact with Ben. The stranger held a black-and-silver sword, its edge gleaming against the layers of black he wore.

Like an inky stain in water, the swordsman flowed forward, leading with his blade.

Ben instinctively rocked his weight to the left to dodge, hand raising as if he could block a sword strike. Searing pain raced up his leg from the strained stitches, and he stumbled to his knees.

Something whooshed over Ben's head. He twisted in time to see the stranger stab the empty air where Ben had been moments prior. The sword struck something unseen. Blood dripped down the blade, over the hilt, and onto the man's gloved hand. Tendons strained in the man's neck as he struggled to maintain his grip against the nothingness.

He twitched toward Ben. "Get back!"

The warrior kicked at the air, and a huge, scaled creature blurred into view. Massive jaws, powerful tail, covered in scales. Ben couldn't believe what he was seeing. Goosebumps broke out over his arms.

Could that be a dragon?

It snapped at the man, missing his face by inches. The man snarled and yanked a dagger from his belt, and drove it into the beast's glittering eye. The dragon reared back with a roar, and the swordsman pulled his sword from its shoulder. He sliced across its scaled throat. It dropped.

Ben scrambled on hands and heels back toward the comparative safety of the hallway where Jade waited. Magic rocks, and now invisible dragons?

Jade knelt, her gaze on the warrior even as she spoke to Ben. "That was close. Are you hurt?"

"I'll be fine." Ben clenched his jaw as he stood and tested his weight on his leg. *I am so not fine.* It didn't feel like he'd popped the stitches, but his leg throbbed with every breath. He'd have to really take it easy now. His heart thumped at the near miss, and he nodded to the creature where the black swordsman stood. "What was that?"

The man wiped his sword on a dark cloth and slid the blade home in its scabbard. He rubbed the back of his hand against his jaw, leaving a crimson streak. "That was a stalker, and you're lucky to be alive." He looked past Ben and dipped his head, wearing a small frown. "If you're out on the deck, please be alert for any more attacks, Jade. I think that was the last one, but there's no guarantee." He looked back toward the med-room. "How's Krista?"

"She'll be fine. But I'm supposed to tell Briar that she's dying and that she needs cookies."

The man smirked briefly. "If she's thinking of cookies, she'll survive." He crossed his arms and appraised Ben without saying anything.

"Doctor Taylor sent us out to see if it was over." Jade clapped a hand on Ben's shoulder. "He offered to come with me."

Ben nodded, unsure of what to say. It wasn't quite hostility that radiated from the swordsman, but it distinctly wasn't friendliness.

"Zak, meet..." Jade paused and looked at Ben, her brows drawn together. "I never got your name."

"Ben."

She flashed him a quick smile and turned back to Zak. "Meet Ben."

Zak nodded a greeting. He dropped his arms and looped his thumbs in his belt, subtly showcasing the dagger on one hip and sword on the other. "Not from around here, are you?"

A crewmember dressed in a bright, headache-inducing ensemble of clashing greens, oranges, and pinks joined them and nodded to the stalker bleeding over the deck. "Hey, Zak, help me drain it before it makes more of a mess."

Zak nodded and shot Ben a look as he turned away. "Yeah, of course."

Jade pressed her lips together and sighed through her nose, then offered Ben a grin that didn't touch her eyes. "Let's find my father."

Once again, Ben found himself being escorted by the petite woman. He stepped cautiously over the crimson and black blood swirled on the deck, unwilling to be the one responsible for leaving sticky footprints.

Jade led him to the staircase, and he gritted his teeth as he followed her up. Each step sent sharp pain shooting up his leg, but he wasn't going to complain about her quick pace. He'd lived through worse. He couldn't remember what exactly, but his body told him this wasn't as bad as he'd experienced before.

The top of the stairs revealed another open deck at the bow of what he realized was a large airship. A blast of wind cut through his clothing as if it were gauze. He could now see over the metal railing that lined the deck. There wasn't a lick of water in sight. Instead, thick green trees reached toward the sky, their tops brushing the edge of the upper deck. Not even those looked familiar.

Jade gestured to a brunet man that strode toward them with goggles hanging loose around his neck and a sword at his hip. "My father, Captain Slate Stohner."

Captain Stohner nodded to Ben as the bald man in pin-stripes, whom Ben had seen earlier, clattered up the steps behind them.

Jade lifted a hand toward him. "And the first mate, Victor," she added.

Ben shifted to face them both squarely and licked his dry lips. "Ben."

Captain Stohner cocked his head at Ben and crossed his arms over his blood-splattered, sleeveless burgundy jacket. "You're lucky to be alive, you know that?"

Ben nodded. "So I've heard. The doctor says I have memory loss." He rubbed his thumb against his index finger, and walked to the edge of the deck rail to point down to where Zak was helping the crew member haul the stalker to an embedded lower staircase. "Jaxton said I was found by a dragon nest. Was I—was I with something like that when you found me?"

Victor peered over the rail and bobbed his head. "With a stalker? No, if you'd been unconscious by a stalker, you would have been dead. We found you by the lake, close to a nest of plodders." A frown creased Victor's brow. "Not exactly the smartest of places to sleep.

And in winter, no less."

Ben frowned and shook his head as he rubbed the worn metal railing with his thumb. "I don't remember being there. Or why I was there."

"Quite a ways from any cities, too." Victor wiped a black speck on his pants and gestured to Ben. "While we're at it, where are you from?"

Ben looked down at the shades of khaki, green, and brown that mingled together on his matching pants and stiff shirt, then at the elegantly casual outfits the other men wore. "I don't know." He caught the skeptical glance Victor and Slate exchanged and forced himself to not clench his fists. Pain radiated up his leg with each breath, and he wanted to finish this soon—without them deciding he wasn't worth their trouble. "I honestly don't remember. I'm sorry."

Captain Stohner squinted at Ben for a long moment, looked askance at Jade, and nodded slowly. "It'll be all right, son. Give it some time."

Victor raised an eyebrow, then shrugged. He directed his attention to the captain, ignoring Ben. "Now we have two stalkers to drag to the coolers, and we haven't even left to search yet. What's your plan?"

The captain grimaced. "The sooner we're out of here, the better. I want our standard setup for teams, and as fast as possible. For this, I want you on one team, and I'll lead the other." He gestured to the expanse of thick trees beyond the airship. "We've already covered the southeast. This time, we'll start where we left off in the south and work our way clockwise."

Ben shifted, and his leg protested. He stumbled and caught his grip on the rail, closing his eyes and focusing on breathing through the pain.

A firm hand rested on his shoulder, and he straightened as best he could.

Concern shone in Captain Stohner's eyes. "You've been through quite a bit. We have a mission to complete here, then we'll be on our way. You're welcome to hitch a ride to Doldra with us, if you'd like."

From the inflection the captain used on the word "Doldra," Ben could only assume that was home, or some equally special place. It didn't sound familiar, and he had to resist the urge to shrug. He'd agree to anything at this point, just for the opportunity to get off his leg. "Sounds good. Thank you."

A smile split Captain Stohner's face. He nodded to Jade. "She can take you down to the crew quarters. Have Briar settle you in." He looked at his daughter and spoke reluctantly. "I think we'll need to bring you on this mission. Tell the crew we're moving out in twenty."

CHAPTER TWO

JADE

Jade gripped the steering wheel as she scanned for the easiest entry into the forest for the buggy. She was only on this mission because Krista had been injured, and while Jade hurt for her friend, this was a rare opportunity that she was determined to not mess up. Maybe today she could prove how she could handle herself—that she didn't need to be protected all the time. Maybe she didn't have to leave.

A patch of lighter green caught her eye, and she twisted the hand crank while angling toward the path. White clouds of steam billowed, and she flexed her feet in anticipation. Would they locate the fabled lair of the Piovant sage today? Maybe she could help her father realize his goal of finding something that could stabilize the keystone that powered the barrier. Then they wouldn't have to live in fear of it suddenly failing. And being enslaved or slaughtered by the Elph in the north.

Being able to redeem the lost time of this morning, the injuries of the crew, everything that went wrong, would be an added bonus.

"Are you ready for this?" Victor's voice was pitched so low that she almost couldn't hear him over the wind as they drove. The bench seat shifted under Jade as he turned to face her. "Are you nervous?"

She looked over her shoulder at Zak and Kerlee to make sure they weren't listening in. "Not really. Maybe. I want this to go well. And...I just—" She blew out her breath as she dialed back the steam for the buggy. It started to slow, and she drummed her fingers against the wheel once she didn't need to grip it so tightly. "I want to really be part of a team. Not always held back because I'm the captain's daughter."

And if this didn't work out, there was always her backup plan with Krista and Briar.

Victor stroked his goatee and nodded with a meaningful glance to the back seat. "Makes sense. For what it's worth, I believe you'll be fine." He smirked. "You've inherited your parents' tenacity. You won't be in their shadows forever."

"Thank you." Jade shot him a smile. "I appreciate that."

Jade drove in silence for several ticks before calling out, "We're here!" and letting the buggy roll to a stop at the trail she had seen. She cranked the steam valve to shut off power and hopped out, circling around to the front of the creaking machine. A swipe on the latch popped open the hood, and the heat from the furnace warmed her chilled face. There had to be a snowstorm coming. The temperature had been dropping ever since that morning. The forest would provide some shelter under the evergreen trees, but it would be a race against the weather for how much they'd get done today.

Lucky for Ben that they found him when they did. Dragons aside, if he'd been unsheltered during this weather, the hypothermia alone could've been the death of him.

"Hey, Jade, I got your bag!"

Jade started, slamming the furnace shut. Warmth that wasn't

from the fire made her cold cheeks tingle. Lost in thought, and she hadn't even done anything useful yet. Brilliant.

She trotted over to the trio and accepted her bag from Kerlee, not meeting his eyes. Last thing she needed was for him to misread her embarrassment.

Kerlee's attention wasn't focused on her, thankfully. He buttoned up his eye-hurting orange jacket and flashed a grin. "I won't lie, it's nice to have you on the team for today, Victor."

Victor strapped his sword to his belt. "I appreciate the sentiment, but I'd hazard a guess that we'll all pay for the captain's decision later. Geist is not one to be content with being left behind, even if it's because the captain wanted a senior officer for this."

"If we actually find the sage's sanctuary, then he'll be even worse, because he wasn't part of the discovery team," Zak reminded in a mild tone. He pulled a black hat over his dark hair. "Geist will likely gripe for the next two days, minimum."

"You're saying you want the captain's team to find it before us?" Kerlee gasped in mock outrage and leveled a loaf of bread from his pack as a sword. "Have you no honor? On guard, you traitorous fiend! We want the bragging rights, Zak, bragging rights!"

Jade laughed at Kerlee's antics as she slipped her bag over her shoulders. She picked up her sword, momentarily caressing the gleaming blue sheath before securing it on her hip. The corner of a brown leather pouch hovered at the edge of her vision, and she looked up to see Victor holding it out to her.

He shook it slightly. "Take it. You can carry our flares." He pivoted and tossed a matching bag to Zak. "You know the drill, gentlemen. Find anything of interest, use one of the flares to let us know."

Kerlee groaned. "Here's to hoping Dr. Jaxton's next batch of stink bombs of color smell better than these. I hope you guys find it. I don't want to be close to one of those flares ever again."

Zak's brow wrinkled as he looked at the matching bag in Jade's hands. "Why does—"

Victor snorted at Kerlee and handed Zak a map. "Jade and I will cover zones one and two, you guys cover zones three and four." Victor folded his map and tucked it into his double-breasted jacket. "Theoretically, this area has fewer dragons, and the cold will keep some in hibernation. That being said, we all know that several are warm-blooded, and they'll be hungry this season. Be alert."

Jade nodded seriously. They were half an hour from the *Sapphire*, and they'd be on foot in the forest. They all had basic medical training, but only Zak could be considered a true field medic. If she or Victor got injured while on their own…

"So you two are a team for this?" Zak asked. He pushed his hand through his hair and glanced at Kerlee. "Any reason we're completely changing the combination?"

Victor raised an eyebrow and gestured a hand between himself and Jade. "I'm not going to hold her back during this mission, and," he waved to Zak and Kerlee, "you two make a good team too."

Jade held her breath as Zak's face smoothed of all expression. She *hated* how good he'd become at hiding his feelings in the last six months. His gaze rested on her, and she forced herself to not react to the concern she could see in his dark eyes. She smiled and shrugged. A muscle in his jaw twitched.

"Do you not trust in my ability to protect the captain's daughter?" Victor held his arms open to invite inspection. Sheathed blades lined his vest, his bag of various tools and supplies crossed over his thin but muscular chest, and his long-bladed sword rested at his hip. He dropped his arms and smirked. "If you can't trust the first mate, then you've got problems, son."

Zak rubbed the back of his neck and nodded slowly. "I trust your judgment, sir."

"Good." Victor pulled out his pocket watch, looked at it, then snapped it shut and tucked it away. "In four hours, I want us all back here." He lifted his gaze to the sky. "We'll be seeing snow by this evening, and we don't want to be out when that happens. Let's cover as much ground as possible."

The first hour passed without adventure, Jade simply following Victor as he led through the dense forest. After they split ways with Kerlee and Zak, they'd found a deer trail, which aided their progress through the thick bramble. By the second hour, the sparkle and excitement of being part of the mission had faded.

Jade buttoned the top of her coat and dodged a thick branch that Victor skirted around. He was so much more graceful in his movements than she could ever hope to be. He carried himself with ease amongst nature, whereas Jade found herself tripping on sticks and getting caught on brambles. Never before had she realized how much she loved the engine room with its clean spaces, everything polished and put in its place. Nothing like the give of vegetation under her boots, the clinging webs of spiders, or the pungent scent of snapped branches.

"Hey, Victor?" Jade pushed down the satisfaction that her voice didn't sound as tired as she felt. "I just had a thought."

The shadow of the evergreen towering above them obscured his features, but a patch of sunlight silhouetted his knife-like form as he paused ahead of her. "What's that?"

"What if what we're looking for has deteriorated?" Jade gestured at the babbling stream to her right. "There's so much moisture here, so much life, that unless the sage built his retreat out of stone or brick, there's no way it could last out here. All the building material readily available would need maintenance. Wood, thatch, it would rot. And this is supposed to be where one of the seven sages would hide away to work. He was alive, what, sixty years ago? Nothing could last that long here."

She caught up to him, and he settled his hands on his hips, pivoting slowly on his heel. "Good thought." He raised an eyebrow at her. "He was one of the seven sages, so he was extremely powerful. What if he used mani-magic to protect it from decay?" He stroked his goatee. "Or what if he used mani-magic to hide it from prying eyes?"

Jade groaned. "Don't even suggest such a horrible thing."

"It could be possible."

"I'm not going to dwell on that idea. If that's true, we could've passed it already." She tugged off her gloves and her hat, and tucked both into her belt so she could re-braid her hair. "Poor father, he was hoping so badly that this lead would actually pay off. He's running out of time before the anniversary."

"Maybe it will." Victor shrugged. "We'll have to wait and see." He beckoned for her to follow. "We've still got an hour to get farther in before we have to turn around. It smells like snow, so we don't want to waste any time."

Each tree looked like the last, but Victor pushed on with the quiet, calm skill of someone who'd spent years in such terrain. He didn't hesitate or dawdle, but somehow found the firm ground, the easiest of the brush to break through, the hidden deer trails. Twice, they each spotted something in the distance that looked out of the ordinary, and twice they discovered it to be just a trick of the eye.

Maybe the rumors of the sage's sanctuary were really just that: rumors.

Despite the guys' banter earlier, Jade didn't care if Geist was upset about being left behind for this mission. They *had* to find the sage's house. He was the only lead they currently had, and if he didn't have a totem, an artifact, or some sort of manuscript or clue on how to fix the keystone, what hope did they have? Her father had been searching for a method ever since the keystone had been attacked so many years ago, and he had run every lead to ground. Something had to pan out. Eventually.

Jade snapped a branch in her way as she followed Victor through the forest. What if this was another dead end? What would her father do? She tossed the branch with a grimace. What would *she* do? Things on board hadn't been getting any better. It felt like the older she got, the more constrictive her father had become. She'd never be free to do what she wished while under his shadow.

Never mind Zak's newfound over-protectiveness.

Relief coursed through Jade when Victor interrupted her brooding to announce it time to head back. Others may have found the scenery soothing, but after parting ways with Zak, she couldn't shake her disquiet. Whatever had climbed into his gearbox and died shouldn't be her concern. But something had changed in their dynamic, and it rankled. After last summer, they'd grown closer. Not in any specific way, but they spent more time together. He'd come to the engine room to talk with her and Krista. He let her keep watch with him and he'd point out constellations in the night sky. He shared fond memories of his older brother, Zane.

She could count on him to be there at any time, with an encouraging word, snarky quip, or just to lend an ear. He was her faithful shadow.

She hadn't even realized how close they'd become till he cut her off that one night. Stopped coming by the engine room, turned her away for his shift, barely talked to her. Yet he was still there— watching. Stepping in and helping occasionally. Protecting her before she had a chance to protect herself.

And now he had the propensity to treat her like a baby bird that had fallen from its nest.

"What *is* his problem, anyway?" she exclaimed, throwing her hands in the air.

Victor jerked to a stop halfway across a log and tilted his head at her. "I beg your pardon?"

Her cheeks heated, and she waved at him to keep moving. Could she ask him his opinion on the whole thing? She eyed him as he moved on, adjusting his cap snug over his bare head while he walked. He didn't come across as someone who had any close friendships, let alone family. But everyone had friends to some degree, so maybe he could offer insight in that arena? She groaned.

"Have you noticed anything…different, in how Zak has been acting toward me?"

Victor turned around, hand on his hip, and batted his eyelashes at her. "Do I look like Krista to you?"

She stuck her tongue out and pushed past him. "Never mind."

He caught up and laughed. "Sorry, it was too easy."

They lapsed into silence that was broken only by the rustling of bushes and the snap of twigs as they forged through the underbrush. She could feel Victor's eyes on her, and when she threw him a pointed look, he offered a half smile.

"I have observed some changes in his behavior toward you, yes."

So she wasn't crazy! And Krista wasn't making a big deal out of nothing. Not if one of the busiest men on board had noticed that there was a change.

Jade broke a lone branch out of the way of her face and snapped the wood in her hands. "Any ideas as to why?"

"Who knows? Humans are stupid."

"Funny," Jade deadpanned. "I was hoping for more of a reason than that."

"Seriously, I don't know." Victor shrugged. "Maybe someone warned him away from being too close to the captain's daughter?"

Jade wrinkled her nose. "Who would do that? And why?" The telltale heat of a blush exploded across her cheeks, and she glanced away. "If anything, someone would warn me away. He's of noble blood. I'm…me."

"Monomi are disgraced, so I'd say you're on the same level with him." Victor paused and raised a single eyebrow. "Besides, isn't your father a noble? You're noble, too."

"True." Jade shrugged one shoulder "But he walked away from that life, so I don't really think about it. It's not like I've ever really been to court, except for day visits. I mean, I guess I've been to a few social noble gatherings, but they aren't my scene." She looked away, a bitter taste in her mouth. "And what little I've had with anything in the regard of royalty hasn't been pleasant."

Victor didn't say anything, and she hastened to add, "But, like you said, the Monomi haven't been a part of the noble life for nearly twenty years, so…" Jade trailed off before stating firmly, "He's noble, but not in the bad way."

A puff of vapor lingering in the air showed Victor's huffed laugh, even though she didn't hear it. Jade plucked at a thorn that snagged in her pant leg, and she chewed her bottom lip. "Do you really think that could be the reason he's suddenly so distant?"

He sighed and pinched the bridge of his nose. "Perhaps he views you as family to be protected. I don't know, Jade. He's not exactly one to discuss his deep, dark secrets."

This wasn't going anywhere that would soothe her mind. She had to change the subject. "Do you have any?"

"Have any what?"

"Family. Secrets." Jade twitched her shoulder. "You've been on the *Sapphire* for half a year, and you don't talk about yourself much. We've got at least an hour to kill as we head back, so…what about you?"

Victor didn't say anything, and Jade bit her lip. Had she insulted him somehow? Was he mad at her? It probably was rude of her to ask about secrets. *Oh, whales, I blundered this, didn't I?*

"I grew up near the border," he said finally.

Jade perked up. "Really? What was that like?"

Victor smiled bitterly. "Like nothing you could ever imagine." He lifted his face to the patchy canopy of needled leaves overhead and breathed in deeply. "It was different than here, more isolated. Cleaner."

"In what way?" Jade asked, curious.

His lips twitched, and he rubbed his thumb against his jaw. "I also was an only child." He rested his palm against a fallen log that came up to his chin and looked back at her. "Once I was older, I traveled extensively, learning various trades here and there. And now I'm with your crew."

"Hauling cargo and chasing myths." Jade shook her head. "I'm sure you had more fun on other adventures than on missions like this."

Victor's eyes glittered. "Oh, I've had many jobs before this one, some more enjoyable than others. This work falls under the category of amusing. It's been surprisingly satisfying to follow your father across Terrene, helping him to search for whatever could help the keystone." He squatted and knit his fingers together and nodded toward the log. "I'm taller than you, and *this* thing's taller than me. Let me give you a boost."

She settled her boot in his hand hold and narrowed her eyes at the top of the log. Icy moss covered every visible inch. She'd have to get a solid grip so she wouldn't fall. He lifted without warning, and her fingers scrambled across the soft green for traction. She hoisted herself onto the log and straddled it to watch Victor haul himself up with little effort.

"What abou—" she fell silent when he lifted his hand, eyes wide. She followed his gaze, hope flaring in her chest before it sputtered out again.

No sign of a sage sanctuary, sage house, or sage anything.

A herd of plodders moved perpendicular to the path that Jade and Victor were taking. Jade counted five of the herbivores as they ambled through the trees. Bright red plates with mottled green and yellow lined their backs all the way to the tips of their tails, and she could barely see their narrow heads as they poked down at the bushes.

Victor crouched on the log, his hand resting on the hilt of his sword. He leaned toward Jade, and she twisted closer to hear him.

"We'll stay here until they pass. No sudden movements."

She nodded. While peaceful, if spooked, a plodder could kill a man with a single swipe of its plated tail. And if they used their ability to manipulate heat and make the spikes on their tails burning hot? As a girl on the *Sapphire*, she'd seen a crewmember return from a mission mangled and burned beyond comprehension by an angry plodder. While it wasn't the first grisly sight she'd witnessed, she'd never been able to get it out of her mind. There was no desire in her body to disagree with Victor's wisdom.

The forest darkened around them as she waited for Victor to signal for them to continue moving. At this point, the guys were probably already back at the buggy. Would they be worried yet? Had they found something and forgotten to use the flares?

What about her father's team? Had their years roaming southern Terrene, searching for clues to fix her father's number one regret, finally come to an end?

A boom thundered overhead, and pine needles rained down onto Jade and Victor. She looked up just long enough to see the streaks of an orange flare, and then a bleating roar ripped her attention to the plodders before them.

"Bleeding whales," Jade swore, horror rippling through her skin.

Victor drew his sword. "Stay on your feet. Try not to be seen. And don't let them hit you."

Jade watched as the group of dragons spread into a star shape in the undergrowth, their heads in the center, tails thrashing the surrounding sparse vegetation. She slid her sword out of its sheath silently. Should they jump back behind the log? They'd be blind to the dragons then, and the plodders were huge—they'd likely just break right through it.

One turned its head from the center and looked back, its beady black eyes staring right at her. It roared, and the others swiveled their heads to look at her.

Victor swore. "Run!"

CHAPTER THREE

SLATE

Captain Slate Stohner used the flat of his sword to push away a leafless thorn branch for his following crew member. He glanced over his shoulder at Ash, who nearly blended in with the shadowed part of the forest they were trekking through, and his teeth shone white against his darker skin when he smiled his thanks.

"Don't lose hope, sir. We've still got an hour before we need to head back."

Slate sighed and let the branch snap back into place. "An hour that's rapidly fading."

Ash shook his head. "We've still got half a zone to search. We may yet find something."

Doubt held Slate's reply behind his teeth. What good would it do to talk about it? What mattered was finding the sage's house. The sage himself was long dead from when he'd helped erect the barrier, but perhaps he'd left something behind. A scroll with instructions or clues, an artifact that a mani-med could identify, some sort of *something* that Slate could use.

It was his fault that the keystone was weakened. He couldn't let another decade go by without doing anything about it. He had to fix the problem now, before it was too late. Before the barrier fell. Before everything *they* had died for was wasted.

I won't let your death be in vain, Sapphire.

Slate motioned for Ash to lead and waited for the taller dragon hunter to pass by. The possibility of finding the sage's lair was slim to begin with, and the likelihood of him having something useful on hand was even less likely, but Slate had to believe it was possible.

What future did Jade have, if her very existence was threatened by something that he was responsible for? He'd already destroyed her family. And he knew she chafed under his rules and secrets, like a gear that wasn't sized for its fittings. But he had to protect her, keep her set apart, ready to someday take on the role she was born for.

But that would mean nothing if he couldn't fix the Doldra keystone.

Slate scanned the underbrush. Everything looked as normal as could be for the Wyld Woods. Dense, uninhabited, the only signs of life being the wildlife typical of a forest. Thankfully, they'd had no dragon sightings—yet.

"Captain."

Slate jerked to a stop, and his gaze followed the direction that Ash pointed.

It took a minute for Slate's eyes to settle on the dwelling, which blended seamlessly into the surrounding forest. He lifted his eyebrows, impressed. They could've walked right past the house, none the wiser, if it wasn't for what must've caught Ash's attention—the quiet creak of a door barely hanging on to its frame. The homestead had been clearly built with camouflage in mind, with no unnatural sharp edges or man-made materials. In fact, the only manmade thing that Slate could make out was the rusted hinges.

Ash tapped his sword hilt with a questioning frown, and Slate nodded. They drew their blades and crept toward the dilapidated home.

Anticipation skittered across Slate's nerves. There was no guarantee that this was the great sage Jace's home, but no one else had ever lived in the Wyld Woods. They were aptly named, after all. Whose house would this be, if not his?

Soft dirt gave beneath the heel of Slate's boot as he neared the door. Ash tilted his head, and Slate let out a breath before silently stepping inside the dark home.

He waited a moment for his eyes to adjust, then moved aside for Ash to duck under the doorway and join him in the cramped room. Moss covered the worn wood beams in the ceiling, and leaves lay strewn about the rotting wood floor. A toppled table and chair were pushed against the wall, and a slashed sleeping pad barely fit in the opposite corner.

"Sparse." Ash commented from behind Slate's shoulder. The debris muffled the sound of his boots as he strode across the room and started looking over the bed.

Slate rubbed his thumbnail along the side seam of his pants, indecisive as to where he should start. Was there anything here that would even prove this was Sage Jace's home? He'd been one of the seven sages to sacrifice himself when magicking-up the barrier over sixty years ago—when none of the sages knew the price of such magic would be their lives.

They'd found this home, so *if* it was the sage's, maybe he hadn't concealed the house or the things inside with magic? Maybe they had a chance of finding something?

An intricately carved whorl above the mantle caught Slate's eye, and he moved closer, optimism kindling. It matched the book of sages that Sam had found and showed him back at the shipping yards. This was what he needed. This was where he had to be.

The hope that had barely begun to rise in Slate sank as he looked around. Only the wood furniture and various metal bits were left. If there had been any scrolls here, they'd have decomposed by now. They had to hope for a stone or a physical artifact that would last in such moist conditions.

Slate moved his hand across the mantle slowly, feeling for any catch or possible mechanisms that would betray a secret compartment. The smooth wood revealed no secrets. He knelt at the edge of the fireplace, pulled a glow stone from his pocket, and lifted it to see up the chimney. Years of soot and dust lined the rocky opening. He pressed and tried to wiggle each stone, but nothing shifted.

Slate huffed a sigh and shifted on his haunches. A nearby fire poker caught his attention, and he used it to push the layers of dirt and dust and ash around in the bottom of the fireplace. Frustration vibrated along his nerves. They had to find something here. Anything. He tossed the metal stick aside and leaned back to avoid hitting his head on the mantle before he stood.

The tip of his boot caught on something. He scuffed at the loose debris that littered the floor, then bent to finger one of three deep gashes in the time-softened wood. *Void take them all. Stalkers.*

A chill ran down his spine, and Slate pivoted on his heel to survey the room again. It was clear that the place had been abandoned, ransacked, even, if the treatment of the mattress was any indicator. They were lucky that stalkers hadn't taken to it for a nest.

Slate caught Ash's questioning side glance, and he tapped the scarred boards. "Stalkers were here some time ago, but I don't see any fresh tracks."

Ash gestured to an empty chest by the sleeping pad. "What may have been here is gone. I'm guessing bandits or sky pirates." He tilted the trunk for Slate to see the age-thinned garments. "There's nothing of value in here or anywhere else." Ash ran his long fingers over a matching whorl carved on the top of the chest, and shook his head. "I'm afraid this is a dead end, sir. Not even a paper weight is left."

"So it would seem." Slate gingerly hefted the table back in place and righted the chair, wary of splinters. Something rolled and touched his boot. He glanced down. "Whales!"

Ash rushed to his side, sword drawn. "What is it?"

Empty eye sockets stared up from the floor. Slate gingerly stepped back. The skull rocked slightly when he moved, then it stilled.

Ash pointed to the side of the bone. "Looks like a dragon got him. Either before he died, or soon after." He shook his head and wiped his hands together, as if rubbing away the taint that hadn't touched him. "Not an end fit for anyone."

Slate rubbed his forehead. What now? "Well, that answers the question of what happened to the sage."

"Yeah, I guess the rumor that he'd survived the Void magic was true." Ash grimaced. "He just didn't survive whatever it was that got him here."

The other side of the room showed signs of Ash's investigation, but no other bones. Slate rolled his neck and sighed. "And you didn't find anything over there?"

"No sir." A crease appeared over Ash's brow, and his shoulders hunkered down. "Should we, uh, perform rites over him?"

"See any other parts?"

Ash's eye twitched. "If I had, you'd have heard me."

"Right." Slate hesitated before picking up the skull. He carried it over to the dilapidated bed and set it down respectfully on the pillow remnants. It was too easy to imagine a residue clinging to his hand, and he resisted the urge to wipe his fingers on the dusty blanket. Instead, he bowed his head and splayed his fingers just above the skull. "Rest in peace in Areilia."

Ash murmured the accompaniment of, "Let it be so," and shifted awkwardly before moving sideways toward the door and peering out. "Should I set off a flare, sir? It looks like we have two hours or less until snow."

Slate grimaced. There was nothing to be found here, and nothing more to do. And a quick glance out the window confirmed Ash's prediction. He nodded. "Do it. We'll head back. There's nothing for us here."

Ash shifted the leather satchel on his shoulder and pulled out Dr. Jaxton's flare contraption. "What's the next step?"

"I don't know." Slate scowled back at the empty room. "I guess we're back to the usual. Hopefully Ellie will have something for us at the next port." He motioned to Ash. "Go ahead and fire that off, then let's get back to our buggy. I want to make sure Jade made it back safely."

A loud pop preceded the streak of orange chalky smoke into the sky, and Ash tucked the flare machine back into his bag. "You coddle her more than you used to."

Slate tugged his jacket shut against the chill breeze and started trudging through the undergrowth. "I know her value."

CHAPTER FOUR

BEN

"I don't want to be alone, Ben."

Ben turned toward the woman's voice. Her face tilted down, hiding her eyes with her blonde hair, so he leaned forward, making sure she would hear his every word. "You won't be alone."

"How can you say that?" Her voice sounded broken, despondent.

"Well, you've already moved in with me." He chucked her chin and brushed a kiss against her forehead. "And I've talked with Nathalie. She'll be your roommate when I'm gone."

That brought her face up, revealing eyes that glistened with tears. "Really? When? You ship out in just two weeks, don't you?"

He squeezed her slender fingers. "Yes. But we'll make it work."

Ben blinked at the bottom of the bunk above him and rubbed at his forehead. Briar, the ship's cook, had dropped him off to rest while the teams were out, promising a tour of the airship later. The nap had done Ben a world of good. His headache had disappeared completely, and the pain in his leg had faded back to being barely noticeable. Whatever magic Doctor Jaxton had performed on it clearly worked wonders. There was no other possible way such an injury should feel as good as it did.

But that memory. What did it mean? Who was the woman?

He frowned. Who had he been before he'd lost his memories? Was he the sort of man who moved in with his girlfriend? Was she a sister? What did "ship out" mean?

The chain around his neck clanked as he moved, and he pulled it out, ignoring the tags to study the ring. Three diamonds nestled in a row, set in white gold. Was this hers? Was it supposed to be, and he hadn't given it to her yet? Or, maybe he had, and something had happened to her. Why would he have a woman's ring, and why did he have metal tags with his name on them? What did it all mean?

There was no way he could move forward with this life here until he knew his past.

No one came down to meet Ben as he left the bunk room, which suited him just fine. He took his time so he could walk slowly and inspect his new environment. Warm-colored wooden walls, lighter wood for the floor and ceiling. Crystal sconces lined the walls and highlighted the metal accents in the hall.

He cautiously rubbed a finger against a sconce and sighed. It was warm, but not hot. Smooth, yet roughly hewn. Nothing here seemed familiar. *And I don't even know what would be familiar.*

Sunshine streamed down on the metal stairs, and Ben blinked as he emerged from below deck. Even the air somehow smelled different than what he'd expected. Sharper. Cleaner.

"Cap'ain, ho!"

The shout came from somewhere above, on the topmost deck. Ben joined the men gathered by the thick metal railing and peered over the edge. Captain Slate and three men came into view from the southern part of the forest. The crew rushed downstairs, and Ben trailed behind, reluctant to return down to the belly of the ship that he'd just emerged from. He watched over the railing at the incoming men. His confusion cleared when they opened a hatch in the *Sapphire's* underbelly, allowing the captain to steer his skiff straight onto the airship.

Ben worked his way down to the bottom deck as quickly as he could while favoring his leg. Who knew how long he had on the airship with the crew, until they left him to be alone and find his own way back to…wherever he was from. He couldn't risk re-injuring his leg.

He came around the corner in time to see Slate nod a weary greeting to the surrounding men and a red-headed woman who looked uncannily similar to the captain—possibly a sister? Ben picked an empty bit of wall space to lean against and watch unobtrusively.

Slate slumped back against his seat and let his head drop back. "Well, that was a waste of time." He lolled his head to look at the empty parking spot next to him, and he stiffened. His shoulders drew back as he sat up. "Where's Jade's team?" He looked at the woman. "Garnet, have you heard from her?"

Garnet's slender eyebrows knit together. "You haven't been in communication with her or Victor while out there?"

Slate shook his head as his men slowly unloaded their gear, eyes shifting between their captain and his sister. "I expected she'd be back by now. Have you seen any flares?"

"Just one, and I'm guessing that was yours."

One of the crewmen carefully deposited a leather bag into a

nearby wall cabinet. "That was us, yes."

Slate slid out of the skiff and stood by the entrance of the airship. "They're still out there. And night is coming." He looked back, his eyes roaming over Ben as he scanned the surrounding crew. "We need to find them. And fast."

CHAPTER FIVE

SLATE

Grief, regret, and frustration roiled in Slate's gut as he stared out the hangar door. Tall blades of grass waved in the chill breeze, and somewhere a bird cawed, but there were no other signs of life out there. Where were they?

Zak would do everything in his power to protect Jade if they ran into dragons or any other dangers. But even Guardians bled...and died. Slate of all people knew this too well.

What if they ran into more than they could handle? Slate ground his teeth together. He'd already been hesitant to send her out, but now he felt absolutely vindicated. Something had happened. He could feel it in his belly.

Garnet stepped up beside him and settled her hand on his shoulder. "The skiff is just about ready. We added some extra blankets, just in case you're out later than expected."

"Good. Thank you." Slate turned from the mockingly peaceful scenery to survey the organized chaos of his crew pulling together for a search-and-rescue mission. The new guy, Ben, watched from a corner of the room, his lips tugged down in a slight frown. He looked about the same age as Jade, maybe a bit older, probably in his early twenties. Ben winced and shifted his stance, reminding Slate of Ben's leg injury.

What if Zak, their field medic, was wounded? Doctor Jaxton could work off-ship when needed, but he preferred having all his tools on hand. Slate turned to the man next to him. "Ash, I want you with me. You're the next best field medic. William, you're coming, too." Slate pointed to Geist. "We don't know what happened or if there's any danger to the *Sapphire*. You're in charge of security here." Slate looked to his sister, his own concern reflected in her eyes. "And tell Jaxton to be prepared for whatever we find," he said softly.

Garnet acknowledged his words with a brief hug. "Be careful. Bring her home."

CHAPTER SIX

JADE

The plodders pursued them.

A stitch spread in Jade's side, and her legs burned, but she pressed on. A quick glance over her shoulder provided another spurt of adrenaline.

Plodders were slower than her and Victor, but they didn't have to weave around brush or duck under tree branches. No, these beasts plowed through obstacles, their superheated spikes scorching leaves and bark as they passed. One plodder pulled ahead of the others, its glossy black eyes fixated on Jade. Its tail brushed a bush and the few green leaves left on it crisped at the edges, curling in.

Jade stumbled on a low shrub and righted herself, one of her father's blistering oaths on the tip of her tongue.

"Down!" Victor pushed against her shoulder, and Jade stumbled into the ground, barely holding on to her sapphire blue sword. A spiked tail swished over her head, and she froze, breath halting in her lungs.

Victor hacked at the tail until it jerked back. Jade scrambled to her feet, dead leaves and debris floating off her clothes.

She scowled at the plodder. "Bleeding Void Born whale of a—"

Victor slipped forward and stabbed at the tail. "Kill now. Swear later!"

Jade gripped her sword hilt hard enough to hurt her fingers and waited for the plodder to swing its tail back in her direction. She dodged it, then leapt forward before the tail could reverse its path. Her blade bit deep—just above the steaming spikes. The plodder roared, and she backpedaled as it stomped its feet, bleeding appendage swaying.

Victor grabbed her hand and pulled. "Move, move, move!"

The four other plodders pushed past the injured one, their noise almost deafening her. How long until they got tired? Jade used her free hand to swipe at the cold sweat on her forehead as she kept pace behind Victor. Their path had more brambles and vegetation to slow them. A thorn bush snagged her sleeve before ripping it and gashing her arm. She clenched her teeth and focused on Victor's back. *I can't keep this up much longer.*

Deep purple plodder blood dripped off her sword while she ran. Cold air bit her lungs as she panted. Tears streamed from her eyes.

Victor leapt over a fallen log, and crashed to the ground with a startled yelp. He twisted and yanked on his snagged boot. Jade clambered over the dead timber to reach him. A flash of motion from the corner of her eye drew her attention. She squinted, breathing hard.

Nothing was there.

No. There *was* something. It was just well camouflaged when it held still. Jade swept her sword just to the side of Victor's face. Her blade struck home. A seeker rippled into view. Victor's eyes widened, and he dove as far away as his trapped foot would let him.

Fresh tears leaked down Jade's cheeks. Not another dragon! Not now!

Blood seeped from the mottled burnt red-and-blue nose of the seeker. It reared back silently, stubby arms grasping for her while its tail thrashed.

No finesse today. Just fear and adrenaline, pounding through Jade's veins as she slashed desperately at the dragon. Zak's voice echoed in her mind as clearly as if he were right next to her: *Seekers have the ultimate predator ability—superior smell, hearing, sight. There is no way to escape if you're targeted. Kill it before it kills you.*

Her first attack must have been too shallow; the seeker only seemed annoyed by her presence. Foul breath washed over her as it bared its teeth. Every tooth looked razor sharp. Jade gripped her sword with shaking hands, praying she wouldn't drop it now. A quick glance showed Victor furiously sawing at a vine entangled around his boot with a dagger, and the plodders were closer than before.

If she could get the seeker to fight the plodders, she and Victor would have a chance at survival.

But how to make that happen?

She stabbed at the beast, and fear iced her back. She over-reached. She was wide open.

Claws rent the air, and she half ducked/half fell to avoid them. Just beyond the seeker, the plodders had slowed. She would need to provoke them.

Victor appeared at her side, his lean face grim. He jabbed at the seeker's belly with a blade.

"Stay here. Don't die," she snapped at Victor as she turned on her heel and ran toward the plodders.

Just as she hoped, the seeker followed. She swallowed her brief grin. Now to survive the next step. Her legs wobbled, and she pushed on with a low growl. There was no way that her muscles could give out now. She was so close.

"Jade!"

Zak's sudden cry distracted her, and she jerked to a stop, eyes wide. She pressed a hand against her hammering heart as she scanned the forest for him. The seeker crashed through the undergrowth. There was no air left in her lungs to scream, so she did all she could and stumbled closer to the plodders.

The nearest dragon reared back at her presence, then trumpeted out a deafening roar when it saw the seeker. The carnivore howled in reply. Jade's boots skidded on leaves. She waited for an eternity of a second while the two dragons stared at each other, then the seeker lunged at the plodder. She turned to double back the way she came.

Zak appeared from the brush, his pale face contrasting with his black clothing. "Are you crazy?" He grabbed hold of her arm and tugged.

She stumbled, leg muscles trembling. He threw an arm around her shoulder and braced the other against her stomach. Zak's hair brushed her jaw as he looked behind them. Then he took off, supporting most her weight.

Adrenaline didn't cover any of her embarrassment at his arrival. He probably thought she needed to be rescued, when she'd had it mostly under control. Her cheeks felt numb from the cold tears, despite the heat pounding through her veins. Zak led her through the trashed forest path, and she risked a glance back.

Plodders surrounded the lone seeker, pummeling it with their tails.

It worked.

She caught sight of Kerlee's orange jacket and Victor's dark hat up ahead. Spots swam in her vision as sweet relief replaced the adrenaline, leaving her weak-kneed. Zak's arm tightened around her middle as she staggered.

"Almost to the buggy," he breathed. "Hang on."

Jade gripped his muscled forearm and gritted her teeth. She wouldn't allow herself to fall to pieces now. Not when she was so close. Not when her plan had worked. Not with Zak next to her. She had to pull herself together, fast. She was the only one who knew how to push the buggy to the limits and not have it break down immediately. Distracted though the dragons were, she wasn't going to take any chances.

This was her chance to prove herself. Maybe after this, her father would accept her as a hunter. And Zak would loosen his stifling protectiveness.

She wouldn't have to leave.

The edge of the forest lightened, and she could make out the form of the buggy just beyond. Her team may not have found any sage house to show for their time and effort, but they had made it out alive. That's what counted in her book today. A living, unmangled team.

Hopefully her father had experienced better luck.

CHAPTER SEVEN

SLATE

Slate slid onto the bench seat next to Krista's father, William, and mentally reviewed his checklist of things to panic over. What if they couldn't locate Jade and the rest of them? It was getting late, and snow was sure to be falling soon. He tugged on his gloves and closed his eyes. Dwelling on what-ifs wouldn't help right now. He glanced at his shipwright. "Ready?"

William shot Slate a tight-lipped grin as he turned a gear and the engine sputtered to life. "We'll find them."

Slate blew out a breath. "I hope so."

"Captain! I see them!" Geist's voice was barely audible over the roaring engine, but Slate whirled in his seat to look out the hangar door. The rumbling of the buggy ceased under him. He all but jumped off the seat to stand by Garnet and clenched his hands to prevent them from trembling in nervous anticipation.

All the crew in the hold pushed to stand at the edge of the large doorway and watched the missing buggy as it tore along the path that had been made earlier that day.

One, two, three, four. Slate released a pent-up breath as he counted the heads bobbing in the buggy. All four were returning. Garnet gripped his arm as a shaky sigh escaped her. Slate shook his head against the jumbled surge of emotions that raced through him.

Red strands of hair streamed behind Jade's head, and Victor hung on to the door frame and windshield.

"Make way!" Slate exclaimed when he realized that Jade wasn't slowing. He didn't see anything pursuing them, but she pushed the buggy to its limits, steam billowing behind them in great clouds of white.

She hit the ramp and cranked gears while turning the wheel, stomping on the brake at the last possible second. It screeched into its parking spot. Silence descended on the hangar for a long moment. Then the crew broke into thunderous applause, relief evident in many faces. Slate grinned in spite of himself. For claiming she didn't have a thing for theatrics, her entrance just now would be talked about for weeks by the crew.

Jade slumped over the wheel, and Slate's smidge of humor morphed back into alarm.

Zak hopped over the bench seat and perched between her and Victor as Slate pushed past Ash to reach her side. Zak cradled her in his arms, and when her head lolled back Slate could see the scratches on her face and hands, the torn sleeve, the blood soaking her clothes.

An iron ball of horror sank to the bottom of Slate's stomach. "What happened?"

A muscle clenched in Zak's jaw, and he nodded to Victor. "Ask him."

Victor slid off the buggy and stretched stiffly. "Jade and I ran into plodders."

At the name *plodders*, Slate immediately scanned over Jade, searching for burns. Zak rolled up Jade's sleeve to inspect the long scratch oozing blood. Garnet hustled to Jade and pressed her hand against Jade's cheek. His daughter moaned, and Jade's eyes fluttered open.

Victor continued, "We survived. And that's that." He peeled off his fingerless gloves and started picking thorns from his clothes. "I know we'd feel better if we closed the hangar, if you don't mind?"

At Slate's nod, William and Ash removed the bracers and started to crank the large door shut.

Victor pointed to Jade, who had pushed Zak away and now sat on her own, chin up and a defiant spark in her eye. "She saved me." Victor's lips twisted. "I got caught in a snarebush when the seeker showed up, and she distracted him long enough for me to get loose. And she executed an excellent—though dangerous—strategy of having the plodders and seeker fight." Slate's first mate offered Jade a genuine smile and half-bow. "I'm glad she was on the team today. Her quick thinking saved us both."

"Her quick acting almost got her killed," Zak groused. He pushed a hand through his hair and hopped off the buggy abruptly, then stalked to the back and pulled out his medic bag. "She—"

"*She* is here and listening," Jade interrupted. She looked over at Slate and smiled. "I'm uninjured."

Zak scoffed at her obvious lie as he set his bag on the seat next to her.

She ignored him when he lifted her arm to examine the scratch. "We made it back. All is good." Her smile sagged and she dropped her gaze, plucking at her rolled-up sleeve. "But we didn't find anything of value out there."

Slate closed his eyes and promised himself that he wouldn't give her a verbal dressing-down in front of the crew. Her recklessness could have gotten her killed. And what would he do at that point? Life without her would render everything else he'd done meaningless. So much rode on her—whether she knew it or not. No, let her enjoy the crew's admiration and the pride of a well-executed plan. He'd address her quick thinking later—and the dangers of it.

"*We* found something." Slate leaned against the skiff and sighed as the familiar sense of depression pulled his shoulders down. Jade had perked up so quickly that it almost physically hurt to say the next bit. "Ash spotted the house, but it was empty."

Jade's smile wilted, and Slate rubbed his palms against his pant leg. "Whatever clues may have been there are long gone. We searched all over, but whatever Void Born bandits were there cleaned it out of anything useful."

Geist spoke up from where he stood by the dragon cold boxes. "How do you know it was bandits?"

Ash answered, "Bandits, scavengers—*bleeding whales*—it could have even been hungry dragons that shredded the place." He shrugged his beefy shoulders and fiddled with a wire between his fingers. "But something else was there first."

"It's another dead end." Slate glared at the worn deck.

"What's the plan, boss? Continue on?" Kerlee asked.

Slate rubbed his forehead with a sigh. "We'll take our cargo to Doldra and talk with Madame Stohner. Hopefully, she'll have turned up a new lead. If nothing else, she'll give us our next merchant itinerary." Slate pushed away from the skiff and stopped next to Jade. She looked up and offered a wan smile. He hugged her. "Get some rest. We'll talk later."

Jade grimaced. Odds were good that she already knew what he'd talk to her about, but if she couldn't obey his "be careful" command, she clearly needed to hear it again.

Weariness seeped into Slate's bones as he strode across the hangar to the narrow hall. He paused when he saw the newcomer, Ben. The man looked uncomfortable under Slate's gaze, but not dishonestly so. Slate chewed his cheek. "Have you had any training against dragons?"

Ben shook his head, slowly. "Not that I can recall, sir."

"Have Zak show you some basics once your leg feels better. I want all on board this vessel to be able to stand a chance against them."

"Yessir."

Slate waited until he was out of sight of the crew before he released his suppressed emotions with a growl, slamming his fist against the wall. A quick shake of his hand helped ease the sting in his knuckles, but did nothing for the ugly facts that mocked him in the face. They were no closer to finding any sort of artifact, instruction manual, scroll, or anything that could fix the barrier. And time had to be running out. Who knew how long the keystone could last after everything that had happened to it?

He rubbed his face and grimaced at the scruff that scratched his hand. He'd need to trim his beard before he saw his mother. Or Sam, for that matter. Neither woman appreciated unkempt facial hair.

Sam also didn't appreciate when he drank, but tonight definitely warranted a stiff drink...or three.

His pride in Jade's quick thinking warred with his fear. Would she be more careful if she knew the truth? Or would she still throw herself headlong into danger? *She's so much like her mother.* Slate balled his hands into fists as he reached the top of the stairs and turned toward his quarters. He knew what Garnet was going to say: tell Jade.

Zak wouldn't say anything, but he didn't need to. He'd mastered quiet disapproval long ago. Slate's own mother would ask if he'd said anything to Jade yet.

He was completely and utterly outnumbered. Jade wasn't ready for the truth, though. And neither was he.

CHAPTER EIGHT

BEN

The wind didn't really whistle. It whooshed—loudly—and no matter where Ben stood on the deck, it beat against him, nearly knocking him off his feet. Two days of travel, and he still wasn't sure how he felt about being in an open ship that flew. How Jade and the rest of the crew walked about so comfortably while in the sky was beyond him.

They used safety belts along the thick metal rail to keep them tethered to the ship. He had one now, but it seemed too thin and small to be trustworthy. He'd mentioned that to Krista yesterday, and she'd laughed and replied, "Then don't blow off."

He still tried to avoid the edge.

Zak, Geist, Briar, the fashion-challenged Kerlee, and Krista's father, William, had gathered on the main deck for an early morning weapons training. As William had explained, they never knew when a terror attack could happen in midair, and being trained to fight them while airborne was essential to survival. Apparently, sparring before dawn was part of the fun.

As far as Ben was concerned, very little of this world seemed friendly to survival. Where in this dangerous realm was he from, and why didn't he remember any of it? With every passing hour, the need to understand his origins became more urgent. How could he live, thrive, without knowing himself? Without remembering his family, his skills, his goals, who he was? Should he make a home here—with the crew of the *Sapphire*—or should he continue on, in hopes that he'd find what he was looking for?

Briar stretched next to Ben and flashed his teeth in a bright white grin. "You keep looking at the railing like it's going to fall away at any moment and suck you off the deck."

Ben couldn't deny it, and he grimaced. "Wherever I'm from, I don't think I used airships for transportation."

"You'll get used to it," Briar clapped Ben on the back with a laugh. "It took me a while to get used to it too. Krista and Jade grew up on the *Sapphire*, and they ran circles around me at first." Briar shook his head with a soft grin. "Those Gearheads may give you a hard time on occasion, but they won't push you off."

"Gearheads?" Ben echoed. He glanced around the deck but didn't see the ladies. "You call them Gearheads?"

Briar nodded like it was no big deal. "They're our mechanics, and they're constantly talking parts and tech. Gearheads."

"Right." Ben snorted as Briar tilted at the waist to touch his toes. "Do you give everyone nicknames?"

Briar snapped up and twisted his torso. "Some, not all. I haven't been able to come up with a good nickname that fits Victor. But I call Kerlee 'Stealthy,' and Zak is 'Spices.'"

William twirled a staff on the other side of the deck, and Ben nodded to him. "What about William?"

Briar's easy grin froze slightly, and he rubbed the back of his neck. "I, uh, figured it wouldn't be the wisest to nickname my girlfriend's father. I want to stay on his good side." His eyes widened and he raised his hands, attention on someone or something behind Ben. "I'm only here for a warmup. I'm not staying for practice, so don't get any ideas."

Zak approached Ben's safe watching zone in the hall. He smirked at Briar. "Noted." Zak crossed his arm over his gray shirt, and he nodded at Ben. "How's your leg?"

Ben flexed his foot back, testing his calf. The stitches pulled, but didn't pop. "Tender, but good enough for mild activity. I just can't strain the stitches."

"Excellent." Zak gestured to a safety line that the crew had winched into place before they took off. It ran parallel the length of the ship from one mast to the other. Perpendicular lines attached to it connected to the edge of the ship. "Hook up, and we'll get started."

"Good luck," Briar said cheerfully. "I'll go find Krista and Jade. They won't want to miss this." Ben narrowed his eyes at Briar, and the ship's cook grinned. "Motivation. I'm providing motivation."

Ben fastened his safety clip onto the main line and cautiously followed Zak to the center of the deck where the other men waited. While he hadn't been hostile the last two days, Zak hadn't been friendly, either. This sudden cordial behavior seemed odd. Had he warmed up to Ben, finally?

Ben leaned into the wind, making sure to plant each step firmly. He forced himself to take deep, even breaths. *Just don't look over the edge.*

Geist thumbed his nose. "What do you want to start with? Sword, spear, hydropack, fists?"

Ben examined the weapons. Swords of various lengths and handgrips lay in one pile, followed by a stack of wired, metal-tipped spears, two large metal cylinders, and several backpacks that each had a long hose and nozzle. Only the swords looked vaguely familiar.

"Let's start with the sword."

Geist picked up one of the swords and handed it to Ben, hilt first. He nodded to Zak and smirked through slanted eyes. "Good luck, Shiny Boy."

Zak sighed as Geist passed him. "No need for insults, Geist." Zak rested a hand on his belt, hand a scant inch from his sword, as he focused on Ben. "We'll begin slow, just to get a feel for what you know. You probably aren't as shiny—new—as everyone thinks you are. Prove it to them, and then we'll really get started."

Ben inspected the smooth leather of the hilt and rotated his wrist, getting a feel for the weight and length. "Sounds good." He shifted his grip to allow both hands on the handle.

Geist's laugh echoed off the main deck. "You sure you know anything about swords, Shiny?"

A glimmer of amusement flashed across Zak's face, and he shook his head. "Unless your memory loss includes loss of sword handling, you aren't familiar with swords. Let's try something different."

Kerlee called out, "Give him a spear!"

Ben shrugged. "Sure." He handed the sword back to Zak and offered Kerlee a small nod. Maybe the spear would be easier. Or, at the very least, one that Geist wouldn't find fault in.

"We use the electro-staff for bigger stuff like stalkers, plodders, and skrull. The point is made of terror claw, so it'll carry a current and zap whatever you touch." Zak's eyes darkened. "It's deadly against people, so be careful. Don't use it if you're not fully awake or alert." He held the spear out to Ben. "See if you can get the feel for it."

Ben wrapped his fingers around the textured grip on the smooth, wooden staff, cautious to not touch the metal tip or the wires that ran from end to end. He inspected the small rectangular box that wrapped around the shaft, housing the energy stone that powered it. A metal emblem at the bottom of the unit showed a symbol of two upright dragons, each holding a sword and a spear. He rubbed the engraving with his index finger. "What symbol is this?"

Zak leaned forward to see where Ben pointed. "That's the crest for Aerugo." He hooked a thumb in his pocket and nodded toward the image, unfazed by the wind whipping his hair every which way. "Do you recognize it?"

Ben stared at the metal a moment longer, then shook his head. "I don't think so. Aerugo. That's a country?"

"Correct." Zak's smile looked more like a grimace. "We move goods for all the southern kingdoms, and sometimes the queen will gift us new weaponry as payment." He tilted his head toward the spear in Ben's hand. "Anything about that feel familiar? Want to give it a try?"

Ben let Zak lead him through several sequences with the spear, and by the end he was able to twirl the pole without getting his arms twisted. Still, he had to admit a surge of relief when Zak called for a break from the electro-staff.

Ben's hands had been rough with calluses before they began, but now the few he'd had felt raw and worn. He handed the spear back and rubbed his shoulder. Spears required a different set of muscles than he was used to using.

Harsh breathing blended with clangs and the shuffle of feet on the other end of the deck. Ben crouched and sucked in air as he watched William and Kerlee move back and forth in a deadly dance of swords. The advantage of height and reach belonged to William, but Kerlee moved with fluid grace, gliding forward, backward, and sideways.

Geist reclined on the deck, his face tipped toward the sun. He opened an eye and glared at Ben. "It was too boring and painful to keep watching you, Shiny."

Irritation tingled Ben's nerves, and he flexed his hands, pushing down the urge to say or do something ill-advised. Picking a fight with a member of the crew that had rescued him probably wasn't the brightest of ideas. No matter how much he wanted to.

The dangerous glint in Zak's expression should've been forewarning enough.

"Geist. How about you and Ben try some hand-to-hand?" Zak suggested. He glanced askance at Ben. "If your leg is up for it?"

Of course, if the opportunity presented itself on a silver platter, who was he to say no? Ben didn't even try to keep the grin off his face. He cracked his neck. "Bring it."

Zak knelt to pick up the small pile of weapons near Ben and paused when he was closer to Ben than to Geist. He appeared fully focused on clearing the deck, but he raised an eyebrow, his voice low. "Don't hold back."

He retreated as Geist stepped forward with a smirk. Zak's gaze strayed over Ben's shoulder, and Ben turned to see Jade and Krista sitting at the top of the stairs. Jade waved and Krista smiled, a hand cradling her bandage-wrapped arm against her chest. Ben offered a brief grin and focused anew on Geist. Now he *had* to win this one.

Their presence hadn't gone unnoticed by Geist, either. If anything, his sneer only grew, and he peeled off his shirt to reveal his tanned chest. He wadded the shirt and turned, revealing dragon scales tattooed across his back and shoulders. He tossed the wadded cloth back toward Zak, then rolled his neck and raised his fists. "Let's see what you've got."

Ben sank back, settling his weight evenly on his feet, and mirrored Geist's actions. *What have I gotten myself into?* He shifted to the right and ducked as Geist threw a straight jab. Ben half stepped forward and slammed his fist into Geist's gut.

Breath whooshed out of Geist as he bent over. His eyes narrowed, and he snapped a kick at Ben's knee.

Ben pulled away from Geist's attack with a small spring. He bounced on the balls of his feet and raised his fists in defense of his jaw, then swooped in. Ben snapped his fist forward, his knuckles connecting with Geist's chin, a shock of bone hitting bone jolting through his nerves. A familiar jolt. Like something he'd done before. And his body seemed to move as if his muscles knew what to do before he'd even decided. As Geist dropped his guard for the briefest moment, shock registering in his eyes, Ben saw the opening. He struck Geist's jaw with a hard hook. The man's head jerked to the side, leaving his stomach wide open. Ben gripped Geist's shoulder and slammed his knee into Geist's gut.

Just like that, Geist dropped with a thud.

Astonished silence followed by raucous cheers and whistles broke Ben's surprised reverie. Everything about that fight felt familiar. Like he'd had training in hand-to-hand combat. But when? Why? He blinked down at the groaning man, and offered Geist a hand up. "Sorry. That may have been overkill."

Geist rubbed a hand against his face as he pulled his legs under him to sit up. "Just maybe." He scowled and worked his jaw. "Whales. Where'd you learn to fight like that?"

"Intuition." It wasn't a full lie. And it sounded better than, *I have no idea, but I'm clearly better at this than you.* There were ladies present, and he didn't want to come off as an egotistical jerk. Still, he made sure to perch his fist on his hip in a casual display of muscle flexing and ignored the screech of pain from his bruised knuckles.

Geist stood and dusted himself off. His eyes darted to where Jade and Krista sat, and he scowled at Ben. "Beginner's luck. We'll rematch later. I'll take you down then."

Ben couldn't help himself. "Anytime."

Zak walked along the safety line to reach Ben's side. He clapped a hand on Ben's shoulder with a grin. "Impressive." He raised an eyebrow. "Are you getting off in Doldra, or staying on for a bit?"

Ben swiped at the sweat on his forehead and shrugged. "No idea. Stay on, I guess." He straightened his leg with a grimace. "I still can't remember where I'm from, so I suppose I'd be better off traveling. Maybe something will jog my memory."

A tiny niggling doubt reared its ugly head. Would it be beneficial for Ben to not remember who he was? To have a clean slate and start from scratch? Or was he missing something important that was imperative for him to recall?

"Seems reasonable." Zak interrupted Ben's sudden wave of indecision. The warrior waved at the relocated pile of weapons. "We'll go over the other things later, after we've been through Doldra. For now, let's pack everything up; we'll likely be landing soon." He shook his head and chuckled. "Seriously. You have good form. You didn't let the safety line get in your way, you held your ground despite being in the air, and you took out Geist. That's not easy to do. He lives for a good fight, and you were at a disadvantage."

"Thanks." A twinge spiked up Ben's leg, and he held in a hiss of pain. "But I think it's time for me to rest this a bit. Especially if we're going to be walking anywhere soon."

"Fair enough." Zak looked to the distance and stilled. A bittersweet smile softened his eyes. "Almost home."

Ben turned and shock rippled up his back and down to his toes, all but gluing him to the deck. Blue sky stretched overhead, fluffy white clouds scattered here and there. But in front of the *Sapphire*? Behind the city that he could just make out in the distance?

The sky was purple.

CHAPTER NINE

JADE

Jade tightened the leather straps of her aviator hat, snugged her goggles into place, tugged on her safety line, and leaned over the railing of the *Sapphire* to watch the turbine spin. Wind whipped around her, puffing her cream-colored blouse under her thick leather bolero, pushing against her back, and causing her to lean forward. She braced her forearms against the wood and counted as the blades whizzed.

One stalker, two stalker, three stalker. She frowned. There was definitely something off-balance in there. She'd have to take it apart when they landed.

She pushed back and dropped her feet on the deck. Doldra had some good supply merchants for airship parts, so they wouldn't have to delay their rounds for that at least. And she loved when Zak's family came to visit him on the *Sapphire*. They always treated her like extended family. That his niece and nephews were adorable was an added bonus.

The sun had finally risen over the horizon, and its golden rays illuminated the surrounding land for Jade to make out where in the air they were. Flat squares of land, filled with growing produce, gave way to rolling green hills. They could already see the unnatural glow of the purple barrier in the mountains beyond the sprawling city of Doldra.

Almost there.

She turned away from the landscape and took a half step back in surprise. Ben stood just behind her, his hands gripping his safety line. The whistling wind had covered the sound of his arrival.

He stared with squinted eyes over the railing, the wind ruffling his short auburn hair. His brow furrowed, and he leaned toward her. "Is that where we're going?"

Sympathy stirred in Jade's heart at his lost expression. She patted his shoulder as reassuringly as possible, and, for what must have been the third time today, wondered where he was from. His shirt material had a stiffness similar to Aerugan or Lasimeon uniforms, but with colors and a cut distinctly not theirs. "Does it look familiar?"

Ben grimaced and shook his head. "I wish I could say it did."

"Maybe something will wind those memory gears when we get there," Jade offered optimistically. "We'll arrive sometime this evening, and you're welcome to come with us when we go into the city." She raised her eyebrows with a grin. "And we'll get you some proper skyfarer goggles, too."

A smile broke across Ben's face. "Thank you. I appreciate the offer."

"Of course." Her heart warmed at the hope in his eyes, and she leaned back against the rail, pressing her spine to the metal to keep her balance against the wind. His fingers grazed the rail, then gripped it as he stepped closer to the edge. He was broad-shouldered—almost what she'd call stout. His eyes didn't stay fixated at one point. Instead they constantly roved, looking over the scenery, moving to every sound, taking everything in. He stared at the rolling hills moving below them.

"Is this your first time traveling by air?" she asked.

Ben's lips pursed. "I don't know." He moved closer to the aft wall, which provided more shelter from the wind. "Seeing the ground from up high seems familiar, but at the same time, not familiar." He lifted a hand, letting the wind buffet it. "Being in a vehicle open to the air like this? I'm fairly certain this is new."

"And you don't like it," she surmised. His startled expression made her laugh. "You've been all but clinging to everything solid since we took to the sky."

Ben rubbed the back of his neck and shoved his hands in his pockets with a sheepish grimace. "Guilty as charged." He nodded toward her. "What about you? You seem comfortable up here." She leaned against the rail and watched his eyes dilate. "Scarily comfortable."

Jade tried to tamp down on her grin and failed. "I grew up on the *Sapphire*," she explained. "Even before I could walk, I've been in the air, traveling Terrene." A stronger gust of wind knocked her forward a step, and she turned to face the breeze with a laugh and raised hands. "I love it up here." She spoke over her shoulder. "Up here, I'm free. I see the horizon, and it calls to me. I want to explore every last bit of the land, know all the secrets, know all the people, know all that I can."

She glanced back when Ben didn't reply, and she dropped her hands, reaching out to him. "Are you feeling well? You look pale."

Ben blinked and shook his head. "Sorry. I–I just…" he trailed off and squeezed the bridge of his nose. "My mind just blanked for a moment there. I don't know why."

Jade hesitated. He looked almost like he'd been spooked, but she couldn't imagine what it was that would have given him such a reaction. She squeezed his shoulder. "You had a busy morning," she offered. "Get some rest. Maybe that will help."

He nodded several times, his eyes darting from the deck to her. She offered what she hoped was a reassuring smile as she turned away. She unhooked her safety line from the side rail and moved it to the line that would take her to the stairs leading down to the engine room. Wind buffeted against her body as she walked across the deck with both hands on the safety line to stabilize her steps. She blinked at the stairs when she reached them.

Zak sat on the top step, where the entire main deck was visible. His green eyes pierced her through his goggles, and he stood smoothly to let her pass.

"What are you doing here?" She unclipped her first safety line and reattached it on the rail leading down, just past Zak's clip on the thick metal line.

Black fabric shifted as Zak shrugged his broad shoulders and inclined his head toward Ben. "Watching him."

Jade glanced over her shoulder, then back to Zak. She switched over her second line and decided to offer an olive branch in hopes that it would reduce the awkwardness that lingered between them. "Sad, isn't it? I can't imagine not knowing who I am. I hope his memories return soon."

Zak's jaw twitched as he nodded. "Agreed." He hesitated before resting his fingers on her shoulder. Heat blazed across her skin under his touch. "Be careful around him, okay?"

She laughed shortly, trying to hide her surprise. "If it makes you feel better, I will. But just so you know, I did invite him to come along with us to the city."

Zak's lips flattened into a thin line. "Don't go anywhere just the two of you."

Irritation reared its fiery head in her gut, and she shot him an indignant look. "Thank you, *mother*, but I already know to be cautious of strangers," she retorted as she passed Zak. She clattered down two steps, then guilt from her acid tone forced her to pause and speak over her shoulder. "I feel sympathy for him and don't want him to be alone. Maybe we can even help him recover his memory. That's all. You don't have to worry so much." She frowned slightly. "And if he causes you so much concern, why did you bother sparring with him this morning?"

"Jade." Zak grasped at her elbow and waited for her to turn and lift her eyes to him. "I'm sorry. I know you're smart enough to look after yourself." He fluttered his hand and huffed a heavy sigh. "I wanted to see what he was capable of, if he was lying about what he knew or remembered."

"And? What did you learn?"

"That he was well trained in hand-to-hand combat but knows nothing of our typical weaponry." Zak rubbed a hand along his jaw. "I still don't know about him." He looked at her, his eyes dark with concern and honesty. "I just want to make sure you're safe."

The chill in her heart thawed a fraction. He did have a vested interest in keeping her protected, and she couldn't deny that she owed him much for his defense of her last summer. Even if he'd overreacted just a few days ago in the Wyld Woods. And before that—Jade slammed the hatch on that thought and repeated, *olive branch...olive branch* in her mind. She looked up, and the rest of her ire melted away at the care shining in his gaze. He subtly bit his lip, giving away his uncertainty and worry.

Jade suppressed her smile, and gripped his hand briefly. "Forgiven.

And I'll be careful. I promise."

A small grin lifted his lips, despite the concern still in his gaze. "Thank you."

She nodded and clattered down the stairs, intent on escaping his concern. But Zak's edginess had leaked through to Jade, and her mind kept turning over new thoughts to worry about after she'd shared her findings on the turbine with Krista. Even the knowledge that Jade would be able to visit her grandmother's shipping yards held little joy. Instead, bittersweet sorrow mixed with irritation weighed her down.

After all, she wouldn't be able to ever walk in Doldra with Zak at her side. He was only permitted at the Stohner Shipping Yards, and that permission had been grudgingly given by the ruling governor overseeing Doldra in Queen Violet's stead. Jade had never walked through her father's home city—Zak's home city—with one of her oldest friends. Her father and aunt weren't willing to risk Zak being imprisoned because of the stupid Monomi peace treaty from so many years ago.

Jade sighed. She'd still take Ben around Doldra, maybe stir some memories for him, but she'd take Krista and Briar with her, too. Promises made to Zak were promises she kept at all costs.

But what did he have against Ben? He seemed like a nice guy.

Her cheeks heated, and she pressed the backs of her hands against them. Nice. And cute. But that wasn't a factor. She genuinely wanted to see Ben regain his memory. And even more than that, she wanted her friendship with Zak to be restored.

Granted, if this mission didn't go well, and everyone continued to treat her like a baby bird, she and Krista would go through with their plan. Briar had no problem with their scheme, but Zak would definitely become unhinged over it.

He was so preoccupied with keeping her safe—from dragons, from Prince Weston, from anything and everything—that he'd forgotten her need for independence. She wouldn't, *couldn't*, be stifled by both her father *and* Zak any longer.

Even if she may lose Zak's friendship by her own decisions.

CHAPTER TEN

BEN

"How much you wanna bet that the overseer will be here within the hour?" Geist asked, leaning against the bunk bed across from Ben. He rubbed at the bruise forming on his jaw and raised his eyebrows at Kerlee.

Kerlee shook his head as he pulled a fresh, orange shirt from his trunk. "No way. I'm not making sucker bets."

Geist grumbled and crossed his arms, rubbing a hand against the faint traces of the ink-drawn dragon scales on the back of his forearm. He narrowed his eyes at Ben. "You're not bad," he decided. "You want to come with us to visit the Hawk?"

"The what?" Ben wrinkled his nose as Ash walked into their bunk room. Whatever soap he'd just used in the showers was strong enough that Ben's eyes nearly crossed. "What's the Hawk? And where is it?"

"The Crimson Hawk," Kerlee explained. He yanked his shirt off and pulled on the orange monstrosity. "The Captain's sister—Garnet—technically owns the place, but she lets the Monomi run it while she's out with us. Best drinks in town."

Ben flexed his leg, considering. He hadn't popped any stitches, but it was tender and slightly swollen after this morning's sparring. "I should probably pass for the night, thanks. Maybe tomorrow?"

Ash shrugged. "Suit yourself." He paused as if a thought had just occurred to him, and he turned, eyeing Ben with a slow-growing grin that Ben could only think of as predatory. "Are you going into town tomorrow? Do you have anyone showing you around?"

"Yeah, Jade said she and Krista would show me around. And I think Briar is going, too?" Ben didn't like the look that Ash exchanged with Geist and Kerlee. "Is there something wrong with that?"

The guys ignored him. Geist smirked at Kerlee. "Ten lut says—"

"I'm not taking sucker bets," Kerlee repeated. He stood and dusted off his pants, shooting Ben what he could only interpret as a look of pity. "So you're not coming with us?"

Ben waved them on. "I'll be fine. Probably go see what I can find in the mess for dinner, though."

"Briar made his 'use everything in the cold box' soup," Ash said as he shrugged on a light suit jacket. "It's good."

Geist grabbed a hat and moved to the door, Ash and Kerlee falling in line behind him. Ben trailed them to the main deck and sucked in a breath of fresh air. For not knowing where he was, or where he was from, he really didn't have it too bad. The crew had taken him in with great generosity in clothing, and they fed him and included him in their training and airship drills. Life on the *Sapphire* with them wouldn't be so bad.

Laughter echoed from the mess hall, and Ben wandered into the room to find Jade, Krista, Briar, and Zak sitting around the table, bowls half-filled with soup.

Krista looked up from her bowl and waved. "Join us."

Ben sat on Briar's left and accepted an empty bowl that Jade slid across the table. Briar ladled a thick, hearty-smelling stew into it and handed Ben a spoon.

Briar pulled a plate of garlic bread toward Ben. "Since you're here, we may as well go over our plans for tomorrow, right?" His gaze flicked to Zak, then back to Ben. "If nothing else, we need to find you proper gear for being aboard an airship."

Ben tried a spoonful of soup and burned his tongue. He set the spoon down and grabbed a metal mug. "Sounds good so far."

"And maybe we'll find something that will help grease those gears," Jade said enthusiastically. Zak cleared his throat and she tilted her head, examining him for a tense moment before she looked back at Ben, her eyes determined. "Maybe we'll go by the markets that sell goods from other kingdoms. See if there's anything there that reminds you of home?"

The click of boots in the hall distracted Ben, and he looked to the door at the same time as Zak tensed.

Zak turned his head just enough that a thick strand of hair fell across his eyes.

A short, scrawny man, whom Ben didn't recognize, walked through the doorway as if he owned the place. His dark eyes skimmed over each of them and stopped on Zak. He straightened his tweed suit vest and moved closer to Zak with mincing steps. "Renegade Monomi."

Zak leaned over his bowl and pressed his palms against the table. "How can I help you, Overseer Nevin?"

Nevin's nose twitched, and he raised an eyebrow at the pot of soup in the center of the table. His nose wrinkled. "I am here on behalf of the esteemed Governor Ethan Bentley to learn how long you and the *Sapphire* plan to be in Doldra."

Zak shrugged even as a muscle in his jaw twitched. "That's up to the captain, not me." He gestured out the door. "I believe Captain Slate is in his room, if you wish to speak to him yourself."

"I'm also to remind you that you aren't permitted anywhere in the city. And if you set foot on Doldran soil outside this property that you have been so graciously allowed to be on, there will be consequences."

"And I thank Mistress Stohner for fighting on my behalf for me to visit my family here. She is a generous woman."

Briar gripped his spoon as if it were a weapon, and Krista practically vibrated in her seat, her eyes narrowed at Nevin in a look of undisguised loathing. Jade's freckles were almost invisible against the backdrop of her flushed cheeks. Ben straightened slowly in his seat as the tension in the room thickened.

Zak swallowed a mouthful before he turned to look at the overseer. "Anything else?"

Nevin adjusted his monocle and peered down his nose at Zak, his eyes hard. "And I personally feel the need to also remind you that Monomi are not permitted to train in any way within the city limits of Doldra—despite being on private property." He sniffed. "And should you or any of your family be found in violation of the treaty, the consequences would be most dire for your clan."

"It's hard to forget such rules. We remember."

"Excellent." Nevin turned on his heel, causing the rubber to squeak. "I recommend you don't plan to stay in Doldra long, Mister Monomi."

Ben waited until the sound of footsteps receded before he let out a low whistle. "Who spit in his ale?"

Briar snorted. "That's pretty typical for Nevin." Briar cocked his head at Zak. "Was it just me, or was he less abrasive this time?"

"We've seen worse sides of him," Zak muttered. He pushed away his bowl with a regretful shake of his head. "He couldn't have waited until I finished dinner."

Jade touched Zak's arm, pulling his brooding gaze away from the table. "Is there anything I can get you while in town tomorrow?"

Zak's shoulders relaxed as he considered her question, and Ben stirred his forgotten soup, hoping it hadn't cooled too much. The quiet clank of metal on metal seemed to draw Zak's attention, and he looked at Ben for an uncomfortably long moment, his gaze hardening. Zak pushed away from the table and adjusted his sword belt, his posture stiff. "You know my opinion of you going out." He glanced at Jade from the corner of his eye, his jaw set. "Just watch your back while you're away." He stalked out of the room.

Awkward silence reigned in the room, and Ben lowered his spoon without letting it touch the bowl. Briar pinched the bridge of his wide nose. Jade sighed and rubbed her face in her hands before excusing herself with a quiet voice and a weak smile.

Ben stared at his bowl of soup and swallowed. What had that been about? Had he inadvertently done something? Clearly Zak hadn't warmed up to him as much as he'd thought. And what did Nevin mean about a treaty and Zak not going into Doldra? What had Zak done?

Briar sighed. "Don't read into it too much, Ben. Things always get ugly around here after Nevin comes by."

"That's an understatement." Krista stood. "I'm going to go check on Jade." A small smile graced her face as she stacked her dishes together. "We'll be ready to go as soon as Jade's done meeting with Ellie in the morning, so you may want to get some rest." She gave a meaningful nod toward the door. "Because who knows what tomorrow will bring."

CHAPTER ELEVEN

SLATE

The brick pavers lining the path to his mother's main office were new. Slate paused to inspect them while making sure his posse was following him through Stohner Shipping Yards. His mother had a knack for administration and used her money wisely, buying land and spreading out the business. Warehouses dotted the acres like mushrooms, each with its own particular type of goods to be stored and moved, and the two buildings closest to the office were reserved as a hostel for the various crews that stayed in Doldra on business.

Slate grimaced at the sight of the joyberry bushes blooming by the front step. True to form, their sweet scent set his sinuses on fire, and he sneezed.

He pulled out his handkerchief with watering eyes, and Jade giggled behind him. "Have I ever mentioned how glad I am that I did *not* inherit your allergies?"

"At least every other month, yes," Slate replied wryly. He shot a look at his twin sister while he opened the door, and shook his head in mock grief. "And somehow, whichever month you don't mention it, Garnet will."

Garnet patted his back as she passed by. "What else is family for?"

"Oh, I don't know. Love and support?"

"I think you'll only find that with your mom," Victor snarked as he hung his hat on the provided rack.

"Even from my own crew? Ouch." Slate tugged Jade's hand, and she turned to give him a quick hug. He tweaked the blue-and-black feathered fascinator resting amidst her braids. "Do you want to check on everyone else after we greet your grandmother?"

"Oh, you know it!" Jade's eyes sparkled. "I'm curious if we can get Ben's memory gears lubed enough to have him remember where he's from."

Slate snorted in amusement as he stepped down after Jade into Elinora's meeting room. *Lubed. What slang will the youth come up with next?*

His mother stood just inside the doorway, greeting each of them with a warm smile. Her rich brown hair had faded over the years, giving way to streaks of gray and silver, and the light in her eyes now shone with the wisdom and patience that only experience and grief could grant. She hugged Garnet and Jade and cooed over their wardrobe choices, then kissed Slate on the cheek while Victor seated himself at the table.

Slate sank into a nearby chair with a small sigh. Elinora's informal meeting room felt warm and cozy, with cream-colored wall paper, a molded ceiling, and family portraits that lined the walls. A genuine Antius-made secretary desk sat in the corner—the only distinctly practical concession to business that Elinora had in the room.

Initial pleasantries passed quickly, and Zebediah and Esther

Monomi arrived soon after Jade had left to join her friends. Guilt and pleasure warred in Slate at the sight of the older couple. The years had not been easy for them, losing their eldest son to the duty of protecting the barrier, and losing their youngest to banishment. Yet strength and dignity radiated from the former Guardians as they joined Slate and the others at the glossy table.

Slate let a deep breath fill his lungs before breathing out some of his impatience to talk about the barrier. Some topics were just as important as the keystone. And whether they ever realized it or not, their familial status as lesser nobles was largely due to his actions so many years ago. He owed it to them. "How are things here for your family?"

Zebediah filled the wooden frame of the chair with little room to spare, and a shrug of his expansive shoulders made the entire seat creak. The lines around his eyes and forehead had deepened, and gray peppered his temples. "About the same as last time you were here." His large hands cradled the fragile teacup that Elinora had provided for him. "If anything, Governor Bentley has gotten worse than before."

Garnet scoffed from Slate's right. "Worse? How is that even possible?"

Zebediah's eyes darkened as he blew out a deep breath. "Small things, mostly. Blame-shifting, taking credit that isn't his to take, so on and so forth. Standard politician." His lips turned up at the corners. "But more people are starting to see him for what he really is, and they're getting fed up with his way of running things."

"Well, that's good to hear." Garnet smiled.

Esther nodded. "Indeed. Overseer Nevin has been relentless in watching our family and associates, waiting for us to do something that violates the treaty. I'm sure he'll visit Zak sometime soon." She leaned over the table, resting her black-sheathed elbows against the wood. "How is he?"

Slate shifted in his seat and side-eyed his sister. She looked at him and pressed her lips together, then twitched her head at him. Slate sighed quietly.

It was one thing to talk to Zak about everything when onboard the *Sapphire*, Garnet at his side. But to mention it to Zak's parents when on Doldran soil? Slate's stomach twisted, even though he knew they would agree with his and Garnet's frank assessment and intervention.

"He's doing well," Slate hedged. "He's extremely skilled in dragon combat, he's a natural when it comes to security, and I have no real complaints."

Zebediah lifted a black eyebrow in an eerily similar manner to his youngest child. "Any non-real complaints?"

Garnet puffed out her cheeks as she traced a finger along the rim of her porcelain cup. "We had to talk to him about boundaries with Jade," she admitted with a small wince. "Nothing happened, but there was, still is"—she waved her hand at the semantics—"a noticeable attraction that we had to address."

Victor snorted into his mug and raised a long-fingered hand to ward off Garnet's concern. "Noticeable attraction to those who aren't as perceptively challenged as your daughter, sir." Slate's first mate chuckled and shook his head. "As clear as it was to all of us, she didn't notice anything until he started ignoring her. With great difficulty, I might add."

Slate winced at the truth of Victor's words. He and Garnet had had to talk to Zak right after the Perennial winter ball, and the next few days had been nothing short of painful. Zak's awkwardness and brooding had been bad enough. But Jade's confusion and hurt even now gnawed at Slate. Three months had eased some of the tension between the two. And it vacillated—some moments they returned to their normal banter and level of comfort. Other days, Zak remembered the boundaries better. It was for Jade's own good—whether she knew it yet or not.

With the opening pleasantries and family matters discussed, he could focus on the question that burned in his mind. He sipped the last of his spicy tea and set the cup down with a gentle *plink*. He leaned forward, and the chair creaked. "How is the keystone holding up? Has anything changed?"

Zebediah and Esther exchanged grim looks.

Elinora answered. "From what I hear through the rumor mill, the time flux around the citadel is getting worse, though Bentley is trying to hide it." His mother frowned, and she crossed her arms with a small huff of annoyance. "None of my men have been able to get close enough to confirm the reports. Void Born, stuffy governor and his goons don't trust us."

"I wonder why," Slate replied dryly. He fell silent as he mulled over her news. If the time flux was worsening, then the keystone was weakening. And if the keystone failed, the barrier would fall. And if the barrier fell, all southern Terrene would be defenseless against the north. The northerners' blood-bond and their desire to have everyone enslaved or dead would become a real threat.

Families would be separated and slaughtered. Slavery would run rampant.

Being controlled, ruled by pain, and under the whim of some ancient Elph wasn't high on Slate's list of things he wanted to also be responsible for—let alone experience.

Esther smiled grimly. She tucked a strand of silvered blonde hair behind her ear. "He doesn't trust anyone who's connected with us. Bentley has been trying to hide the problems at the citadel, and refuses to let any Monomi near it—even though we're the only ones who have some understanding of the keystone and are the trained Guardians for it."

Silence fell on the table as Garnet, Victor, and Slate absorbed the news. Grief punched the air out of Slate's lungs, and he bowed his shoulders. He absently rubbed at the knobby scar over his eye. If only things had turned out differently that day. If only he had said, "no." If only they had all lived. If only...He sighed. *If regrets and wishes were currency, I'd be a rich man.*

The world was too large, hiding away the one man he needed to find.

One of the alarms triggered by the keystone had given him a single clue: an Elph had been there. An Elph had masterminded the entire fall of the Doldras family, and whoever it was must have also been the one responsible for the near-collapse of the keystone and barrier—nearly dooming the entire southern Terrene population to slavery. And that man had murdered Zak's brother Zane.

Slate clenched his fist. He would find the son of a whale. Eventually.

Wrongs had to be righted. Blood spilled in reparation. Vengeance.

Victor sighed. "So we're no closer than we were before?"

"Not exactly." Elinora pushed away from the table, and she ducked into the adjoining kitchen before returning with the kettle. She refilled Slate's empty cup and topped off Garnet's and Zebediah's teacups before returning the pot. She sank back into her seat with her usual grace, straight-backed in her burnished brown-and-gold corset. "Haven't you heard the rumors?"

"Rumors?" Slate stopped tracing the whorls in the tabletop with his finger and gave Ellie his full attention. "What rumors?"

Ellie tilted her head with a raised brow. "How have you not heard? There are stories circling of ghosts that came through the barrier, over by Loore's Landing."

Slate stared at her blankly, his brain trying to make sense of her words. Ghosts? Through the barrier? "How...how would there be ghosts? And through the *barrier*?"

Victor perked up. "Well, that's an unusual sighting."

"That's why the rumor mill is going crazy," Zebediah replied. He stared at his palms and frowned before meeting Slate's eyes. "What else could go through the barrier, if not ghosts?"

Slate shivered. What, indeed? "I guess we'll make our way over to Loore's Landing," Slate said as he leaned back in his chair. "Ask around, see what we can find."

"I'm afraid that will have to wait," Garnet replied, her tone regretful. "We still have that shipment that we need to deliver to Aerugo first."

Ellie sighed and nodded. "I need you to focus on deliveries for a bit. We're down two airships for repairs, and I need you to help keep things running smoothly in the meantime."

Slate's stomach clenched at the thought of putting off the lead, but loyalty and responsibility forced him to agree. "Soon, then."

"Hopefully." Ellie took a sip of her tea. "Anything else happen on your trip?"

Garnet lifted a shoulder in a half shrug. "Well, we did find a dragon nest, and Ben."

Slate rolled his eyes. "Yes, that's true. We found trouble in the form of stalkers and terrors, and an amnesiac with no fashion sense."

Amused curiosity arched Esther's brow. "You found someone?"

Slate gently swirled the tea in his mug as he nodded. "Found a guy passed out by a herd of plodders. Jaxton is convinced Ben's got memory loss, and in the meantime, Zak's keeping a close eye on him."

Esther accepted Slate's news with serene interest. "I'm glad you found the poor soul." Her eyes glinted. "And I'm even gladder to hear that you aren't taking anything for granted, and keeping an eye on him, regardless of what the esteemed doctor says."

"I'm not taking any chances. And I'm not giving up." Slate stared at the grainy reflection in the table of the elder Monomi. The distortion and natural lighting made the man look younger somehow. Almost like Zane. Slate swallowed the lump in his throat and blinked away the moisture of sorrow. If regrets were wishes...

"Well, I'll be returning to Aerugo within the week," Elinora announced, tapping her fingers against her teacup. "And I'll keep an ear out for any more rumors of interest." She traced the handle with a manicured fingernail, her brow wrinkled. "I don't know when I'll be able to spare you to investigate all the way over there, but we can at least try to stay apprised."

Slate nodded and set his jaw. "I'm going to restore our keystone to full strength, no matter how many years it takes me." He looked up at Zebediah and allowed his determination to show through. "I'm not going to let so many lives continue to be endangered. And I'm going to fix my mistakes."

CHAPTER TWELVE

JADE

The brisk Fervar breeze sent a chill down Jade's back, and she pulled her coat tight.

It would have been faster to take one of the streamtrans into the City Circle, but the group had ultimately decided to walk. Ben was clearly enraptured by the tall brick buildings and the billowing smoke from chimneys in High Doldra, and Krista and Briar didn't mind a longer jaunt together away from the *Sapphire*. And maybe something would spark a memory for Ben.

What bothered Jade about the day trip was Zak's attitude right before her group left the shipping yards. He'd returned to being distant, with a cool gaze and neutral words. No pleasant goodbye, just a simple "Don't trust anyone," as if he didn't think she'd already heard that enough from him—or her father—after last night. And when she'd glanced back to her grandmother's property, he'd been standing by the fence, a dark silhouette, with only his single hoop earring gleaming in the morning light.

Jade huffed and shook her head. Whatever had made their friendship start progressing to something more was gone. He was clear enough with his unspoken words—he only considered her a friend. If that. It was high time for her to accept it and move on. Somehow.

A patch of fog wafted in front of her, and she wrinkled her nose, waving her hand to try to dissipate it. Buildings towering on either side of them belched white steam and hazy smoke, causing currents and eddies in the brisk spring air as it mixed with the warm humidity. If only Doldra would adopt newer steam-tech. Like Piovant's superior venting. The narrow street opened up far ahead, widening into the City Circle of shops, stores, and merchants.

Krista broke Jade's reverie. "Remind me before we head back, I need to get a new hair potion."

Jade glanced at Krista's tight, dark curls. The hair potions they'd picked up in Aerugo hadn't done Krista's dry hair any favors. "I'd let you use what I have, if it worked for your hair type."

"If only life were so simple." Krista sighed dramatically. "What do we need to get for the ship before we can start our personal shopping?"

Jade pulled her list out of the deep pocket in her duster and held it out to Krista. "We have enough in the budget to buy brand new headlamps if we want. What do you think? Replacement crystals, or new tech?"

Krista bit her lip as she walked, then shook her head. "I don't like the gas-light tech coming from Lasim. Let's just get replacement crystals if we can find them." She shot Jade a grin. "Maybe we can save some of that budget for that shiny condenser upgrade."

"Yes! Great idea." Jade folded her list and returned it to its pocket with a decisive nod. She looked over her shoulder, to talk to the guys, and frowned at the frizzy red strands in her line of sight. She pressed her hands on her curls in an attempt to subdue the damage done by the humid air as she waited for Briar to stop talking to Ben so they could make their plans.

Bless Ben, he looked enthralled in whatever story Briar was weaving for him. He smiled and followed along, asking questions whenever Briar paused for breath. Ben's warm laugh echoed off the brick buildings, and his eyes sparkled with amusement. Too late, she realized that she'd been caught staring. Ben winked.

Blushing, Jade turned to look at Krista, letting her hair hide her face. Of all things. Caught ogling a guy she barely knew. *Barrier, take me now.*

Krista leaned into Jade's space, and she wrapped her good arm around Jade's shoulders. "I saw that," she whispered. "Moving on from Zak, finally?"

Jade pulled away, biting back her shriek of protest. She clutched Krista's arm and leaned close to her friend. "No, I'm not 'moving on.' There's nothing to move on from!" she whispered vehemently. "And it's not as if I like Ben. I was just…" *Think of something, quick.* "I was admiring how the sun brings out the red highlights in his hair."

Krista's shoulders shook as she raised an eyebrow and smirked. "For your sake, I hope you never have some big secret to keep. The world would know it within a minute."

Too embarrassed and irritated to admit the truth of Krista's words, Jade chose not to respond. Adding fuel to the fire of Krista's imagination wouldn't help any.

"Miss Stohner!"

Jade looked up from the cobblestones and searched the nearby faces for the owner of the voice. A strapping young man about her age stalked toward her with earnest eyes and a carefully curled moustache. He stopped several paces away and bowed.

"James." Jade smiled, and ingrained etiquette made her bob in a shallow curtsy. "It's been a while." She motioned toward an emblem on his gray uniform. "Is that new?"

Her father had only a handful of family friends that he'd made a point of her meeting specifically, and James was one of them. Something about his grandfather being one of Slate's commanding officers "back in the day," or something along those lines.

James adjusted his gray military police cap and nodded with a broad smile. "It's Ensign Brigley now. Is your family well? Anything new?"

"Nothing out of the ordinary." Jade chuckled. "All are well, and life's been full with our usual brand of misadventures."

"Excellent." He noticed Briar and Ben and nodded to them, his gaze lingering on Ben's outfit. James half raised an eyebrow before schooling his face into neutrality and returning his attention to Jade. "I hope the Monomi didn't get too hard a time from Overseer Nevin's visit last night." He tapped a finger against his sword hilt and dropped his voice. "Please, let Zak know that the Monomi don't stand alone."

Jade pushed down her rising emotions at the mention of Zak, the Monomi family, and Nevin, and dipped into a short curtsy again. "Thank you. Your support means much."

A small, tight smile spread on James' face. "Of course. Now, if you'll excuse me." He tipped his hat and melted into the flow of the morning crowd.

Ben crossed his arms and frowned as he looked off in the direction that James disappeared to. "Is something going on? Why didn't Zak come with us?"

Briar's lips puckered out, then in, and then pressed into a flat line. His eyes flicked to Jade and back to Ben. "Zak's not allowed in Doldra. It was a battle to get permission for him to be allowed at the shipping yards, but because he's part of the *Sapphire* crew, and the shipping yards are private property, he's permitted." Briar shrugged. "He's the exiled Monomi. Overseer Nevin comes by every time we're in port to remind Zak that he's the renegade, the banished, the unwanted."

"Monomi, as in Zak's family?"

"Zak's clan, yes," Krista answered, tucking her arms behind her back. "They're a noble family here in Doldra that became the Guardians of the keystone back when the barrier went up."

Jade nodded. "His clan excels in stealth and fighting and all the secrecy and stuff needed to keep the citadel safe." She scowled. "But the massacre of the royal family messed up that system, and now his family is not only a lesser noble class, but not very loved here."

"And there's a treaty with a long list of what the Monomi can and can't do." Briar rolled his wrist in a fluid motion. "Nevin likes to rub it in that Zak broke the treaty as a teenager and got exiled. Bleeding Void Born scum. I'd love to give him my thoughts on the matter."

Jade gripped the hem of her duster and bit back her opinion of the government. Something that happened so long ago shouldn't affect her friend now.

"What did Zak do?" Ben asked as he idly scratched at the beard scruff that had started to grow in. "Scowl at the wrong person?"

Briar huffed a laugh and ran his hand through his short black hair before dragging it down his face. "How do I even explain all that?" He blew out a breath and glanced out of the corner of his eye. "It's a sore spot, so don't try asking him unless you're ready for whatever his reaction is."

Jade quirked her lips at Briar's words. He wasn't wrong. Zak talked about his banishment rarely, and his early childhood even more rarely. And if he did talk about either, oftentimes he'd be in a funk for at least a day after.

Jade motioned to lead them on through the crowd, but she stopped when she realized Ben hadn't kept pace. He stood in the middle of the street, arms folded and mouth gaping as he leaned back, his eyes trained above her head. Jade dodged a horse and rider and moved back to Ben's side to see what held his attention. Briar and Krista trailed behind her.

A mauve haze stretched toward the sky like a large curtain that hung from invisible hooks. It curved away on either side, as far as one could see. Ben skipped forward a few steps, then stopped.

He pointed to it as he turned to them. "I didn't get a chance to ask before. Why is there a huge purple..." He glanced back at it and turned back, an unsure expression puckering his lips. "*Thing* in the sky?"

Jade couldn't help the small giggle that escaped her. Somehow, Ben made confusion look cute.

No. Stop that thought right there, lash it down, and leave it to die.

"Wherever you're from, I'm guessing it's midland and not by the barrier." Jade gently tugged his sleeve, and Ben reluctantly tore his eyes from the sight to look at her. She tucked her hands behind her and walked backward slowly, trusting Krista to stop her before she ran into anyone. Jade shifted her tone to a scholarly drawl. "The barrier is what protects southern Terrene from the great evil of the blood-bonded Elph in the north. It is a curtain of time and Void magic; instant death comes to any who touch it. Without it, we would all be enslaved and turned into mindless zombies."

Krista doubled over with a burst of laughter, clutching a hand against her corset while she wiped tears from her eyes. "You stole that last line from Zak, didn't you?" She rubbed her hand against her skirt, still chuckling.

"Silence!" Jade commanded, trying to hold humor out of her voice despite Krista's scoff. "I am educating our recruit." Jade narrowed her eyes at Ben and lowered her voice, as if telling a scary story. "Nearly twenty years ago, the Doldran keystone was sabotaged during an attack by the Reformers on the royal family here, and ruin had a chance to sweep the lands." She gestured grandly and almost hit Krista with her hand. "But brave heroes fought against the evil renegades," she brought her fisted hands together in front of her chest, "and we are safe today because of their sacrifices." Jade shrugged, and the twinkle in her eyes dimmed. "The keystone still has issues though, making it fragile, so wherever we go in Terrene, we're searching for anything that can help stabilize it, as it powers the barrier."

"What is the keystone, exactly?"

Jade blinked at him. "It's one of six other keystones that are linked together to make the barrier. I've never gotten an actual explanation of how it works. Focuses the manipulation of time and Void, I think. Either way, no keystone, no barrier. No barrier, no safety."

Ben's brow furrowed, and he rubbed his jaw as he stared up at the barrier again. "I've never seen anything like that. I would remember something that majestic."

Krista tucked her hands in a pose that mirrored Jade's and shot her a crooked grin. "I still say you stole all that from Zak."

Jade pushed Krista's shoulder with a light-hearted scowl. "Of course not!" She laughed. "I got it from Mister Monomi."

"And Zak got it fro—" Krista started before Briar interrupted, slinging an arm over both girls' shoulders.

"If you ladies don't mind, before the next history lesson starts, I'm going to escape with our friend and find him clothing that normal people wear."

Jade and Krista laughed as color rose to Ben's cheeks. Dressed in borrowed clothes, he didn't stand out too badly, but Zak's black shirt pulled tight on Ben's chest and hung loose in the sleeves. Kerlee's crimson pin-striped pants may look halfway decent on Kerlee, but on Ben they were downright comical. Better than Ben's odd, swirled, multi-hued pants and stiff shirt with the foreign three-color patch on the sleeve, but only by a bit.

Jade slipped her hand through the slit in her jacket to reach her money pouch. She pulled out four deep blue lut and passed them over to Briar. "Father gifted this to Ben for clothing, but I'm willing to bet that Ben doesn't know his money."

Briar held one out for Ben to examine.

"Can't say I've seen anything like this before." Ben held up the lut and bounced it in his hand. "What is this? Some sort of rock?"

Krista rolled her eyes and propped a hand on her hip. "It's actually a mineral, but we use it as a currency. And that's quite a bit there."

The unfamiliar currency rolled in his palm and slipped out of his fingers. He squatted to grab it off the cobblestones, but Krista beat him to it. She dumped the lut back into his hand. "Don't lose all that!" she exclaimed.

"Sorry, sorry." Ben handed it back to Briar. "I'll let him handle my finances for now."

Briar snorted and tucked the money away. "Better in my hands than these two—they'll spend every last bit you own on some sort of tech."

"Will not!" Jade protested, cheeks burning. She dug the point of her boot into a cobblestone and muttered, "I'd save some for clothes and necessities."

Ben laughed. "But important things first."

"Basically."

"Like I said." Briar shook his head before kissing Krista and looking over his shoulder at Ben. "Better in my hands than either of these two." Briar leaned toward Jade and lowered his voice. "How about you ladies discuss the plan while I distract our new friend?" She nodded, and his cheek dimpled with a grin. Briar pointed to a nearby tailor's shop and steered Ben toward it.

Jade and Krista turned to walk down a side street lined with stores for airship parts and mechanical inventions, with the odd café or gambling den peppered into the mix. Old metal signs hung over each doorway, and several vendors had wares displayed on tables in front of their shops.

Jade's gaze snagged on a faded sign in one of the windows that stated in bold letters, "Monomi not welcome." She hunched her shoulders with a sigh and kicked at a pebble in the road. "Everything happened almost twenty years ago. Can't they get over it?"

Krista didn't even glance at the sign. Jade moped and complained about this topic often enough whenever in Doldra that Krista had probably been expecting the comment. True to form, Krista silently patted Jade's shoulder.

Jade believed Zak's side of the story regarding the fall of the

Doldras family: the Monomi had defended the royal family and the barrier as best they could when in the face of betrayal. And the Reformers that led the attack had done a wonderful job of turning the public against the Guardian clan, despite the losses the Monomi suffered. It was simply too hard for the public to look beyond the deaths of the royal family.

"I think I'm going to go by the royal mausoleum later," Jade announced. It had been over a year since she'd last laid flowers at her uncle, aunt, and baby cousin's family monument. She'd also go by the cemetery for royal staff, and lay flowers at Miss Clara's grave on behalf of Uncle Andre. And then finish her rounds by stopping at Zane's plot, and tell his memorial stone of Zak's latest adventures. Zak couldn't visit his elder brother's burial spot, but Jade could—and would—on his behalf.

Stupid law against Monomi. Jade kicked at a weed growing through the cobblestone cracks. Won't even let a good man visit his own family in his own house, or pay respects to a fallen family member, or—

"I'll go with you." Krista interrupted Jade's mental tirade and stepped behind Jade to allow a couple enough space to exit a shop. Jade ignored the wide-eyed looks the two gave her loose, multi-pocketed pants. Krista pointed to a shop that advertised luminary crystals and tilted her head. "Do you think it could happen again?"

"An entire royal family being wiped out overnight?"

"Yes." Krista followed Jade into the store, and they both nodded to the shopkeeper, who greeted them. They reached the back counter that held wooden racks of loose crystals that would fit into the headlamps. Krista continued, "I mean, it's not like it'd happen here in Doldra again. Not with your queen living in Aerugo."

Jade hummed as she picked up a blue crystal, turned it over, frowned at a crack in the facet, and returned it to the display tray. "It could happen. Maybe in Lasim, but the politics there aren't bad right now. Aerugo…is too powerful and scary for anyone with half a brain to consider doing that there."

Krista's laugh chimed pleasantly against Jade's bitter chuckle. Anyone with half a brain would avoid Aerugo as if it were a pyrodragon.

"Change of steamtrans." Krista leaned against a pillar to the right of the tray and crossed her arms with care to not hurt her still-mending arm. She tugged her gloves up with a shiver. "What's our plan?" She cast Jade a speculative glance. "You seem fairly invested in helping Ben."

Jade sucked in a breath and clutched the pink crystal she was inspecting. She shook her head and set the stone back on the velvet tray. "I only want to help him remember where he's from. There's nothing more to that." Jade skimmed her finger over a smooth blue stone and turned with a small sigh to face her friend. "As for leaving, I'm torn. I want to help my father, but…"

"But we've gone over this before, Jade. It's your choice. If you decide to leave and work on an airship that will let you work up to being a captain, Briar and I will follow you."

"I know." Jade scuffed the pointed toe of her boot against the wood floor. "And Zak's already starting to steam me with his mother-hen act, but I *do* want to help Ben. And he's probably going to be staying on for a few more runs."

Krista nudged Jade with her shoulder. "Then we'll stay till Ben has his memory back." Krista pulled on one of her dark curls, and it sprang back into place when she let go. A small smirk played on her lips. "Unless you change your mind at that point."

Jade rolled her eyes with a scoff. "I have no plans for anything of that nature, thanks." She handed Krista the two stones she'd picked out. Krista held them up toward the window to examine them. Then she nodded. They strolled through the store, checking out other crystals of interest and ogling a luminary crystal that stood as high as Krista.

"He likes you, you know."

"What?" Jade froze mid-step and grabbed the bronze stand by her to keep her balance. She stared at Krista with wide eyes. "Zak or Ben?"

Krista grinned and casually rubbed the back of her gloved knuckles against her cheek as if the conversation didn't amuse her as much as it clearly did. "Possibly Ben. Definitely Zak."

Jade offered the shopkeeper a wan smile as Krista placed their purchases on the counter. Jade leaned a hip against it and turned back to Krista, trying to understand how her friend had reached such a conclusion. "You're teasing me. If Zak liked me, he wouldn't act like he has been. And Ben?" Jade shook her head and tried to ignore her traitorous heart flutter.

"I'm perfectly serious."

Jade huffed a small laugh and closed her eyes.

"No, listen to me." Krista widened her stance and crossed her arms. "Aerugo happened in summer, you two started getting closer, then suddenly," Krista snapped her fingers, "he's brooding and distant and can't stay consistent in how he acts toward you. He likes you. I'm betting he got warned off by some over-protective family member."

She smirked.

Jade's stomach sank, and she pulled out her leather money pouch, counted out three yellow lut, and handed them to the shopkeeper. "There's a difference between liking someone and mothering them."

Krista shook her head. "A mother hen doesn't follow someone around, protecting them and moping over it." She scooped up the bag of crystals from the shopkeeper and helped tuck them in Jade's satchel. "What if your father warned him away? Trust me, there's more to his feelings than you think."

Jade wrinkled her nose skeptically. "Since when does Zak listen to anything my father says? Besides," she took a deep breath and released her words in a gush, "I've decided to move on. I can't keep up with his distance and then stifling protectiveness." She stared out the window and tried to ignore Krista's dropped jaw and the shopkeeper who lingered by the counter. "If he wanted to pursue something with me, he had a chance, and he left it. I *need* to move on."

"I...uh...wow." Krista stepped back to appraise Jade. "I'm impressed."

"Thanks." Jade hefted her bag and nodded goodbye to the shopkeeper, then raised a hand against the glare of sunlight. She followed Krista onto the bustling street, her mind in turmoil as her feet moved without conscious thought to direction.

Jade had once harbored the idea that there may be more to Zak's devout protection of her, but once the injuries he'd received on her behalf were healed, nothing else was mentioned. Not one thing changed at all, really, except the dynamic between them in their normal interaction had something...more to it. One day she'd look up from replacing a pipe or tubing, and Zak would be nearby, watching with a smolder in his eyes that caused her heart to flutter and her cheeks to heat. Other days, he'd barely look at her when passing a plate at the meal table.

Then the ball had happened.

Jade laughed aloud as Zak spun her away then tugged her back into his arms, his grip on her firm, yet still so very gentle. His eyes shone with merriment as he smiled down at her, and she beamed up at him as she swayed to the music, her aquamarine gown swishing around her ankles.

"I'm pretty sure this is the most I've seen you smile at a ball," Zak commented, his tone conversational. A lock of dark hair fell across Zak's forehead, and she lifted her gloved hand from his shoulder to brush it back. His eyes crinkled in thanks.

Heat suffused her cheeks, but Jade held his gaze and settled her hand back on the shoulder of his formal black jacket. "Probably because this is the most fun I've ever had at a ball."

"Oh really? Any idea as to why?" His voice was low, just loud enough to be heard over the music, yet she could hear the teasing lilt in his words.

She bit the inside of her cheek, trying to hide her smile as she shook her head. "No clue. Maybe some things just get better with time?"

Amusement lit Zak's eyes, and she looked away, trusting him to lead her in the next few steps of the dance. Surely he could feel her heartbeat through their joined hands. What if he kissed her tonight? The whole evening had been magical enough, and he hadn't left her side since they arrived in the Perennian palace.

She caught her father's eyes and beamed at him as Zak twirled her again. Maybe things were starting to look up for her.

Jade clenched her fist as she willed away the memory. She didn't know if it was something she'd done or said. Maybe he'd decided he wasn't interested in getting close to the captain's daughter. She was only a mechanic—and she'd mentioned that night how much she loved being one, how she never wanted to leave her position. He'd fallen silent at that. Maybe that was it? He was a Guardian. He far outranked her in importance. A mere mechanic shouldn't be worth his time. Her heart twisted.

Who would consider someone of her station as worth pursuing?

"You mentioned Ben, too," Jade prompted, finally.

Krista shot her a glance, and a slow grin spread. "Why? Are you thinking of moving on from Zak to Ben?"

Jade lifted her face to the sun and shrugged. "I don't know. He's nice. Attractive. Talks to me more than Zak does."

"True." Krista pursed her full lips with a glint in her eye. "You know, you could always try kissing Ben to see what Zak would do. It'd give a good impression of how they both feel about you."

"No!"

Krista cackled, and Jade turned her friend away from a pair of military police that stopped to watch them. She offered a quick nod to the men as she steered Krista from their watchful gaze.

"I don't know what you want to do more," Jade hissed at Krista, "embarrass me to the point of death, or attract unwanted attention."

Krista sobered and patted Jade's back. "Sorry. You make it too easy. But you're right. I don't think we usually go this way, do we?"

Jade shook her head and increased her speed through the narrow alley, suddenly more aware of their surroundings. They had wandered into an older part of High Doldra, where the buildings sagged and the air felt musty. Men without elegant hats wore rough clothing and had steely eyes that wandered. Women who lacked the customary flowing dresses and parasols lingered in doorways, wearing swooping necklines and skirts hitched high enough to show their knee-high laced boots and a touch of flesh above the leather.

Jade suppressed a shiver and tried to surreptitiously glance behind her. This was one of the times she'd welcome Zak's company—mother-hen syndrome and all. She touched the pommel of the dagger hiding in the folds of her loose mechanic pants and swallowed as a burly man slowed in the street to openly appraise them. They had to get out of this neighborhood.

"Is that Geist?" Krista pointed, and Jade shaded her eyes to squint.

Jade raised her brows as she watched the umber-toned crewman duck out of a signless doorway. He shoved his hands in his pockets, scowl visible even from across the street. She watched his shoulders rise and fall with a deep breath. His eyes snapped open, and he looked up at them, his lips twisting in a frown.

Relief trickled down Jade's spine as Geist walked over. Even though he wasn't what Jade would call a friend, he was more trustworthy than any of the people in the street around her. He nodded to her as he drew close, but his eyes stayed on Krista.

"What are you two doing here? And without the other two?" Geist's gruff tone rankled, though Jade couldn't fault it. They really should have paid attention to the direction they were going.

"We got turned around," Krista replied easily. "And the guys are buying Ben some new clothes."

Geist leaned back as he nodded and crossed his arms. "He needs them." He glanced back at the building he'd come from, and the skin around his eyes tightened. "And you two need to get out of here. I'll escort you back to the City Circle."

"We'd appreciate that, thank you." Jade couldn't hold back her curiosity. "What were you doing out here?"

Geist's dark eyes flicked to her. A muscle in his cheek twitched, and he pointed behind her. "We're going that way." His hand grasped her elbow as he bulled forward. "And it's none of your business."

CHAPTER THIRTEEN

BEN

"You've stalled long enough." Ben picked up a pair of rose-lensed goggles and held them up to his eyes before hanging them back on the peg with a minute shudder. He picked up another pair and tilted them to better see the reflective film. "Krista made a comment yesterday—something about Zak and Aerugo? And today that MP mentioned to Jade about standing with the Monomi. And that Nevin prick from last night? What was that about?"

Briar turned away from the leather knife holster he had been looking at and snorted at the goggles Ben held in his hands. "Those are for mechanics." He tapped a finger against the gears that held smaller monocles on the side of the lenses. "You don't need these unless you're planning to join Krista and Jade. Which I recommend against."

Ben sighed and set that pair aside before grabbing another to inspect.

"Early last summer we were making a delivery in Lucrum—that's Aerugo's capital—and we stopped by the palace for Jade and family to visit her uncle. The prince there disagreed with Zak in regards to Jade." Briar leaned against the counter and grimaced, twirling a dagger in his hands. "Zak hit him and got punished for striking a royal." He sighed, slid the blade back in its sheath, and set it aside. "It was nasty."

"Oh." Ben paused. "So he's Jade's protector? Why is he not here?"

"Sort of?" Briar hedged. He picked up a brown pair of goggles with deep red tinting. "Try these."

Ben slipped them on, and Briar nodded in approval. He then led Ben to a shelf of leather and scaled pouches.

"Zak and Jade have been friends together on the *Sapphire* for years," Briar continued as Ben looked over his options. "But their friendship has hit a…rocky…patch."

Ben bobbed his head slowly, trying to match Briar's description to what he'd witnessed of the brooding, black-haired swordsman. He'd definitely noticed the rocky patch, if that's what they called last night. "There's something about her. Something familiar."

Briar turned and raised a single eyebrow, clearly sizing Ben up.. "You serious?"

Ben nodded. She was one of the few on the crew who didn't hold him back at arm's length. And something about her reminded him of someone. Maybe the woman he'd had that brief memory of? He couldn't think of who she was—if it was a lover, a family member, a friend—but he wanted to get to know Jade. Maybe she could help unlock his memory somehow.

He fingered the metal tags around his neck. Maybe he could ask this store clerk if they'd seen anything like his necklace. Any clue would be helpful, and clerks saw a lot of people. He could probably help.

Briar led him to a long display of larger pouches, where a dark green, soft leather hip bag caught Ben's eye. He hefted it and examined the tiny stitching along the side and the swirled design across the front. He tossed it on his growing pile of items to buy.

"As for why Zak is banished from here, that's a longer story. And one that he would tell better—*if* you can get him to talk about it." Briar rifled his hand through their bag of clothes and necessary accessories for Ben. "We need to get you a skyfarer hat, too."

Ben followed Briar through the racks of goggles and top hats. Briar stopped in front of a shelf of folded leather hats of various colors and stepped aside to let Ben sift through the selection.

Ben tugged on a brown cap. "I'm not sure if Zak would want to open up to me." The leather squeezed his skull, and he yanked it off with a muttered, "Nope."

Briar tossed him a dark green leather cap.

Ben eyed it critically and pulled it on, adjusting the straps to fit snugly. He worked his jaw and nodded, pleased.

Briar nodded to the hat that Ben wore. "Put on the goggles. Make sure they fit comfortably together." He leaned against a shelf and crossed one leg over the other casually. "Zak tends to be suspicious of newcomers. Give him time. Show him you're trustworthy." Briar crossed his arms and made a show of looking Ben up and down. "You *are* trustworthy, right?"

Ben snorted. "As far as I know, yes." He pulled the goggles on and shifted them until satisfied. The shop looked both darker and rosier with the goggles, but they felt good, and they'd be excellent protection against the wind when onboard the *Sapphire*.

"Zak's had a rough life," Briar said finally. "More than we know, I'm sure." Briar shot Ben a look. "He has his secrets, just like you have yours."

"There's a difference between secrets and not remembering, you know."

"True enough, I suppose." Briar hitched a thumb in his belt loop. "Do you remember anything at all?"

Ben shook his head and pulled out the chain with the two metal strips around his neck. "This is all I have, aside from what I was wearing, and I don't even know what these mean." He closed his eyes, shutting out Briar's concerned expression and the various racks of merchandise that surrounded them. "All I can remember is my name, a boom, and pain. That's it, really."

Ben slid his feet farther apart to anchor himself while he breathed deeply, eyes still closed. Something niggled at him, an anxiety or urgency that he was forgetting something—or someone—important. A flash of gold and the warm glow of happiness was all he had to go by. Nothing concrete or even remotely helpful.

Pressure on his shoulder made Ben's eyes snap open, and he let Briar shepherd him to the bearded shopkeeper.

"I wonder what it'll take to get you to remember everything," Briar said.

Ben shrugged as he helped pile his purchases on the counter. "Knowing my luck here thus far, it'll be something unpleasant."

"Good day, gentlemen. Did you find everything you hoped for?" The clerk pulled out a paper pad and started jotting down a list of their items.

"Yes, thank you," Briar replied. He nodded to the man behind the counter. "Lance has been working here for…" He turned back to the shopkeeper. "How many years has it been?"

"More years than you've been on that airship of yours." Lance softened his words with a humored smile as he started to add numbers next to the listed items.

Ben tugged out his metal necklace. "Then you probably see a range of things come through from all areas, right?"

"Of course. The total is seventy-two lut, by the way. Did you have something in mind that you're looking for, or something—" Lance looked up from his notepad, and his gaze fell on the necklace dangling in Ben's hand. His brow furrowed, and his eyes slowly widened. Lance hesitantly lifted the flat rectangle that hung on the chain and angled it toward him. Color drained from the shopkeeper's face, leaving his skin looking like bleached sand. He stumbled back and hit the cubby-holed wall behind him. A bolt of cloth tumbled to the ground. He lifted a shaking finger. "Put that away. Now."

Ben and Briar exchanged puzzled looks.

"Lance?" Briar's hands froze on his money bag. "Are you—"

"Put it away!" Lance exclaimed.

Ben fumbled in his haste to slip the metal under his shirt. Lance pressed both hands against the counter, and he leaned forward, his pupils so dilated that Ben could see his own reflection in them.

"Do *not* bring those out in public again. No good will come of it. You hear me?" Lance's cheeks hollowed, giving him the appearance of one who'd just tasted something sour. He closed his eyes and whispered, "Another one, *here*." He let out a shuddering breath. "You need to leave. Now."

"Uh, payment." Briar set three dark blue lut on the counter. He retracted his hand as if he expected Lance to jump out at him.

Lance fumbled for the money, and he handed Briar two crimson lut without a word. He didn't look at either of them, his eyes trained on the counter as they moved their items into the large bag that Briar had insisted Ben bring from the *Sapphire.*

Irritation ebbed from Ben and was replaced with a pang of fear when Lance finally looked up at him. His eyes held Ben captive while Lance gestured at Ben's necklace. "If you value your life, and the lives of those around you, destroy those and never think of them again."

CHAPTER FOURTEEN

SLATE

It had been a full month since Slate last saw Samantha, and thirty-five days' time was far too long to go without his wife. He sighed as he checked his compass and corrected the course of the *Sapphire* accordingly. They'd had to loop down south through Florence to make a quick delivery, and if his calculations were accurate, Sam and the *Phoenix* would be flying through Perennia right now, too. Hopefully they'd both land in Lucrum on the same day, so they could make the most of their land-docked time.

Oh, the joys and difficulties of a marriage between two airship captains.

Getting Sam's thoughts on the new guy would be interesting. She was as protective of Jade as Slate was, and he wanted Sam's insight on Ben's mysterious background and lack of general knowledge. Slate liked the young man thus far, but he wanted a different judge of character than himself.

He knew better than to trust his own judgment on anyone.

And maybe Sam would have a lead for his crew to follow, or new rumors of Loore's Landing and their so-called ghosts. If nothing else, she would encourage him with her ever-flowing optimism. Too many years of no solid clues wore on a man.

How could they repair the keystone?

Was there really an artifact that could do that?

Where would it be?

Where would Zane's murderer hide?

Slate's grip on the wheel tightened as shame flooded his heart and memories poured into his head.

It wasn't supposed to happen this way.

He brushed blood-stained fingers down Sapphire's face, closing her eyelids. A sob choked him, unable to free itself of his chest. This whole endeavor was to protect her and her family—not get her and the rest of the royal family killed. This was his fault. He'd trusted the wrong person.

A blue jay squawked, pulling Slate from the memory. It glared at Slate with one beady eye, then the other, before ruffling its feathers and flying off the banister. He swiped at the moisture threatening to leak from his goggles. The sun glanced off the lenses, glinting crimson.

The barrier rippled, flaring orange and red, illuminating Zane's drawn face. His eyes blazed even as his blood ran out. "If this is your fault, you need to redeem yourself. Live with what you've done."

"How?"

"If the princess is alive, protect her."

She didn't want to be protected.

"Lie if you must."

My entire life has become a lie, Zane.

Slate groaned and rubbed at his forehead, willing the memories away. He couldn't let anyone else die for him. And he couldn't lose any more family. He had to focus on the here and now. Samantha.

Where was she? Was she safe? How had her travels gone while

they were separated?

He gazed over the helm and railing, and tried to admire the clear blue sky and rolling green landscape while he turned the questions over in his mind. The sun's warmth loosened the tense muscles in his back, and the cool bite of the air on his face kept him wide awake.

Motion caught his eye, and he turned to see Garnet's customary emerald-dyed hat bobbing over the railing. His sister popped into view, switching over her safety lines and coming alongside him, leaning into the stiff breeze. Her loose-fitting jacket smacked him in the leg, and she grabbed the wool edges and buttoned it down.

"Sorry." She flashed him a quick smile and leaned against the rail. "So. What are your thoughts on Ben?"

Clawing out of the depression that pulled at Slate prevented him from replying to her peppy tone.

She caught his eye, and her shoulders sagged. Her fingers slid over his. "We'll find them."

"Yeah." Slate took a deep breath and shook out his hands, as if he could fling the reminiscence away. Wind buffeted the *Sapphire*, and he grasped the helm. He brushed a finger across the starboard turbine controller as a cross breeze rocked the ship. "I *was* thinking about Ben earlier."

Garnet tucked a flapping strand of hair under her hat. "And?"

"I haven't decided yet." Slate shrugged. "I think I like him as a crew member. He and Briar are getting along well, and for not remembering where he's from, he's a quick learner. He's done well with basic duties and working in the galley."

Garnet grinned and tapped her goggles. "And he looks normal, now that he's in proper clothing."

Slate snorted and shook his head. Only Garnet would be concerned about someone's garb fitting in with what was fashionable. Then again, she was the businesswoman. She enjoyed and excelled at finances, communications, and marketing, and her dedication to the *Sapphire* allowed them the side missions to chase clues for the keystone. And even little details like Ben's strange clothes wouldn't escape her scrutiny.

The wind whistling made hearing Garnet's sigh impossible, but her shoulders raised and dropped clearly enough. She ran her hand along the brass railing and tilted her head to look at Slate. "He gets along with Jade. Quite well."

Slate inhaled deeply through his nose. He scanned the sky for the telltale flash of terrors. "I don't think this is the best time to talk to her about it, though."

"When will be a good time?" Garnet waved her hand as she spoke. "Last summer wasn't a good time, nor this winter, and now we have this going on, and—" She broke herself off and pinched the bridge of her nose before looking up at him, blue eyes a filmy gray from the tint of her skyfarer lenses. "I don't think there's anything there besides friendship, but neither of them knows the truth."

Slate drummed his fingers against the helm and resisted the urge to bang his forehead against it. "And Zak's keeping his distance. Mostly. And she's miserable and confused by it." He sighed. "Who knows? But I want to decide on keeping Ben or not before we add that gear to the chaos machine."

Garnet pressed her lips together. "What is Zak's read on Ben?"

"He thinks Ben could be telling the truth about not remembering, but Zak still doesn't fully trust him." Slate suppressed a wry smile.

Zak's hesitancy on their unexpected recruit could be from more than just Jade's safety. "Maybe we can train Ben to be a dragon hunter," he suggested. "We could always use another set of hands in that regard. Of course, we'll need to test him and see how he does with fear under pressure; that's imperative for making or breaking a hunter."

"He beat Geist easily enough in the last sparring match, from what I overheard from the girls. I think it's Ben: four, Geist: zero," Garnet commented, her expression thoughtful. "So that's a good start; he's no weakling or pushover. But if he's going to be trained in dragon hunting, it'd be best to have Zak teach him."

Slate could imagine how *that* conversation would go over with Zak right now. He winced. "Maybe we should—"

The metal stairs by the railing vibrated as Victor popped into sight, his dark eyes wide open. He kept a hand on the rail as he snapped his line over from one safety bar to the other. "Captain! The *Phoenix* has been sighted!"

Fierce joy fluttered like butterfly wings and then spluttered in Slate's chest at the sight of his first mate's clenched jaw and knitted brow.

"Sir, terrors are attacking them! They're circling below, and Kerlee swears he saw what may have been a stalker." Victor's eyebrows tightened as he pointed northeast and down. "Just over the side, sir."

Slate slammed his hand down on the black-and-silver gem that controlled the gravity stones, and he held it there to hasten the ship's descent. He flicked open the hatch on the voice-pipe with his free hand and shouted, "Dragons below, attacking the *Phoenix!* All able hands, get ready for a rescue!"

His stomach lurched into his heart, and he gritted his teeth as the *Sapphire* plunged down toward the ground. He could hear Briar swearing in the galley through the closed voice-pipe. A quick glance showed that Garnet and Victor held onto the safety railing as the ship tilted under them. The floor bounced as they landed, and Garnet dropped to a knee while Victor bent his legs to absorb the shock. "Victor, stay onboard for defense. It's Geist's turn to go out," Slate ordered.

Victor nodded, tight-lipped. He and Garnet hustled down the stairs the moment the *Sapphire* settled. Slate unclipped his line, hefted a hydropack, and scrambled down the stairs after them. The *Phoenix* gleamed in Slate's peripheral. *Hang on.* Victor disappeared below deck, and Garnet waylaid Jade as she rushed toward the side rail.

"No!" Garnet exclaimed, holding her arms around the struggling Jade. "You need to stay on board."

"I can't!" Jade cried, twisting out of her aunt's grasp. "Mother needs help!"

"Jade!" Slate stepped in her way and clutched her arms, spinning her around to face him. His pack shifted and poked a sharp edge into his back, but he didn't let go of Jade.

Wild blue eyes stared up at Slate, and he suppressed a flinch as a flashback surfaced like a bubble released from dark waters. *Strands of red hair escaping her bun, eyes burning with fear and anger, dimming soon after.* Slate swallowed hard and willed the unwanted ghost of his past away.

"You need to stay where it's safe. I'll get to her. She'll be fine." Doubt soured the words in his mouth in the wake of the memory.

Garnet nodded earnestly by Jade's side. "Let the men go help."

She craned her neck to watch the *Phoenix*. "I left my spyglass in our room. I need to go get it."

Ben appeared next to Jade, tense and wary. His eyes flitted over the edge of the ship and toward the *Phoenix*. His fingers twitched, as if wanting a weapon.

Slate held a hand on Jade while lifting the other to point at Ben. "You!"

Ben whirled around with wide eyes and held a finger against his chest, questioningly.

"Stay on the *Sapphire*." Slate pushed Jade in Ben's direction. "I want you both to stay here, away from the danger." He leveled a glare at Ben and pointed at Jade. "Keep her safe. I need to go rescue my wife."

CHAPTER FIFTEEN

BEN

Ben fisted his hands and bounced on the balls of his feet while he watched Slate, Zak, and the dragon-hunting crew rush down the gangplank of the *Sapphire*. He wanted to help, but all the training he'd done with the crew thus far had been focusing on what he knew with hand-to-hand combat. He knew practically nothing of dragons.

Jade stood beside him at the railing, her freckles stark against her pale cheeks as she gripped the worn metal bar. Krista came up from somewhere below deck and hugged an arm around Jade, both girls silent and tense. Large, bird-like creatures with narrow heads swooped down on the wooden-and-metal airship nearby. Shouts of pain and anger and ghastly avian shrieks sent chills down Ben's spine. The din of the battle echoed in his head, compounding his unease.

Why did the yelling, the cries of pain, the clamor, sound so familiar?

Victor joined them, his jaw set and arms crossed as he watched.

Ben pointed to a group of people clustered on the top deck of the *Phoenix*, shooting what looked like water into the air. "What are they doing?"

"They're using hydropacks," Victor replied without tearing his eyes away from the battle. "One of the best tools to kill the lightning-element dragons without damaging valuable scales."

Ben tapped his fist against the railing as a bellow from the other airship sent shivers down his back. Fear of the unknown dragons concerned him, but something about the racket of battle crawled under his skin, lodging there, taunting him with wisps of memory that wouldn't take shape.

"Is the bottom deck closed up?" Victor asked suddenly.

Jade started and turned to face the main deck with wide eyes. "I don't remember."

"I'll go check," Victor decided, his hand on his sword hilt. He pointed at each of them. "Stay out of trouble."

The ladies chorused their promise to be safe while Ben nodded. He watched Victor steal down the stairs, his steps slow and cautious, not making any sound.

"Hey, let's go to the top deck. Maybe we can get a better view there." Krista tugged on Jade's arm.

Ben followed behind them with slow steps up the stairs, unable to turn away from the scene before him. He counted at least six terrors, and he spotted a blurred movement on the ground below the *Phoenix* that seemed somehow familiar. The crew of the *Sapphire* reached the gangplank of the *Phoenix*, and Zak pointed to the hazy image. Four of the dragon hunters broke off to join him as the rest rushed up to the deck of the ship.

A strange shadow flitted over Ben, and he looked up. Adrenaline pumped through his veins with icy alarm, melting away the vague shadows of recollection. *Terror! Apt name.* He pounded up the last two steps and rushed around the corner, a shout of warning lodged in his throat.

An ear-splitting *kree-yah* rattled Ben's bones as the terror swooped closer. Krista and Jade both looked up, and their eyes widened. Arcs of electricity crackled on metallic claws that reached for them.

Krista shrieked and grabbed Jade's arm, dropping to the floorboards as Ben ran forward, waving his arms at the dragon as if he could shoo it away. It clearly wasn't a timid sparrow, but he had to do *something*, and this was the best he could think of without a weapon in hand.

Sharp claws grazed Ben's arm, and agony blazed, highlighting every nerve ending. He dropped and writhed as his muscles clenched and released in rapid succession from the electrical shock. Wisps of steam wafted from the four open gashes where the metallic claws had brushed him and seared his skin. He pushed away from the deck with his good arm, watching the terror as it circled ahead, screeching.

Krista dragged Jade under the control panel. Blood soaked Jade's white blouse, and she clutched her bleeding forearm. She must have hit her arm on the copper board when Krista pulled her down.

Krista held a trembling wrench out as a weapon, her eyes blown wide. Something in Ben's gut stirred at the fierce glint in Jade's steely glare as she watched the terror above.

I have to protect them. How?

The stairs leading down to the covered parts of the ship were open—easy access for the terror wheeling overhead. Ben's gaze snagged on a metal-and-leather pack with a coiled hose sitting next to the helm. Captain Slate had had one when he left for the *Phoenix*. Victor had called it a hydropack, and Zak said that they'd go over those later.

No time like the present.

He lurched for it and knelt beside the bag, holding his bleeding arm close to his chest. The gauges showed full—of what, exactly, he didn't know—but he trusted that whatever state the water was in, it wouldn't need to be primed. Hopefully it could pack a punch against a flying lightning dragon of doom.

Sunlight behind the terror rendered it a dark blur. Ben gritted his teeth and stood in front of where Jade and Krista sheltered. He steadied his hand and aimed the hose. The terror swooped down toward them. He waited a full heartbeat, then yanked the lever.

A high-pressured stream shot out of the cannon. The terror squawked as the water hit it in the chest. It fell to the deck by Krista's foot. Jade screamed.

Ben jerked the lever down to stop the water before the spray reached the women. Krista scrambled out from under the control panel desk. She raced forward and kicked the terror in the head. The menace skidded away from where she and Jade had sheltered, its claws scratching at the wood boards. Ben refocused the water attack on the creature as electricity arced over its body, smoke and steam billowing. It scrambled away from the harsh water jet on the leathery little hands on the bottoms of its wings.

Pain blindsided Ben as steam vented from the hydropack and rolled over his unprotected hands and arms. Heat lit his nerves on fire.

Scarlet anguish overloaded his senses, and he collapsed as black boots raced across his line of vision toward the terror.

Ben saw nothing more.

A male spoke: "When do you think he'll show up?"
His own voice: "Wish I knew. I'm ready to go home."
"Ugh, yes. I'd kill for a cold beer." A different intonation, younger.
"Technically, that's what we're doing."
Laughter.

"Ben? Ben!"

The woman's voice sounded frantic. Ben groaned, and the memory evaporated like water on a hot day. He shook his head against the pain that threatened to pull him under. A familiar, firm-yet-soft surface under his body gave him a clue to where he was.

Not the infirmary again.

Something cold touched his arm, and he jerked upright with a yell.

Krista, Briar, Victor, and Jaxton swam in his blurred vision. Ben squeezed his eyes shut and counted to five before opening them again. This time he counted exactly one of each face.

Jaxton blinked at him. "You're awake." He turned away and plucked a small pink stone from the counter and dropped it in Ben's lap. "Hold on to that, please." He waited for Ben to pick it up with stiff, trembling fingers. Jaxton raised a black eyebrow and pressed the wet cloth against Ben's arm.

Coarse fabric rubbed against scorched skin, and Ben tensed against the crimson agony that lapped at his nerves. The sharp pain faded as quickly as it came, leaving a dull, muted ache that made his stomach roil.

"Clean," Jaxton announced. He sank onto a stool, next to the bed that Ben sat on, and slid a metal tray over the counter toward him. "I'm going to stitch your arm." He poured an amber beverage and pushed it toward Ben. "Drink up. And you may want to look away."

Ben had barely tasted the bitter alcohol before Jaxton jabbed the needle into his arm. Ben choked and swallowed hard, sinuses burning, as his free arm cast about for something to grip.

"Briar, get Ben a nullification stone!" Zak's voice snapped from the corner of the room, and Ben twisted to look over his left shoulder.

Zak stitched Jade's arm, which was clean of blood and already had a few neat stitches in her skin. Drying blood browned the edges of her crimson-stained shirt. She offered Ben a wan grin that dimpled her cheek, and held up a mottled blue stone, barely blinking when Zak touched the needle to her arm to weave another stitch. Her dimple deepened as she looked at Ben, and her gaze dropped as a blush colored her cheeks.

"Here." Briar slipped a cool rock into Ben's hand—the same hand that already held the pink stone. Immediately, the dull pressure of pain disappeared, leaving a numbness in his body.

Jaxton snorted. "Use that up now, and we won't have one for later."

"Better to use it now than to needlessly torture the man," Zak shot back from the corner. "He helped protect them. Let him have a break from the pain for at least a few minutes."

After the last week of Zak keeping Ben at arm's length, hearing his praise rang oddly in Ben's ears. Pleasant and deserved, certainly, but shockingly strange. *Maybe I just needed to prove myself to him.*

Ben glanced back to reply to Zak, but his words disappeared when he saw Jade. She sat straight, posture elegant enough for a formal event. Her eyes closed, and a soft smile curled her lips up.

"You're pretty."

Jade's eyes snapped open, and the smile slid from her face.

Ben's cheeks burned. That thought wasn't supposed to leave his head. "I—sorry," he stammered. "I didn't mean to—"

The glare Zak aimed at him was almost enough to give him fresh burns. Krista and Briar laughed in the background.

"I suppose it's safe to assume you're one of the people who doesn't handle mixing painkillers well." Victor's voice was low, conspiratorial almost, but humor shimmered in his words. His eyebrow twitched at Ben's confusion. "Most of us can combine nullification stones and alcohol without a problem." He gestured at Ben with a small smirk. "Some, when under the influence of both, have difficulty controlling what they think and say."

Ben opened his mouth.

"Ah, ah." Victor waggled his finger. "This is one of those times you should really practice 'think before you speak.'"

Ben simmered at that and resisted looking back at Jade. He hadn't meant for it to sound the way it did. But judging by the glee in Krista's eyes and the amusement radiating from Briar, no one would believe him if he said so. And, just his luck, Zak had witnessed it. Whatever camaraderie he may have had a chance at with the moody swordsman was assuredly gone now.

Briar leaned against the wood paneling and shook his head at Ben, mirth still crinkling his eyes. "You know, if you want to use the hydropack, it's recommended to wear gloves and protective clothing. A leather vest, at least."

Ben closed his eyes with a low groan as he tried to steady his arm against Jaxton's relentless tugging. He focused on his words before gritting out, "A bit late to tell me that."

"He did well enough." Victor looked at Ben with a mix of sympathy and pride. "Krista finished the terror off while you napped on the deck."

"Seriously, though," Briar's voice softened, and he gripped Ben's shoulder. "You did good. Thank you for being there with them."

Ben dipped his head in a shallow nod. "It was the right thing to do." *Really? Why couldn't I have just said, "of course" or something suave like that?* He dared to look down at his arms and swallowed at the sight of the swollen, shiny red skin. Blisters wept clear fluid on his fingers. "I'd do it again. Preferably with training first." Good. Didn't flub that one.

A laugh huffed out of Briar, and he snapped his fingers. "I know! I hereby dub you Steamboy."

"Steamboy?"

Victor rolled his eyes and nodded to Ben as he left.

Krista circled around Ben to lean against Briar. Her eyes shone with sympathy and gratitude. "Briar likes to give everyone nicknames."

Ben absorbed that and winced when Jaxton tugged sharply on his arm. He looked down to see the doctor tie off the last stitch and snip the excess thread.

"Done." Jaxton flicked a tawny hand toward Briar and Krista. "One of them can wrap your burns. I need to get to the *Phoenix* to help there."

"Thank you."

Krista plopped down on the seat that Doctor Jaxton vacated and picked up a roll of gauze. "Normally, it'd be Zak who helps, but since he's currently preoccupied, I get to help."

Ben glanced over his shoulder again. Zak and Jade leaned in close to each other as he wiped away fresh streaks of blood from her arm. Ben pressed his lips together, not trusting his inhibitions. He didn't want to make another comment when his mind was befuddled by Jade and by the dim memory that ghosted over her when she smiled.

Did he know someone who was similar to her? Why did he have to say that "pretty" comment earlier? Some things, though true, were best left unspoken.

And he didn't want to interfere with whatever was going on between her and Zak. Ben looked away to meet Krista's knowing eyes.

She quirked her lips and sighed dramatically as she tugged her chair closer. Krista lowered her voice. "It's how it goes right now. Zak keeps his distance until something like this happens, then he becomes all protective of her. Then he freaks out and backs off again." She gently lifted Ben's arm to start wrapping the gauze. "As much as I wanted them together—I used to call the two of them Zade when they weren't within hearing distance—he hasn't been able to make up his mind."

Ben watched her hands as she deftly wrapped his arm. While all she said was interesting, where she was going with it, and how it involved him, was something he was hesitant to guess. He rolled the two stones in his burned hand. He didn't trust his lack of a filter right now.

Briar leaned in and tapped his finger against the med-table. "The point of what she's saying is that we want to see her happy. However that may come about."

CHAPTER SIXTEEN

JADE

Jade didn't look up as Doctor Jaxton left the med-room to help over at the *Phoenix*. She desperately wanted to know what was going on over there and if her mother was safe. Just as desperately, she wanted to escape the awkward tension of the room.

You're pretty. Ben's words echoed in her mind, and she blew out a breath. Judging from the surprise in his eyes, he hadn't meant to say it aloud, but it did add some credence to Krista's theory. Him saving them from the terror was a point in his favor too. She glanced out of the corner of her eye as he talked with Krista and Briar. The terror burns were going to leave him permanently scarred, and they'd hurt like shehalla while they healed. She owed him. Big time.

And while she heard Krista's voice in her head telling her to maybe move on, maybe give Ben a chance, she couldn't. She was open to the idea, but it was one thing to think about it—let alone say it—and another to follow through on it.

Especially when sitting this close to the one man whose presence simultaneously soothed and aggravated her. Zak.

He bent over her outstretched arm, breath ghosting across it as he carefully inspected his handiwork on her stitches. He lifted his shoulder to brush a loose strand of dark hair away from his narrowed eyes, and then gently set her arm down to reach for a roll of gauze.

Jade bit her lip and flicked her eyes up to where Krista stood near Ben and Briar. Ben hadn't looked at her again since his unintended declaration, but Briar shot her a wink while Krista grinned mischievously. Her twinkling eyes spelled certain doom for Jade.

Jade sighed and turned away from her friend.

Bad enough to be injured from something as mundane as falling—even if it was to avoid a terror—but worse to be stitched up by the man she had just declared herself done with. His proximity alone threw off her internal temperature regulation. Her skin felt like it was on fire, and her heart twisted every time she met his eyes. She examined the stain in her blouse to avoid looking at Zak.

Krista's theory only rubbed salt into the open wound in Jade's heart. Of course, the first guy that she loved wouldn't look at her the same. She'd probably scared him away with her clumsiness and constant need to be protected from preying princes. And if not that, then it was the constant grease, sweat stains, and bird's-nest hair that she sported as one of the ship mechanics.

It doesn't matter. I'm done. There's no reason to keep thinking about him or us. Never mind the fact that his hands on her arm gave her goosebumps. *Moving on. I'm moving on.*

"I'm glad you're safe."

Jade's thoughts derailed at Zak's low tone, and her mouth abruptly felt dry when she realized he was talking to her. She hesitated before deciding to adopt his same nonchalant attitude. "I feel bad that Ben got so injured, though."

"Yes, but he protected you and Krista. I'm indebted to him for that." Zak's green eyes held her gaze until he dropped them to focus on her arm. He smoothed the bandage with his long, tan fingers and pressed her pale hand between his two warm palms.

Jade's heart skittered erratically at the tenderness in his eyes, and she fought to keep her breathing even as her nerves jittered. What was he doing? Was Krista watching this? Ben?

Zak's shoulders hunched, and he sighed. "Maybe we should—"

The door swung open with a bang, and Samantha stood in the threshold, brown hair disheveled and her right sleeve stained with drying blood. Her eyes met Jade's and tears welled in them. "Jade!"

"Mom!" Tears slipped down Jade's cheeks as relief threatened to overwhelm her at the sight of her mother. Alive. Whole. *Praise the Author.*

Zak dropped Jade's hand, and he jumped off his seat in a blur of black clothing. "I should get to the *Phoenix* and help." His voice was gruff. He pulled carefully marked vials out of the cupboard and shoved them into a leather bag without looking back at Jade. Then he disappeared out the door.

Jade swallowed hard as the turmoil of emotions in her gut threatened to pull her apart. Elation, now...disappointment? She couldn't identify the feelings that roiled in her gut, and this wasn't the time or place to melt down over it. Not when her mother was alive.

Family came first.

Samantha took Zak's seat, and all Jade's lingering concerns over the ever-annoying male race faded as she took in her mother's slumped posture and weary eyes.

"Are you okay, sweetie?" Samantha leaned over and brushed back a stray lock of Jade's hair. "I came over as soon as I was able."

"I'll survive. It's a mere flesh wound." Jade lifted her bandaged arm with a wry grin, burying her confused emotions. "What about you?" Jade reached out and lightly touched her mother's sleeve. "I see blood. The crew? What actually happened?"

Samantha sighed and leaned back in the chair. "Terrors swarmed and forced us to land. Keene and Steban have light burns, but Schultz says they'll survive." Her mother's lips pressed together, and she stared down at her bloody sleeve with distant eyes. "Elise didn't make it."

The air left Jade's lungs in a rush. "Oh, no. I'm so sorry." She lunged from her chair to squeeze Samantha in a tight, one-armed hug.

Her mother returned the embrace and pressed a kiss on Jade's head, then shifted in her chair to tug at the stiffening sleeve.

"Uncle Michael? Aunt Becca?"

"They're fine. They're supervising cleanup and medical needs." Laugh lines crinkled around Samantha's eyes. "They scared a year off my life though. Your uncle distracted a stalker long enough for Becca to take it down."

Jade lightly snorted at the mental image of her aunt yelling like a banshee while stabbing at the dragon. "They make a good team."

"That they do." Samantha nodded to where Ben sat with his back to them. "Tell me. Is that the new guy that your father mentioned?"

Jade nodded and sank back into her seat. She jostled her arm and muttered a soft curse. "Yes. He helped save us, but he didn't understand steam-tech and got burned in the process."

Samantha winced. "I used to know an herbalist who made amazing burn cream. I wish I knew where he was now, so I could get some. We could really use some on both our ships."

"Oh, that would be amazing," Jade agreed with a wistful sigh.

Her mother studied the back of Ben's head. "Burns aside, from what I can see, he's pretty good-looking."

Jade's jaw dropped. "Mother!"

Samantha grinned—humor momentarily overshadowing the sorrow in her eyes—and shrugged. "Just saying what's true. Why? Have you not noticed?"

Jade *had* noticed, but that wasn't the point.

Samantha continued with a thoughtful tone as she rested her chin in her hand. "You need someone to help you smile through the day." She rubbed Jade's knee. "I know things between you and Zak have been tense lately, and you've not been yourself." Her smile softened, and a crease of worry briefly wrinkled her brow. "I just want to see you happy." She tapped Jade's arm. "And safe. No more injuries for you, dear. And I need to go talk to that young Ben and thank him for his help."

Jade tensed. *Please don't say anything embarrassing.*

Samantha stood and helped Jade to her feet, hand braced under Jade's elbow. "Where are you going to go for now? What's your plan?"

Jade hesitated. "I want to get off the *Sapphire* for a bit. I'll go see if anyone out there needs my help." She'd be distracted, at the very least.

Samantha pulled her in for a quick hug and leaned back with a sly grin. "Are you sure you trust me to talk to the new guy without you supervising?"

Jade flushed and raised her bandaged arm with a glare. "Be nice. I'm injured." She stuck out her tongue and turned to the door as her mother's laugh rang clear and free.

Ben's blue eyes sparkled at Jade as she walked by, and she couldn't stop herself from smiling back. Krista hovered over his shoulder, a broad grin stretching across her face. Jade turned away and fled out the door before her blush could be noticed.

If only it were so easy to escape the whirling questions in her head.

CHAPTER SEVENTEEN

BEN

Ben cradled his bandaged arms close to his chest as he leaned his hip against the rail of the top deck and looked out at the night that stretched on. Stars shone brightly in the Perennian night sky, and he recognized none of the constellations. While aspects of Terrene echoed familiarity, the rest of it was strange, wild, and different. Even the air had a unique flavor to it, like it had something extra to it, some sort of spark or just, *more.*

It niggled at him. Like Jade's smile. Mocking him with a ghost of a memory that wavered just out of reach. He was certain that he didn't know Jade from before, but there was something about her, some connection, that he'd be a fool to ignore. Did he know a relative of hers? Or did she remind his subconscious of that blonde woman that he knew back home? And who was that woman? What was she to him? He touched the necklace under his shirt, confirming the ring was still there.

Ben set his elbows on the rail and leaned back to drop his head between his arms with a groan. When would he find answers? How could he find answers?

"Ben?"

Ben whirled around at the voice before he fully registered his own name.

Zak blended in with the barely lit deck, his dark clothes merging with the shadows. He held up a gloved hand. "Easy, man. It's just me."

Surprise held Ben's tongue for only a moment. "How are the ladies?"

The rail vibrated under Ben's elbows as Zak leaned his back against it. He tilted his head and closed his eyes. "Good." He cracked an eye open and shot Ben a sympathetic grin. "They'll be healed of their scratches long before you of your burns."

Ben huffed a laugh. "Figures." A cool breeze ruffled his hair, and he watched a nearby tree sway in the wind. "I'm glad to hear it, though. I'm disposable. They're the only mechanics on board."

"True, but also not true." Zak slid his hands in his pockets. "William has mechanic experience, and so does Kerlee, to a limited degree. You, while not currently assigned a position here, aren't 'disposable.' You're…" Zak hesitated, his brow furrowed, as if searching for the right word. "You're the filler guy. You fill whatever role we need at whatever time." His grin flashed in the dark. "We just need to train you in all the other responsibilities here so you can properly *fill in* that role."

"I see what you did there," Ben dead-panned. Then he chuckled and shook his head. Who knew that the quiet swordsman had a bad sense of humor?

"I need to thank you." Zak's voice interrupted Ben's musing.

"Thank me?"

"For saving Jade and Krista." Zak shifted, and the light of a distant luminary lamp highlighted his serious expression. "They might have been able to handle that terror on their own, but their injuries would've been much more grievous." He took a step away from the railing and bowed deeply. "I'm indebted to you."

Ben took a step back. "Uh, you're welcome." He waited until Zak straightened before deciding to take Briar's advice. "Can I ask you something?"

Zak raised an eyebrow and nodded, sliding his hands from his pockets to rest on his hips. "I'll answer as best I can."

"Thanks." Ben ran his forearms against the smooth coldness of the railing, thinking of what he wanted answers to first. Maybe working up to the bigger questions would be best. "That was the captain's wife we rescued today, yes? Why doesn't she live on the *Sapphire* with him and Jade?"

A small smirk crossed Zak's face, and he rubbed at the scruff on his jaw. "You probably haven't gotten to know her really well yet, but she's cut from the same stubborn cloth as Slate and Jade. When he met her, she already had her own airship and captaincy. Neither of them wanted to be the one to yield their ship, so they decided to keep things as they were and just make do with whatever land time they could get together."

"And Jade? She's with her father and not," Ben squinted and tried to remember Jade's mother's name, "Samantha?"

Zak shrugged. "It's safer for Jade to be with her father. A woman captain already draws more fire from air pirates; having her daughter onboard would only worsen things."

Ben nodded slowly. "And I understand now why Slate's mission is so important. But why are *you* here? Briar says you're a Monomi, and your family is in Doldra, as Guardians."

Zak's hand froze, and he slowly ran it through his hair, then let it drop. He grasped at the rail and blew out a breath. "Yes, I'm a

Monomi. And yes, we're known as Guardians in Doldra."

Curiosity simmered in Ben. "Guardians of what?"

"The keystone, and the barrier," Zak replied simply. He peered out over the railing, his eyes distant. "Our role is to make sure nothing happens to it."

"But something did happen to it. That's why the captain is searching for something to fix it." Zak furrowed his brow at Ben and Ben shrugged. "I'm just trying to figure out all these pieces and how they fit together."

Zak's cheek twitched, and he nodded. "An attack happened on the keystone. That same day, the captain lost his younger sister and the royal family was wiped out." He dropped his head and his voice lowered. "And I lost my brother."

A weight settled in Ben's chest, and he started to rub at it—stopping when his burnt hand flashed with pain. Had he ever experienced loss like this? He must've, if the lead in his gut was anything to go by. "I'm sorry."

"He died a hero." Zak raised his face to the stars. "As did many others who fought to protect the barrier."

"So why are you here, and not there?" Ben tugged his thick jacket closer as another chill breeze blew across the deck. "I mean, what's to guard here?"

Zak glanced back at Ben. "I'm here to help Captain Slate."

Ben nodded slowly while taking in Zak's stiff shoulders and focused expression. Maybe changing the subject would be good. He chose the most cheerful thing he could think of. "And Jade?"

Zak twitched and turned to face Ben fully. His eyes burned and his voice dropped low, steady. "Jade is none of your concern."

"Woah, easy, there." Ben pulled back slightly and waited for Zak's jaw to unclench. He let out a breath when Zak's tenseness eased some. "I do want to get to know her better," Ben admitted. He ignored Zak's crossed arms and set jaw. "There's something...familiar about her. I'm hoping she can help me remember who I am."

"I'm all for you getting your memory back." Zak rocked where he stood, as if he couldn't decide whether to step into Ben's space or not. "But you'll keep your distance from her, if you know what's good for you." He nodded stiffly, then spun on his heel and walked away.

CHAPTER EIGHTEEN

SLATE

Slate sighed in relief the moment his boots hit the spongy grass at the Lucrum airship dock in Aerugo. Too many side trips and unwanted adventures had drained much of his limited sanity. He smiled at the quiet scuff of steps behind him and turned to see Samantha stretching, the morning light haloing her fit form. She yawned and wrinkled her nose at him as she straightened her thickly embroidered vest.

"For the record, I'm not adverse to the idea of using the night to sleep," she commented with a raised eyebrow and small smirk.

Slate shook his head and slid an arm around her shoulders to peck her cheek. "No way. Gotta make up for lost time."

"I'm going to pretend I didn't just hear all that."

Slate laughed aloud and turned to see Jade at the edge of the gangplank, her expression just as disgruntled as her voice.

Jade grimaced as her eyes bounced between him and Samantha. Garnet stood behind Jade with an amused smile. Jade's red braid swung back and forth as she shook her head, a blush dotting her cheeks. "Maybe I'll visit Grandmother later."

"No, we'll all go together." Garnet lightly pushed against Jade to get her moving again. "You and I can walk ahead of them, to avoid any more bedroom conversations. If she stayed on schedule, she'll have been here for only a day ahead of us. Maybe she'll have some news of interest for us all." Garnet nodded to Slate as she passed him. "Victor is handling land rotation and will be taking a crew out to haggle prices on our loose merch."

"Excellent. Thank you." Slate looped his arm through Samantha's and moseyed down the smooth road behind his sister and Jade. He frowned at the bandage wrapped around Jade's left arm and what light-heartedness he'd felt dissipated, leaving sorrowful frustration to weigh his shoulders down. "She shouldn't have been anywhere near the terrors."

Samantha squeezed his arm, and he felt her sigh against him. "In a perfect world, no. But this is what her reality is." Her brown eyes searched his, understanding and love shining in their dark depths. "All we can do is prepare her for what's to come."

Slate dipped his head in a short nod. If not for him, Jade would have grown up with the constant love of both parents, privileged beyond compare, and safe from renegade skyfarers, lecherous princes, and dragons.

Samantha had often argued that Jade now had freedom to make her own choices, a well-diversified upbringing, and still had the love of a family.

But guilt weighed heavy on Slate's shoulders in the dark of night. The blood of the dead cried out in the silence, and not even his wife or a bottle of mead could quiet their anguish and hatred. Would he ever be able to atone? Could he fix what was broken?

What if he'd thought through his actions more?

What if he'd listened to the counsel of others? What if that day had turned out differently? How many lives could have been saved? How many families whole, unbroken, unshattered? What if she'd been raised where she belonged?

"Sweetheart."

Slate shook his head to clear it of his musings and blinked as he looked up. Smooth gray plaster covered the two-story building, the edges lined with brickwork in mimicry of pillars. Two small boxes filled with purple and pink flowers on either side of the wooden door offered the only reprieve from the bland colors that blanketed Aerugo. Garnet and Jade waited on the small front step. A breeze blew, and Slate sneezed.

"I'm glad that between the two of us, you're the only one with allergies." Garnet teased over her shoulder.

"I love you, too," Slate muttered with a sniff.

The door opened, revealing Ellie. She stood back and smiled warmly. "Good to see all of you. Come in."

Ellie waved a hand to where they could hang their jackets and swords, then led them to her parlor. She turned a lever on the wall, causing the gaslight sconces to brighten and showcase the plush amber couches and dark wood furniture. Settling regally in a chair that the other couches turned toward, Ellie lifted a hand and gestured. "Come. Sit. Tell me of your latest adventures."

A small laugh escaped Slate as he plopped down on the nearest couch. *Mother and her theatrics.* Samantha settled next to him. He leaned his head back with a sigh before straightening and inhaling deeply. The familiar fragrance of lavender, cedar wood, and ink soothed his nerves. It didn't matter if it was Ellie's home in Doldra or Aerugo—they always smelled the same.

"How did your last few stops go since I saw you?" Ellie asked, posture perfect as she lifted a delicate cup of tea from the end table next to her.

Garnet smoothed her skirt with downcast eyes. "We had a terror attack."

"And Sam lost a crew member. So not the greatest." Slate shrugged and slumped into the couch cushion. "And, of course, no new leads."

Ellie leaned forward and tapped her index finger on the rim of her teacup. "I take it you haven't heard the newest rumors?" She raised a thin eyebrow at Samantha. "Before I share, have you found anything of interest?"

Samantha leaned back against Slate as she shook her head and yawned. "Not at all. Unless you count the curious coincidence of several groups describing a pirate band asking similar questions about the keystone as we did."

Ellie cocked her head and set her teacup down on her saucer with a tiny *plink*. "That is odd. But nothing like the news we've just heard." The fine lines around her eyes deepened as she frowned. "The keystone on the Isle of Heather was attacked."

Slate straightened so abruptly that Samantha had to fling out a hand to catch herself from sliding off the couch. He gaped at Ellie. "But the barrier is still up?"

"If it weren't, we'd be having a very different conversation right now." Ellie tucked a silvery curl behind her ear and reached into a polished wooden basket next to her seat. She pulled out a paper and handed it to Garnet. "The attack failed to damage the keystone there, but it definitely shook up the other citadels."

"No kidding." Slate rubbed at the goosebumps on his arms. Nearly twenty years later, and another attack. Would it happen again? If so, where? "Was anyone killed? Did they catch who did it?"

"They lost five guards from the isle. And unfortunately, no. They couldn't find who did it." Ellie hunched her shoulders and tilted her head down, swiping a hand by her eyes. "As a result, much of the Void Born animosity has been stirred up again."

"Lovely," Garnet said flatly. Her knuckles whitened around her teacup as she drew her shoulders back. "Because there aren't enough problems going on, now we have to deal with the crazies." She shot Slate a look.

He sighed. Though it wasn't the same, it *felt* similar. This time people were stirred up against imaginary bogeymen, whereas last time the population was stirred up against a hot-headed ruler-to-be. Last time, the riots preceded the attack on the Doldran citadel and keystone. This time, it was the assault on the keystone that brought about the madness.

"But enough of that for the moment." Ellie pursed her lips before turning to Jade. "I've waited long enough. What happened to your arm?"

Jade described the terror attack and Ben's heroic efforts to protect her and Krista—despite him not knowing what to do—complete with gestures and sound effects, to Ellie's clear amusement.

"I miss such adventures." Ellie's eyes sparkled with memory. "I'm glad you have this opportunity to see the world while you can." She sighed dramatically and fluttered a hand in the general direction of the palace. "As if the new panic isn't enough to worry about, Lord Everett has raised taxes recently for some pet project of his, and it's bleeding me dry. I may need to downsize the company if he keeps it up."

"What project, dare I ask?" Garnet glanced sideways at Jade, who had sunk back against the couch with tightly pressed lips at the mention of Everett Windsor.

"He wants to claim some of the Arid Plains for Aerugo, and that requires an obscene amount of money to pipe in water and persuade Aerugans to move that direction. I'm sorry to say that I won't have as much funding for you to pay your crew when not on an active job." She paused, her eyes settling on Jade and softening. "Jade, could you do me a favor while you're here?"

Jade straightened, and she flipped her braid behind her back. "What do you need?"

"There's a clock in my bedroom that I haven't had time to take in to a repair shop. I know it's not the same as an airship engine room, but—"

"I can fix it," Jade interrupted with a small laugh. "Shall I take care of it now, before we forget?"

"Yes, thank you."

Jade excused herself and left the room, her hand trailing along the textured wallpaper.

Ellie waited until they heard the quiet click of the door upstairs before she continued, "As you know, Lord Everett has only grown more corrupt over these years." Her brow wrinkled in sorrow as she looked at Slate. "Tell me, how is Zak doing, now that he's back here? Has he fully recovered yet?" Her eyes flicked to the ceiling where they could hear the floorboards creak as Jade walked into the room. "And how is she faring, since you talked to him?"

Slate and Garnet exchanged glances, and Samantha intertwined her fingers with his. "He's doing better," Slate said finally. "He's back on for dragon hunting, and he hasn't commented much on the whole ordeal. Jade's been more vocal, of course. She hates coming to Lucrum now, and I know she's dreading our visit to the palace."

"And it's a bit more difficult to be here this time around, with things so awkward between her and Zak," Garnet added with a sigh.

Ellie nodded slowly before taking a small sip of her tea. "Andre comes by occasionally. Rumor has it that the prince isn't quite the man-whore that he had been."

Slate loosed a cynical laugh at the same time as Garnet coughed. Garnet fanned herself with a hand. "Sorry, but that's a bit hard to believe."

Ellie shrugged. "Rumors, Garn, they're just rumors." She paused again, taking her time to look at the three of them. Ellie tapped her fingers against her leg. "I know you've talked with Zak, but I also know you haven't talked to Jade yet. When are you going to?"

Samantha and Garnet turned to look at Slate, and he dropped his eyes from his mother's scrutiny. He ran his thumbnail along the piped edge of the couch. "I don't know when," he admitted after a long pause. "But not anytime soon. I don't expect her reaction to be good, and I feel that we need more distance from last summer."

"The longer you wait to tell her, the harder it will be when the truth comes out," Samantha pointed out in a gentle voice. She twisted in his arms to look at him apologetically. She pressed a tender kiss on his jaw to soften her words. "Sooner would be better."

Slate offered her a wan smile that he knew didn't reach his eyes.

"Agreed." Garnet scooted to the edge of her couch and gripped the cushion under the folds of her golden yellow skirt. "We're already at the point that whenever she knows, it will be difficult and painful. That's inevitable." She skewered him with a stare. "And now there's possibly a new interest for her? Slate," she lowered her voice and glanced at the doorway before meeting his eyes, "Jade has to know she's the Princess of Doldra, and *soon.*"

"It would be better for her heart, son," Ellie stated with a stern, practical tone. "Spare her and the young Guardian further heartache." She arched a brow in Garnet's direction. "And the feelings of any other possible beaus for her. We can't let her heart get entangled with others. Not when she's going to need to marry another crown to appease the other rulers."

Slate closed his eyes against the onslaught of their words and shook his head. Memories of crimson hair, sparkling blue eyes, and a life-loving laugh assaulted him. "We wait." He cracked his eyes open and put what firmness he could in his voice. "Soon, probably this summer. But not now."

CHAPTER NINETEEN

BEN

Doctor Jaxton pressed the two wires against Ben's upper arm, above his burns, and dabbed a cold gel on them to adhere them to his skin. Ben twisted his arm to get a better look at them as Jaxton tightened the straps that held down Ben's legs, arms, and torso.

"And what will these do, exactly?"

Jaxton walked around the table that Ben reclined on and patted a hand on the contraption he'd pulled out and set on the counter. The wires ran from Ben's arm to a squat cylinder, filled with metal coils that attached to a board with several dials, switches, and gauges. Jaxton shot Ben a grin, his eyes bright with excitement.

"It's called electroshock therapy." Jaxton turned a knob, glanced at Ben, then moved the dial a bit more. "I'm going to pump a very precise amount of lightning into your body in hopes that it will restore your memory."

Ben twitched his burned fingers. "And that won't make this worse?"

Jaxton paused, as if only just remembering that Ben was injured. "Oh, yes. That." His lips twitched. "I suppose we should take care of that first." He pulled a black stone from a drawer and stood in front of Ben. "This will feel odd, as I'm going to accelerate the healing. Just hold still."

Ben could make out the tiny glimmering flecks of blue and purple in the rock now that it was closer. He tensed as Jaxton blew out a breath and touched the healing stone to his burns. Jaxton closed his eyes, brows drawing together. He frowned. His eyes opened, and he held up the rock to the light, then tapped it against Ben's arm again.

"Is something wrong?" Ben asked as Jaxton stepped back, still examining the stone.

"Not exactly." Jaxton drew the words out, his mind clearly in another place. His black eyes flicked up to Ben, narrowed. "And you can't remember anything about where you're from, still? What about things here? Are there still things that you don't remember?"

Ben eyed the stone that Jaxton set on the counter, mentally debating how honest he wanted to be. *He's a doctor. If he's going to help me, I need to be honest.* "I don't remember my past. And I'm still not sure what the keystone or barrier is about. Or how they work."

Jaxton leaned against the counter and ran his fingers up and down the crease in his white doctor's coat. "The keystones link together Void, time, and death magic. They're all reaching out for each other. If we want to use Lasim terms, we'd say they're connecting a circuit." He cocked his head, eyes speculative. "Do you remember what the Void is?"

"Something bad?" Ben shrugged. "I'm sure it'll all come back soon." He nodded to the wires on his arm. "Maybe we should try that, see if I remember everything then?"

"Of course," Jaxton pushed away from the counter and pulled his goggles up from around his neck, looking over his shoulder. "You ready?"

Ben set his head back against the cushion of the table. "I think so—" Before the words were even out of his mouth, pain arced through his arm and raced along his nerves, setting everything on fire. He jerked, straining against the leather straps. Stars sparked in his vision.

The current stopped, leaving Ben gasping for air. He blinked away the spots in his eyes and focused blearily on Jaxton.

The doctor raised his eyebrows. "Anything?"

Ben closed his eyes, mentally reaching for anything new. Shadowy recesses in his mind offered nothing. Whatever secrets his memory held were still inaccessible. He sagged against the table, refusing to give in to the frustration and depression that whispered at him. "Nothing."

"Hmm." Jaxton pulled a pad of paper from a drawer and scrawled something on it. "Do you remember who I am?"

"Doctor Jaxton." Ben frowned. "Was there a chance that this would take *away* my memory?"

"I never said that." Jaxton's reply was a bit too quick for Ben's liking. The doctor tapped his pencil against the counter. "Let's try a different question, something a bit harder. Do you remember Kerlee's story from last night?"

Ben sucked in a deep breath and stared up at the ceiling. "About his hometown being wiped out?"

Jaxton wrote on his pad again. "Good. Any details beyond that?"

"It was after the attack on the Doldra keystone." Ben frowned at the memory. "Dragons moved into the area, when they had been staying away before. Most of the city was wiped out; his family fled before it was too late." He lifted his head to look at Jaxton. "Why?"

"Checking your memory—immediate, short, and long." Jaxton

pulled the wires off Ben's arm and wiped the gunk away, then lifted the seat and started tugging at the leather straps. "Your short term and immediate memory seem unaffected, though your long term is still problematic. But you knew that already."

Ben stretched his arms once they were freed from the restraints. "So we're no closer to a solution?"

Jaxton tossed a rag into the basin. "Yes and no. You've given me some ideas to work on. It'll be a few weeks though. I need to make sure I think through it all before I try it on you."

"Oh. Okay." Ben sat up on the bed and swung his feet over the edge. "Is there anything else for today, then?"

The door opened, and Geist poked his head in. He nodded at Ben and turned his attention to Jaxton. "Do you have a minute, Doc?"

"*Doctor*," Jaxton emphasized. He pointed his pencil at Geist, eyes narrowed. "Bad enough that Briar doesn't show proper respect. Don't you start too."

Geist smirked and pushed the door all the way open. He strolled in. "You know I live life on the edge."

"And one of these days you're going to come in from a fight, and I'm not going to fix you up." Jaxton crossed his arms. "What do you want?"

Geist propped his hands on his waist. "Looking for a favor." He shot a quick grin at Jaxton, and then at Ben. "Would either of you be good for a small loan?"

"Captain's not going to like it when he finds out what you're up to," Jaxton warned. Geist chuckled, and Jaxton rolled his eyes as he handed over two crimson lut. "And you'd better pay me back, or not even your lucky stars will save you."

Geist tossed a quick salute at Jaxton. "You know I will. I always pay my debts." He slapped the back of his hand against Ben's shoulder. "Come on, we're heading into town, we've got some errands to run."

CHAPTER TWENTY

JADE

Jade followed Geist and Briar and tried to not think anything of Ben's shoulder rubbing against hers as the crowd moved around them. This was a simple trip to the marketplace. Not a date or anything to be nervous about. Even if Zak's glower at Ben as they left made her wonder if there was more to the day than she thought.

The scent of roasted meats, sweet fruits, and fresh bread rolled over Jade, but instead of being tempted, her stomach roiled. This was a bad idea. Maybe after Briar picked up the food supplies he needed, she could volunteer to carry it all back. They didn't really need her help, did they? Ben's hands were still burned, but they had been healing well these last two weeks, so her help wasn't as necessary as they made it out to be. She could make it back to the *Sapphire* and have plenty of time to get psyched up for the tri-discus game tonight. And then she wouldn't have to stress right here and now.

Krista would be disappointed but understanding. Neither of them could have imagined how much worse it was for Jade to actually be so close to the palace, and if Jade had had any idea how stressed she'd become, she'd never have let Krista rearrange the schedule to allow Jade to go into the city with Ben. Jade's mind felt like it was tearing itself into pieces. She could think of little else—Ben, Zak, and *him*.

Her skin prickled at the remembered touch of Prince Weston. Never again would he lay a hand on her. Zak had made that evident to the entitled prick.

Just as Weston had made it clear to her, through Zak's torn flesh, that she was powerless in his nation.

But Krista heard Jade claim she was moving on from Zak, and she seemed determined to see Jade actually follow through. And while Jade didn't mind admitting that Ben was attractive and interesting and that she wanted to get to know him better, she wasn't ready to throw herself at him like Krista wanted her to. She couldn't.

At least, not yet.

Just being in the grid-like marketplace, so close to the Aerugan palace, made her jumpy. She specifically wore her most Aerugan-looking mechanic clothing: fitted trousers with a double-slit skirt over them, and a blouse and bodice that closely resembled the uniforms that the people here loved. It was uncomfortable, but in a sea of people who wore similar clothing, she didn't stand out. She kept her distinctive red hair securely tucked under the black headscarf that Garnet had loaned her.

But it didn't feel like enough. Being in Lucrum without Zak by her side left her feeling more exposed than she would've dreamed. Geist was their tracker and a skilled spearman, Briar had talent with knives beyond what she believed humanly possible, and Ben had proven his ability with hand-to-hand combat.

And despite having these three men with her, she felt vulnerable without *him*.

Barrier take me, have I really grown to be so dependent on Zak? No wonder he's scraped me off his boot.

A woman laden with bolts of fabric pushed past Jade, and Jade stumbled into Ben. His hands gripped Jade's shoulders, and he glared over her head at the ignorant woman. Jade muttered her thanks and turned away without meeting his eyes. She knew she could trust him. Could trust Briar and Geist.

But they just weren't Zak. When had she grown so accustomed to her broad-shouldered shadow, his snarky comments, his light laughter? How had he gotten so under her skin that she couldn't survive a trip to the market without him constantly on her mind?

Granted, he'd also physically defended her from a fate that she'd considered worse than death, but in her heart, she knew it was more than that.

"Jade?" Ben's voice was barely audible in the babble of sellers hawking their wares, customers asking questions, and children playing. His hand touched on her shoulder, feather-light. "Are you all right?"

Moving on.

Jade lifted her face and met his concerned gaze. How had she not noticed the tiny scar above his lip? She pasted on a smile. "I'm fine. Sorry."

They walked past a bustling fruit stand, and a man slipped between them and the guys up ahead. Jade saw only the strong posture, the dark curly hair, and she stiffened, breath seizing in her throat.

Ben seemed to sense her stop. He glanced back, and immediately whirled to face her, his back to the oblivious man. "Jade? What's wrong?"

The stranger waved at the seller, and Jade caught a glimpse of his pale skin. Her muscles relaxed as she sucked in a lungful of air. Her vision momentarily blurred. *It wasn't him.*

Briar shouldered past Ben to reach her side. "What happened?" he demanded. His hand dropped to the knife strapped on his waist. "Is he—"

"Not here." Jade interrupted. She wiped her clammy palms on her beige pants and forced herself to smile. "My mistake. I'm good. Just..." she looked at Briar and let herself show her fear. "I thought I saw him. But it wasn't. I need to relax. That's all."

Briar rubbed his thumb over his knife hilt and shook his head. "You're allowed to be nervous. Whales, *I'd* be nervous."

Jade ignored Ben's curious gaze and looked around Briar. She could just make out the cart he'd been heading toward. "Where'd Geist go? Did you send him on ahead?"

"What?" Briar spun on his heel and pushed his hand through his hair. "No. I don't know where he went."

"Somehow, I'm not too surprised," Ben commented. "He's been on edge all day."

Jade stepped between the two men and did her best to scan past them while pushing her paranoia down. There was no connection between Geist and the royal palace, so wherever he was, he should be safe. But where would he go?

Briar touched her shoulder. "C'mon. The sooner we find everything, the sooner we can get back to the *Sapphire.*"

"But Geist—"

"Is a big boy." Briar cut her off. "He can take care of himself. Honestly, he's probably looking for some wrestling match or something to give him his adrenaline fix. Now, I want to get some fresh meat and whatever sorry excuse they have for vegetables." He grinned at Jade's slight scoff. "Perennia has superior produce, and you know it. How about you and Ben start looking for garlic and get the rest of this list?" Briar carefully split his paper and handed half to Jade. "I'll be right over there if you need me for anything."

Jade nodded, reluctant to split up their group any more.

She led Ben past a stall brimming with leafy greens and followed her nose to the pungent cart. Large braids of the herb hung from the framework of the stall, and baskets overflowing with loose bulbs took up half the counter itself. Minced garlic in jars of various sizes lined the front half of the other side of the cart, with larger bottles of whole cloves and oil in the back.

The shopkeeper smiled broadly as they approached, and he scooped freshly minced garlic into a glass bottle, stoppered it, then set aside his cleaver. He wiped his hands on his apron and nodded. "What can I get for you two today?"

Jade stepped forward, fingering one of the garlic braids, testing the firmness of the bulb. She skimmed her fingers over two other braids before answering. "We'll take two, please. And—" she leaned forward and tried to sniff for the bread stall she'd smelled earlier, "do you know where we'd find a loaf of bread, that we could get a spread?"

The portly shopkeeper laughed. He leaned down and pulled up a half a loaf of golden bread. "Would you like two slices for you and your husband?"

Jade stammered, her mind suddenly blank, and flushed, waving her hands in the air in denial.

"Oh, no, we're not married." Ben laughed, sparing her the need to find cohesive words. He grinned when the man apologized. "It's no problem, really."

Ben slipped the garlic braids into his bag as Jade paid the shopkeeper and accepted two slices of well-buttered, pungent-scented bread. She handed Ben a slice and consulted the list, unable to maintain eye contact. Her cheeks still felt hot from her tattle-tale blush.

He nudged her and thumped his slice of bread against hers in a toast. "Thanks for the bread, *wife.*"

Ben's teasing tone soothed some of the burn in her face even as it made her heart flutter. Jade shook her head at him and couldn't contain the giggle that bubbled up inside, even while her subconscious still moaned at lost dignity. "Why, you're welcome, *husband.*"

He waggled his eyebrows at her, and she glanced down at the list to avoid staring at his sparkling eyes. "Next is jerky. That way." She pointed, and Ben began to weave through the crowd with her on his heels.

His steps slowed, and he turned toward a group that argued loudly in the street. Jade caught up to him, and set a hand against his linen shirt to urge him on. The lady closest to him stamped a foot and shrilled loudly enough for Jade to overhear.

"—those Void Born are probably the cause of it!"

A man in a top hat, too formal to be in a marketplace, pounded his cane against the smooth concrete. "We really need to get rid of the bleeding veebs."

"When will Lord Everett take care of those—"

Jade sighed and rolled her eyes before pushing at Ben with more force than necessary. *They need to find something better to do with their time than clog up the aisles here with their theories and complaining.* Ben half-skipped to avoid being bowled over by her.

"What are they talking about?" Ben asked with a quizzical expression. He tilted his head back to watch, and a lady in the group raised her voice and waved her arms.

"Conspiracy theorists," Jade replied curtly. "Ignore them."

He cocked his head as the man shouted something behind them. "Kind of hard to ignore. What's a Void Born?"

Jade sighed. "No one real." She raised a hand and let it drop while she searched for words. "Void Born aren't real, they're…they're the ones who get blamed for bad things. When a newborn dies, they say a Void Born must've cursed the baby. When crops wither, they say a Void Born must've spat on the field or something."

"So a Void Born is basically a legend?" Ben used the back of his knuckles to rub at his chin. "Interesting."

"It's an excuse for people to not accept that life happens, and sometimes, life just bites." Jade scowled. "The worst of the whole Void Born issue is that people will get so worked up that they go mobbing, and they've killed innocent people whom they believe to be Void Born. It's barbaric."

She caught the flash of blue from his eye as he gestured at the paper crumpled in her fist. He shot her a wry grin. "Let's find that jerky, and anything else on that list, before it's unreadable."

Jade grimaced and smoothed out the paper as they reached the jerky cart. Ben ordered, and she settled the wrapped meat in the bottom of her sack. She motioned to the next stall, and they fell into an easy rhythm of chatting between errand locales.

Ben leaned against a wood pillar of the salt stall. "What was it like, growing up on the *Sapphire*?"

"I don't know." Jade furrowed her brow as she looked over a pillar of black charcoal salt. "I mean, I don't have anything to compare it to." She dipped her finger in a small tray of sample salt and cautiously touched it to her tongue. It tasted completely normal. Weird. "I got to travel all over the world and experience and see so much; I can't imagine living in just one place."

Ben held the small package of salt while Jade paid the lady. "Do you think you'd ever want to just settle somewhere?"

"No, I don't think so." Jade shrugged. "I don't know where I'd settle, if I did. Or how to stay settled." His eyes roamed over the crowd as she answered, and she used that distraction to examine him. He held an easy smile on his face, revealing the openness that she found so refreshing. His white button-up shirt accentuated his stocky build, and he carried himself with a strength and a calm depth that reminded her of the restful lakes in Lasim. The self-confidence of a warrior. Achingly similar to Zak, now that she thought about it. She turned on her heel and let the cowl of her scarf brush over her cheek and hide her eyes. "What about you?"

Ben caught up to her with one full stride. "Where would I settle?" He blew out a breath. "I don't even remember where I'm from. I can't really think about where I'd live until I know where I have lived." He paused. "Does that make sense?"

Jade met his gaze and smiled, pouring as much hope into the expression as she could. "Yes. And we'll figure out where you're from. Don't worry."

Briar met them on the edge of the food and tech quarter, and Jade let him take over the price haggling that she detested. She left him and Ben at the booth while she meandered to the stall across the road that had caught her eye. Gears of all sizes and metals were neatly arranged in trays. Tiny gears smaller than her pinky nail, gears the size of her hand, two gears as large as her head.

"We're at the crossroads for this section." Briar's voice sounded from behind her. "Hey, princess, do you actually need anything in the tech quadrant, or can we head over to the clothing? I want to look for something for Krista."

Jade rolled her eyes at Briar's nickname for her, and put the gear in her hand back on the cart with a rueful smile. "Nothing actually needed. Just greatly desired."

Briar snorted. "Gear head."

"Egg head."

"Grease monkey."

"Cupcake."

"Hey, that's low," Briar protested. "You broke the name-calling rules. You are hereby on name-calling probation."

Jade rolled her eyes and started walking down the wide aisle between the tech and food quarters.

Ben caught up quickly and leaned over her shoulder. "Cupcake?"

Jade grinned over her shoulder. "Long story involving his first week on board and his 'celebration cupcake special.'" She giggled. "They were—" She paused, searching for the right word. She gave up with a laugh. "Horrible. They were horrible."

"I'll have you know that was because nobody warned me that Zak shouldn't be allowed in the kitchen." Briar broke in. His eyes wrinkled in amusement despite his scowl. "I don't know what he was thinking, but rosemary did not belong in those cupcakes. That was a spectacular failure. In an absolutely mortifying kind of way."

Ben chuckled. "So there's something that Zak can't do?"

"Oh, never let him by the kitchen." Jade laughed. "And if you find him skulking around it, push him into the mess room where we keep a few snacks on hand. For the sole purpose of not letting him go into the kitchen to find food."

"So much makes sense now." Ben smirked. "Glad to finally understand his grumbling about the kitchen."

Jade spotted a display of vivid scarves and hustled over, leaving Ben and Briar. Deep blue with specks of green and lighter blues drew her attention first, then a beautiful rich purple pulled her away. She lifted it and examined the weave. This would look amazing on Krista. She turned to show it to Briar and paused.

Ben and Briar had stopped several feet away, their pose mirrored in each other, arms crossed and creases in their brow as they talked too low for her to hear. Briar shook his head, and Ben's eye twitched. Ben asked something, and Briar shrugged, gesturing toward the direction of the palace. Briar noticed Jade watching them. He rubbed his head with a sheepish grin and walked over, gently taking her elbow and turning her back to the scarves.

"What did you find? Anything interesting?" he asked as he focused his attention on the table. Briar spoke rapidly, not letting her get a word in. "This one looks good." He picked up a sage-green scarf and held it up by Jade. "Hey, Steamboy, think this would be a good color for Jade?"

Ben blinked at Briar and scratched his chin, his eyes roving over Jade's face. He joined them at the cart and leaned past her, his hand barely touching her shoulder. He tugged on a green-and-blue swirled scarf and stepped back, handing it to Jade. "This would be better. It'll either bring out the blue in your eyes, or make them that mysterious seafoam color."

"Seafoam?" Briar raised an eyebrow. "Interesting choice of word. Are you from a city by the ocean?"

Ben stared at the scarf, his eyes distant. "I...don't know. But it fits." He looked at Jade and held his hands up in a shrug. "I stand by it."

Jade accepted the lightweight fabric, her shoulder mourning the lack of Ben's hand. She dropped her gaze from his, under the pretense of examining the scarf. It *was* beautiful. And she wouldn't mind having something so elegant. Maybe she'd even wear it to hide behind when she visited the palace tomorrow.

"Here, I'll get it for you." Ben handed the shopkeeper two lut.

Jade looked up quickly. The protest forming on her lips died as Ben shook his head, hands up.

"Nope. Done deal. Already paid for everything."

"But you just earned that money!"

"It's too late, Jade." Briar laughed. "Just let the man give you something nice." Briar shot her a grin. "It's not like you're required to wear it in Vodan."

Jade's heart seized at Briar's words and their implications.

People at the nearest entrance started murmuring and moving back. She sent Briar a we'll-talk-later look and stepped away from the cart to try and see what was going on.

Her eye caught the flash of silver and black, and blood drained from her face so quickly her head spun. The previously delicious scents of garlic, roasted meat, and fresh fruit now turned her stomach. Her knees wobbled, and suddenly Ben's arm was around her, offering support.

"What's wrong?" He straightened, pulling her up with him, and surveyed the crowd. "What did you see?"

Jade pulled away from the protection of his arm, and she yanked on Briar's sleeve.

He turned with the purple scarf in his hands.

"Prince Weston is here."

Briar's eyes widened, and he tossed his lut at the shopkeeper and shoved the scarf into his bag. "Bleeding Void Born," he swore. He gripped Jade's shoulder. "Let's get you out of here."

Fear and anger lent Jade enough strength to look through the crowd to where *he* was with his guards. He stood, profile visible, talking with a shopkeeper in the tech quadrant. Two bodyguards stood on either side of him, a small ring of guards beyond.

She swallowed hard. It was one thing to be at the palace and know there was a high chance of seeing him. To see him here was unexpected, especially after all her fretting earlier. He looked in her direction, and she spun around with a gasp. Did he see her?

Jade fought the nerves that threatened to take away her clarity of thought. Would she rather deck him in the jaw or collapse in a ball of fear?

"I have to get out of here," she whispered.

Briar nodded and hefted his sack of food while Ben did the same. "Ben, you take up the rear. I'll lead. No stopping. Try to act somewhat natural."

Ben nodded, his eyes hard. "Let's go."

Heart pounding so hard that her ribs hurt, Jade followed Briar, her eyes on his boots as she kept a death grip on her own sack of purchases. Of all times. Of all places. Why would Weston be at the marketplace? He had servants for that! Her fear of being here this morning had been that a guard would see her and inform him of her presence—not that he himself would show up!

Her nerves jittered as Briar paused to let other pedestrians cross in front of them. Shivers ran down her spine from every little breath of breeze that swept across the hairs on the back of her neck. She glanced back and only saw Ben, closer than she expected, his eyes sharp as they roamed the crowded market street.

They broke through to the edge of the square, and Jade tried to suck air into her tense lungs. *Just need to*—she caught Briar's wide-eyed expression and followed his gaze, only to have ice shoot through her veins.

Prince Weston and his guards were following them.

They weren't actively looking at Jade, but they were close enough that she could see the silver gleam of piping on Weston's guards' uniforms. A shopkeeper bent, revealing Weston's gleaming white grin as he leaned over the counter, presumably ordering the poor soul around.

Jade whirled, heart hammering in her chest. She tugged on the black scarf to reassure herself it was still covering her hair. Why was he taking his time catching her? Was he trying to prevent a scene?

Jade broke into a run, dodging a horse and its rider as she darted into a nearby alley. She wouldn't let him touch her. He wouldn't get that close again. Not in any way. Never.

The worn cobblestones darkened with the dirt of less use, and the sounds of the crowded outdoor shopping faded in favor of the clatter of their mad dash. Briar pulled ahead of her and pointed which direction to turn as they came up to a T.

They pounded down the next narrow alley, and Jade slowed her pace a fraction. The sound of her harsh breathing masked almost all others, and she needed to be able to hear. She slowed to a fast walk, and the guys kept pace.

Briar caught her eye. "We'll be back to the *Sapphire* soon."

"Hey, wait!"

Ben's arm swung her against the wall, and she shrieked. He blocked her body with his. She stared at his back, trembling. Briar stood side by side with Ben, providing the best screen they could to hide her. At this point she couldn't even feel ashamed for her weakness, not with the fear flooding her system. Had they been followed after all? Best she could do was hope that the wall and the guys would provide enough cover.

Briar spoke first. "Geist?"

Ben's tense shoulders relaxed, and he stepped back, letting her see past him and Briar. Ben offered her a sheepish "sorry," but she shook it off with a trembling smile. She didn't move from where she leaned against the cool bricks as she watched Geist jog up to them.

"Where have you been?" Briar asked.

His question blended with Jade's "Where did you go?"

Geist hesitated, then shrugged as he shoved his hands in his pockets. "I went exploring. Did you find everything?" He raised an eyebrow at Jade. "And what did I miss? Why were you all running?"

"Exploring?" Ben challenged. He half lifted the bag on his shoulder. "We've been working and trying to stay out of sight of..." He glanced back at Jade, and the skin around his eyes tightened before he looked back at Geist. "Unwanted attention."

Geist took a step forward, hands fisted.

Jade closed her eyes and leaned her head against the wall. Did they have to start on this right now? *Deep breath.* "We'll tell you on the way." She pushed off the wall and scooped up her small bag of goods. "And you can tell us where you disappeared to."

CHAPTER TWENTY-ONE

BEN

Cream-colored walls towered above Ben as he followed the *Sapphire* crew through the crowd. Multiple sets of stairs led up to the stadium seating that lined the bowl-shaped Aerugan tri-discus arena. Ben smelled roasted meat, and he stopped to look for the source. Kerlee stepped in front of him, effectively blocking the view of the sausages on sticks.

"You're going to get lost here if you stand around and gawk," Kerlee admonished. He waved a crimson-sleeved arm at the rest of their group. "Don't worry about your stomach. Briar tends to sneak in snacks, and once we get our seats, we'll send out a team to grab food." Kerlee clapped a hand on Ben's shoulder and steered him to walk between Victor and Zak. "And there's food from all over the land here, so maybe you'll find something familiar from home."

Zak half-turned to acknowledge Ben's arrival. His eyes flicked to Ben's, then away, his lips pressed into a flat line. "Any luck with remembering anything recently?"

"None." Any hope that Zak was over his funk from last night sputtered and died. Clearly whatever progress he'd made in befriending Zak had returned to square one. Who knew that Jade would be such a touchy topic? He had to somehow let Zak know that he had no intentions or interest in Jade in that way, and that he specifically wanted to get close to her for the purely selfish motives of trying to figure out his own past.

"Back home, we had a brew that was helpful for memory loss," Victor commented. He rubbed his bald head and shot Ben a small smirk. "You're not grossed out by desiccated lizards, are you?"

The mental image of a withered and dried lizard flashed through Ben's mind, and he wrinkled his nose. "If they're not something I'm supposed to ingest, I have no problem with them."

"Oh. Well, I'm not sure how interested you'd be in this particular recipe." Victor chuckled.

Zak's eye twitched as he looked over at Victor. "Note to self, never ask you for any potions or memory help." He waved at Jade, and let her, Krista, and Briar cut in front of him in line. "I can think of much better uses for dead lizards."

Jade whirled and stuck a finger under Zak's nose, her eyes blazing. "If you think you're going to get away with that little prank in *my* engine room, one more time, so help me, you are going to regret it!" She stepped closer and glared up. "Let me remind you that I have the power over all the hot water in the ship, and it would be very, very easy to make sure you have cold showers for the next month!"

Ben swallowed his snort as Zak raised his hands in an exaggeration of wide-eyed innocence. Zak as a prankster. Unexpected, and yet unsurprising. After all, it was always the quiet ones who seemed to cause the most trouble.

"It's always the quiet ones, you know." Laughter framed the words.

Ben grabbed a nearby glass and guzzled it, water dribbling down his chin as his mouth burned with what had to be liquid fire. Tears streamed from his eyes and rendered the faces of the guys around as nothing but blurs. "I hate you all. That was the last mug they had."

"Hey, man, ever heard of Mexican hot chocolate?" Someone plopped down next to him, but Ben ignored him in favor of blowing his nose, then grabbing at a water bottle. "I just added a touch more spice than typical."

"My tongue is numb, Laurent. You better watch your back."

"Ben!"

Ben squeezed his eyes shut and tried to block out Jade's voice, desperate to hold on to the memory. A name. *Laurent.* His gut told him it was a friend. And a prankster, at that. What happened to Laurent? Where were they when that memory had happened?

"This is your first tri-discus game, right?" Jade bounced into view, and the wisps of recollection faded from Ben's mind. Red paint swirls with gold highlights covered most her face, and she wiggled where she stood.

"First to my knowledge, yes." Ben raised an eyebrow as she twirled in place with a happy laugh.

"You need to sit with Zak and me!" She spun around and grabbed Krista's arm. "Don't sit with this *traitor* or Briar."

Krista's face was painted with purple and green floral patterns, and she laughed as she released her arm from Jade's grip to walk into their aisle of seats. "Just wait. He'll suddenly remember that the only team worth cheering for is Perennia."

Jade gasped in outrage and threw herself in the chair next to Krista. "Traitorous fiend!"

Ben didn't follow her lead, and instead stood by Zak at the end of the row. "I take it they're really into the sport?"

Zak grinned. "What gave them away?"

Victor stopped by their row, squinted, then raised an eyebrow. "I'm actually going to sit somewhere else," he smirked. "I just saw someone I know." He waved and disappeared into the crowd of people streaming up the stairs.

Wait. Had Geist disappeared again too? What was with that guy? Ben pivoted to look at the row that the *Sapphire* crew had taken over. No short brown hair. The spearman had left without saying anything. Again.

Zak shifted his feet awkwardly and glanced over where the bickering girls sat before nodding at Ben. "I owe you an apology. I may have overreacted last night." He rubbed the back of his neck. "It's fine for you guys to be friends, and it's not like you need my permission for that. I genuinely hope that she can somehow help you with your memory. Just," his eyes strayed toward Jade, "be careful with her."

Ben hadn't realized he was tense until Zak's words eased the rigidity of his spine. "Of course." He lowered his voice, hoping Zak would be able to hear him over the din of the crowd. "And I know she's yours. I won't be making a move on her or anything."

Zak jerked and stared at Ben. "What?"

"Nothing." Ben gestured at the row of seats. "After you."

Zak shook his head with a small scoff. "No, you can sit between us. She'll love the opportunity to convince you Doldra is the superior team."

"Joy." Ben settled in the smooth stone seat and arched his spine into the back of it. For being a solid piece of rock, it was surprisingly comfortable. He scanned the arena and gestured a lightly bandaged hand at the green. Grassy ramps and mounds littered the ground, with no symmetry or discernable equality. "Nothing here looks familiar, so I'll need you to explain why the field is uneven."

Zak crossed his ankle over his knee and leaned back in the seat. "Well—"

Jade tapped Ben's elbow. He turned, and she held out a bag for him to take. "Pass those to Zak." She reached out, and Briar handed over another sack. "These are for you. If you want anything more, you're on your own."

"Thanks." Ben dropped the bag in Zak's waiting hand. Ben pulled the paper apart to peer into his bag and grinned at the mix of nuts and fruits he saw. "Thanks, man," he called over the ladies. Briar's dark hand waved over Krista's head.

Zak pulled a bright blue piece of rock candy out of his bag and dropped it into his mouth. "Just like it should be." He stared down at the field and absently rubbed the heel of his hand against his chest. "When I was a kid, the game was only discus, as it hadn't grown into a three disc sport yet. My brother, Zane, would take me to games and let me fill up on rock candy." A bittersweet smile crossed his lips as he popped in another small piece. "Briar found out a while ago, and has kept me supplied during games ever since."

Ben nodded silently. What was there to say?

"But you asked about the game." Zak dropped his feet to the floor and leaned an elbow on his knee while he pointed. "The teams draw sticks to see who has first pick. The team that wins first pick gets to either choose which side of the field they want, and get only one disc at the throw-off, or they can let the other team pick which side, and then they get the advantage of two discs at throw-off. You follow?"

"So far, yes." Ben fished a raisin from the bag and chomped on it. "What are the obstacles for?"

Jade leaned into Ben's seat, interrupting whatever explanation Zak would've given. Her eyes glowed in the stadium's gaslights. "Those are for the extra challenge. And it's *awesome*." A shrill whistle sounded, and she whipped back to join the rising cheer.

Zak chuckled at Ben's furrowed brow. "Watch, and you'll see."

The two teams filed out on opposite sides of the field, the green and purple of Perennia on Ben's right, and the Doldran red and gold on the left. The Doldran team knelt on their side of the field, while the Perennian team huddled together, passing something white among them.

"Most Doldran teams pray to the Author of Life before playing, whereas Perennia may pray to Ganum of Determination, or Gladus of Honor." Zak nodded to the field. "Looks like they've got a gladiolus tonight, so I'm guessing Gladus."

A leader from each team met in the center of the field with a referee in gray, and after a few moments with the sticks Zak had mentioned, the Doldran team was given two discs.

Jade whooped and Ben twisted away, ear ringing. He rubbed at his head with a wry smile.

His ears rang as she cheered. She jumped from the bleacher and wiggled her hips in a little dance as she pumped her arms. The stadium was doing the same, everyone on their feet, yelling and shouting as a man in a blue jersey ran across the field, kicking a white-and-black ball in front of him. The player kicked, and the ball flew into a net. Sara shrieked, and her popcorn went flying as she danced.

"Sara." Ben whispered.

Zak waved his hand in front of Ben, leaning close enough for Ben to hear him over the crowd. "Are you feeling all right?"

He touched the ring on his necklace, closing his eyes against the dizzying bright colors and noise. *Sara. Who are you to me?* His head spun, and determination welled up in his chest. Was this Sara's? *I will find you.*

CHAPTER TWENTY-TWO

BEN

Ben breathed in the cool night air and enjoyed the invigorating fresh scent as he followed Zak and Briar. The tri-discus game had gone into the night, and it felt good to stretch his legs and get his blood flowing again.

Zak's black clothes turned him into a smudge of darkness as he and Briar reenacted a play-by-play from the game.

Briar shot around Zak and mimed throwing a disc back at Ben. "He throws, he—"

"Interception!" Zak exclaimed, grabbing the imaginary air disc and squatting down to look around Ben to where Jade and Krista walked. "Jade! Catch!"

Jade's head shot up at the sound of Zak's voice, and she hunkered down before jumping up and clapping both hands together. She landed with a fierce grin made terrifying with her painted face. "Victory!" She bumped her knuckles against Zak's, her eyes sparkling with laughter. "Team Doldra: one. Team Perennia: zero."

Krista laughed. "I didn't even know I was playing!" She reached out to Briar and twined her fingers with his, tapping his nose with a smile and a wink. "Next time, let your teammate know when we're playing invisible games."

Briar flushed and pointed to Zak. "He started it."

Zak pointed back at Ben. "He was on your team, too."

Ben slipped his hands in his pockets in silent mirth as Krista continued to tease Briar. Ben still didn't fully understand the intricacies of the game, but it'd been fun and fast-paced. Parts of it seemed maddeningly familiar, though no more new flashbacks came to him.

Just who is Sara? Why do I remember her but not who she is?

Zak pointed to a painted wooden sign of seven cups tipped together. "There it is." He flashed a bright grin back at the group. "The Tipsy Paladins is one of the few establishments where no one cares who we are. And it's clean enough for our ladies to visit."

Jade and Krista laughed at that as they entered. The pub had already started to fill with the crowds leaving the tri-discus game, so the girls claimed two seats at the gleaming bar next to another lady, while Ben followed Zak and Briar to a table offset from the center of the room. Zak sat facing the door, his eyes roaming over the people coming in. Briar chose the chair that let him watch the women, so Ben picked one of the two chairs left available and dropped into it.

He let Zak and Briar place their order once the waitress flitted over. He hung an arm over the back of his chair as he balanced on the back two legs and studied the decor. Globular gas-lanterns lined the walls between each booth, casting shadows across the faces of the customers. Individual flames flickered and danced. Low-hanging metal circles with smaller gaslights illuminated each table in the middle of the room, like a miniature island of socialization. Wall-to-wall wooden floors gleamed in the ambient light. Nothing about this triggered a memory.

Briar stood. "I'm going to go clean up before food comes." He looked pointedly at Zak. "Don't start any fights without me."

"Wouldn't dream of it. Besides, you're the troublemaker," Zak snarked back.

Jade's laugh cut through the din of the room, and Ben glanced over to see Krista waving her arms in some grandiose story. He turned away from them and shook his head with a small smile that slipped away a moment later. Did *he* have a close friend? Laurent, maybe? Was he worried about where Ben could be? Was Sara concerned about him?

A glass of frothy amber liquid slid just into range of Ben's vision. He blinked at it curiously.

"On me," Zak said, pushing it closer with two fingers encased in black leather that cut off at the knuckles. "Consider it a 'thank you' for helping the girls last week."

"Thanks." Ben reached out to the handle of the mug and grimaced when his stiff fingers couldn't fully grasp it. Maybe he had overdone it this morning with hauling around bags from the marketplace. He rotated the mug and awkwardly picked it up with his left hand. Though his hands had recovered from the worst of the steam burns, he clearly needed to finish using the burn cream Jaxton had given him. Ben took a sip, closing his eyes to enjoy the heady rush of joy as his taste buds celebrated the rich flavor. He swallowed a second mouthful before setting the mug down. "That's some good stuff there."

Ben didn't see Briar yet. He sighed and thumped his finger against his mug, wincing a moment later when the pain reminded him of his injury. "Hey, Zak?"

Zak stirred, as if drawn out of deep thoughts. "What's up?"

Just get it over with.

"Quick question for you." Ben hesitated for half a second and prayed that his friendship with Zak wasn't about to plummet back to the coldness of last night. "Jade. It's clear she's a sore subject, and you like her though you seem to deny it. What's going on?"

Zak became completely still, a dark statue in a bustling room of amber light. He didn't say anything, just stared at his mug, lips pressed together and a crease between his eyebrows. Finally, he sighed deeply through his nose. "It doesn't matter if I lov—like her, I can't be with her. And nothing good would come if I encouraged that line of thought."

Couldn't be with her? Or wouldn't be with her?

"What? No food yet?" Briar plunked himself down in his chair with a moan. "I'd hoped that talking with the women for a while would guarantee the arrival of sustenance."

Zak smirked and sipped from his mug, eyes downcast.

Finishing that conversation with Zak would have to happen later. "So, how are they, since they've been so far away from your sparkling presence? Have they survived?" Ben asked.

Briar's chair creaked as he stretched. "Krista and Jade think my pickup lines are bad. They just don't appreciate my inspiration."

"If you likened them to food, no, they wouldn't appreciate your inspiration," Zak replied dryly. "I've yet to meet any female who appreciates that."

"Hey, Krista didn't mind when we first started dating," Briar defended.

"Krista was too overjoyed that you finally got over your cold feet and asked her. At that point, she was willing to overlook such grievous mistakes in character." Zak leaned back and crossed his arms. "She's smarter now."

Briar recoiled with a laugh. "Ouch, man. Talk about a burn."

"So what line did they hate so much?" Ben asked. He smiled his gratitude as the waitress slid several plates onto their table. He plucked a piece of meat from the steaming plate and blew on it. "Or do we even want to know? And why do you even need pickup lines?"

"I use them on Krista whenever we're out of the *Sapphire* like this. Keeps the romance alive, you know?" Briar grinned at Ben and leaned across the table on one arm. "If you were a vegetable, you'd be a cute-cumber."

Ben cracked up while Zak groaned.

"Briar, that's awful." Zak shook his head with a pained expression. "Please don't ever say something that horrible again. It's a blight on the male race."

Amusement bubbled within Ben as he looked at Zak. "Life without you would be like a broken pencil—pointless."

Zak shot him an unamused look. "I'm not joining in on this."

"You don't have to. You're the one sitting here." Ben chuckled as he brandished a leg of chicken at Zak. "And the less likely you are to participate, the more amusing it is for us."

An evil spark entered Zak's eye, and he grinned slowly. "Participation? How about this. Next girl that walks in, you have to use a pickup line on. That should be amusing."

"Deal."

Ben and Zak shook on it and returned to their food.

Briar coughed. "So, Ben, it's time to make good on your deal."

"No problem. Where is she?" Ben swirled the liquid in his mug and quickly washed down his bite of potato. He followed Briar's finger and felt his confidence waver.

An angel walked behind their table toward the bar. The glittering light highlighted sharp, tan cheekbones, and her raven hair glimmered and shone as she moved. Her gaze flickered over their table, and Ben's body tingled at the depths of her dark eyes. A deep blue tunic hugged all the right curves in all the right places, and the sword on her hip only heightened the image of perfection. Her casual grace and confidence suggested that the weapon wasn't merely for show.

Ben pushed his mug away from the edge of the table as he stood clumsily. Zak slouched and covered his mouth with a hand, already wincing. Silent laughter shook Briar's shoulders. Ben ignored them.

She stood by the counter, waiting for the bartender to finish mixing her drink.

The closer he sauntered, the more nervous he felt. Though he'd felt a draw to Jade, this was a different draw. Jade needed a friend, a protector, someone to walk alongside her. This woman was special. Confidence radiated from her, and a sense of something else that Ben couldn't put his finger on. Need a champion, she did not.

Never had he regretted taking on a dare this much.

He took a deep breath before leaning an arm on the polished wood and flashing her his most dazzling smile. "Anyone ever tell you that you're gorgeous?"

A single black eyebrow rose, and she frowned at him.

He wouldn't be deterred. He *had* to get to know her. There was something about her that pulled him in like a moth to a flame, and getting burned would be well worth it. "Because you are. I'm Ben." He held out a hand. "And you are?"

She sighed and paid the barkeeper with a quiet "thank you." She lifted two mugs, pausing only then to look him in the face. "Raine." Her voice was flat and emotionless as she answered, ignoring his hand.

He dropped his hand to his hip in a suave gesture. "A lovely name for a—"

"Please, just stop." Raine rolled her eyes and shook her head before walking away.

Ben watched forlornly as she sat with an older gentleman in a corner booth. He sighed and returned to his table to find Briar gasping for air, tears of laughter visible in the corners of his eyes. Zak's hand had moved to cover his eyes instead of his mouth. They both looked at him when he dropped into his chair. Briar started snickering again, and Zak dragged his hand down his cheek with a grimace.

"That was more painful than amusing." Zak shook his head. "Absolute torture."

Briar wiped tears from his eyes. "Better luck with the next girl."

"Oh, no." Ben sipped from his mug, his eyes traveling to the corner where Raine sat. "I'm not giving up."

Briar spluttered and coughed, pounding on his chest before looking at Ben with watering eyes. "Oh, really?" His gaze traveled past Ben, and Ben turned to see Jade watching him from the bar, her eyes filled with questions.

He fought to keep the grimace off his face. Had Jade mistaken his friendliness with her for something else? It wasn't like he'd done anything to lead her on. The shopkeeper's comment about them being married rose in his mind, and he froze with a wince. He'd have to talk to Jade and make sure that he hadn't somehow given the wrong impression in his playful banter that he'd meant to ease her tension. He nudged a potato on his plate with his fork and resisted the urge to look at Raine again. "I at least want to meet her properly. Someday."

Zak's green eyes darted in Raine's direction. "I think I'm willing to encourage that. But that will have to be a different day. We should finish up and head back before it gets much later."

Briar pulled his plate closer and slid his arms around it as a shield. "I'm finishing my potatoes first."

"I know." Zak's eyes tightened with a smile as he rubbed a hand through his hair. He blew out a deep breath. "Ben. I need to ask you for a big favor."

Ben tensed at Zak's tone. "What's the favor?"

Zak hunkered over the table, his jaw tense. "When Jade next goes to the palace to visit Queen Violet, I need you to escort her."

Cold fluttered through Ben's gut. He kept his voice even as he racked his brain for everything that Jade had mentioned in passing about the palace and the prince there. "That sounds deceptively easy. What's the catch? Why can't you go?"

Briar coughed and pounded on his chest. He raised a hand to forestall Ben's additional back thumping, his eyes watering. "I'm good."

Zak shot Briar a sidelong look and pursed his lips. "The prince there has already proven to be handsy when it comes to Jade, and we've…disagreed over his intentions toward her." He scowled at his mug. "I'm forbidden to be on palace property, and my presence is barely tolerated in Lucrum because of it."

Jade laughed beside Krista, and Ben consciously relaxed his aching fists. He'd been willing to do whatever it took to get her to safety while in the market this morning, but that had been in free territory, where it was easy to run or hide her. In the palace, it would be different. Rules and etiquette, and in the prince's own playing field.

Ben would be sorely outmatched for what would be considered

politically proper. "Will my presence make things more difficult for her?"

"Not particularly, no." Zak's jaw twitched. "We'd rather risk some political affront than her safety."

Ben raised his eyebrow. "We?"

"Captain Slate and I."

Interesting. Ben tapped his fingers against his mug, considering. From what he'd gathered before, if it really came down to it, he could be in the crosshairs of the rulers here. *Crosshairs?* Ben shoved the odd word choice aside and focused on Zak's request. He didn't want to start any issues here—didn't want to risk anything that would interfere with his goal of figuring out his past.

But he'd be damned if he let something happen to Jade when he could defend her.

Ben drew his shoulders back and looked Zak in the eye. "You can count on me. Consider her protected."

Zak nodded once, then tossed back the last of his drink and set it on the table with a note of finality. "Tomorrow, the captain meets Lord Everett, and it'd be best if we're all sharp and prepared for whatever Slate will need us for after that."

"What could he need us for tomorrow?"

Zak twitched his shoulders and shot Ben a dark look. His voice lowered, barely audible over the din of the tavern. "When it comes to Lord Everett and what he thinks of our crew, anything is possible."

CHAPTER TWENTY-THREE

SLATE

"With all due respect, my lord." Slate filled his lungs with the stuffy air, smoothed his brown dress coat with his palms, and dared to move a half a step closer to Lord Everett. Then Slate bowed. "The money from your taxes would be best spent in defense of the barrier. You know there was an attack on Heather Isle, and the Doldran keystone—"

Lord Everett raised both black eyebrows and leaned forward, the single gem in his gold crown glittering under the throne room lights. "Are you presuming to tell me that *my* plan for my money is not what *you* think it should be?"

Smooth, Slate, smooth. Insulting him is not going to do anyone any favors.

Maybe staying up late the night before hadn't been the brightest of ideas. But here he was, sluggish brain and all, meeting the one man in all of southern Terrene whom Slate distinctly did not want to steam. And yet, he had to make the ruler see reason.

He caught Queen Violet's wince from the corner of his eye and tried to backtrack with as much logic and humility he could muster this early in the morning. "No, my lord, it wouldn't be my place."

Slate bowed as low as he could, and came up, ready to try again. "But, my lord, dragons have been steadily increasing in numbers around Doldra, and the time flux has only worsened at the keystone since the…" he swallowed past the sudden lump in his throat, "fall of the royal family, and we must stabilize it. On top of that, we don't know who attacked the Heather Isle keystone, and if they're going to attack again. If we can find something that will, in fact, secure it, we can protect all the southern nations."

Everett stood and paced with long strides on his glossy gypsum dais, turning on his heel with a snap and flourish as he reached one corner. He shook his head and paused where the light cast dark shadows across his pale face. "Governor Bentley keeps me apprised of the situation in Doldra, and it's not as severe as you make it out to be." He smirked at Slate. "If I didn't know better, *Captain*," he emphasized Slate's title as if it were fit for a child, "I would think you've heard a few too many blood-bond bogeyman stories in your youth. As for the Isle, the keystone there received no damage. It's of little concern."

A flash of heat broiled through Slate, igniting his skin and burning away the vestiges of exhaustion that clung to him. He ground his teeth to prevent himself from retorting something rude. Insulting the ruler of two countries while in that ruler's palace would not go over well. Even if Lord Everett wasn't the King of Doldra, his marriage to Queen Violet clearly had gone to his head, giving him the audacity to act as if he were the rightful ruler. "Maybe so, but would you still permit us to search for such an artifact in our travels?"

Lord Everett snorted and waved a hand dismissively before tugging the bottom edges of his black uniform jacket. He sniffed. "Of course. If you can keep up with your schedule for our deliveries here, what do I care how you spend your time?"

"Thank you, my lord." Slate's bow wasn't as grudging this time.

"Captain Slate." Queen Violet finally spoke from where she sat on a couch to the side of Everett's desk, her spine straight and gaze unrelenting. "I do have a mission for you to undertake, immediately, should your men be available."

Slate shifted his stance to face Violet directly. She was the only source of color in the otherwise stark Aerugan room. White walls, black floor, gray and white furnishings–only the obsidian thrones held a bit of color with crimson veins shooting through them. Violet's deep chestnut skin complemented by a sapphire-toned dress offered a pleasant respite from the monotony.

"My men can be called together very easily, my lady." Slate smiled warmly at her, and the edges of her mouth tipped up in return. "What can we do for you?"

Her smile slipped away as apprehension etched lines around her eyes and her skin lost some of its warmth. "Advisor Samuel was expected to return from Piovant and report with his convoy four days ago. He hasn't arrived." Her fingers twisted in her skirt before quickly smoothing the fabric. "Please, try to find my uncle. We can supply you with maps of the route they typically use."

The idea of Samuel Thistle being in possible danger concerned Slate just as much as it did the queen. Samuel had been a voice of reason and justice for as long as Slate had known him—even before the deaths of Prince Richard and the Doldras royal family, and before Violet's remarriage to Lord Everett. Slate pushed back the unease and tilted his head in a sign of acceptance. "We'll begin the search as soon as we have the maps."

"Captain, we're almost to the Wyld Woods."

Here they were again. Slate nodded to acknowledge Victor's words and peered through his telescope, sweeping it to and fro across the horizon, hoping and praying for a flash of metal or a glimpse of an airship. But where could such a large ship disappear to?

"Continue on along this path." Slate glanced down at the map provided from the Aerugan palace and traced the *Sapphire's* path over the marked route of the *Dauntless*, his gloved finger skidding along the protective glass casing. "We'll continue along this direction until we reach Piovant, and if we don't find them, we'll double back and widen the search."

A flash of Victor's bald head indicated a nod, but the man had already returned to the helm. Slate drummed his fingers against the rail and sighed. While Advisor Samuel Thistle didn't know Jade's true identity, he had a sympathy for Slate's family and was a valuable ally within the royal palace. To lose Samuel through some accident would be grievous. Slate wanted to avoid that at all costs.

A glint to the right attracted Slate's attention, and he snapped the telescope back to his eye, carefully panning from left to right. There! Through the thick canopy of trees, he could just glimpse the shiny black material of the *Dauntless's* helium balloon.

"Victor!" Slate shouted over his shoulder. "Bear ninety degrees starboard!"

"Aye, sir!"

Hope rose in Slate's chest as they drew nearer to the downed ship. Not a dragon in sight, and two men on the ground next to the egg-shaped airship waved and cheered when they saw the *Sapphire*. Slate spun around and clattered down the steps to the engine room. He popped his head in and rapped on the wall to get Jade's and Krista's attention.

"Ladies, we are about to land by the *Dauntless*." As he spoke, the turbines whined outside the walls, indicating their descent. "And if first looks are to be believed, I'm going to guess she ran into some sort of technical difficulty, not a dragon-related problem."

Krista snorted and moved away from the bronze boiler as she dropped her goggles to rest around her neck. "No surprise there. Steamy ships have so many issues."

"Yeah." Jade wiped the back of her hand against her face, smearing a black glob of grease across her pale cheek. "Those new ships are so much less reliable than our good ol' grav stones." She patted the floorboards lovingly. "Hopefully, their problem is running out of water for their boiler and not helium-related. That'd be a pain to fetch."

Slate leaned against the doorway, staying as far out of the humid room as possible, and grinned at Jade's dirty face and Krista's rumpled hair. "Either way, I'll be bringing you two along to talk to their mechanic and see what we can do to help, so you may want to look somewhat presentable."

He trotted back up the stairs where the fresh, cool breeze ruffled his cotton shirt, and he mulled over what the two had said. It was true enough. Ever since the barrier went up some sixty-odd years ago, grav stones had become harder to mine, then impossible to further excavate, due to the location of the barrier over the mines. Piovant worked hard to create other airships that weren't reliant on the grav stones, but the new steam-tech vessels weren't built the same in any way, shape, or form. They weren't as sturdy as the *Sapphire*, with her solid wood and metal. These new ships were light-weight wood and canvas, they were run by minimal crew, and they weren't meant for hauling cargo.

Please, let it be a simple fix.

Victor landed the *Sapphire,* and Slate walked down the gangplank with Zak and the girls to where a bearded man in a black Aerugan military uniform stood at ease.

The *Dauntless* captain shook Slate's hand with a strong grip and a relieved smile. "Am I glad to see you!"

"Likewise." Slate quickly introduced himself and his party, the *Dauntless* captain did the same, then Slate gestured to the burnished silver-and-black airship. "What's her problem? How can we help?"

Captain Thompson scratched at his short beard with a grimace. "Ran out of water. Should've had our mechanics double-check before we left port, but they slacked off."

"Sorry to hear that." Hands on his hips, Slate rotated to look at the dark trees that surrounded the clearing. "Have you had any dealings with dragons this deep in the Woods?"

"Some trouble," Thompson hitched a thumb over his shoulder to point to the *Dauntless*, and Slate noticed the furrows in the metal by the door. "Second day here, we let the men out to stretch their legs, and some plodders came by with stalkers close behind. We got everyone on board without injury, but it was pretty close. Void-cursed stalkers ruined my paint job." The captain grinned and slipped his hands into his coat pockets with a shrug. "Better a cosmetically challenged ship than dead men, though."

Slate huffed a short laugh and nodded. "Very true. Sounds like you guys got off easy."

"We did." Thompson gestured to the *Sapphire.* "We have a royal advisor on board who needs to get to Aerugo immediately. Please tell me you have space for him."

Slate nodded. "Of course. Queen Violet wouldn't send us to you for just a drop-in greeting."

"Glad to hear it." The captain smiled. "That's good of her majesty. I don't know how long we'd be stranded without help." He turned to the crew member behind him, boots squeaking on the damp grass. "Go get the advisor and his attendant. Tell them help is here and they're switching ships." Thompson looked back to Slate. "Can you send another ship with water for us?"

"Of course." Slate shrugged, "Do you need any parts or just water?"

"Eh." The captain's eyebrows drew together. "My mechanic would know the answer to that better than I."

Jade stepped out from around Slate and bobbed in a mimic of a curtsy, despite her stained, loose-flowing mechanic pants. "Krista and I can check it out, talk to your mechanic, and get a list of whatever else is needed. Be back in two sparks!" She waved a hand at Krista, and the two girls jogged to the *Dauntless* with Zak trailing behind.

The trio passed a tall black man, impeccably dressed in ebony slacks with matching coattails and a top hat. The man smiled when he drew close enough to see Slate.

"It has been a long time. Good to see you again, Captain." Samuel's hands moved gracefully through the air as he signed, and the words came to Slate's mind, Samuel's stone ring visible on his left hand.

"And it's good to see you as well, sir." Slate spoke aloud and bowed. *Marvelous things, those interpretation rings.* "My crew and I will see you safely returned to Aerugo, and we'll bring a report of what is needed to get the *Dauntless* home."

"Thank you." Samuel's smile slipped away, and he gave Slate a significant look. *"Time is of the essence, as I bear news of great importance for Lord Everett and Queen Violet—I daresay you will find the information most crucial for your endeavors."*

CHAPTER TWENTY-FOUR

JADE

Jade watched in the mirror as her aunt took the final curler from Jade's hair and pinned the curl in place under her hat. Krista's reflection nodded in approval, and Garnet's hands fell away from Jade's head, landing on her shoulders.

"You look lovely, dear." Garnet's no-nonsense attitude shifted into something softer, and a bittersweet smile touched her lips. "If only your mother could see you."

Jade shrugged as she ran a critical eye down her reflection, her heart aching. She'd been to formal events with both her father and mother, and Samantha wouldn't be distraught over not seeing Jade in her outfit today. It was the same dress that she'd worn for the ball in Perennia, when she'd danced with Zak and everything in the world seemed to be going right. How things had changed. But the gown still fit like a glove cut from the latest fashion—fitted in the bosom with a skirt meant for dancing and twirling. Even the corset had extra give to it, allowing for breathability and movement.

The side trip to rescue Advisor Thistle had bought her a few days' reprieve before she'd have to come visit, but time never slowed enough for her to avoid the palace altogether. She shivered despite the warmth of their room. She'd much prefer to be wearing this for a ball than for today's purpose.

"Ben's escorting you, right?" Krista scooted off the bunk and circled around Jade, fluffing the skirt as she moved. "He won't leave your side."

Garnet nodded. "You'll be safe, dear." She leaned away to look at the clock, then sprang back to Jade's side. "We need to get you going, or you'll be late!"

Jade rolled her eyes at her aunt. "Your idea of being late is not being early. I plan to arrive at the exact moment I'm supposed to be there. No earlier, no later." The fabric rustled softly as she walked to the door, and she paused, leaning a hand against the frame as she lifted a foot and tugged at her slipper. "Do I have to wear these?" She cast a longing eye at her boots. "These are too tight."

"Yes," Garnet replied firmly. "You are meeting with the Queen of Doldra and Aerugo. You need to look the part of your station and carry it with dignity and respect."

Jade sighed. "Yes, ma'am."

"Let's go find your escort," Krista said, sympathy in her voice though her eyes twinkled with amusement. "And am I glad it's you and not me who has to go see her," she whispered as she clutched Jade's arm. "It's so freeing to not be a noble."

"Low-ranking noble," Jade muttered.

"Still noble enough."

Jade wrinkled her nose at Krista and cut in front of her to take the stairs leading up to the main deck. She lifted the hem, cautious to not let it get caught on the metal tread or brush anything that would dirty the aqua fabric.

Kerlee passed the stairs just as she came to the top step, and he paused, blinking at her before he grinned and bowed. "You look simply beautiful, princess."

Jade groaned. "Don't you start, too! Bad enough that Briar calls me that."

"Princess Gearhead," Kerlee rolled the title off his tongue and snapped his fingers, "of the Engine Room."

"Fine. Whatever." She shook her head at him as he laughed.

He pointed and winked. "They're over there."

She didn't have to ask who "they" were. She closed her eyes for a brief second before stepping out onto the main deck and turning to face Zak and Ben.

Ben cleaned up well. She took note of his top hat, polished boots, and matching sword belt. But her attention drifted to where Zak stood, just a step behind Ben, his lips parted and eyes shining with the same look that he'd given her the night of the ball. Like she was his whole world.

She stopped before the duo and let herself bask in the rare moment of enjoying being dressed up. She smiled up at Zak, a thrill of delight racing through her as his breath hitched.

"I've said it before, but I'll say it again." Zak shoved his hands in his pockets and licked his lips. "You're beautiful."

"Absolutely stunning," Ben agreed.

She dipped into a playful curtsy. "Why, thank you."

Garnet hustled to her side, waving her pocket watch. "It's time to go, Jade." Garnet studied Ben straightening his collar and tugging on his vest. "Good, good. I'm glad we found something that works for you. Did Zak show you proper etiquette for meeting the queen? Of course he did." Garnet laughed to herself as she circled around Ben. "Zak is an excellent teacher."

What joy Jade had been floating on slowly sank as her aunt bustled about, being the business woman that she excelled at. She watched as the light in Zak's eyes faded, as if he'd put up a shield, not letting her see inside.

He gave her a perfunctory nod before gesturing to Ben. "He'll be by your side the whole time." Zak's lips twisted and he turned halfway, speaking over his shoulder. "You should probably hurry if you don't want to be late."

Jade lifted her skirt in a final curtsy as Ben held the door open for her to escape the queen's meeting chamber. The door whispered shut behind her, and she closed her eyes with a sigh of relief. She'd done her required duty of seeing the queen, and now she was as free as she could be when within the stifling confines of the palace. Time to escape. She glanced to the left and then right, pleased to see the stark hall clear of all but the customary guards at the queen's door. *From here, down to the main floor, through the gardens, out the—*

"That wasn't so bad." Ben's voice broke through her mental calculations. He slipped his hands into his slate-gray pant pockets casually and cocked his head at Jade. "Where to next?" A small smile crossed his lips. "Are you sure you really needed me in there? You were definitely more well-mannered than I was."

Jade caught the eye twitch of the silver-and-black-clad guard and gritted her teeth. She grabbed Ben's shirtsleeve and pulled him after her. "That's because it was just the queen, and I've been raised to know multiple etiquettes for multiple kingdoms." Her next words threatened to stick in her throat. "And some places here aren't safe for a female to walk alone."

I thought Zak would have told him before we came here. Maybe he didn't?

Ben stumbled after her, matching her pace, and she released him when he reached her side. He glanced over his shoulder, his eyes hard. "Jade. I know only fragments of what happened here last year. And I know you need to avoid the prince. That about sums it up." He hesitated. "I don't know the details of what happened, nor do I know if I want to."

They passed an open window, and Jade glanced out at the lush green garden and the vibrant flowers and winced. "Give the man a cookie; he figured it out." She sighed and pinched the bridge of her nose as she walked as fast as her flowing dress would allow. Great. Now her sarcasm was coming out. As much as she'd been enjoying Ben's presence the last few days, having Zak here would have been better for her nerves.

Then again, after this morning, maybe it was better that he wasn't with her right now. She needed to keep her wits and not be distracted. Not that Ben wasn't distracting in his own way. She thought he'd been interested in her, but then she'd seen him flirt with the girl at the bar last week. What was his deal? Had she been misreading him at the market?

No, Ben was just as distracting as Zak would have been. All that mattered was that she'd had a relatively good visit with their family friend, Queen Violet, and now was Jade's chance to visit her uncle before returning home. Quickly. Her shoes pinched in the toes, and walking so fast made them hurt even more. Further motivation to find Uncle Andre, and get back to the *Sapphire*.

"I know Zak isn't allowed at the palace as an escort." Ben's voice held no reproof, just mild curiosity. "And, to use his word, the prince is 'handsy.'"

Memories of blood, despair, and fear washed through Jade like an ice bucket over the head. Air caressed the nape of her neck as Ben nearly rammed into her back. She ignored his startled apology and shut her eyes, shaking her head, trying to dislodge the vision. How could she tell him Zak had been whipped last time they were here? And that her uncle had been the one to suggest that punishment—to protect Zak from worse? All because he'd defended her when Weston forcibly kissed her?

One of her closest friends was permanently scarred because of her. And Weston didn't like hearing "no." What if he tried claiming her again? "I…" She licked her dry lips and tried again. "Yes. And—"

"Miss Stohner."

If Ben's question had been frigid water to her body, the voice she heard now froze everything in her core. Despite every cell in her being yelling for her to run, she couldn't move her feet. Her lungs couldn't pull breath.

He'd found her.

Prince Weston stood in a nearby doorway, his eyes as wide as hers. He fumbled with a velvet-wrapped package in his arms when he realized she was looking at him. "Oh, uh…" He pulled himself upright with an imperious tilt of his pointed chin and offered a minute bow. "Have your travels treated you well?"

Speechless, Jade stared. The brief glimpse of him in the marketplace hadn't prepared her at all. Same light hazelnut skin, dark eyes, and tight curly hair. He had filled out a bit since last summer—no longer lanky, but lean and well-muscled. His gaze didn't stray from hers. She closed her mouth and shook her head, backing up into Ben, whose hands braced her shoulders.

Weston pressed his lips together, gaze downturned at the bundle he gripped, before looking down his nose at Ben. "And you are?"

Ben squeezed her arm and stepped out from behind her to bow— not as low as he should've. He settled his hands on his hips, his stocky shoulders tense. "Ben."

"Ben?" Weston's eyebrows rose, and his gaze flickered from Ben's borrowed boots up to his brownish-red hair. "No title? No last name?" Weston smacked his mouth in distaste and looked past Ben to Jade. "Your replacement for Zak?"

At the mention of Zak's name, all the ice in Jade's body melted away in favor of hot anger, leaving her trembling from the sudden change of emotion. Just enough fear kept her from grabbing the entitled princeling prick and hurtling him into the doorframe.

Weston must've caught her shift in mental state; he shuffled his feet awkwardly. He dropped his gaze and sucked in a cheek, then he looked up at her through his thick eyelashes. "I'm sorry." He swallowed with an expression that suggested he'd just tasted something sour. "That was unnecessary. And...cruel." His lips puckered. "What happened last year, I mean." He scuffed the toe of his shiny black boots against the marble floor.

She didn't reply. What was there that she could say?

Silence stretched, broken only by the distant sounds of servants moving about in other hallways.

Ben eyed her and clapped his hands together, startling her and Weston. "Well, pleasant conversation. Thank you. Time for us to go." He pressed his hand against her shoulder blades and gently propelled her toward the door. "After you, my lady."

"Wait."

Ingrained manners barely held Jade in place. She turned slowly to see Weston holding a hand out to her, his eyes panicked. He extended the velvet-wrapped package.

"I…I've been learning metalworking," Weston said. "Pistoia— my master—suggested I try making something that could be used against flying dragons. It made me think of you and your crew, and I wanted to somehow say I'm sorry about last year. I made this. Well, I made it with the help of my master, of course, and I know you probably don't want anything from me, but," he held it out again, insistently, "please, I-I'm sorry."

Jade accepted the gift hesitantly, cautious to not touch his fingers or get too close to him—just in case it was a ploy for him to grab at her again. She shuffled back two steps once she grasped the bundle securely.

A smile of relief split Weston's face, and he nodded. "Open it, and I can explain." The tension in his shoulders dropped as she flipped back a corner of the fabric to reveal a coppery handle. "I call it a steam-pistol. It can propel a lead ball the length of an entire hallway." Weston gestured to the passage they stood in as an example of distance. "It's deadly, and it can maybe be used for dragons or bandits. Maybe you'll find it useful on your travels."

Jade ran her finger along the ridged handle and inspected the narrow barrel and the pistons on the side. A small glass tank, filled with water, was attached to the bottom of the barrel. The design was unique, she'd give him that. But to accept a gift from him? Even an apology gift? Jade bit her lip. She'd take it, but she wasn't going to keep it.

"If it's steam, where does it vent?" Ben asked.

Jade peeked around her curled hair at Ben's still somewhat shiny red hands. Why hadn't Jaxton used a time-spell to heal him already?

Weston ignored Ben, but pointed to four small vents on the right side of the pistol. "It vents to the right, so don't have anyone stand too close, unless they're in proper protective gear."

"Thank you." Jade spoke softly to the gleaming floor, unwilling to look up at Weston.

"You're welcome."

She waited, silent for a few moments. "Well, I have to go. Thank you for the steam-pistol." She didn't move as she listened to Weston's footsteps fade away in the opposite direction. Jade finally looked up when Ben touched her elbow.

His blue eyes analyzed her, and he stepped closer, keeping his voice low in the echoing hallway. "Are you okay?"

Jade wrapped her arms around herself to ward off the sudden shiver that rippled through her body. "I'll survive."

He gestured to the door. "Shall we escape while we still can?"

"Yes. Please." She swallowed hard and held the pistol and velvet wrapping out to Ben. "You want this? I don't."

He accepted it with a quiet nod, his eyes searching hers for answers that she didn't want to explain. "About what just happened—"

"I'll be fine." Jade turned toward the stairwell and stopped when Ben's hand clasped onto her wrist. She looked back and watched the struggle on his face as he started to say something, stopped, closed his mouth, and finally nodded to himself.

The gentle warmth in his eyes kept her still even when he released her. "Jade, I want to be your friend, and I want to do all I can to help protect you. But part of being friends is honesty, openness." He sighed and rubbed the nape of his neck. "I don't have much to share, because I still don't remember much worth sharing." His brow furrowed. "And I'm not asking for you to dig through painful past stuff, or to spill whatever dark secrets you have. Just, be honest."

Jade stared at the blurry floor through watering eyes. The last man she had been open and honest with hadn't talked to her the next day, and had only just started acting normal around her again. And she still didn't know what she'd said then that had pushed him away. Did she dare make the same mistake now?

"For now, I'm going to assume that you aren't fine," Ben said quietly. "I'm also going to assume you don't want my arm for a proper escort. So if you know how to get out of here, I'll follow your lead. Otherwise you can follow me."

"I-I want to find my uncle still."

He nodded, brow furrowed, and a small frown tugged his lips. "As long as you're still comfortable being here. Let me know if you need me to make a ruckus and let you escape or something drastic."

A hollow laugh escaped Jade. The last time something drastic had happened in this palace on her behalf, her friend had been whipped. She wasn't going to let that happen again.

CHAPTER TWENTY-FIVE

BEN

Ben followed Jade out into the garden and frowned when she swiped a hand by her eyes as she walked. *I hadn't meant to make her cry. Or was that because of the prince?*

Honestly, between what Briar had shared with him on their supply run the day prior, and what Zak had mentioned before Ben had left with Jade, he knew exactly who Prince Weston was. He didn't know the full story of what happened, but what he did know was more than enough—and if the prince had tried anything with Jade, Ben was prepared to do whatever was necessary to get her out in one piece.

But physically defending her was one thing. Emotionally protecting her was another. She hadn't turned around since they entered the gardens, but her face dipped forward, and every time she moved her hand by her eyes, he could see the telltale glisten of tears. Ben clenched the steam-pistol. He had to get her back to the *Sapphire*, where Krista could cheer her up.

They passed through a white marble archway and into yet another hallway. He'd known the palace would be large—but it was another thing to see just how sprawling it was. Countless corridors, rooms, hallways, and offshoots leading to who-knew-where created a maze that left Ben at the mercy of Jade's memory of the layout. He easily kept pace behind her and glanced over his shoulder occasionally, making sure the prince wasn't following.

"Where do you think your uncle is?" he asked.

Jade paused at a split in the hall. She bit her lip and shrugged. "I'm not sure. Right now, he could be anywhere, and I don't want to risk running into *him* again."

Ben nodded, unsurprised, and moved to block one of the entryways. He ducked to look up at her downturned face. Red-rimmed eyes shifted away from his gaze. "Hey." He tucked a finger under her chin and gently raised her head, then dropped his hand. "Let's ask a guard if they know where your uncle is. Then we can go directly to him and reduce the risk of running into Weston again. Right?"

Jade chewed on her bottom lip before nodding with a sigh. "I suppose we could ask."

Ben pressed his hand against his pocket, confirming the crinkle of paper there. He couldn't afford to forget to deliver the letter if they did find her uncle. He looked around the bland hallway—*Haven't these people ever heard of a thing called color?*—and spotted a guard standing outside a doorway. Ben turned back to Jade. "Wait here." He trotted over to the silver-and-black-clad man.

"Excuse me, sir." He stopped an arm's length away. "My friend and I are looking for her uncle Andre. Do you know where he might be?" Ben grimaced to himself. He didn't even know her uncle's last name. *The captain's never mentioned a brother, so I assume it's not Stohner.*

Metal clanked as the guard turned on his spot to see Jade. His eyebrows disappeared under his black cap. "I assume you are referring to Sir Catalina?"

"Uh, yes." Ben bluffed.

The guard shifted his grip on his spear and pointed to a doorway on Jade's left. "Down that way; check the library or the study room."

"Thank you, sir." Ben bent at the waist in an awkward bow and walked back to Jade. He offered her his arm and a reassuring smile. "Let's go find your uncle."

Jade hesitated for a heartbeat, looking from his arm to his face. He smiled softly, hoping she could somehow feel his desire to shield her. Her fearless friendship and now vulnerability had awoken a protectiveness that had been buried under the foggy murk of his mind. The sorrow and uncertainty in her eyes faded, replaced with the spark that he'd grown accustomed to seeing on her.

A flash of a smile. Blonde hair. A feminine whisper, "You'll come home, right?"

His own voice, "I'll be back. I promise."

Ben blinked away the memory, shaken. *Sara.* Now he recognized her voice and could match it to her name. But he still didn't know who she was to him. But she wanted him to come home to her. He lifted a trembling hand to the ring that dangled on the necklace buried under his shirt. *Am I married, and I don't even remember my own wife?*

Jade touched his arm, uncertainty swimming in her eyes. "Are you all right?"

"Yeah, fine." Ben sucked in a quick breath. "Just"—*honesty*—"another hint of a memory. Nothing major, but still, something."

"That's wonderful!" Jade enthused, the tension in her shoulders disappearing entirely as she beamed. "Every little bit counts. What did you remember?"

"Sara." Too late, Ben realized that perhaps that wasn't the most tactful of things to say, as Jade's excitement visibly dimmed before she plastered a smile on.

"Well, that's something," she replied before turning in the direction the guard had pointed. "Maybe you'll be able to remember where you're from soon, too."

Ben let his arm drop and followed her into a cavernous library. She hesitated in the doorway, then started a clockwise search through the room. Her face lit up when she found a muscular man with bits of gray streaked in his brown hair reading and taking notes at a table.

"Uncle!" Jade called out, and his head snapped up, his pen raised above the paper. Sorrow flashed through his eyes even as he smiled, and Jade embraced him. She turned to introduce Ben.

"Meet my Uncle Andre." Jade's tremulous smile reached her eyes fully.

"A pleasure." Andre bowed as he clasped Ben's forearm in a firm shake, his eyes clear and warm.

"Likewise." Ben looked at Jade, then Andre. "I'm guessing you're related through Samantha?"

Jade laughed and shook her head. "Uncle Andre is actually a family friend who worked for my Doldran relatives before the fall of the Doldran royalty. He survived, obviously." She smiled brightly at Andre, and he reciprocated with a brief nod, his lips twisted in a half grimace, half smile. "He's been looking out for me my whole childhood, and he taught me most of what I know about weapons." A shrug caused Jade's curls to bounce. "He's my uncle."

"I suppose that makes sense." Ben set the steam gun on the table. He pulled a sealed letter out of his pocket and held it out to Andre. "Zak asked me to deliver this to you."

"Did he now?" Andre accepted the envelope and inspected the green-and-black wax imprint before he edged the knife blade under the hard seal and popped it open. He leaned back in his chair and scanned the letter with a thoughtful expression, his left hand casually twirling his knife. His eyebrows twitched as he read, and after several minutes of silence, Andre harrumphed, folded the paper, and slid it into the breast pocket of his open gray jacket. "I don't always have the luxury of time to leave the palace to visit him when he's in town, so I appreciate you bringing this."

"Of course." Ben stood back, legs hip-width apart, arms clasped behind his back, while Jade and Andre sat at the table and caught up with small pleasantries. Deep blue carpet sprawled through the library—the first concession to color that he'd seen in the palace that wasn't under Queen Violet's direct control, as her meeting room had been. Two balcony floors stretched up over their heads, and bookshelves lined the walls in an impressive display of literary knowledge.

"So, Ben." Andre closed the book on the table and leaned back, his blue eyes analyzing. "I've heard you know a bit about fighting."

Ben turned and looked over his shoulder at Andre and Jade. "That's right. We've been able to determine that hand-to-hand is my best form. But Zak has been trying to teach me how to use a staff."

Andre rubbed his chin and nodded. "And I heard you helped save Jade and Krista from a terror several weeks ago." His eyebrow lifted. "And you got injured in that adventure."

Ben flexed his stiff hands and held them up with a halfhearted shrug. "They've healed quite a bit already, thanks to Doctor Jaxton and his abilities." Light reflected off his shiny skin, and he rubbed a knuckle absently. "They're sensitive around heat, of course. Jaxton tried doing some sort of time-spell to speed the healing, but it didn't work, so we're only using potions and poultices."

"Ah," Jade said from the chair that she perched in. "I wondered why he hadn't healed them faster. That makes sense."

A gleam in Andre's eye put Ben on the defensive. "Why do you ask?"

Andre tapped a finger against the steam-pistol that Ben had laid on the table. "I see his highness gave you the pistol, Jade."

Jade rubbed her forehead and grimaced when her corset prevented her from slouching in the chair. "I don't want it, so I gave it to Ben."

"Sounds like a fair idea." Andre stood and smoothed out the creases in his burgundy shirt and tugged his jacket into place. "I can only assume you haven't been shown how to use it. I'd feel more comfortable with you escorting my niece, knowing you've gotten some practice in on that thing."

Ben gripped the back of the chair in front of him as he watched Jade's face turn pink. "Fine by me. When would be a good time for some practice?"

Andre's eyes dropped to Ben's hands. "No time like the present, if you can handle it."

Ben flexed his fingers into fists, evaluating their tenderness. The uncomfortable tugging in his palms might make things difficult, but no more so than carrying the heavy bag of food yesterday in the marketplace. "Now's fine. Lead on."

Andre led Ben and Jade through the palace and to an outdoor ring that was clearly used for combat or training. A rounded wall opposite them held a variety of weapons on racks, but it stood alone, allowing air to flow freely through the open training area. Black marble pillars held up the ceiling, and gaslight sconces flickered on each obelisk.

Ben pivoted on his boot and craned his neck as he surveyed the open-walled room. "Nice place."

"Indeed." Andre shed his formal jacket and draped it over a low bench by a rack of swords. He removed his tool belt and several low-slung pouches, then walked over to a locker and pulled out two heavy leather jackets and two sets of gloves. He tossed Ben a jacket and held up the gloves. "See if you can get these on your hands. You really don't want to risk getting re-burned."

Ben shuddered. "Burns on top of burns. No, thank you." He held his hand up against the glossy leather to compare fit before he slipped them on, wincing as the material rubbed his sensitive skin.

"Jade," Andre called. He pointed to a target on the far side, by a large rack of bows and arrows. "Could you please move that to the center of the room?"

Ben waited until Jade was halfway across the training arena before he decided to ask the question that had been on his mind ever since he learned that Andre and Zak had been friends for years. "Can I ask you something?"

Andre nodded as he set a handful of metal spheres on a nearby table. "What's on your mind?"

Ben glanced over to make sure Jade wasn't within earshot. "Do you have any idea why Zak is treating Jade the way he is? What scared him off from pursuing her?"

Andre dropped one of the bullets and he picked it up, stuffing it into the pistol with a muttered curse. His lips compressed into a thin line as he watched Jade finish dragging the target to its location. He looked at Ben, his eyes filled with a promise of deadly intent that sent shivers down Ben's spine. "It wasn't me, if that's what you're wondering. But if I had heard of his attraction first, I would've been the one to warn him away." He picked up the pistol, loosened a rotating handle, and flipped a switch, then added, his tone mild yet dark, "Her place is not with either of you."

Ben nodded silently as Jade approached, her smile easy and eyes bright.

"Ready when you are!" She passed them to stand by the table, out of the way of where they'd be shooting.

Ben tried to push the conversation to the back of his mind while Andre showed the specific order of how to load, unload, refill, clean, and shoot the steam-pistol. But something in Andre's words niggled at Ben: *her place.*

Where was Ben's place? And how would he get back?

Did he *want* to go back if he couldn't remember everything? Would it be better to start a new life here, with the friends he was making, and help the captain protect the lands?

Could he really consider starting a new life here, when he didn't know who was waiting for him to come home?

"Your turn to try." Andre handed the steam-pistol to Ben, and he realized to his chagrin that he'd zoned out for the last half of Andre's instructions.

Ben held the weapon in his hands, familiarizing himself with its weight. He lifted it and looked down the sight at the target, visualizing it and pushing away all distractions until it was just him and the target. He squeezed the trigger. Steam puffed and swirled around his arms, but didn't touch him.

Andre took a few steps forward as he stared. "Did…did you hit the center on the first shot?"

Jade whooped. "Looks like it to me!"

"I'm surprised," Andre admitted. "It took me quite a while to even hit the edge of the target. Do it again to prove it wasn't luck."

Ben reloaded the pistol with ease, his hands moving almost of their own accord, as if the action was remembered by his muscles, not his mind. He aimed and shot again. A second near-bull's-eye.

Andre whistled lowly and shook his head, eyebrows raised. "You're a natural. I've never seen anyone pull that off. Everyone who's ever tried that contraption took a long time to even get close to the mark. You've hit it twice. And," he lifted a bullet and handed it to Ben, "you remembered how to reload without any reminders. You must be an incredibly fast learner."

Ben hefted the metal ball in his hand and looked between it and the gun. How did he know how to use this? Why was he so good at it?

"Shoot it again, please," Jade begged, her eyes sparkling. "That was amazing."

Ben obliged for several more shots before the water tank needed to be refilled. He set it down and unscrewed the glass holder.

"I can do it for you." Jade offered with a grin. She touched the steam-pistol with a cautious finger. "Funny, how it's not nearly so ugly a thing when it's in your hands, versus his."

Andre's lips twisted as he looked aside. "He's improving, Jade. Give Weston time."

She huffed an incredulous laugh and shook her head with an eye roll. "When whales fly." She grabbed the water tank and stalked over to a large cylinder of water.

Ben lifted the gun and ran his fingers over it, wondering at his mind's insistence that there should be a bump here, a smooth spot there. *Why does this seem so familiar?*

Andre pulled out the note from Zak and jotted something down on the paper, then slipped it back into the original envelope. He strolled to a nearby gaslight sconce and flicked open the glass. He drew a slender wax stick from his pocket and stuck it into the flame, rotated it slowly for several moments, and moved it over the envelope, allowing the crimson sealant to drip over Zak's seal. A quick press of Andre's ring into the soft wax finished his business, and he blew out his burgundy stick.

He handed the letter to Ben. "Please return this to Zak."

"Roger that."

Andre blinked, and his brow knit in confusion.

Ben shifted. "I mean, of course."

"Thank you." Andre's eyes roamed over Ben and rested on the chain around his neck. He gestured. "May I?"

Ben hesitated, remembering Lance's panic over the metal necklace. *Jade's uncle is trustworthy, right?* He slipped it off and handed it to Andre. Jade leaned over the table to look at the plates as well. This time, Ben's gaze was glued to the innocuous-looking ring that lay next to the plates.

Andre rubbed the metal and peered at the numbers and name imprinted on them. "I've never seen anything like this." He handed them to Jade to scrutinize. "And you still don't remember where you're from?"

"No." Ben accepted the chain back from her and slipped it over his neck, taking care to tuck the two bits of metal under his shirt.

Andre seemed to sense Ben's discomfort and turned away, scooping the bullets into a small pouch. "I'll locate the mold to make more spheres, as you won't be finding anything like this in the market for quite a while." He handed the bag to Ben, then looked to Jade. "Do you know when your father will meet with the advisor?"

Jade shrugged and brushed a hand down her skirt. "I think this afternoon? Not too sure, but I'm hoping that we'll have a clue or something to follow. Life is never dull when we're hunting after Dad's goals."

Andre snorted at Jade's words and shook his head with an odd expression. "Life is never dull with Slate as your father, no." He pulled a pocket watch from his pants pocket and glanced at it. "I'm truly sorry to say this, but I need to get going." His blue eyes flicked up at Jade, then away as he clicked his watch together. "Prince Weston is expecting me in five minutes to review politics between Doldra and Perennia."

Jade wrinkled her nose and hugged Andre. "I'm glad we got to see you."

"Me too." Andre brushed a kiss against the crown of her head and held a hand out for Ben to shake. "Good to meet you, Ben. I enjoyed watching you practice. And I'll get the rest of the supplies sent to you as soon as possible." Andre dropped his gaze down to his niece's head. "Thank you for escorting her," he added softly.

Ben turned to follow Jade out the doorway when Andre called out. Ben turned to see Andre slip his formal jacket back on, his eyes burning with some unfathomable emotion.

"Zak mentioned in his note that you're training for dragon hunting. Good luck. And train hard—dragons aren't the only danger a skyfarer has to worry about."

CHAPTER TWENTY-SIX

SLATE

"My contact has learned of an artifact that may be the one we're hoping for," Samuel Thistle signed from where he sat at the gleaming table in the Aerugan meeting room. Slate quirked an eyebrow as Samuel continued, *"He has been searching in Vodan for us, and he's been in contact with a bandit group that claims to have found a cache of relics that belonged to the Sage of Piovant."*

Victor shifted in his chair next to Slate and shot him a side glance before lifting his fingers from the tabletop to gain Samuel's attention. Samuel nodded and Victor asked, "How do we know that this group is to be trusted?"

Samuel inclined his head and pressed his thick, dark lips together. *"We don't. Ezekial says this is a mercenary group that has some unsavory rumors about it."* He caught Slate's skeptical expression and added, *"More unsavory than one would expect with a mercenary group. Ezekial can't meet them alone, as he doesn't have the manpower or the lut required to pay for the relics."* Samuel rested his hands on the table for a moment, letting that sink in before he lifted them again. *"His lordship and my queen have agreed that this is a mission worthy of your crew."* His dark eyes sought out Slate. *"It will be dangerous, as I'm sure you've already ascertained. Additionally, we want to be cautious to not cause an incident between Aerugo and Vodan."*

Slate drummed his fingers against his arm as he nodded. "We're in, of course." He looked to Victor. "Maybe we'll have Garnet find us a load to take to Vodan for cover?"

Victor scratched at his cheek and dipped his head. "Good idea. King Varium would never allow an Aerugan mission like this in his territory without his involvement. I'll discuss details with Garnet this afternoon."

A rap against the table brought their attention back to Samuel. *"Aerugo will provide the lut necessary to pay for the artifact, of course. Ezekial said he'd have a meeting set up by the time we have our men out there, so Lord Everett wants you there as soon as possible."*

Slate nodded and mentally tallied the distance they'd be traveling. "We'll need a day to get everything in order. So, if we leave the day after tomorrow, we can be in Vodan in eleven days. Sooner, if the winds are in our favor."

"Very good." Samuel paused, then added, *"We will send some royal guards as well, for extra protection."*

"Thank you. That is most generous. They will need to be plain-clothed, of course, no Aerugan uniforms." Slate stroked his goatee. "Will they be under my command or Lord Everett's?"

A hint of a smile at the edge of Samuel's eyes told Slate what he already suspected. *"They will be under Lord Everett's directions to be of help to you—but, no, they are not yours to command."* Samuel's dark eyes focused on Slate. *"They are loyal to only his majesty."*

Victor stirred. "Sounds like I have some arrangements to make. With your permission, I'll get started."

"Of course, thank you, Victor." Slate lifted a hand from the armrest of his chair. "I'll join you soon."

Victor left, and Samuel rose, Slate following their lead. Samuel came around the corner of the table and loomed over Slate, his back to the guards in the room.

He held his hands close to his body, his black suit jacket hiding his signs from all but Slate. *Be cautious of Lord Everett. He doesn't fully trust you.*

A trickle of fear slid through Slate's veins, but he kept it from his voice and face as he bowed. "Thank you for the lead and the advice. We will be off as soon as possible."

Slate left the meeting room and decided to head straight back to the *Sapphire* to get as much prepared as possible while he still had daylight. He'd let Briar know that if he needed to get any extra food supplies before the trip, he had until morning to gather everything. And Slate would let the girls know that the engine room had to be put back together before their scheduled departure.

"Captain Stohner."

Slate suppressed the groan that rumbled in his chest. He cleared his face of annoyance, turned, and bowed crisply. "Lord Everett."

Black knee-high boots tapped against marble as Everett drew closer, the gold buttons of his ebony suit jacket flashing in the light. He stopped just within Slate's personal space and clasped his white-gloved hands behind his back as he studied Slate with cold eyes. "Your daughter was here earlier."

"I'm aware. She was meeting with Queen Violet and then her uncle Andre, if I recall."

Everett nodded once and circled Slate in a manner reminiscent of a dactyl sensing fresh meat. Slate held himself straight and refused to allow himself to be intimidated by the other man's close presence and gag-inducing cologne.

"I was struck by how much she doesn't resemble you," Everett finally said from behind Slate. He moved into view. "She looks quite like her late aunt Sapphire. Much more than she resembles you or your wife."

Slate forced himself to keep breathing regularly. "Yes…funny thing, genetics." He shrugged as if ice wasn't churning in his veins. "Our mother complained that Garnet and I looked more like her brother than like herself. It's common enough to not always resemble one's parents."

Everett thinned his eyes at Slate before turning on his heel. "If you say so." He looked over his shoulder. "It would be curious, if one could compare your daughter to what the late princess would've looked like now."

Everett walked away, and Slate watched him go, his mind whirling. Maybe he should talk to Jade soon, after all.

Slate scarcely noticed the bustle of the *Sapphire* as he boarded it, his mind still whirring with Everett's veiled threat. It had to be a threat. Everett didn't have a single kind bone in his body, and he didn't go out of his way to speak to people for no reason.

Should he talk to Jade now? Yes. Right away. She should know that Everett had his attention on her, and that might prove unpleasant.

Laughter rang out from the engine room before he reached the bottom of the metal-tread stairs.

Krista's voice rose above Jade's maniacal cackle. "Don't you dare!"

"He'd love to know!"

Slate warily poked his head in the doorway to see Krista brandish a wrench at Jade.

Jade held her own ratchet out against Krista, humor dancing in her eyes.

She looks just like her mother.

"There's nothing you can say that will make me—oh!" Jade caught sight of him and whipped the ratchet behind her back in a belated attempt to look innocent. She smiled, her eyes wide with suppressed mirth. "Hello, Father dearest. However can I help you this fine day?"

He couldn't do it. He couldn't squash her joy, her freedom. What value would it be to tell her something that would only increase her stress, and about things that she couldn't do anything about? Forewarning meant little when it came to Everett. Better that she could laugh freely, right now, than be burdened with knowledge she didn't need. And she didn't need to know that her time on the *Sapphire* was running out and that she'd soon be thrust into a world of politics just because she was of royal blood.

"We have a mission to Vodan," he said instead. "It would be quite helpful if you ladies could get the engine back together for us to leave in time."

Krista inched closer to Jade and gently rapped the wrench against Jade's shoulder. "Assuming this one actually helps instead of distracting me all day, we can get this beauty working in just a few hours."

Jade slipped to the side from under Krista's wrench and raised her ratchet at Krista. "You started it."

Slate's heart hurt too much to roll his eyes at their antics, but he managed a small smile before he stepped out of the hot room. He closed his eyes and leaned his head back against the wall.

Coward.

Slate opened his eyes as he felt movement pass him. Ben lifted two apples in greeting and shot him a quick grin as he entered the engine room.

"Ladies! I have brought a gift of sustenance from the kitchen above!"

The girls chorused "thank you" with laughter.

Slate sighed. He was going to need to talk to Ben about Jade soon, too. He rubbed at the scar above his eye. If he could just wrap her in a safety blanket and put her away, maybe she'd be safe from any and all interested men.

He knocked on the door of the ladies' bunk room. The door creaked open, and Garnet raised her eyebrow and wordlessly gestured for him to come in. She shut the door behind him and leaned against it. Slate stared at Jade's perfectly made bed with its simple pillowcase and blankets. She deserved so much more.

"Everett suspects, and I'm positive that Ben is interested in her," Slate said without preamble. He pinched the bridge of his nose while looking at his twin. "I don't know what to do."

Garnet's pale face had turned a sickly greenish-white hue at his first announcement about Everett. "You've had plenty of perfect opportunities to tell her, and you didn't." Disapproval dripped from Garnet's voice, and Slate looked away from her hard eyes.

"I can't tell her. Not yet."

Garnet flung her hands in the air and turned away with a little growl of frustration. She whirled back, her finger inches from his chest as she jabbed. "Why not? You're a masochist for pain. All you're doing is prolonging the torture. She needs to know!"

Slate shook his head, a bitter taste filling his mouth. "You know why I can't."

"And you know why you need to. She deserves to know." Garnet sighed and laid a gentle hand on his arm. "She's old enough. It's time for her to hear the truth."

"And have her look at me like that? No. I want her to be happy. This won't make her happy. She just needs to be protected." Slate rubbed his thumb in the crease of his pant leg. "I don't know what she'd do," he admitted. "But I know she won't be happy with us. With me."

Garnet rolled her eyes. "Well, yes, you're right. We've kept this from her for her whole life. She won't be thrilled. But maybe it won't be as bad as you think. If nothing else, she'll understand why you keep dragging her to whatever noble event you can get an invitation to."

"She needs the training."

"If she even takes on that role," Garnet exclaimed. She stalked to her bed, sat, and popped up a moment later to pace the tiny room. "You've decided her future for her without her permission. She's comfortable here. She's happy. Do you really think she'd be happy with what you have planned?"

"I'm not planning anything." Slate's shoulders sagged under the weight of his memories. "I'm only giving her what she deserves." He puffed out a breath. "And what our people need."

"Deserves, maybe. Wants, I doubt it." Garnet's eyes softened. "Our people have survived without their rightful ruler this long. They'll continue to survive without her, if that's what she decides. Either way, it's past time for her to know, and we need to be the ones to do so. We can't risk someone like Everett suspecting and her figuring it out the hard way. Think how much worse she'll take it then."

Doubt, guilt, and frustration roiled in Slate's stomach. He swallowed back bile. "I'll tell her soon."

"When?"

"Soon enough," he amended. "I just need to find the right time."

"Don't let it pass you by." Garnet shot him a look. "Again."

CHAPTER TWENTY-SEVEN

JADE

Jade laid her folded undergarments into the cedar chest at the foot of her bed, then returned to the small pile of clean, lemon-scented garments waiting to be put away. She tugged the sleeve of her blouse, pulling it out of the pile. She shook it out before folding along the lines, trying to minimize wrinkles. Aunt Garnet would likely get on her case later about not taking the time to press her clothing in the name of propriety, but what did a mechanic need such frivolities for? Jade smirked as she set the folded garment aside and pulled her blue blouse from the jumbled clothing.

Besides, who has time to care so much about appearance and clothing and makeup? Not this mechanic!

Someone knocked on the door, and Jade glanced at the shirt in her hands before setting it aside with a shrug. All her unmentionables were put away. Whoever was there shouldn't be put out by seeing her laundry or her barely brushed hair.

Jade blinked in surprise to see Ben on the other side of the door. *I take it all back.* He looked up from the floor and flashed her a small smile. She resisted the urge to smooth a hand over her static-y hair as she let the door swing wide open.

"Hey, Jade." Ben rubbed the back of his neck as his gaze traveled across the small room and came to rest on her pile of clothing. "If this is a bad time to talk, I can come back later. I—"

"No, it's fine." Jade stepped back and hesitated a heartbeat before sitting on the bed. She grabbed a pair of coarse pants to fold and looked up to see Ben leaning against her desk. Jade tried for a smile, ignoring the flutter of nerves coursing through her. What could Ben want to talk to her about? Yesterday, at the palace? The market? Jade tamped down on her growing panic.

"So, what's on your mind?" she asked as she watched Ben fidget.

Ben glanced at the open door and closed his eyes with a sigh. "I came to apologize."

"Apologize?" She stopped folding her white blouse and wrinkled her brow. "For what?"

"I—" Ben clasped his hands in front of him as he looked up, his blue eyes shining with uncertain sincerity. "I have this feeling that I somehow led you on. That I was interested in pursuing you, romantically, and I...I can't."

The light-hearted morning dimmed around Jade as Ben's gaze dropped to the wood boards below his boots before he met her eyes again. "I can't remember where I'm from. I don't know who Sara is to me." His brows creased. "But every time you and I are together, you remind me of her, somehow. I don't understand it." He lifted his shoulders and dropped them with a heavy sigh. "I want to be with you, be your friend, have you teach me this world that I don't remember, but I want to do so honestly." His lips twisted to the side, and he rubbed the back of his neck again. "Nothing romantic involved."

Jade nodded, her gaze falling to the metal-wire laundry basket next to her. Her fingers traced over the cool knobs where the metal wires had been melted together to create the snag-free basket.

First, Zak didn't want me, now Ben. At least Ben told me himself. And why.

Jade took a deep breath before she looked up at him. He'd folded his arms and started picking at the brown buttons on his cuff. His expression blended sorrow and frustration so perfectly that the ache in her heart eased.

"I understand," Jade stated quietly. She knelt to put away the rest of her clean laundry, keeping herself focused on the task, so she wouldn't have to make eye contact until she was sure the ache was buried. "It's not your fault that you can't recall. But," she turned to raise an eyebrow at him, "if you can't pursue anyone, what was that at the bar with the girl?"

A blush darkened Ben's face as he winced. He shuffled his feet and shoved his hands in his pockets, hunching over slightly. "So you did see that."

"Hard to miss it."

"Zak and Briar dared me."

Amusement wormed its way through Jade, and she dropped the pretense of organizing her chest. She closed it and sat on the lid. "They dared you to do what, exactly?"

Ben lifted a hand to cover part of his face. "Briar was talking about pickup lines, and I may have said that I could do better than him, and one thing led to another."

Jade lifted an eyebrow and cocked her head.

Ben groaned into his palm. "Are you going to make me spell it out?"

She grinned. "You came to me," she pointed out. "And you told me that you couldn't pursue anyone because you can't remember anything. So yes, spill."

"Fine," Ben mumbled. "Zak dared me to use a pickup line on the next girl to come into the bar, and it was her." He dropped his face fully into both hands. "I did it. She probably thinks I'm an utter fool, and I wish I could apologize to her for it." Ben pulled his face back and rapped his knuckles against the wood desk in frustration. "But we're leaving tomorrow, so…" He trailed off with a sigh.

Sympathy stirred in Jade at his obvious distress. Poor Ben didn't seem to have any luck going for him. She swallowed the small giggle that she felt as he continued to make little sounds of anguish.

"First, we will be back in Aerugo after this mission." Jade stood and stretched. She leaned against Krista's bunk and shook her head at Ben. "Second, we'll likely go to the same place tonight, and maybe she'll be there and you won't make an utter fool of yourself. Third," Jade pushed away from the wood frame and reached out to instinctively hug Ben. He stiffened at her first touch, then relaxed into the hug as she continued, "we'll be fine. Friends?"

Ben squeezed her, and leaned back, his hands resting on her upper arms as he searched her eyes. "Friends sounds great." He hesitated. "I feel awkward even bringing this up, but I have to know. Did I just hurt you with all this?" His shoulders tensed. "If I did, I am sorry."

Jade dropped her gaze and drummed her fingers against his back as she bit her lip. "Honestly? I don't even know yet." She squeezed her eyes shut and sucked air into her lungs. "I've been too confused lately." She opened her eyes as she blew out a breath and stared at the buttons on his shirt. "I haven't gotten over Zak, entirely."

"Good. He's not over you."

Jade's eyes widened and she stared at Ben, her mouth open. "What? How do you—"

A rap on the doorframe broke her question. Zak walked into view, already speaking, "Have you seen—" He stopped and rocked a half step back.

Jade gaped at Zak as he stared at her. The warmth of Ben's shirt under her hands mocked the conversation she'd just been having. She pushed away from him. Ben stumbled against the desk while she propelled back into the bunk bed. "It's not what it looks like!"

Zak said nothing, his eyes shuttered as he looked to her, then to Ben. He turned on his heel and left.

Tears pricked at Jade's eyes. This was not supposed to happen!

"I'll go talk to him," Ben offered softly. He paused in the doorway and spoke over his shoulder, not looking back at her. "Let him know it wasn't what he thinks it is."

Jade didn't reply. Gloom seeped in her heart as she sank onto the bed. She was literally in Ben's arms!

And Ben didn't even know who he was or what he was doing in life. But he was going to talk to that girl again.

And Jade was all alone.

Misery wanted company.

Jade checked the engine room, the storage hangar, and the showers, but couldn't find Krista. Jade's nerves jittered as she peeked over the edge of the stairs. She absolutely, positively, could not run into Zak right now. She had to talk to Krista first and get all the scrambled thoughts in her head organized.

Odds were good that this late in the afternoon, Krista had relocated to the galley with Briar. Ben had been helping Briar with breakfast and lunch, but evening remained Krista's specific time to help her boyfriend.

Please, don't let Zak be there, too. Jade mentally begged as she followed her nose to the galley. The scent of roasted meat usually made her stomach rumble with hunger, but this afternoon, it just made her gut clench. Her emotions were too unstable right now for her to consider food.

Jade rushed past Zak's closed bunk room door, and she turned her face away from the mess hall as she passed it. There was no guarantee he was even in either of the rooms. But she couldn't help being cautious.

She pressed her face to the galley window set in the door, and relief trickled through her when she saw Krista chopping vegetables beside Briar. Jade slipped into the narrow kitchen, relaxing infinitesimally as the familiar humid warmth washed over her.

Krista used the back of her hand to push a strand of black hair out of her face as she took in Jade's watery eyes and trembling hands. She set the knife down and yanked off the sunset-orange apron. "Are you all right? What happened?" Krista pulled Jade into a fierce hug, and Jade closed her eyes, savoring the lavender scent of Krista's braids. Krista released her and guided Jade to a closed barrel. "Sit and talk."

Briar handed Jade a metal bowl and a large sprig of rosemary. "If you want something to do with your hands, you can strip that."

"Thanks." Jade settled onto the wood and angled herself to see Briar and Krista, her back to the door. She set the bowl on her lap and twirled the fragrant herb in her hand. Briar and Krista shared everything, so there was no point in talking to Krista without him. And he tended to have useful insights or methods to talk through problems. Jade pinched at the thin, needlelike leaves and started to pull and drop them into the bowl.

Jade floundered, trying to think of where to start. The rhythmic sound of Briar continuing to prep dinner soothed her nerves, and Jade spilled everything that had happened between her and Ben, including how Zak had found them. She clenched her hands, rosemary biting into her palms as she remembered Zak's expression of surprise, then—nothing.

I hate how he does that. Shuts his emotions down. It makes it impossible to understand him.

Krista hummed to herself as she dumped the chopped vegetables into a large pan. She leaned her hip against the counter and pointed her knife at Jade. "You know what you need to do? Just take Zak and use those lips of yours to—"

"*Communicate,*" Briar exclaimed, throwing his girlfriend an exasperated look. He looked up to the ceiling and raised two fists dramatically. "How hard is it? Really now."

Briar wiped his hands on a nearby towel, and Jade pulled her legs close to the barrel to avoid tripping him. He pulled a large pot out from under the counter, filled it with water, and carried it back. Krista tapped on his flexed arm with a low whistle, and he winked at her.

Jade dropped her eyes to her hands, and she fiddled with the bare stem. "I don't know what I'd even tell him."

Krista nudged Jade's foot with her own. "Pretend we're him. Look,

I'll even be silent and dour." Krista drew herself up and pushed her lips into a neutral line, her eyes laughing as she struggled to maintain composure. She collapsed on the counter with an exaggerated flop and sigh. "Never mind. I can't do that."

Briar rolled his eyes and grabbed an orange washcloth off a nearby rack and tossed it on the counter next to Krista's hand. "You dirty it, you clean it."

"Sir, yes, sir." Krista grabbed the cloth and started scrubbing. She turned to Jade. "Seriously, though. Talk it out. We'll listen. Maybe just having a long rant will help to ease some of the tension in that internal boiler of yours."

"I'll make it easier." Briar ran his finger along the controller of the heating stone. It glowed in response. He stood in front of Jade and looked down, brown eyes soft in sympathy. "If you could tell Zak what you're thinking right now, what would you say?"

Jade sighed. "I don't know." A whisper of movement pulled her attention away, but Briar reached over her and grabbed a spoon from the wall.

He tapped the handle against her head. "Yes, you do. Let it out."

Jade handed the bowl to Krista and buried her face in her hands. "What would I tell him? Everything I think of is stuff that I wouldn't be able to say to his face!"

"Then tell us," Briar urged. "Get it out."

"I like Zak."

Krista made a little squeak, and Briar shushed her. "That's a start," he said neutrally. A pot clanged. "Continue."

"I've liked him for at least a year." Jade shifted her hands to balance her head on her fists so she could stare at her wool skirt.

"I thought we were getting somewhere, getting closer." Her voice cracked, and she closed her eyes again. "I don't know why he dumped me like he did."

Jade flung a hand out in Krista's direction without looking up. "Was she right? Did my father warn Zak off? If so, I'm going to kill him."

Krista snorted. "Who? Your father or Zak?"

"Both." Jade's laugh sounded suspiciously like a sob to her own ears. "I know Zak. He wasn't toying with me—not on purpose, at least. He's too thoughtful, too methodical. I know I can trust him with my life."

Jade sighed and stared at the barrels lining the other side of the wall. "I miss his hugs." She huffed a small laugh. "Sorry Briar, but your hugs just aren't the same as his." He nodded with an understanding smile and she ran her fingers down the cool edges of the bowl, trying to tame her turbulent emotions. "I want…I want him to know that there's nothing going on between Ben and me." She looked down and twined her fingers together over the dish, her words barely a whisper. "I'm still available."

Irritation swallowed the hurt in her heart, and she stood abruptly, tossing the metal bowl onto the counter, angry. "I'm going to be available all my life, because no guy wants me. I don't know why. I don't know what's so wrong with me. But I'm going to be alone forever, while my friends get married and have someone to share their lives with. And I have no one!"

Briar stopped, lid in hand, mid-stir. Krista stared at Jade.

Embarrassment heated Jade's cheeks. *Well, they wanted to know what I would say to him.* She whirled to the door, intent on escaping her friends' silence. She stopped short, her own breath frozen in her lungs.

Zak stood in the doorway, his eyes wide open, mouth ajar.

The sound of boiling water echoed in the quiet.

Zak's eyes brimmed with emotion as his hand reached out toward her. Something flashed in his gaze, and his hand dropped. A muscle in his jaw twitched. "Briar," he said, his eyes not leaving hers, "Captain Stohner wants to know if you'll be ready to leave in the morning."

Jade could barely hear Briar's response over the rushing in her ears. Zak's green eyes pierced her, seeing far too much. *How much did he hear?*

Zak nodded at Briar's answer, his gaze locked on to Jade's, as if something tangible connected them. "Nothing is wrong with you. You are exactly who you should be." Pain glimmered in his eyes, and he swallowed hard. "You won't be alone forever. I can promise you that."

He opened his mouth, stopped, and turned his face away, breathing deeply. His knuckles cracked as he curled his hands into fists and set his shoulders. Zak looked back at her and dipped his head in a formal, somber nod. He pushed against the door and left.

There wasn't enough air in the room for Jade's spinning head.

She sat on the barrel and cried.

CHAPTER TWENTY-EIGHT

BEN

Ben lifted his mug in a silent toast with Briar and Zak. "So we leave for Vodan tomorrow?"

Briar knocked back his small shot. "Yessir. Back to the humidity and fish." He grinned and started ticking off his dark fingers. "We'll get fresh tuna, salmon, crab, lobster—" Briar cut himself off and shot a sideways glance at Zak. "And we'll see how many admirers Jade gets this time."

Zak closed his eyes and drank deeply. Then he set down his mug with a firmer hand than necessary.

Ben's eyes automatically sought out the redhead at Briar's words. She sat at the bar with Krista, William, Slate, and Garnet—the five of them laughing as the barkeep served them. Jade looked over and caught his eye, offering a wide smile before Krista pulled her attention away. Ben turned a speculative gaze to Zak.

Something had occurred between Zak and Jade beyond the awkward afternoon interaction that he had been involved in. Ben had found Zak easily enough and explained what happened, urging Zak to go smooth things out between him and Jade. Zak hadn't said if he would or wouldn't, but something had changed in their dynamic, as now Jade had lowered her guard around Ben even more, and she all but tip-toed around Zak, her eyes everywhere but on him.

As for the shadow-clad swordsman, he had reached a whole new level of introversion. Even now, he let Ben and Briar lead the conversation, his eyes roving over the room, and constantly lingering on Jade.

Time to draw him out.

"She had admirers in Vodan?" Ben asked.

Briar leaned back in the booth and grinned at Zak's deepening scowl. "Oh yes. Pale skin and red hair is rare out there, so she's considered a lucky charm of sorts, like a terror claw, or a blue rose. Last time we were there, she had two guys vying for her attention the whole trip. Drove her crazy, and made this guy," Briar elbowed Zak, "a jealous, brooding wreck."

"Did not." Zak didn't look up from his mug.

"Did, too, man. We can ask Krista, if you doubt me."

Zak glared into his mug without reply.

"You should talk to her." Ben sighed.

Zak's jaw clenched, and he hunched his shoulders. "It's not that easy."

"Yes, it is." Ben studied the fine lines around Zak's eyes. Maybe this wasn't something to push right now. The Guardian clearly had something on his mind, and Ben wanted to respect his friend.

Ben tapped the table. "Can you answer a different question for me?"

Zak's eyes flicked up from the polished wood. "Depends. What is it?"

Ben lifted a hand from his mug. "The captain refers to Queen Violet as 'his' queen. But, from what I've heard, Slate's from Doldra, and she's the Queen of Aerugo. How is Slate even on such friendly terms with a queen?"

Briar plucked a strip of meat off the platter in the middle of their table and nibbled on it, making a face. "Whoever made this needs a lesson in seasoning." He nodded to Zak. "He's had the most time with the captain."

"But you know the story, too," Zak said mildly. He looked up from his mug. "She's originally the Perennian princess who married Prince Richard Doldras. He died in the massacre, as well as all the other royalty who could have led the country. She became Queen of Doldra until she married Lord Everett of Aerugo." A wry grin flashed across his face at the confused expression Ben wore. "To simplify, she's the Queen of Doldra *and* Aerugo."

Ben mulled that over as he grabbed a piece of meat for himself. One bite and he agreed with Briar. Someone definitely had a heavy hand with the pepper. He sucked down some ale to wash away the burning of his tongue. "Is Queen Violet Jade's aunt?" Ben leaned back and Briar blinked when Zak whipped his head up, eyes wide. "I mean, Jade mentioned that she lost family during the slaughter, but she has her father here, and I met her mother, so—"

Zak's tense shoulders relaxed and he settled back in his chair, nodding. "You're partially right. Lady Sapphire was Slate's younger sister, and she was married to Prince Richard's younger brother, Brandon." His eyes dropped, and the distance in his gaze hinted at old memories. "Queen Violet is a close family friend for Slate and Jade." He shook his head and his eye twitched when Ben nudged the meat plate toward him. "It's a good thing for survivors to stand together."

Shadows of memory danced in Zak's haunted eyes, cluing Ben in. "You were there, weren't you? You must've been just old enough to remember it."

The skin around Zak's mouth tightened, and Briar shook his head slightly. Zak took a long drink from his mug and stared into it as if it held the answers to all the misery in the world. "Yes. And I lost my brother there." He took a deep breath. "Zane defended the keystone to the very end. A hero above heroes."

Ben ran his hand over the table, brushing away little crumbs. "I'm sorry if I hit a nerve."

Zak shook his head with a heavy sigh. He stretched his shoulders forward, straining his shirt before he sank back into the chair. "No, better to ask me than Slate or Garnet. The memories are harder for them. We were all there, as well as Jade's uncle, Andre. They lost multiple family and friends." He looked down, a deep crease in his brow as he pinched at the leather of his fingerless gloves, momentarily revealing what looked like a black ring. "I lost my brother, and some of the royal family that I counted as friends."

Briar sipped from his drink, silent.

Zak continued. "Zane," he coughed to clear his throat. "I wanted to be him. He embodied all that our clan stands for as a Monomi, and he still made time for his kid brother." Sorrow aged Zak's eyes. "But no one, no matter how well-trained, could have been prepared for that mob of Reformers. Or their new pyrotechnics."

"That's why you don't do weapons that make loud sounds," Ben murmured.

Zak's face paled, and he nodded stiffly. "Neither Andre nor I do well with explosions. We were both there when one of our friends was—" He swallowed hard and dashed a hand across his face. "Anyway, I'm better than I used to be, but it's a weakness."

Ben glanced down in his mug to give Zak a moment. "And you haven't found who did it?"

"No." Zak gripped his mug with both hands. "We know he's an Elph, but that's about it."

An image of a slender, pointy-eared humanoid crossed Ben's mind. He quirked his head. "An elf?"

Briar groaned. "Seriously, man, you have the worst memory of anyone I've ever known." He rolled up his sleeves before leaning his elbows on the table. "An Elph. Like, the immortal guys that live in northern Terrene–started the blood-bond, tried to wipe out all us southern nations, the guys we want to avoid at all costs?" Ben shrugged and Briar sighed, rubbing his face with a hand. "You know what, it'll come back to you soon, I'm sure. Few people could forget what's on the other side of the barrier."

Ben nodded slowly. Unless they didn't know to begin with. He sipped his drink, watching Jade and Krista over the rim as they talked with Garnet and their fathers. Slate said something that caused Garnet to choke for air before she pushed him on his stool, both of them laughing. "Did the royal family protect the keystone better or worse than Everett?"

Zak frowned. "About the same in word. But in deed, the Doldras family worked much harder to keep it secure. They took the testimony of the Monomi very seriously."

"So it'd be better if there were an actual Doldras on the throne?"

"If Aerugo's power over Doldra was severed, and any other Doldran of royal blood survived, yes." Zak slid his mug across the table from hand to hand. "If anyone else lived, they would be the rightful ruler, and Queen Violet could abdicate the throne, assuming

Lord Everett would allow it."

Captain Slate leaned toward Jade, the two of them deep in discussion. What little Ben had seen of the Aerugan royalty didn't lend any hope to Zak's words. Prince Weston didn't seem too bad when Ben had met him, but he didn't strike Ben as the type to stand back and just give up what power he had. And he had quite the reputation—not one that suggested good things. Queen Violet, maybe, but her husband, Lord Everett? Definitely not.

"And everyone was killed?"

Zak dipped his head, his hair falling forward, hiding his face in shadows. "It's assumed, yes." He spun the plate and selected a small sliver of pale meat. "We never found the bodies of Prince Brandon or his daughter, Princess Adeline."

Ben's eyebrows rose. "So there's hope. Maybe they survived by some miracle, and just haven't stepped forward."

"After nineteen years?" Zak laughed, a hollow sound in the midst of a noisy, bustling tavern. "Unlikely." He shook his head, keeping his head low. "Right now, Lord Everett and his leads are the best bet we have for strengthening the Doldran keystone and thus the rest of the barrier." His eyes flicked over to where Slate and the others sat. "Someday, we'll be out from under Everett's thumb."

Briar lifted an eyebrow at Zak. "It's rare that you talk politics."

Zak shrugged. "It's been an odd day."

Ben scanned the room and tried to ignore how his heart sank. What if Raine didn't come by tonight? It niggled on his conscience, her expression of annoyance from their brief conversation. Even if it was short, he had to apologize to her.

He watched Jade as she interacted with a brunette barmaid, who was refilling her drink. It wasn't Jade's appearance that reminded him of Sara, he finally determined. It was her mannerisms, like the way her eyes lit up when she laughed. It filled him with warmth, made him feel at home.

But is Sara my home? Ben clenched his hands into fists as he dropped his gaze to the table. If only he could just turn on the faucet of memories and let them flow. It was past time to know everything.

Doctor Jaxton's electrical shock therapy hadn't worked, nor had Geist's attempts to "knock it out of him."

Jade coughed, and he glanced up at her. She raised an eyebrow and nodded toward the door with a faint grin. He followed her gaze and felt relief trickle down his spine. *Speaking of.*

Raine scanned the crowded pub and sat at table near the captain and girls, her back to the bar. A barmaid came by, and Raine smiled and chatted amiably before the girl bounced away. Ben took a deep breath and scooted his chair back.

Zak wordlessly watched him, while Briar cocked his head and asked, "Where are you going?"

"I have an apology to make," Ben replied, his eyes on Raine. She hadn't seen him yet, and that might be a good thing. He wasn't sure if it'd make it easier or harder if she had a moment of forewarning.

Quit stalling.

He hurried to stand behind the chair next to her. "Excuse me, miss?"

She looked up with a warm smile that faded away once she recognized him. "You."

Ben couldn't let her flat voice deter him. He gestured to the chair. "May I please take just a few moments of your time?"

Her shoulders rose and fell with a deep sigh, and she lifted a hand while looking away. "If it will make you disappear faster."

Ben dropped onto the hard wood seat and examined the edges of her slender jaw, the tense angle of her toned shoulders, and her white-knuckled grip on the handle of her drink. He sighed and dropped his head down. "I'm sorry that my presence aggravates you."

Raine rolled her head to look at him, her eyes dull with irritation. "I'm not on edge. I'm just allergic to arrogant idiots."

Ben heard Captain Slate's snort behind him and Jade's muffled groan. Were they all eavesdropping on him? This was not going anywhere close to how he'd dared to hope. "Well, I'm not what I'd call arrogant, but I *am* an idiot."

She looked at him out of her peripheral. "If you're trying to impress me, that's not the best way to go about it."

Ben traced a finger along the grain of the table as he shook his head. "I'm not. I want to apologize for how I annoyed you the other day. I was sent on a dare by my"—*what's that word again?*—"Void Born of a friend, and I managed to completely make a fool of myself and make you uncomfortable. I'm sorry."

Raine's posture had started to relax as his apology unwound, but she stiffened at his use of "Void Born." Ben panicked internally at the coldness in her eyes. *I used that wrong, didn't I? I should've asked Zak or Jade first. I just made this so much worse.*

Before Ben could apologize for his newest blunder, he felt someone stand beside him. He twisted in the chair and looked back to see the same older man he'd seen Raine with last time.

Wrinkles lined the gentleman's eyes as he rested a firm hand on Ben's shoulder. "Another suitor, Raine?"

Raine harrumphed and looked away, her voice icy. "No."

The older man chuckled lightly, and his grip on Ben tightened. "You heard her. Time to leave my granddaughter alone."

Heat rushed to Ben's face as he stood, the chair screeching with his movement. "Of course, sir." Ben looked back at Raine. "I truly am sorry if I caused offense." He bowed.

This time Ben was sure that Captain Slate was listening in. He peeked over his shoulder, eyes speculative, and Slate stole his attention.

Slate whirled on the stool and took a half step forward, reaching a trembling hand toward Raine's grandfather. "Finn?"

Raine twisted in her seat, hand dropping to her sword hilt while her grandfather merely turned. The gentleman peered at Slate for a long moment before taking a step back. "Slate? My boy, is that really you?"

Ben leaned back to avoid being hit in the jaw by Slate's sudden back-pounding hug with Finn. He glanced at Raine and felt a bit better at seeing her equally confused expression. Her eyes met Ben's, and she offered tiny shrug while somehow keeping her face impassive and eyes cold.

Ben lingered, listening in, just as everyone else in the group was.

"Am I glad to see you after all these years," Slate exclaimed. "Sam said you arrived safely, but aside from your letter, I hadn't heard anything. I've missed you."

Finn chuckled and crossed his arms. "Are you still in contact with Samantha, then? I—" He broke off and raised a pointed eyebrow at Ben. "You're still here?"

"He's one of my men." Slate spoke before Ben could. "New to my crew." He gestured to his right. "And this is William, my shipwright."

Finn nodded and shook hands with William. Finn examined Ben

from head to boot tips. "Good to meet you both." His gaze switched to Garnet and he stepped forward with his arms extended, a warm smile crinkling his eyes. "Garnet, my dear, it's wonderful to see you again."

Garnet slid off her stool and hugged Finn before brushing at invisible dust on her green jacket. "Likewise, Finn." A welcoming smile brightened her face as her eyes sparkled with fondness. "It's been far too long." She gestured to Raine. "Did I overhear you say 'granddaughter'?"

Raine pushed away from the table to stand by Finn's side. She stood comfortably, her posture relaxed, but her shoulders set, as if ready to flee.

"Indeed." Finn wrapped an arm around Raine's shoulders and turned to talk to her. "Technically, you met them, but that was back when you were a baby."

Raine smiled slightly before raising her hand to Slate. "Pleased to meet you officially."

Slate smiled and gripped her forearm in a solid shake, then stepped back to let her greet Garnet. "Likewise." He gestured to where Jade and Krista sat at the bar, watching. "My daughter, Jade, and Krista, her best friend." He smiled at Finn. "You know Jade's mother, Samantha. And you've already met Ben."

Raine and Finn greeted the girls appropriately, and Finn gestured to the table that Raine had claimed previously. "Will you two join us? I'd love to catch up on your news."

Slate and Garnet seated themselves, and Ben drifted back to his own table where Zak and Briar were watching keenly.

"So," Briar didn't wait for Ben to get settled on the bench, "who's the old guy?"

"Raine's grandfather, apparently." Ben watched as Finn and Slate chattered away like old friends. "Finn."

Zak's eyes gleamed. "Finn?"

Ben looked between Zak and the trio. "You know him?"

"I think so." Zak pursed his lips as a shadow darkened his eyes. "I'll ask the captain about it later."

Ben's misery over the failed apology made him ask without second thought. "Where from?"

Zak's hair fell across his eyes as he tilted his chin down. "From Doldra."

CHAPTER TWENTY-NINE
SLATE

Slate rubbed the condensation off his mug as he listened to Finn talk to Garnet and William. Slate couldn't say that he had been worried about Finn—not when he'd received the letter saying that Finn and baby Raine had arrived safely in Piovant so many years ago. But nineteen years of silence had taken its toll, as had become apparent to Slate as he tried to shake off the light-headed relief that had plagued him since he first hugged Finn.

"Raine, how about you join the girls?" Finn suggested to his granddaughter. Raine raised a dark eyebrow, and Finn smiled gently. "You won't be as interested in our conversation, I'm sure. And it would do you good to make friends your own age." His eyes sparkled with the amused glimmer that Slate remembered from his childhood. "I'm sure they won't make the same mistakes as your new beau."

William snorted into his drink, and Garnet coughed to cover her own laugh. Raine wrinkled her nose and stood, pulling her beverage with her. She nodded politely to them, then shook her head at Finn with narrowed eyes before joining Jade and Krista at the bar with a shy smile.

The warmth of the room threatened to overwhelm Slate, and he rolled his beige sleeves up to his elbows. The bar chair creaked as he leaned back to soak in Finn's appearance. The years had worn on his friend: lines wrinkled around his eyes, tanned leathery skin, and hair almost completely gray with white streaks. "So, Finn, how have you been?"

A soft smile curled Finn's lips as he shrugged. "Well enough." He tipped his head at Raine. "She's good company for keeping me on my toes and young at heart." Finn quietly thanked the barmaid that delivered his steaming tray of food, and he continued after a brief moment of silence over his plate. "We've traveled all over southern Terrene, getting by with my healing skills. We settled in Sordes for a few years while Raine was young, but the last decade has been constant moving." He rested his fork on his plate. "We'd been in Loore's Landing most recently, and moved as soon as the locals started getting riled up about Void Born after the keystone attack."

Slate frowned. "Last I heard, they haven't caught who did it, either." Dark memories led to other dark memories. He swallowed. "Any clues as to the murders?"

Finn finished chewing the bite in his mouth and shook his head, shadows from the orb lights dancing in his eyes. "Not much." His gaze flicked to Raine. "But we're both alive and safe, and that's what matters."

William paused, his fork partway to his mouth, his head turned to where Jade and Krista sat. "Constantly moving? So she really doesn't have any friends her own age?"

"I'm afraid not." Finn wiped his fingers on a cloth napkin. "Friends were a luxury that was hard to afford when on the road so frequently."

Garnet rested her elbows on the table while Slate worked to swallow past the lump in his throat. "Are you living in Lucrum now, or just passing through?"

"We actually just arrived last week." Finn drank deeply from his mug and pointed to the west wall. "We're still deciding if we're staying or moving on."

"I'm glad you came out when you did," Slate said. "How is Raine doing? She's grown so much."

Finn raised an eyebrow and looked over Slate's shoulder to where the girls sat at the polished wood bar. "Same to your daughter. I'm guessing she's just a year or two behind Raine, as I don't recall you having a girl when we saw each other last?"

Slate plastered a smile on his face. "I learned about her soon after you left."

"Mmhmm." Finn paused, twitched his eyebrow, then continued. "Raine is an accomplished swordswoman now. She's excellent at it, and she trains wherever, whenever."

"She didn't follow your lead in becoming an apothecary?" Garnet asked, surprised.

Finn shook his head, and his shoulders shook with a huff of laughter. "She and I both agreed that herbs and such are not her strong suit. She's good enough in a pinch, but she prefers the physical. Swordplay is what greases her brain-gears—not figuring out which herb combats which ailment."

"Fair enough." Garnet smiled and reached across the table to touch Finn's elbow. "It's really good to see you again."

"Likewise." Finn's chair creaked as he shifted and looked between Slate and Garnet. "What have you two been up to?" His expression darkened. "I'm truly sorry for what happened at the palace and for Sapphire. I was heartbroken to hear the news." He pressed his lips together, grief shadowing his eyes. "I'm sorry I couldn't come back for her funeral, or Zane's."

Slate inhaled sharply and let it out in one deep breath. He traced his thumbnail along the grain of the table and shook his head. "Thank you, but it was better that you two stayed away and stayed safe. Since then, I've become a captain of an airship, and we," he gestured between himself and his sister, "have started working for Mother as her merchants."

A burst of laughter from the girls behind him drew their attention for a moment. Raine and Jade gestured animatedly while Krista laughed. Contentment warmed Slate's chest as he watched Jade laugh, tears of merriment sparkling at the corners of her eyes. He turned back to Finn.

"The Doldran keystone hasn't been working the way it should since the Fall, so we're keeping our eyes and ears open for anything that may possibly help it while we're out and about." Slate pursed his lips and chose not to mention their new mission. "It's been hard to find anything helpful."

Finn nodded, concern glowing in his eyes. "I've heard rumors of the problems plaguing the citadel, but I don't know of anything still in existence that could work. Everything I've ever heard of is surely gone by now."

"Well, if there is anything, we'll find it," William stated with a firm voice. His brow creased. "We've looked for too long to fail now."

Slate frowned into his mug before sipping his ale. Finn's words bothered him, but he opted to ignore the feeling. He had to keep up what optimism he could. He had to fix his mistakes of the past. He had no choice.

"I...I'm also looking for the one who killed Zane," Slate added quietly. He glanced up to see a shadow cross Finn's face as he nodded. "He gave his life to keep the barrier from falling, despite being stabbed in the back. I need to fix the keystone and avenge him."

Silence fell across the bar for several long moments before William stood and held his hand out to Finn. "It was good to meet you, sir, but I need to get back to the *Sapphire* and check on the state of things before we go on our next mission."

Finn set his bread down on his plate, wiped his fingers on his napkin, and clasped William's hand. "Likewise."

William tapped Slate's shoulder. "See you in a bit, boss." He nodded to Garnet, dropped a kiss on Krista's forehead, and left.

The rest of the night passed in a blur of laughter, memories, and tears as Finn, Garnet, and Slate whiled away the hours together.

Garnet checked her pocket watch and straightened with a gasp. "I'm sorry, Finn, but we really need to get going. We're leaving port in the morning, and we've only a few minutes before we're officially *in* the morning."

Finn pulled out his own time piece and blinked at it before nodding. "Of course, my dear." He rose and bowed as Garnet stood stiffly and stretched. "I'm glad we had this time to catch up."

She leaned over and kissed Finn's cheek with a smile. "Leave a note at our mother's next time you'll be by. Maybe we can meet here again."

Slate's knees popped as he stood and shook Finn's hand. "Exactly what she said. We can't let it be another nineteen years."

A quick glance to the corner showed Zak, Ben, and Briar all bright-eyed and alert. Zak tilted his head toward Jade and Krista with an eye roll and a shrug. He shook his head with the hint of a smile and turned away to reply to Ben.

Slate yawned and smiled. The young people would likely be here a while longer. And Zak knew his limits.

Slate stepped out of the bar, and the cold night air chased away the tired fog induced by the warm pub. He paused on the wooden porch and waited for Garnet to adjust her lightweight jacket.

She tipped her head back and breathed deeply. "That was a pleasant surprise."

"Indeed." Slate shoved his hands in his pockets as they strolled down the quiet street. Pale moonlight reflected off the white buildings, illuminating their path just as well as the gas lights that lined the edges of the paved street.

Garnet returned to the topic they had been discussing hours earlier, right before they had begun eavesdropping on Ben and Raine. "We'll need to set up a team to haggle for our unplanned delivery in Vodan."

Slate shrugged. "Let's send Jade and her little group." He grinned at Garnet's exasperated sigh. "What? There's nothing wrong with using Vodan's cultural superstitions in our favor."

His twin shook her head at him with a tight smile. "Had it been me suggesting it, you'd have protested out of fear for her safety." Garnet tugged her thin jacket closer. "And I suppose you'll suggest that they also be our mingling team?

"Maybe." Slate frowned as he thought and slipped his hand over his sword hilt as they passed a swaying drunk. "I want a second group to blend into the populace and try to find Ezekial, but odds are good that Ezekial will find us. And Everett's men will stand out like new cogs in an old clock if we send them into town."

Garnet snorted and rubbed her hands over her arms as a chill breeze blew down the street. She smiled her thanks as Slate slipped off his heavier duster and dropped it over her shoulders. "Two redheads on one ship? Ezekial will likely show up on our deck within hours of our arrival. It's not like we blend in."

"Hopefully this will be a quick, easy mission, and we'll be back with what we need in just a few weeks."

Garnet cast him a doubtful frown. "When are we ever that lucky?"

Slate blew out his breath and kicked at a stone in the street. "First time for everything."

CHAPTER THIRTY

JADE

Jade tugged at her half-bodice and grimaced when it peeled away from her sweat-soaked shirt. They'd made great time across country to Vodan—just in time for a blistering heat wave that caused the typically warm engine room to positively swelter. She made a face at Krista, who snickered from her corner on the floor and fanned herself with a sheet of scrap metal.

"Hey, girls." Zak leaned against the door frame.

Jade scrambled to sit up and not look as if she was melting against the condenser coil. Though they'd spoken cordially over the last week since Zak found her talking with Ben, and he'd deflected several odd questions from Everett's guards, she struggled with embarrassment. Ben assured her—twice—that he'd explained what'd happened to Zak, and "it was all good." But Ben's read on the situation was far different than hers. It was easy to say things were good when one wasn't personally invested in the outcome.

As for her, she respected Ben's reasons for not pursuing anything— even if it meant, with the distraction of Ben gone, her heart was wide open and it still held far too much love for Zak.

A flash of amusement lit Zak's eyes as he swiped at the perspiration on his forehead with the cuff of his sleeve. Jade looked down and fiddled with a wrench on the floor next to her. Of course he still looked amazing, even in this miserable weather. A bead of sweat ran down Jade's back, and she closed her eyes in wordless frustration. *While I look like I've been living in the boiler.*

"Captain suggested that you two come with us into the city," Zak announced. "We need to find some buyers for the steam cannons that Aerugo sent."

Krista groaned. "There's sunshine out there. And more heat."

Zak smirked. "There's also a cool breeze. And Briar." His gaze shifted to the side of the hall, and he raised a dark brow.

Jade understood the look. *And none of Everett's creepy guards.* Getting away from the unwanted Aerugan men would make the morning heat well worth it. It seemed that no matter where Jade went onboard the *Sapphire*, one of the six Aerugan guards would be nearby. Captain Trevor, specifically, was always where she was, asking random questions: Where had she traveled? What did she think of Aerguo? What did she think of Doldran politics? It was unnerving to say the least. She bit her lip and lifted a shoulder in a half shrug at Krista. The Aerugans were under orders to stay aboard until the meeting. She'd be free from their watchful eyes and ears.

Krista bobbed her head from shoulder to shoulder as she considered Zak's words. She nodded at Jade while mock-glaring at Zak. "You just had to bring him into it." A grin creeped across Krista's face, and she climbed to her feet then held a hand out to Jade. "Come on. We're going into town."

Jade laughed despite herself and allowed her friend to pull her up. "You just want more time with your boyfriend." She raised her voice so any guards lurking outside the engine room could hear.

"Mmhmm." Krista winked at Jade before sauntering past Zak, then called out over her shoulder, "I do appreciate Vodan customs!"

Jade stumbled and swore as she passed Zak. She fought the blush that threatened to rise to her already flushed cheeks. *I'm not ready for dealing with these superstitions again.*

Unfortunately, just as she had feared, within half an hour of leaving the ship, Jade had a follower. She strove to ignore him as graciously as possible as she meandered through the sea-shell paved street. Fresh, salty air soothed her irritations, and she shaded her eyes with her hand as she followed Krista and Briar. Jade twisted to look back and couldn't decide what emotion she felt at the sight of Ben and Zak, deep in conversation, effortlessly dodging the pedestrians that crowded the area.

It was good that they were getting along, right? It meant that whatever happened between them earlier had eased up?

Briar carried a leather tube that held the schematics of the Aerugan steam cannons they were hoping to sell. He tapped it against his shoulder as he walked hand in hand with Krista. Briar shot Jade a look that blended sympathy with amusement as her new love-struck beau approached her side again.

Her suitor-of-the-day kept pace alongside her and pulled a rolled mat from a deep pocket on his thigh. He leaned back with a large smile, twisting just enough to let the sun highlight the muscles on his dark chest before gesturing at the fish hooks carefully arranged on his mat. "These have brought in much food for my family. I can provide food aplenty for you and me, and our childr—"

"Thank you." Jade interrupted him for what had to be the third time already. "But I'm not interested in marriage right now."

He puffed out his chest and flexed his arms, showing off his admittedly impressive biceps. "I am a strong and capable fisherman. I will protect your honor and   "

"And she said she wasn't interested, so go away," Zak snarled from behind her.

Jade whirled around to examine Zak even as a rush of gratitude surged through her. Unlike her, he didn't mind being blunt when the times called for it. Zak met her eyes for a long moment before looking away, his jaw set. She sighed and followed Krista's bright scarf as she and Briar led through the bustling street to the next shop.

Ben started talking to Zak, and she slowed down to listen in. "Well, you scared that one away, but you aren't going to step in, take his place?"

"No."

Ben was audible over the breeze in the tall sea-trees and the voices hawking wares in the streets. "Well, why doesn't she just give him a shirt and send him off?"

"That would be accepting his proposal." Zak's terse tone caused Jade to wince.

"Well, it looks like competition is supposed to be shirtless, which works, because it's too hot to be wearing layers here anyway—so why not go for it?"

Jade twitched and ignored the shiver that traveled through her spine at the mental image Ben's words conjured. She held her breath as she walked, wondering what Zak would say. No matter what happened here, she couldn't imagine Zak taking off his shirt in public. Not with his scars.

Besides, Zak had no interest in her.

"I…can't," Zak said finally.

Sorrow and uncertainty warred in Jade's gut. Why had she even listened in? He'd made it clear before that he wasn't interested. Even if he'd been warmer to her in the last two weeks, it didn't mean anything. She kicked the toe of her boot against a dusty seashell and bit her lip. *And he hasn't said anything about when I was talking with Krista and Briar. I don't even know how much he overheard.*

"Hold up," Ben called out.

Jade stopped, and Briar and Krista moved on without her. She lost sight of them in the crowd, and she turned around with a sigh.

Ben held a limp envelope in his hand as he talked to Zak. He flashed Jade a grin as she approached them.

"Doctor Jaxton asked me to deliver this for him." Ben lifted the paper. "He said to just deliver it to the nearest post center, and that his friend would find it."

Zak used a free hand to billow his black shirt for air as he pointed to a large cream-colored building. "That's probably the closest option available for you."

Ben nodded and jogged across the road, leaving Zak with Jade in the middle of the pedestrian street. Jade chewed the inside of her cheek while examining Zak's silhouette through her eyelashes.

Balmy sunlight highlighted the strands of his beach-tousled hair, and even with his charcoal-black belt of vials, knives, and other "necessities," he somehow didn't stand out in the mixed crowd. He stood, relaxed, hands on his hips as his green gaze roved over the people. A dimple appeared in his cheek as his eyes met hers. Jade snapped her head to the side, conscious of the heat rising in her cheeks.

Bloated whales!

"Done!" The sound of rocks and broken shells crunching announced Ben's return. He raised a speculative brow at Jade and suppressed a smirk. "We should catch up with the others."

"Great idea," Jade agreed, grateful for his thoughtful opening for her to escape. Not knowing what was going on in Zak's mind made her embarrassment at being caught staring at him all the more acute. Whether Ben realized that exact detail or not was irrelevant—that he had inadvertently saved her from further mortification was.

They passed a row of pedestals, each with different sea creatures—a kraken, a mermaid, a squid, a whale. Ben slowed to look at each one. His brow furrowed, and he hitched a thumb toward it. "What are these?"

Zak crossed his arms as he looked up at the huge, gleaming whale. "These are—what?" He glanced at Jade. "The top four gods of Vodan?"

"Yes, the top four." Jade took a step back, examining each of the idols. They were devoid of offerings, so they must have been ceremonially cleansed recently. "Most Vodans worship the sea, but some are considered more important than others."

Ben stared. "They worship a whale?"

"Balnic," Jade corrected. She inclined her head at the statue. "She's a magnetic whale."

His gaze switched to her, and he blinked, looking more confused by the second. "A whale that's magnetic?"

"Don't ask." Zak shot Jade a strange grin. "Jade's well versed in all the religions of southern Terrene, and she may give you a lesson in them if you ask too many questions."

Jade glared. "Not my fault my father wanted me tutored in everything about everyone."

Krista approached from the side and tugged on Jade's arm, pulling Jade several steps away from Zak and Ben. "You guys walk slow," Krista complained. "Hurry it up. We have a possibly interested merchant, and I want to get inside."

Jade tugged on the pink scarf that draped loosely around Krista's neck and strove to calm the rapid beat of her heart. "I thought you liked the customs here."

"I do, when it comes to watching the guys try to woo you." Krista laughed, the flash of her white teeth contrasting with her dark skin. "But Briar doesn't want to be shirtless all day, and he's too jealous to have me walk around without my wrap."

Jade grinned at that. Vibrant scarves around the neck showed that a woman was engaged or already spoken for, whereas kerchiefs tied around the head were reserved for married women. In that regard, walking around Vodan while single worked in her favor—fewer layers in the heat.

"We'll be there soon." Jade shaded her eyes to scan the various shop fronts with their colorful signs and vibrant fabric awnings. "Which one are we going to next?"

"Pearl's Weaponry and Shipping." Krista pointed to a translucent blue-and-green shade covering an adobe doorway decorated with shark teeth.

As Krista spoke, a trio of men exited the shop and stood in front of it, talking amongst themselves. Jade turned back to urge the guys on and stopped at Zak's expression.

All color had drained from his bronze face, and his eyes were wide, the green barely visible. Concerned, Jade stepped closer and settled her hand on his arm, startled by the clammy feel of his skin. A shudder ran through him. Dilated eyes focused on her, and he shook his head with a wince.

"Are you feeling ill? What's wrong?" Jade stared up at him, disturbed to see him sway a moment before he steadied himself. Ben moved to stand on the other side of Zak, his hand hovering over Zak's shoulder.

"I'm fine." Zak looked past her at the trio of men, and she turned to look at the group as well. Zak cleared his throat and forced a smile as he gently steered her forward, the sword on his hip clinking with his movement. "I just thought I recognized one of them, but that's impossible."

"Oh?" Jade watched the men as she approached the building. None of them popped out to her. One man stood just a bit taller than her, a scruffy blond beard and long hair pulled back in a ponytail gave him the appearance of a rough-and-tumble mercenary or dragon hunter. A unique blood-red sword and sheath hung from his hip. The other two men clearly deferred to the blond. He pointed and said something, and they both nodded and bowed.

Jade stepped into the building and sighed in relief at the coolness of the shade, and twisted to look back at Zak. "Why is it impossible?"

Zak spared the trio one last lingering look before shaking his head with his lips pressed together. "A dead man can't be alive."

CHAPTER THIRTY-ONE

BEN

Ben stepped from the gangplank to the main deck with Briar and the rest of the group on his heels. The *Sapphire* had been home to him for only three months, yet he already attributed the scents of lumber, grease, oily potions, and cooked food as the perfume of safety. Here, he had friends who didn't care if he couldn't remember his own history. They were his viable future, until he could remember his past, or who Sara was.

Captain Slate poked his head from the hallway by the med-bay and held out a hand. "Crew meeting in two minutes!"

Jade and Krista scurried below deck in a rush to deposit their purchases, while Zak followed Slate into the hallway with a straining bag of lut from their successful selling in the city. Doctor Jaxton, Victor, Kerlee, Geist, and the rest of the crew assembled on the main deck within moments of Slate and Garnet coming out to greet them. Six royal guards from Lord Everett stood near the back of the group, silent. Their leader, Trevor, eyed Jade as she came up the stairs with Krista. Ben glared until the muscular man looked away with a cough. Jade, Krista, Briar, and Zak joined Ben where he stood.

"Ezekial left a message," Slate began without preamble, hands stuffed in his duster pockets casually. "We need to send two of you to meet him and learn the details of this mission. He specifically doesn't want anyone who's known to be on the crew, so if you've been on high-profile missions with us, go ahead and step back for now." Slate waited for some of the crew to dissipate, then he counted those left. He didn't even glance at the men Everett had sent. "Jaxton, you came on after Victor, but I would rather keep you here than send you out for this."

"Thank you." The raven-haired doctor stepped back and leaned against a nearby mast, his bored eyes scanning over the group. He lifted an eyebrow at Ben. "If you go, don't get yourself injured again."

Ben scowled at Jaxton in mock outrage, suppressing his laughter at the jab. "Hey—"

Slate spoke over Ben's reply. "I'm thinking we'll send Ben and Victor." He looked at his first mate with a small sigh and lifted a hand to forestall any protests, despite Geist already grumbling. "Like I just said, you've been on with us just a bit longer than Jaxton, but I know you're good at blending in." Paper rustled as Slate waved an orange envelope at Victor. "Zeke's message, along with location and code word." Slate looked past Victor and pointed at Kerlee. "You're similar enough in build to Ben. See if you have anything formal for him to wear for this. Nothing too outrageous though, he's supposed to blend in."

Jade snorted. "Kerlee thrives on the abnormal. Good luck."

Ben grinned down at her. "You're just jealous you don't get to go back out there. You like the attention, admit it."

"Do not!" Jade pushed against his side with a smothered laugh.

Zak watched with folded arms from behind Jade. A crooked smile tweaked his lips. "I don't know, Jade. I think he's right."

Jade's jaw dropped, and her eyes narrowed. She waved a finger at both of them. "Away with you two. Ben, go get ready. And, Zak? Go polish your daggers or something."

Ben chuckled to himself as he followed Kerlee down to his bunk room. Witnessing Zak open up to Jade, and her reactions to him, were downright amusing. Just because Ben couldn't remember anything important and couldn't move forward with his life, didn't mean his friends couldn't move forward themselves.

He crossed his arms and let out a long breath through his nose as Kerlee opened his chest, revealing an array of vibrant clothes. Hopefully, they'd find something suitable in that mess. Victor shook his head with a skeptical look.

Luck was with them, though. They found a formal pair of navy blue pants and a matching jacket buried at the bottom of Kerlee's trunk.

Ben changed into the outfit, and Kerlee wrinkled his nose at the muted colors. "Do me a favor, keep it." He slammed the wooden lid shut and leaned against a bedpost, shaking his head. "That is so lifeless."

Ben raised a brow and nodded at the trunk. "And all that hurts the eyes."

Kerlee grinned. "True. But when you're relatively average in a group of talented fighters and skilled people, don't blend in. Be the one everyone remembers."

Victor rolled his eyes and nodded his approval at Ben's outfit. "Do you have a hat that Ben could borrow, too?"

"A hat?" Ben looked up from smoothing the wrinkles out of the velvety fabric. He was going to die in the heat and humidity outside. "What kind of hat?"

Victor twirled a white top hat in his hands before setting it on his bald head and tilting it rakishly. With his blood-red vest and white suit, he popped against the warm wood tones of the room. "A hat, you know, for your head."

"Ha, ha. I know what a hat is for." Ben wrinkled his brow at Victor as the lean man polished his black shoes. "I thought the goal of you and I going was to *not* bring attention to ourselves."

"Close, but not quite." Victor reached around his bunk and pulled out a black-and-gold walking cane. He tapped it against the floor with a haughty air. "I hate to admit that he's right, but wearing something distinctive draws attention. Then, should we need to disappear in a hurry," Victor opened his jacket and tugged on the vest to show the muted gray shirt underneath. "Ditch what people remember, blend in with the crowd, and you're gone."

Impressed, Ben nodded. He eyed his mission partner. "Your pants don't look bulky enough to be wearing something extra under them."

Kerlee snorted. "Did you see the fishermen while you were out there by chance?"

Ben frowned as he thought back. "The men who wore loincloths?" He hesitated at the sudden mischievous grin that Victor grew. "On second thought, let's just go. I don't want to know."

Kerlee laughed while Victor pointed at Ben's belt on the bed. "Don't forget that."

Ben patted the steam-pistol and slipped the leather around his waist. "I won't. But I don't have many shots left. I used most of them during our training round yesterday."

Victor grunted. "We'll look around for a shop that can sell us the metal we need to make more." He straightened his vest and jacket.

"Let's get this over with."

Sweat dripped down Ben's back and ran down his face by the time they reached the sturdy adobe-and-wood restaurant. Victor patted a crimson kerchief against his forehead and gestured toward the cloth-draped doorway with his cane.

"After you."

Ben stepped into the dim room, and a light breeze of cool air washed over him. He sighed in relief. A smiling young lady greeted them, her flowing dress a brilliant shade of green that contrasted with her purple neck scarf.

"Can I help you?" she chirped.

"Yes." Ben paused and looked to Victor. "We're meeting with Mister…"

"Nathaniel." Victor inclined his head to the hostess. "Is Mister Nathaniel here yet, ma'am?"

Her eyes lit with recognition, and she shook her head. "No, sir. But I can take you to his usual corner table, if you'd like.

Victor rewarded her with a winning smile. "Yes, thank you."

She led Ben and Victor through the restaurant, her stride matching the rhythm that a young man drummed out from the corner. Each table had a vibrant tablecloth covering it, and a glass lamp filled with oil in the center. No gas lamps in sight, nor the luminary crystal lamps of Doldra.

The hostess led them to a table against the back wall, next to a door marked "staff only." She twirled to face them and bowed with a small flourish. "Mister Nathaniel favors his back to the wall, and I'm sure he'll be here soon, if he's expecting you."

Victor tipped his hat with a wink. "I'm sure he will. Thank you, miss."

Ben swallowed his chuckle at the blush that rose to the lady's cheeks. She turned away with a flustered smile, and Victor nodded to the table.

"I'm claiming the wall. He can deal with disappointment." Victor sat in the chair closest to the staff door, leaned his cane against the wall, and raised a black eyebrow at Ben. "Are you going to stand there until he arrives?"

"No." Ben pulled out the chair next to Victor and plopped into it, automatically half-turning to let his gaze roam over the few patrons of the restaurant. Everyone seemed focused on their own table and group, chattering amongst themselves, ignorant of whatever dealings happened around them. "I'm just wondering if Ezekial is going to be willing to give us what intel he has if we took his favorite spot."

"Intel?" Victor gave him an odd look. "He'll give us what information he has, whether we tick him off or not. He works for Aerugo, and he's being paid for what he learns. He won't risk the entire mission just because he's steamed." Victor drummed his tan fingers on the linen tablecloth and smirked. "Besides, if he wanted to sit somewhere particular, he should have gotten here first."

Ben snorted. "Right."

They waited in companionable silence after a waitress came by for their drink order. Victor glanced over. "How's training with Zak going?"

"Well enough, I suppose." Ben stared at his hands and flexed them. "I'm good with the steam-pistol, decent with a staff, and, in Zak's words, 'atrocious' with the grappling hook."

Victor removed his white top hat and set it on his cane and rubbed his hand across his head with a small grunt. "Knowing how to use a grappling hook is an important skill for a skyfarer. He's probably told you before, but if we need to get off an airship in an emergency, while it's still in the air, that glove is our best bet for escaping alive. You need to learn how to use it, and how to do so with skill."

Ben smiled his thanks as their waitress delivered his water and Victor's fizzing blue drink. "I know. It's something I need to work on."

He meant every word, too. Zak had explained, several times, the importance of being able to safely disembark in case of emergency. He'd had interesting examples of emergency, too—ship fire, skyfaring pirates, Jade's wrath. Whatever the reason, Ben wanted to master the skill. Dying on an airship from some random mishap because he didn't learn the safety procedures wasn't what he had in mind for his future.

"I'm pretty handy with the grappling hook," Victor said finally. "I can give you a few pointers when we get back, see if we can get you up to speed."

"Thanks."

"Mmhmm."

Ben picked up his glass and rotated the cup, letting the water get as close to the rim as possible without spilling any. "Hey Victor, what's a Void Born?"

He could feel Victor's curious stare without even looking up at him.

"A Void Born is what everyone in these lands fears," Victor said finally. "In the north, Elph used the blood of Void Born to create the blood-bond that allows them to control the humans that live with them." He took a long sip of his drink, his lip curling up at the corner as he savored the flavor. "Rumor has it that Void Born aren't able to be touched by Void magic, and possibly a few other types, but I haven't ever heard of those being confirmed. Most people are too freaked out by the fact that Void Born don't have the same spark of life as everyone else here does."

"Spark of life?" Ben echoed. "What is that supposed to mean?"

Victor shrugged. "That's just what you always hear when people talk about Void Born. They're like walking dead, without the spark that allows them to manipulate the magic or elements. Who wouldn't fear people who aren't really alive? And if their blood can create the blood-bond, well," Victor looked away with a small smirk, "what else can they do?"

Ben absorbed Victor's words in silence. So he'd told Raine that his friend was a Void Born, essentially someone without magic or life or something. Maybe she didn't like zombies? What about that upset her so much?

A dark-skinned man approached them, his shaved head gleaming in the steady light of the surrounding tables. His eyes narrowed at Victor and Ben, and he stroked his goatee as he stood before them, a large, menacing show of muscle. His black eyes flicked from Ben to Victor and back.

Victor spoke first. "For the sake of our people."

"And for the safety of our families," Ezekial replied. His tense shoulders relaxed infinitesimally. He studied Ben for a long moment. His eyes tightened and he looked back to Victor. "You just had to take the wall."

Victor shrugged. "You want the wall, you come sooner."

Ezekial grimaced at him and muttered, "Bleeding Void Born," as he pulled out a wood chair and sat on the edge of it stiffly. He nodded when the waitress delivered his drink moments after he sat.

"Been here often?" Victor asked wryly.

"A few times." Ezekial smirked as he pulled the mug of frothy liquid closer. "I'll keep this short. I have somewhere to be."

Ben leaned forward, setting his elbow on the table. "You won't be going with us?"

"No." Ezekial didn't look away from Victor. "I have a lead that just opened up after years of digging. I'm not letting it pass by." He took a long sip and wiped foam from the stubble over his top lip. "What I need to tell you is simple. The bandits had a leadership change recently, and I don't know this new guy. I'd set up the meeting with Lupin, their former leader. The exchange is still set to happen, but this new leader may not have the same goodwill that Lupin had. You need to be extra cautious—more so than before."

Victor nodded, a crease forming between his eyebrows. "When is the scheduled meeting?"

Ezekial swirled his mug before setting it on the table. "Tomorrow evening." He tugged a folded paper from a pocket inside his jacket and slid it over the deep purple cloth to Victor. "Coordinates and time. You'll need to hike for part of the way," he warned. "These guys either know a back way to fly their airship in, or they're paranoid. They want to meet up in the hills, past the shepherding communities."

"Thank you." Victor picked up the paper and opened it before re-folding it and slipping it into his own jacket pocket. He steepled his fingers and looked over to Ben. "If that's all you have, we'll be on our way."

A vein in Ezekial's forehead throbbed, and a frown tugged at his lips. "I know I've already said it, but I'll say it again: be careful. I didn't trust Lupin, and I know even less of this new leader. Don't get cocky going in. Whatever relics they can sell you is great, but don't forget your own safety."

Ben nodded when Victor didn't say anything. "We will, thank you."

"Oh." Ezekial lifted a finger off the table and pursed his lips. "Rumor has it they have a warrior with a demon's strength. A berserker with blond hair and a crimson sword. Stay away from him."

Victor nodded his thanks and stood, gathering his hat and walking stick. Ben followed, mind churning. Ezekial's description sounded familiar somehow; if only Ben could place it.

CHAPTER THIRTY-TWO

BEN

The setting sun streaked the sky with gold and brilliant fire-orange clouds, providing more than enough light for them to get to the destined meeting site in the middle of seemingly nowhere. Thin air filled Ben's lungs and left him wanting more as he trekked through the green wilderness and the scattered shrubbery. A quick glance ahead showed Slate comparing his compass to Ezekial's coordinates.

One of Everett's guards—Captain Trevor—sneezed, and Ben shot the man a sympathetic grin. Having wool allergies while walking through the sheep-inhabited countryside had to be pure torture. Still, Trevor marched on, eyes narrowed on the trail they followed. They'd landed the *Sapphire* half an hour ago and left the airship in the care of Garnet and the other non-combatants. Since then, the group Slate led had passed a flock of sheep and their goggled, glow-eyed shepherds leading them home for the night. If the magic stones hadn't been enough, the strange technology further cemented Ben's belief that he wasn't from here.

And who knew? Maybe they'd find something for the keystone and barrier, and maybe even some sort of clue or potion that could help Ben with his memory. He shuddered. As long as the potion didn't include desiccated lizards. *Still not sure if I'm that desperate.*

Ben studied Slate's tense shoulders and ran his gloved fingers on the staff Zak had insisted he carry in addition to the steam-pistol that hung on his hip. The captain had been fairly talkative while they were preparing to go, and he'd shared how the crew had had many such meetups over the years—each with its own perils and uncertainties. But something about this one had Slate's nerves on edge, and he wanted every crew member armed with multiple weapons, "just to be safe." What good Ben would be with the staff, he didn't know, but they wanted him to come along, so he'd do his best to help and not hinder the cause. *I think I trust the gun more.* Ben frowned. No one else called it a gun, and yet that was the word that came to mind.

Is this something from...before? Smooth glass curved under his free hand, and he shook his head. *Maybe it's similar to something I've handled before.*

The captain wasn't the only one on the ship who was out of sorts. Ben's meetings with Jaxton had been more scattered of late, as the doctor had been unusually preoccupied ever since Victor and Ben gave their report.

Up to now, Jaxton Taylor had carried himself with an unflappable air and dry humor. But when Ben last saw him, the doctor had been muttering and agitated the whole time they were preparing to go. Finally, the white-coated man had emerged from his med-room with two glass spheres. Yellow fumes swirling in one, blue mist in the other. Jaxton explained that he'd heard some unpleasant things about the new leader, Kadar, and his pet berserker. And because of his concern, Jaxton created something new for their mission: a paralyzing agent. He'd warned that once the two globes were smashed together, everyone who didn't want to be affected would have to move away from the resulting toxic cloud to avoid the numbing effect.

Victor volunteered to be the one to carry the orbs, and thus it was his job to find the berserker and, at best, incapacitate him—if he could. If the warrior proved stronger than the doctor's creation, Victor would eliminate the threat—permanently.

Ben blew out a breath and looked at Zak in his peripheral vision. The swordsman marched after Slate, his eyes dark and mouth set in a grim line. While none in the crew *wanted* any killing to happen, Slate made it clear back at the *Sapphire* that the bandits had a reputation, and Slate valued the lives of his crew and Everett's men over those of the others. They were to do whatever they needed to insure their health while on this mission.

"We're almost there," Slate announced.

Ben slowed to match Slate's steps. Anticipation skittered along Ben's nerves, and he shook out one hand, then the other.

The captain perched a hand on his hip while he gestured. "I'll meet them with Trevor as planned. Victor, I want you free to roam and find their berserker. Kerlee, you take our purchases and get them back to the *Sapphire*. I want everyone else loosely spread out in pairs. Be prepared for anything." Slate ran his thumb over the edge of his belt and lifted his eyebrows. "Geist. Keep an ear out for any double-crossing or back-stabbing."

Geist lifted a clenched fist and pounded it against his chest, his eyes gleaming. "Yes, sir."

"Everyone know what they're doing?" Slate's eyes roved over Ben, and he nodded along with the rest of the men. Slate turned back to the path and gripped the pommel of his sword. "Good. Let's go."

Although the staff didn't give Ben any confidence, he remained loose-limbed and alert as he entered the bandit camp. Smoke rolled lazily across the ground from three small campfires, and the scent of cooking meat wafted in the air. The bandits watched them enter, their eyes glittering in the firelight.

Slate swaggered forward and stopped in front of a man who scowled at them from a campfire in the center of the bandit camp.

The bandit leader stood with all the relaxed calmness of a cat who'd been sunbathing, and glared up at Slate. "Did you bring the money?" he demanded, hands on his hips by the two hilts hanging from his belt.

Slate raised his eyebrows and mirrored the leader's posture. "And you are?"

"Kadar," the man spat. "The leader and one you should be indefinitely grateful to be talking to."

"Really? I'd think it'd be the other way around." Slate replied casually as Trevor turned his head in an obvious scan of the tense bandits.

Ben had already finished his initial reconnaissance. All the men were armed. Geist and Kerlee stepped closer to Victor, all three resting their hands casually on their sword hilts. Slate exchanged glances with Trevor, then looked back at Kadar and crossed his arms. "Seeing as how we're here to make a deal with you, and we're giving you our good money, I think we should see the merchandise first."

Ben slid his left hand down the shaft of the staff, tense. Kadar sneered and waved his hand, and Slate took a half step back at the same pace as Trevor. Trevor's sword rang clear of its scabbard as Ben gripped the staff with both hands.

Kadar laughed, an ugly sound. "Jumpy, aren't ya?"

Ben breathed through the brief jitter caused by the adrenaline pumping through his blood and waited as a young man–a boy, really–knelt before the trio and opened a chest. He tilted it, allowing Ben and the rest of the *Sapphire* crew to see two scrolls, two stones, a crystal, and what looked like a black ring.

"You've seen our goods. Let's see yours."

Slate gestured, and Trevor moved forward, his eyes not leaving Kadar as he knelt by the boy and opened the mouth of the bag. Blue and black stones glittered in the dying sunlight's rays, and Kadar's eyes glinted. Ben silently slid his foot to the right, widening his stance.

Kadar nodded appreciatively and lifted his hands to his men. "See, boys, this is what I'm talking about. Clearly, these are worth quite a bit, and Lupin was going to practically give these relics away."

Slate's voice sounded tight. "Deal?"

Kadar dropped his arms and raised his eyes from the money bag with a grin. "No deal. I'm keeping these relics. And the lut, of course."

A heartbeat of silence passed, and then men all around exploded into action.

Ben whirled and smacked a nearby bandit on the head, dropping the man before he could draw his sword. Clanging metal and yells echoed eerily in the hills as chaos abounded.

Zak appeared on Ben's left and slashed. A man that had just come into Ben's peripheral fell. Kerlee slid to his knees and tossed the lut bag into the chest. He slammed the lid shut. A wild-bearded bandit raised a sword behind Slate. *He's too far away!* Ben dropped his staff, yanking the steam-pistol from his belt. He cranked the lever, aimed, and shot. A hiss of steam whirled over his gloved hand. The bandit dropped.

Ben whipped his head around, seeking another foe as he fumbled to reload. Zak backed up next to him, bloodied sword held at the ready.

"I'll cover you," Zak shouted over the clamor. "Keep shooting!"

Ben dropped a bullet in the chamber and nodded. Zak fought off an attacker and sank a dagger in his opponent's side. The man gurgled and fell. Ben shot a bandit fighting Ash.

Victor sprinted past Ben.

Trevor had moved away, fighting Kadar and a second man by himself. Ben turned, seeking the next target in the lull immediately by him. He swore when he saw why. The bandits had banded up against several of Everett's men, leaving three bodies in the blood-churned mud. A blond ponytailed man stalked after another, his scarlet blade dripping crimson fluid. Ben aimed.

"Watch yourself!"

Something jostled Ben, and he pulled his finger off the trigger. Slate stumbled away from Ben, his cheek bleeding. Zak's blade crashed against Kadar's, turning a killing strike away from Slate at the last moment. The metal sliced down Kadar's arm, ripping through sinew and muscle until it shattered a metal bracelet. Zak stalked after the leader as he fell.

Ben turned back to the ponytailed man. The blond berserker slumped on the ground, clamping his head with bloody hands. Glowing yellow and blue gases swirled and mixed into a sickly green. Victor watched, upwind, sword in hand, dark eyes burning with a visible hatred. *Jaxton's potion worked. Good.*

Zak moved away from Kadar's body. He met another adversary with a mighty clash of steel. Slate yanked his vest off and dropped to a knee next to Everett's captain. Trevor groaned, blood pouring from his wounded face, and he yelped when Slate pressed the thick material on the wound.

A cursory inspection showed Kerlee had the chest with the lut and had halted by Geist. Geist sprinted past Ben and stopped suddenly, showering Slate and Trevor with dust and pebbles. He leaned over, panting. "Captain, something doesn't smell right."

Slate's head whipped around. He focused on the tracker. "What did you notice?"

Geist waved a hand at a nearby campfire. "Remnants of smoke and men." He pointed to where their crew had come in. "Over there. Couldn't have been us. We didn't have any smoke on us coming in." His eyes danced with the zing of adrenaline even as his face hardened. "I had to backtrack. There are footprints on a deer path. Maybe four men?"

Ben's heart seized, and Slate swore. The captain pushed to his feet. "To me!" he yelled. "Fighting retreat!"

Zak appeared from the deepening shadows, eyes dark with anger. Blood dripped from his upper arm. "For how many bedrolls and dead campfires they have here, men are missing."

Slate nodded. "Geist pointed out that some aren't here."

Zak's entire body stilled. "We left the *Sapphire* undefended."

Ice shot through Ben's spine at Zak's words. *Jade!* He turned on his heel to sprint at the same time as Zak and Geist.

CHAPTER THIRTY-THREE

JADE

Jade leaned against the upper deck railing and stared out over the countryside as the sun finally set behind the western mountain ridge. She settled her chin into her hand with a heavy sigh.

"They'll be back before we know it." Krista dropped the chair she'd dragged out of the mess hall and up the metal stairs with a clatter. She scooted it next to Jade and plopped into it with heedless abandon, stretching her long legs out. "And even if something were to happen and push came to shove, Zak's with them. It'll be over before it starts."

Jade turned away from the railing to face her friend. She could see below to the main deck over Krista's shoulder. Garnet crossed beneath them toward the captain's room with a sheath of papers in hand, her white skin nearly glowing in the soft deck lighting. Her aunt nodded briefly up at her before focusing her attention on the documents again.

"It's not that I'm worried about them, per se," Jade griped. "I want to be out there with them! How many years did we train with Uncle Andre? Zak?" She paced away from the edge of the ship, her boot heels clicking against the deck. "What good was all that for if not for us to go out and help, be part of the action?"

"And what would they do if something happened to you and me, and they had no mechanic?" Krista pointed out reasonably. Jade grumbled a reluctant agreement, and her friend chuckled. "If I didn't know better," Krista teased, "I'd say you just want to be near the guys."

Jade touched the sconce by the helm wheel, and it warmed under her hand, illuminating the center of the topmost deck. "That's not it, and you know it."

"Really?" Krista straightened from her languid posture in the chair and pressed her palms together, dark eyes glittering in the luminary light like a night predator. "Then what is it? At the very least, you have to admit that things have been very interesting between you three lately."

"And I've told you everything." Jade shoved a hand through her loose red hair. "Ben isn't interested because he can't remember anything. He's a friend now, and just that." A red curl snagged on her finger and she fiddled with it, considering. "He's protective, but not in a romantic sense. Almost like what I'd imagine a brother to be like." She released the strand, and it bounced back into place while she sighed. "And Zak is...confusing."

Krista's white teeth flashed in the dark as she chuckled. "That's a good word for him."

Jade rapped her knuckles against the control board, eyes closed as she shook her head. "He's been more friendly and more open lately. I don't know how to interpret it. It's not my fault that he's—"

A bang rattled below the ship, and Jade froze. She looked at Krista, and found her friend with equally wide eyes.

"Briar and my dad are in the galley, Jaxton is in his office, Garnet's in your father's room. Who's below deck?" Krista asked, her voice low. "They couldn't be back already, could they?"

"They would've called a greeting if they were back." Jade crept to the side railing as quietly as she could and stole a peek over the rear gate. She dropped into a crouch and pressed her back against the wood with a blistering oath. "Bandits!"

"Bleeding Void," Krista swore. She grabbed a hydropack and slung it over her shoulder. "We need to get to the others."

Jade followed Krista as she crept down the stairs, and Jade thanked her lucky stones that she wore mechanic pants today. A fight in a dress would not have been easy. Only one sconce had been lit on the main deck thus far, providing them plenty of shadows to hide in.

Four men slunk into the corridor going to the captain's quarters and med-room.

Adrenaline coursed through Jade, her hands trembling. Belatedly, she realized that neither she nor Krista had their swords. Who would have thought they'd need them while on board their own ship? She felt along her belt as Krista peered around the corner into the hallway. Jaxton bellowed, and something crashed. Jade yanked her heavy multi-tool out of a thick pocket and charged down the hall on Krista's heels.

They barged in the open door of the med-bay, and Jade froze for an eternally long second. A man twitched on the floor. Three thugs surrounded Doctor Jaxton, backing him into the corner.

Krista snatched a scalpel off a tray and shouted a challenge. She darted forward. Jade dropped her multi-tool in favor of the heavy metal tray on the counter. She swung with all her might against the closest man. Metal dented in her hands. The bandit collapsed.

Gripping the metal tray, she saw the man by Jaxton drop. She pivoted to check on Krista. Jade's right shoulder muscles clenched in agony as something sliced through them. She stumbled against the medical table and cried out, tears blurring her vision as she clung to the bed.

Krista screamed.

A shrill screech echoed through the room, ringing in Jade's ears. She snapped her head up to the doorway. Garnet stood there, teeth bared as she fired her electro-staff. Electricity arced through the room, hitting the bandit in the face and neck. He fell back with a yell like a terror's. The scent of cooked meat wafted from his body. That took care of all of them.

Jade wilted her head against the bed again. Her stomach churned from the agony of breathing and the stench of enclosed battle. Fingers probed at her shoulder, and she flinched away with a swallowed scream.

"Are you hurt anywhere else?" Garnet's urgent voice commanded Jade's attention, and Jade lifted her eyes to meet Garnet's frantic gaze.

"Just," Jade sucked in a breath, "my shoulder. The others?"

Krista sank onto the bed, careful to not jostle Jade. Her friend held her cheek with a grimace. "No one taught him to never hit a lady." She dropped the hydropack on the floor with a wrinkled nose. "I couldn't use it in close quarters, useless thing."

Jade tried to smile and groaned instead. She craned her neck to look in the corner for Jaxton and ignored the bodies on the floor. "Doctor? How are you?"

The doctor held a thin, metal bracelet in his bloody hands, scowling. He slammed it down on the counter, and a red gem rolled out of its socket. He shook his head, slanted eyes narrowed so much she couldn't even see them. "I'm alive, thank you." He glared at the metal jewelry and gripped his bleeding wrist. "The Void Born broke a priceless artifact of mine."

"Sorry to hear that." Garnet's voice rang sharp. "But we have two ladies bleeding here, and I need to check on the men."

"Please," Krista's voice trembled. "Let me know if my father and Briar are—" she broke off, and Garnet squeezed her shoulder.

"I'll be back," she promised. She glared at Doctor Taylor. "Any time now."

"Of course, of course." Jaxton shuffled forward and plucked a roll of gauze off the floor, rescuing it from a slowly expanding blood puddle. He wrapped it around his wrist absently as he inspected Jade's shoulder. He raised an eyebrow at Krista. "I'll need to get to her first, before she bleeds out anymore."

Krista nodded and slid off the bench. She braced a hand around Jade's middle and helped slide her onto the exam table.

Jade's head spun with the motion of moving, and she tensed as she heard yelling outside. Krista brushed back her dark hair with her less bloody hand. "I'll check on it."

Jaxton's fingers probed Jade's shoulder, and she gasped as agony blazed down her back and arm. He yanked on the material, swore softly, then grabbed shears to cut the blouse around her injury. Something soft and wet pressed against her shoulder, and it started burning a moment later. He stilled and brushed his knuckles against the skin of her shoulder, raising goosebumps over her arms. "Have you always had this mark?"

It took a few moments before Jade could unclench her hands

from her pant legs, move them to keep her shredded blouse in place, and speak. "My birthmark? Yes." She tried to look back at the doctor and gave up when the room lurched around her. "I don't like it, so I keep it covered."

"Interesting. I didn't know that." Jaxton's voice sounded odd.

"My shoulder. How bad is it?" Jade asked, trying to keep her tone steady.

Jaxton snapped back to attention and continued scrubbing at it. "You'll live." He walked out from behind her to pull a fresh roll of gauze from a drawer. "You're lucky; it looks mostly superficial. You'll still have use of that arm."

"Jade!"

Zak burst into the doorway, his green eyes widening as he took in the bodies on the floor and the blood soaking her blouse. He reached her side with long, loping steps and knelt next to her, taking her free hand into his. "We came back as fast as we could when Geist realized they sent men here. Praise the Author you're all alive." His eyes roamed over her, coming back to her shoulder. "Are you hurt anywhere else?"

Ben appeared in the doorway, chest heaving as he leaned against the doorframe. His expression stilled as he met Jade's eyes. Zak looked at Ben and though they said nothing, Jade could've sworn that they communicated.

Ben came over to her side and squeezed her uninjured forearm. "Your father is fine, so don't worry about him right now, okay?" He glanced down at the floor and the bodies that she refused to acknowledge. "I'll get some help to clean this up."

She nodded, still taken aback by Zak's concern—and now Ben's.

Zak's hand warmed her cold fingers. The click of Jaxton's shoes warned Jade that he had returned from fetching the gauze. Something sharp jabbed into her shoulder, and she gasped, twisting away. Zak's eyes looked thunderous as tears slipped down her cheeks from the doctor's ministrations.

"I need to re-spell the nullification stone before we can use it," Jaxton explained as the stabbing sensation continued. "You'll have to tough it out, princess."

Jade grimaced at the mocking tone in Jaxton's voice as he used Briar's nickname for her. She was no princess. And being the captain's daughter didn't give her special privileges or a softer life, as Briar had first assumed. She would show Jaxton that she could withstand the pain just as well as anyone else on the crew. A fresh wave of pain rolled over her, and she bit on her lip, trying not to cry out.

Zak sprang up from his knees and straddled the medical bed, facing Jade. He pulled her into a hug and dropped his shoulder so she could lean into him comfortably. "Do what you must," he told Jaxton, then wrapped an arm around her waist and the other braced her good shoulder against his chest. He tilted his head down to murmur in her ear, "I've got you."

Tears leaked from Jade's eyes as she leaned against Zak, promising herself that she wouldn't get used to having his warmth, his closeness, back. He'd likely retreat the moment she did. Her shoulder burned as Jaxton poured something over it, and she clutched Zak. Embarrassment warred with pain, and she gave up the pretense of toughness that she desperately wanted to hold on to. *Princess, indeed.* Misery forced her to press her face against Zak's sweaty black shirt. *I need to become stronger. But, for now, I need a distraction.*

"The mission? Was it worth it?" She dug her nails into Zak's arm as Jaxton tugged against her back. Her head felt light in the sea of torment. "Briar and William were in the galley. Are they—"

"They're unharmed," Zak assured her as his grip tightened. "The crew's on their way back. Some of us ran ahead when we realized everyone here was in danger." His sword clanked against the frame of the table as he shifted slightly. "I'll catch you up on everything that happened after you're cleaned up and feeling better."

Jade pressed into Zak and breathed deeply as Jaxton finished stitching her shoulder. The bitter tang of adrenaline and sweat that clung to Zak helped to mask the odor of the room. She slid her hand up his sleeve with shaking fingers and encountered damp fabric. She lifted her hand and gasped when she saw red on it.

"You're injured!"

Zak's grin came out more like a grimace. "It's not too bad."

Jade twisted to look at the gash on his elbow peeking out from his slashed shirt and glared up at him. "Were you going to say nothing? We need to get this cleaned and taken care of!"

Jaxton's hand settled on her uninjured shoulder. "Hold still. I can't finish bandaging you if you keep moving."

Jade *thunked* her forehead against Zak's chest again, her hair catching on his chin's stubble. Her shoulder ached as Jaxton rubbed something cold that eased the sensation of pain. She shot upright when she heard the muffled sounds from the main deck and her father swearing loudly. Jaxton muttered behind her as he started bandaging her shoulder.

Zak shook his head, one corner of his mouth barely curled up. "See? Slate's alive and kicking." He raised a hand to her forehead and brushed her hair to the side. His eyes widened and his gaze flicked between her and his fingers. He looked away and swallowed hard. "The crew comes first," he muttered.

Before what? Jade tilted her head as she opened her mouth to ask.

"Done." Jaxton stepped back awkwardly around the body on the floor. He scowled. "Get Ben and William in here to clean up this mess."

Zak slid off the bench and helped her to stand, his hand under her elbow. "Go find Krista and get yourself washed up a bit," he suggested. "I'll help get us ready to go. We'll likely head to Aerugo as soon as everything here has been taken care of."

Jade bit her lip, unsure if she really wanted to go out and see what condition the crew had arrived in. If her father hadn't come directly here after being out there, it meant he was with bodies downstairs. It was rare that they lost men on missions, but it was memorable enough that she had no desire to find her father this exact moment. She'd wait till he was done performing rites.

Curiosity of why they were attacked and who they'd lost roiled in her gut. She looked down at her boots and flinched into Zak. Blank eyes stared up at her from the bloodless face of one of the invaders.

Zak gently pushed her toward the door. "Go rest. I'll send Slate to check on you as soon as he's done, and we'll be out of here soon enough."

CHAPTER THIRTY-FOUR

BLADE

Blade panted and clutched at his pounding head before gripping Kadar's arm and pulling his former leader's body to the mound of other corpses. He dropped it, then paused to rearrange the still-loose limbs.

For over half his life, he'd been controlled by others. For over half his life, he'd obeyed direction mindlessly, unable to do something as simple as show a modicum of respect for the deceased.

No more.

He was aware of the looks that the men in his company gave him. They could tell he'd been freed. How, exactly, he'd been freed, he didn't know. But he'd had time to puzzle it out while under the paralyzing effects of that green fog: Kadar had one controlling bracelet, and Master Jaxton had the other. Both had to be destroyed for him to be free.

And free he was.

Was Jaxton dead? Probably. He wouldn't relinquish control over Blade for anything.

It meant Blade couldn't exact his revenge.

But anger burned through his veins as he recalled the scene only hours earlier. Slate, walking through their simple camp, bold as brass, with that man from the citadel so many years ago. A change of clothes and hairstyle couldn't hide those cold eyes. It proved all that Blade had ever heard.

Slate *had* been behind everything in Doldra. The blood of the royal family stained Slate's hands. As did the unstable barrier. So many deaths. So many potential deaths if the barrier were to fall for good.

Blade motioned to one of the men, and dried blood flaked off his hand as he gestured. "Light the pyre. We're moving on."

The man scurried to obey, and Blade turned away from the bramble and oil heap to watch the sky for the airship that Slate commanded.

He was finally free. But what did he have left? A few bandits that he could call his own men? His family was dead. He had no friends. Two faces popped into his mind, seared there by the hatred that had buoyed him through the years of mental slavery.

The man whom he had once called brother had to pay the price. And the man who walked with him. They were responsible for all his loss, and they would pay for it.

Fire crackled behind Blade, and an oily black smoke rose from the pile of corpses. His men muttered as they watched the flames lick at their comrades and the few dead men who'd been left behind by Slate. What kind of captain left behind his own men?

He gripped his sword hilt and stalked forward. "I'm claiming leadership. Does anyone wish to challenge me?"

The ragtag group all stepped back, none looking him in the eye. One by one, they either dropped to a knee or saluted a hand over their chest. Grim satisfaction set Blade's shoulders back—a position they hadn't held in nearly two decades.

"We're going to follow that airship." He ignored the surprised whispers and gestured at the blazing pyre. "Smell that? Remember it. That's the cry of your comrades demanding revenge." He paced before the men, his boots sinking into the blood-soaked ground as he looked each one in the eyes, trying to impress upon them the same fire that drove him. "We will conquer them, take back what is ours, and make them pay blood for blood."

He reached the edge of the handful of men and looked back. "Are you with me?"

CHAPTER THIRTY-FIVE

SLATE

Fresh guilt tied knots with Slate's gut as he neared the gleaming white Aerugan palace. Two guards pulled open the arched double doors, and Slate's stomach plunged to the toes of his boots as he passed the uniformed men. *I left them behind. My men. Everett's men. I left their bodies. How much lower can I sink?*

It had taken them several hours to get the *Sapphire* and her crew fit to fly. It didn't matter that the sun had already set. Kerlee and Geist dumped the bodies from the med-room, while Ben scrubbed blood from the wood floor. Jaxton and Zak had their hands full with wounded to stitch, wrap, and heal. They'd wanted to get out of Vodan.

Only Jaxton's report had offered some modicum of comfort to Slate.

As usual, Jaxton had been taciturn when revealing his findings with Slate, but he'd announced good news amidst the chaos, so the doctor's distracted attitude could be easily overlooked. Jaxton had spent hours with Everett's man, Trevor, working hard to preserve what eyesight he could, and after that, the two were frequently talking in low tones, falling silent when approached. But according to the documents that Jaxton studied in the solitude of his office, the bloodstone in the box they'd recovered on the mission was what they had been searching for all these years. At long last, the keystone could be stabilized.

Maybe then, some of Slate's shame could finally be put to rest.

A guard ushered Slate and Victor into a spacious office where Lord Everett sat behind a gleaming desk that was larger than Slate's bed on the *Sapphire*. Prince Weston lounged on a nearby navy blue couch, flipping through a book. Sunshine streamed in from the glass wall behind Everett's head, and dust motes danced against the beams. Dark shadows fell across his pale face as the light highlighted his dark hair.

Prince Weston straightened hastily when he made eye contact with Slate. Everett raised an eyebrow in his son's direction and leaned forward, pressing his elbows against the rich wood with his fingers steepled.

"Captain Stohner, you made it back, I see." Everett's cool gaze traveled to the box under Victor's arm. "And it looks like you had a successful errand."

"Yes, my lord." Slate bowed and gestured to the desk. "May we?"

Everett nodded and stood imperiously. "Show me and report."

Victor set the chest on the desk and stepped back as Slate moved forward.

The door opened behind them, and Queen Violet entered with Andre and her handmaiden, Deisy, just behind. Violet dipped her head in a shallow nod to her husband, then her cheek dimpled with a small smile as she sank onto the couch beside Weston. "We heard you'd returned." Her hands fluttered over her silken skirt. "What news have you?"

Slate sighed and pressed his palms against the rough-hewn wood of the chest. "We arrived and met with Ezekial as expected." He raised his eyes to where Violet listened intently. "He found a new lead that he had to leave immediately for, so he gave us," Slate gestured to include Victor, "what information he had, and that was that. We found the bandits easily enough, but they had a new leader who wasn't interested in selling to us."

Everett touched two strong fingers against the desk and ran his other hand over the lapels of his smooth obsidian jacket. "And yet, here you are with the relics."

"Yes." Slate swallowed and continued, his words halting. "Despite our preparations, they did, in fact, double-cross us." He took a shallow breath and released it. "We took heavy losses. Several of my crew, and…"" Slate dropped his eyes and stared at Lord Everett's reflection in the polished wood. "I'm sorry, but only one of your men survived." He winced. "Captain Trevor will be permanently blind in one eye. Silva died on the way back."

He explained the sneak attack and the panic and confusion that ensued. Slate closed his eyes, brow knit as he trembled against the imagined onslaught of ghostly voices crying out. "Due to the attack on us and their concurrent invasion on the *Sapphire,* we had to leave the bodies of our fallen men behind." His back tingled as he looked up at Everett. "I'm sorry," he repeated.

"I see." Lord Everett's stony countenance betrayed none of his thoughts. "You obtained the chest, however."

"Yes, my lord." Slate lifted the lid and reverently pulled out the black-and-red flecked stone that Jaxton had identified as their saving grace. "Our ship doctor is a mani-med, and he has studied the scrolls in here." Slate set the rolled parchment on the desk. "He's determined that this is a bloodstone. It's what we've been looking for."

Everett reached across the table and picked up the smooth stone. He raised it high to look at it in the sunlight, then rolled it in his fingers. "Well done. I will have my own manipulators study the scrolls, of course, but we will begin plans to fix the Doldra keystone as expediently as possible." The ruler set the rock down on the stack of papers before his chair and nodded once with a pleased expression. "I assume you will stay in Lucrum?"

"Possibly. My sister is looking in the Merchant's Market for cargo for us to move, but we'll return here immediately after." Slate coughed, his mouth dry. "About the injury and loss of your men…"

"Not important." Everett frowned. "Bring the captain to the palace later, and we'll have our own mani-med look him over. I am displeased that my soldiers are gone, of course. And the fact that you didn't bring back their bodies is regrettable. But you found what has been long sought after, and that makes such sacrifices worth it."

Slate swallowed and nodded. Buoyant relief battled with heavy guilt in his limbs, and he deliberately avoided looking at the nearby couch. There was no way he'd be able to sit and keep his composure. Not when he desperately needed a strong drink to combat the new voices that had joined the ghosts in his memory.

"Shall I get him and escort him here now?" Victor asked, his gaze focused on Lord Everett, back straight, hands clasped behind his back.

Everett narrowed his eyes at Victor, silent, analyzing. He nodded once. "Take him to the infirmary."

Victor bowed, his head gleaming in the beam of sunlight that lit Everett's desk. "Yes, my Lord."

The guards opened the doors as Victor strode out.

"Captain Slate." Violet's smooth brow crinkled, and lines of concern were etched around her rich brown eyes. "You mentioned that there was an attack on the *Sapphire*. Is everyone well?"

Chagrined to have worried her, Slate nodded hastily. "Yes, your majesty. A few wounds, but nothing time can't heal." He hesitated, studied Weston's downcast eyes, and added, "Jade received stitches and will not be by to visit anytime soon."

Violet pressed her lips together and nodded. "May she heal quickly."

"Thank you, yes."

"If that is all the information you have, then that will be all." Everett clapped his hands, and a guard appeared in the doorway. "We'll notify you when we have communicated with Governor Bentley, and I'll update you on your orders at that time. Dismissed."

Slate bowed and turned to the door.

Some of the weight on his shoulders sloughed off after he left the palace's looming shadows. He tilted his head back to enjoy the warmth of the sunshine on his face and dared to let himself feel hope for the first time in years. It simmered beneath the surface of his skin like tiny bubbles begging to burst free.

The meeting he'd been dreading was over. An artifact had been found, and it looked promising. Maybe it would be enough to fix some of the wrongs in his past. Maybe the dead would be appeased. It wouldn't—couldn't—fix everything he'd done, but it might be enough.

CHAPTER THIRTY-SIX

BEN

Ben leaned an arm against the sun-warmed railing and stared at the white clouds that billowed from the chimney stacks in the distance. Now that the *Sapphire* had been scrubbed clean of all traces of bandits, and Slate had delivered the chest to Lord Everett, they were finally on an "easy" mission to pick up supplies from Lasim.

Every nation or kingdom that Ben had experienced thus far had its own unique style, and this city proved to be no exception. Brick buildings supported the flues, and white-robed people bustled about in an orderly fashion from structure to structure. He squinted, but couldn't guess what they were doing.

A whisper of movement announced Zak a moment before he came into view by Ben's side. Ben frowned as someone in the distance dropped a flask and several others scurried around, upsetting the purple smoke billowing from the shattered glass.

"What's so special about this place, again?"

Zak crossed his arms and nodded his chin toward the industrial workings. "Lasim specializes in medical potions, stones, and such. That's one of the biggest factories they have currently."

Ben turned away from the semi-organized chaos and let the

railing support his weight. "Think they'd have anything that can help with memory loss?"

Zak shrugged with a small sigh. "If anyone has anything of that sort, my hut would be on the mani-meds here."

"Mani-meds?"

"Manipulator-medics," Zak clarified. "Those with an aptitude for manipulating specific elements that help with healing tend to train here at some point or another."

So people who were definitely not Void Born. Ben braced his elbows against the metal digging into his back. "Are you a mani-med?"

A wistful expression crossed Zak's face, and he shook his head. "No. I wish I were; it would have been a very useful skill on many occasions. Jaxton is the only mani-med we have."

Ben scuffed the toe of his boot against the wooden deck. Jaxton still hadn't had any luck with releasing any memories or anything of relevance from Ben's mind. All Ben could remember thus far was a few scattered memories, Sara, Laurent, and blood. Lots and lots of blood.

"Zak! Ben!" Jade appeared from the stairs leading below deck, and she bounded over to them with a large smile, her eyes sparkling. "We've got at least four hours before we'll be ready to head back to Lucrum. Let's go out, stretch our legs, and see what interesting things they've come up with since last Decembri!"

Ben didn't miss the way that air whooshed out of Zak when Jade first approached, then the softening in Zak's gaze as he talked to the enthusiastic redhead. Jade waved her arm in circles, miming something that must have occurred in the engine room, if her grease-stained sleeve and apron were anything to go by.

A small smile tugged at Zak's lips, and he raised his eyebrows at

Ben from across her head. "I'm up for it. You want to come, too?"

Ben shrugged amiably and pointedly looked over the gleaming, empty deck. "Chores are done. I've got nothing better to do."

"Actually, Ben, could I borrow you while they're away?" Doctor Jaxton lurked in the hall, a white smudge contrasted by dark shadows. "I have a new protocol I want to try in regards to your memories."

Ben weighed his options. A new city to explore with friends, or staying on the ship even longer—but with the possibility of learning some of his history. As much as he wanted to forge ahead with his life, he couldn't, not without knowing his past.

"If you think it's worth a try, let's do it." He flashed an apologetic smile at Jade and Zak. "Sorry."

Jade waved both hands in front of her chest, red wisps of curls whipping into her face as she shook her head. "No, no, that's much more important." She offered him a soft smile. "Good luck." Her hand reached out and snatched Zak's black sleeve, and she tugged him to the stairs leading below deck. "Briar and Krista are waiting, so let's go!"

Ben laughed as Zak's face turned red as he followed Jade into the stairwell. Zak glared at Ben before pulling his shirt out of her grip. She instantly stopped.

Zak jutted his jaw forward. "I'm following. I just don't want to break my neck on the stairs with you dragging me."

Ben missed her indignant retort as the two continued into the belly of the *Sapphire*. He skirted around the square capstan grate in the deck floor and joined Jaxton in the shaded hallway. They walked together to the med-bay.

"My hands have improved quite a bit since you last looked at them. Thank you for the ointment," Ben said.

"My time-spell should have worked, and your hands would have healed faster." Jaxton sniffed and closed the door behind Ben. "Sit and get comfortable."

The rotten scent of spilled blood made Ben's nose wrinkle. Despite all their work to scrub the floor, blood from the bandits had leaked into the wood, and now it needed to be replaced. He could try to get comfortable—but the sour smell guaranteed he wouldn't be able to truly relax.

Ben plopped onto the med-table and tapped his fingertips together idly as he watched Jaxton putter around the room. First, a pad of paper and a writing instrument. Then, Jaxton dropped to his knees in front of a cupboard to pull out a metal box, which he set on the countertop. Jaxton's slanted eyes studied Ben for a long moment before he pressed his thumbs onto dual squares that released the lid with a squeak.

"I was hesitant to try this at first," Jaxton said as he turned around, holding a delicate silver circlet in his tan hands. "But I think this may help to answer the mystery of where you're from, as well as your memory problems."

Ben tilted his head to the side as he studied the circlet, and he raised a single eyebrow at the doctor. "You're telling me that jewelry will help me?"

Jaxton compressed a small smirk as he stepped forward and slipped the circlet on Ben. "No, I'm telling you that this will answer some of *our* questions—if my hypothesis is correct."

Cool metal brushed against Ben's forehead, and his entire body felt strange. Almost numb. He tried to touch his thumb to his forefinger, but found he had no control over his hand.

Panic surged through him when his head wouldn't lift as he

directed. *What is this?*

Fingers pressed the circlet down until it fit snugly. Jaxton said, "Look at me."

Ben's head turned to obey Jaxton's order, allowing Ben to see the doctor. The doctor showed all his teeth in a rare smile that sent involuntary shivers down Ben's spine.

"You may be a bit disconcerted to learn that you cannot control your body anymore. I can control it for now. This circlet was originally meant for pain nullification during surgery, but I've made adjustments over the years to suit my needs." Jaxton sat on his stool and slid his paper and pen across the counter. "Maybe we can unlock your mind with it. Let's start easy—what's your name?"

Without thinking, Ben heard himself reply: "Benjamin Dubray."

Jaxton made a note on his pad and nodded. "Excellent. Next question. Where are you from?"

Hazy images swam under the murk of Ben's mind, but nothing broke through. "I don't know."

A harrumph. Then Jaxton said, "Tell me what you know of Jade's identity."

Jade's face flashed into Ben's head and he found himself nodding. "She is Captain Slate Stohner's daughter, his only child. She is a mechanic here. Krista is her best friend. Jade likes Zak. She—"

"Enough, enough." Jaxton wrinkled his nose and scribbled again on his paper. "What do you know of the Void?"

The question rattled in Ben's brain but found little answer. "It has something to do with the barrier."

Ben still couldn't lift a finger as Jaxton continued questioning him. Sometimes answers rose up from the haze in his mind, like someone standing up in the midst of thick fog. Concern niggled through Ben while Jaxton continued his inane questions. *He's barely asking anything about my past. Why? What does he think I know?*

Jaxton set down his pen and looked at Ben over steepled fingers. "I'm sure I already mentioned that the circlet nullifies pain. It doesn't heal anything." He leaned back with a quiet sigh. "Sometimes pain has to be a catalyst for unlocking memories. Blood can also be used, depending on why the mind is hiding." Jaxton jiggled a stone in his hand. "But I can't use the cleaner methods that involve those options, as those spells don't work on you." He narrowed his eyes. "Tell me. Why don't they work on you?"

Bile roiled in Ben's gut. "I don't know."

Jaxton pressed his lips together and sighed through his nose. "Maybe we will need to try the hard way after all."

CHAPTER THIRTY-SEVEN

BLADE

Blade held his hand over his hilt as he prowled the hallway of Slate's airship. Having the clang of metal give away his presence would be most annoying. It had taken several days to track Slate's ship to Lucrum, and Blade had arrived just in time to witness Slate leaving the city. He'd tailed him again, this time to Lasim. Now he'd just confirmed his suspicions of the identity and guilt of Slate's man.

It had been nearly two decades since Blade had last seen Slate's crew member. Back when Blade was a free man, and everything was just starting to disintegrate. Back then, the man had a ponytail and carried himself with a haughty air. Now, he'd disguised himself as a bald man, but such a ploy didn't fool Blade. And even for having a room all to himself, the man—Slate's first mate, if his quarters were accurate evidence—kept incriminating records that those who knew such details would recognize. So careless.

Anger boiled in Blade as he thought of his former friend. He refused to refer to Slate's airship as the *Sapphire*. How dare Slate name his ship after *her*? After all that he'd done, he dared to parade her name? Truly, Slate deserved what was coming.

It would be best if he could find Slate or his first mate before everyone returned to the ship. Blade wasn't about to share their due deaths with his own men. He pulled his garrote out of its pocket and opened the med-bay door with blasé ease. Shock rippled through his body.

Doctor Jaxton wasn't dead. Not yet. And one of the men from the camp sat on a bench, a silver circlet pressing down his reddish-brown hair.

Jaxton's head whipped around and he froze, gaping. His pupils dilated. "You!"

"Me." Blade stepped into the organized room and shut the door. He didn't want any interruptions. Not for this unexpected prize. He'd wondered where he would find his former master, if he was still alive. Finding him on Slate's ship was a shock—and yet it further proved Slate's treachery. Blade slipped the thin metal string back and pulled his crimson sword free of its matching sheath. The small room would be difficult to maneuver in. But it was only fair that Jaxton taste what he'd created.

Jaxton stumbled over a chair in his haste to put the medical table between himself and Blade. The young man separated them, his face blank, as if free of thought or emotion.

Memories of suppressed rage and helpless horror raced through Blade, leaving him breathless against the tumult. He raised his sword and looked at Jaxton over the tip. "You will not destroy another life like this."

Jaxton dropped his hand into his coat pocket as Blade lunged across the room. Before Jaxton could grasp whatever he reached for, the edge of Blade's sword bit into his neck, severing the artery there. The traitorous doctor collapsed on the floor, legs akimbo. The white of his uniform rapidly changed to crimson. His fingers trembled as they lifted to the blood pouring from his neck. His eyes widened in shock. Jaxton's hand slipped down, leaving bloody streaks on his neck as the light in his eyes dimmed.

It wasn't enough.

It wasn't nearly enough.

How *dare* he die so easily? How *dare* he not pay for his crimes with the same pain and blood that he'd forced Blade to experience?

Blade hacked at Jaxton, uncaring of time, noise, or mess. Finally he stopped to wipe at the fluid dripping off his face. Blood stained everything in sight, including the man that still sat on the med-bed.

Rage appeased by his act of justice, Blade wiped his sword clean on a linen bandage, then sheathed it. He came around the bench and looked at Jaxton's most recent victim. Splashed blood dripped from the back of his head, and only his vibrating pupils indicated any sort of emotion.

"Leave, or you risk death," Blade said as he tugged at the sticky circlet. "Anyone left on this ship will meet a similar fate as him." The silver band popped off, and the man's blue eyes rolled up into the back of his head before he collapsed on the medical bed.

Blade nudged the unconscious man and shrugged. "I'll give you a day to recover. You've been warned."

CHAPTER THIRTY-EIGHT

JADE

Jade tried to be subtle as she eyed the large airship and walked past it. Smooth, clean lines made it appealing at first glance, until she spotted the large water tank tucked under the deck. *A steamy.* No, she wanted to avoid transferring to one of the modern ships if she could help it. The whole point of leaving the *Sapphire* was a fresh start in a place where her skills would be used and appreciated. Being one of many mechanics on a ship like that wouldn't do her any favors.

"She looked good at first, huh?" Zak's voice broke her musings, and Jade startled, heat rising to her cheeks. Zak didn't know what she, Krista, and Briar were planning, and she couldn't let him suspect anything until they'd already left.

"At first, yes," Jade stammered. She'd specifically avoided any sort of conversation that could put her in such a tricky spot, and now she had to finagle her way out, and without lying to Zak. She looked ahead to where Krista and Briar walked, hoping that one of them had overheard and could offer a distraction of some sort.

Briar brushed his nose against Krista's, and he whispered something before kissing her. Jade's stomach clenched, and she looked away. Was she really thinking of leaving with those two lovebirds? Ben was getting his memories back in fragments and didn't need her anymore. And Zak was starting to warm up to her again. He seemed to be reclaiming his position as her friend. Things were looking up.

Jade shook her head. No, she had to do this. Her father's overprotectiveness hadn't abated at all, and she knew better than to try to ask him about her apprenticing to be a captain. He'd give her the wide-eyed look and then monologue about how she could be so much more, and not to sell herself short, and to just wait a bit longer and she'd find a better station in life.

"Jade. Are you feeling all right?"

Jade flashed a quick smile up at Zak. "I'm…fine. Just, a bit on my mind right now. Sorry."

Concern ebbed in Zak's eyes, and a corner of his mouth lifted as he nodded. His fingers skimmed over her hand. "If you ever need to talk, I'm not Krista, but I'm good at listening."

"I know." A tiny fissure opened in Jade's heart as she dipped her head, avoiding his gaze. "Thank you." Did he have to be nice now? It wasn't making things any easier for her. Krista. She'd be a good distraction. Jade jerked her head up to call out, saw her friend, and wrinkled her nose. "Really? You two need to just get married already."

Krista pulled away from Briar and mock-glared at Jade. "You're just jealous." Krista shot back. She waggled nimble fingers between Jade and Zak. "Maybe if you two were a couple—"

Jade inhaled sharply as Zak choked next to her.

"—you wouldn't feel so awkward about this." Krista pulled Briar's head down and pressed her lips against his.

Jade ducked her head and listened to the smoothed gravel road crunch underfoot as she avoided making any eye contact with Zak.

Unseen electricity between her and Zak raised the hair on her arms, and she bit her lip. *Krista,* she moaned to herself. *That was not the distraction that I needed.* She flicked her eyes up to judge how close they were to the *Sapphire.* Almost home. *Good.*

Minutes passed as she walked in awkward silence by Zak's side. Should she leave more space between herself and Zak? Stay as they were? His knuckles nearly brushed hers, and her entire arm tingled.

Something about him was magnetizing, and she wanted to be by his side as Krista and Briar were with each other—close to one another, no gaps between their bodies. She wanted to feel his arm wrapped around her waist. But any time the topic of her and Zak being together came up, tension would rise. He radiated it. His smoldering glances warmed her belly, while the hard set in his jaw warned her away.

What was so bad about liking a mechanic?

They arrived at the airship, and Zak disappeared downstairs under the excuse of helping load cargo. Jade whirled on Krista the moment he vanished from sight and she could no longer hear the soft clatter that his leather boots made on the metal steps.

"I can't believe you said that!" Jade's hands flew up to her burning cheeks. "Why would you do such a thing?" She waved her finger under Briar's nose. "And quit your laughing, blimp-for-brains, you're just as guilty as she is!"

Briar waggled his thick eyebrows at her and winked. "Who do you think gives her all these fantastic ideas? It's time you guys start communicating." He grinned at Jade's speechlessness. "Now, if you don't mind, I actually need to get started on dinner, and I need Krista's help with all the prep work. We're going to try something new tonight—pancakes!"

Krista laughed and followed Briar, leaving Jade alone on the abnormally quiet deck to bemoan the death of her dignity. She spun and hit her palm against the thick mast, then *thunked* her forehead against it with a heavy sigh.

A keening groan raised gooseflesh on her arms and she twirled around, back against the wood as a superstitious shiver ran down her spine, causing a flash of pain to radiate from her injured shoulder.

She rubbed lightly at the bandage as she held her breath. Muted thuds below deck told her that the crew still loaded merchandise, and odds were good that her father and aunt were still in town. The groan sounded again, and this time she could tell it was coming from the med-bay.

Ben. Had he and Jaxton had any luck? Jade shook off her unease and trotted across the deck to investigate. Ben had proven to be a good friend for her. Maybe he could distract her from her earlier mortification.

She knocked on the med-room door and waited. No one said anything, but the low moan sounded again, and this time she recognized it as Ben's voice. Interrupting Doctor Jaxton wouldn't be favorable, but no one answered. She turned the brass knob and pushed it open slowly.

"Hello? How's it goin—" Jade froze, her question dying on her lips. Along the back wall, written in bold crimson letters, were the words *"I KNOW."* Blood coated the ceiling and painted the wood paneling scarlet. She recognized Jaxton's black shoes, but everything else that she could see around the bed resembled raw ground meat. Her lunch begged to come up as the stench assaulted her. She stumbled back, hitting the hall wall. Her shaking legs wouldn't support her. She slid down the sturdy partition.

Ben had collapsed. His arm and head dangled off the med-table. His fingertips grazed the bloody floor. He exhaled, and his moan rang in her ears.

Shock, terror, and horror finally made their way up and out of her. She screamed.

How much time passed, she didn't know. A second, an hour—it all blurred together. Her vision swam. Blood, gore, flayed flesh, so much blood, then green. Green like Zak's eyes. Zak.

Jade shook as she blinked at Zak. He held a hand out, and voices babbled somewhere nearby. He answered them, not breaking eye contact with her. She couldn't look away from him, couldn't hear anything over the rushing in her ears.

Zak walked forward on his knees and pulled Jade's face into his chest before lifting her to her feet. She clung to him as he moved her out of the hallway and into the sunshine and fresher air. He ducked his head to look at her directly.

"Jade." He spoke slowly, his eyes searching hers. "I need you to stay here with Krista." He released Jade and Krista hugged her tightly. Zak didn't leave. His hand rested on Jade's back. "I need to check on Ben. Can you stay here with Krista?"

Jade nodded dumbly as Krista rubbed slow circles by her uninjured shoulder blade. "Doctor Taylor...the blood. He..."

"I know, love. I know." Zak squeezed her good shoulder and looked over at Krista. "Take her to the top deck so she stays in the sun." He pulled a dagger off his belt and handed it to Krista. "See anything unusual, call for me. Do not look over the edge until someone comes for you. You don't need to see this, either."

Krista gently tugged on Jade. "Come on. Let's do as he says."

Tears overflowed Jade's eyes, and she couldn't stop them from streaming as she followed Krista past the flight wheel on the top deck. The cloudless blue sky and chirping birds seemed to mock the horror that had happened below. "Who would do such a thing?" she asked, her voice nothing more than a hoarse, broken whisper.

Krista led her to a corner that they could sit in. Once they were settled with their backs to the short, wooden wall below the metal railing, her friend replied, "Evil. Only someone evil could do this."

Jade wiped away the tears and sobbed as the waterworks still came. She hiccuped and buried her face in her hands, but the memories were too fresh to disappear. The shadow of her palms made the image of blood flash in her mind's eye, and she tilted her face to the sun, trying to burn out the sight.

What had happened to Ben? Had he been injured during Jaxton's murder? He had to have been. There was so much blood. What had happened to him? He was breathing. So he had a chance at survival, right? Would she lose her friend in addition to losing the doctor? She shuddered. "No one deserves to die like that. Except the one who did that to him."

CHAPTER THIRTY-NINE

JADE

Jade stared at the toes of her boots, cold despite the warmth of the dropping sun on her face and the heat of Zak and Krista sandwiching her. A shiver ran through her, and Zak wrapped an arm around her shoulders. Krista held her hand. Jade's tears had dried for the moment, and she didn't want to move, didn't want to risk anything that would require her to feel more than the numbness in her chest.

Why? Who would murder a doctor? And in so brutal a fashion? It had taken William, Kerlee, Geist, and Ash hours to clean the med-bay, and Zak had spent a good chunk of that time trying to determine if Ben was actually injured or not. At this point, he concluded, it seemed that Ben had no physical injuries, but had fallen unconscious, probably his mind's way of protecting him from whatever he'd witnessed.

Jade tucked chin to her chest and curled in on herself. What horrors had Ben seen?

The deck vibrated under her as someone walked by them, but she didn't look up from her legs. She didn't want to see any more blood. Not today.

"Jade." Kerlee's gentle voice drew her gaze. He knelt on one knee in front of her, a clean black shirt that she recognized as Zak's draped over him. He offered a small smile. "Your father wants to talk to you."

Zak's arm gently squeezed her.

"You're wearing Zak's shirt." Why that was her first thought, she didn't know. But the words were out her mouth before she could think of anything else to say.

Kerlee's lips twitched in a small grimace, and he gave Zak an apologetic nod. "I needed a clean change after...cleaning up, and I wasn't about to wear something...red."

"Right." Zak's voice was low, soothing. "Not a problem." He stood and helped Jade to her feet. "Want me to walk with you downstairs?"

Jade hesitated, and Krista replied for her, "That sounds like a good idea."

Jade trailed after Zak, eyes downcast. She didn't want to look at the med-bay door. Actually, after all the cleanup...Jade focused on the back of Zak's shirt, unsure if she wanted to see the floorboards in the hallway.

He left her at her father's door and quietly excused himself. She touched her knuckles to the door in a semblance of a knock, and then walked in.

Aunt Garnet sat at the little desk, just beyond the door, and Jade's father stood by his bed. Seeing the fresh lines of grief lining their eyes and Garnet's pale face proved to be too much, and Jade lurched forward and sobbed in his arms. "Why, just, why?"

Her father steadied her and led her to the second chair at Garnet's table. She sank onto the wood and shook her head, tears still dripping down her face. Garnet pulled out a handkerchief and slid it across the table.

"Jade," her father said softly, his eyes flicking to her, then down to his hands. "I don't know how to tell you this."

Oh no. Was Ben dead too? *I've lost two friends today.* Fresh tears welled up in her eyes, and she watched him inhale deeply. She held her breath.

"But your real name isn't Jade." Her father swallowed hard. "And I'm not your biological father."

She blinked. Blinked again. *What?*

Garnet's lips quivered, and she reached out to hold Jade's still hand on the tabletop. Jade stared at her father. What was he saying?

"Your birth name is Adeline Grace Doldras. You are the daughter of Prince Brandon; you are a princess of Doldra. I am only your uncle." He lifted his hand with a broken, weak laugh. "Garnet is still your aunt. Nothing changes there."

Jade tilted her head, and her lips moved, despite no words coming out. Her mind was blank. Finally, a question. "But…my mother… Samantha?"

Her father—*uncle?*—shook his head. "She's my wife, but not your birth mother. Lady Sapphire Stohner-Doldras, my sister, was your real birth mother." He rubbed his thumb along his pant leg and didn't meet her eyes.

Not my mother? If finding Jax and Ben had numbed her, this was the step beyond. She couldn't process everything that had happened today, and then this new news. Her father wasn't her father? Her mother wasn't her mother? What?

Garnet spoke softly in the quiet. "We never found Brandon's body after the massacre. And after losing Sapphire in the same night, along with the entire Doldras family, we just couldn't risk knowledge of you being alive. We couldn't lose you, too." Garnet braced her elbow against the table and rested her hand in her cheek while she watched Jade with sad eyes. "We did what we had to do to protect you."

Slate knelt by the table, looking up at Jade. "But with Jaxton… we can't hold off on telling you. Someone may have figured out who you are, and that person might be trying to get to you."

Jade's heart seized. She grasped at her blouse, struggling to pull in breath, and her father's eyes widened. "You mean," her voice was unrecognizable to her, too ragged and raw to be hers. "Doctor Taylor died because of *me?*"

"No, no, of course not." Garnet soothed. "But if someone is coming after those with connections to the palace, they may come after you, or us, or even Zak, and we need you to be aware, and—"

No. Just, no. Jade straightened, her head light, almost feverish. "I'm not a princess. You're in shock. Delusional." The room spun, and she gritted her teeth against nausea. Her father wasn't her father? *There is no way I can believe this.*

"Sweetheart, I'm sorry, but that's the truth." Garnet offered a tremulous smile, her fingers shaking as she touched Jade's hand. Jade flinched back and Garnet retreated, slipping her hand into her own lap. "Think about it. Haven't you always hated how we've done things different than Krista and William?"

Her aunt's words hit her like a wrench to the noggin. Jade fell silent, her already torn heart shredding as the truth sank its claws in. It made sense now. Her father's over-protectiveness. His comments about her finding a better place, a better station. He meant her role as a princess. He meant her—Jade's thoughts screeched to a halt and she rocked back.

"That's why you've both discouraged me from being too close to

Zak. It's not that I'm not enough for *him*, it's that I'm a princess, and he's not enough for *me*. Is that it?" She stared at her father, mentally begging him to deny it. "It was you. You scared him away, didn't you?"

He winced, and when his eyes met hers, she could read the painful truth in them.

Jade huffed an incredulous laugh. "I can't believe this. All this time, I thought I was the problem. That *I* wasn't good enough. Wasn't smart enough. Brave enough. But no. It's because *you* think I'm a princess." She gripped the excess fabric of her mechanic pants and tried to not sway as her mind spun. "Unreal. You've both lost a cog."

"Jade. We're telling you the truth," Garnet said quietly, her voice betraying her desperation despite her calm attitude. "We wouldn't make this up."

Jade hunched forward, burying her face in her hands, blocking them from her sight. *What more could we add to make this day any worse than it is?* She stiffened. "If this is true, then what else have you lied to me about?" Jade stood and teetered as the room spun. She gripped the table. "All these years, you've been my father. My mother, Samantha. And now you rip that away? Did you expect me to be happy to hear that I'm supposedly a princess?"

"Maybe not happy," Slate replied, his shoulders hunched as he hung his head. "But it's the truth. And you'll need to take the throne back someda—"

"No!" Jade shouted. Her chest ached, and she pressed her palm over her hammering heart. "I'm not a princess. I'm not having anything to do with royalty. I've seen royalty. I've seen what it does." She pointed out the door, her hand shaking as tears streamed down her face. "My best friend got *whipped* because a stupid prince"—she hissed the title—"saw a body he wanted and didn't like being told 'no.' I'm not entering that world. Ever. I'm an airship mechanic! Someday I'll be an airship captain! That's all I am, and that's all I ever want to be."

"Jade, please, sit—" Garnet started, but Jade shook her head.

"No. I'm done. Goodnight." Jade yanked open the door and slammed it shut behind her. She trembled where she stood for a long minute, before fleeing to the one safe place she could still call hers—the engine room.

CHAPTER FORTY

SLATE

Slate stared at the closed door, dazed. "What have we done?"

Garnet curled in on herself, her eyes red-rimmed and puffy as she shook her head. "We did what we had to. We told her the truth."

Slate needed to move, to pace, but his feet didn't step. All his energy had been sapped away, leaving a shell of himself behind. He collapsed in the chair that Jade had been in moments before. "Yes. We told her. But at what cost?"

"We waited too long. And now it's so much harder." Garnet blew her nose and took a shaky breath. "But there's no way we would've been able to keep the secret after this."

"I should've told her sooner. I should've told her from day one." Slate ran his fingers through his hair, catching on knots and pulling, but he welcomed the pain. It was easier to bear than the agony in his heart. "I did this," he whispered. "I was too scared to tell her the truth before, and now I've just ruined everything."

"I doubt you've ruined everything," Garnet tried to soothe. "Your timing was off by several months, at least, but we'll work through this. We always do."

Slate scrubbed his face with his palms, trying to erase the images burned into his mind. Jade's shock. Jaxton's blood. "Whoever killed him was looking for something." He dropped his hands and braced against his knees as he stood. Two long strides brought him to his nightstand, and he pulled out a bottle of mead and two glasses. He plunked them on the table and filled both. "Geist said most of the room had been rummaged through. And Victor will need to replace almost everything in his quarters."

Garnet eyed her glass for a long moment before lifting it to her lips. "Did whoever do this find what he was looking for? Or will he be back?"

Slate felt like his emotions were processing through slushy ice, everything slow and dull. He couldn't panic right now, couldn't process everything sufficiently to think that far ahead. The scent of blood clung to everything, and even now it permeated his sinuses. The message left behind had been written in Jaxton's blood, and what it said had shaken Slate to the core: *I KNOW.*

Know what? Slate's involvement? Jade's identity? Fear iced Slate's spine and he shook his head, numb.

"Jade knows who she is now, so there's that. And now we can do all we can to protect her," he said finally. "We can only hope that changing locations and having a guard or something will be enough."

Garnet's eyebrows drew together. "It's going to have to be."

CHAPTER FORTY-ONE

JADE

Jade finally uncurled from her warm corner on the floor next to the boiler and wiped her eyes.

Princess. Losing Jaxton has snapped them. They've both lost a gear if they think I'm going to believe such a crazy story. She heaved a shaky sigh. It did make sense, though. Her father's insistence on her going to noble balls when an invite was extended to them. Garnet drilling her on manners and etiquette. Zak's changed attitude toward her after last summer when her father warned him off.

The sudden clarity didn't help.

How much of her life would be different if she had been the true daughter of Slate and Samantha Stohner? Would she have had to fight to learn to be a mechanic? Would she have been dragged to and fro across Terrene, learning cultures and how to properly interact with them? Would she have been free to pursue her dream of being an airship captain?

Would Zak find her desirable? Attainable?

I don't want to be a princess.

The trappings of royalty stifled all freedom and creativity. She wanted to be responsible for a crew, not a whole nation! If she were to take on the crown of Doldra, she'd never again be able to stay up all night with Krista, laughing and crying and swearing in the engine room over a failing condenser coil. She wouldn't be able to walk through the fields of Perennia with Briar while he waxed eloquent on his love for herbs and how they made everything so good. She wouldn't be able to walk freely through Lasim, devouring local fare and gawking at the newest potions with Zak.

Instead, she'd be in a gilded cage, never to see the horizon again.

Fresh tears threatened to spill, and Jade scrubbed at them before they could fall. Maybe fresh air would ease the bitter ache that squeezed her heart. She slipped out of the engine room and rushed up the stairs to the main deck, hoping to not run into anyone. At least it would be easy to explain her red eyes and swollen nose. It would be expected after just losing Jaxton.

She shook her head and gripped the wind-chilled safety bar. What had her father—no, uncle—been thinking? Dropping a bomb like that on the same day as a savage murder? Bad enough to lose Jaxton. Worse, to find him. Adding in this news of who she was…

Stars glimmered overhead, and Jade breathed in the cooler air. What would she do now? Did Slate expect her to change what she did? Would she be forced to go into hiding, in case his fears were correct? Would she still be allowed to be a mechanic? Would she have to start something ridiculous, like princess training?

She snorted. *No way.*

"Jade?"

Jade whirled at the sound of Zak's voice, and he emerged from the hallway by the captain's quarters, blocking the doorway to the med-bay. Even in the dim light, she could see him cock a black eyebrow.

"Are you feeling all right? I'm surprised to see you up and about." Zak strode closer and stopped an arm's length away, his hands stuffed in his pockets. "Ben is still unconscious. We're going to try to find Finn in Lucrum to get more experienced help for him." He studied Jade, his gaze lingering on her puffy eyes. "Can't sleep?"

"Did you know?"

Zak furrowed his brow and tilted his head. "Know what?"

"Who I am? That my real name is Adeline?"

Zak froze. He opened his mouth, closed it, then spoke slowly. "I take it they told you, finally?" He shook his head and muttered, "And tonight, of all nights."

She nodded, and he sank against the wall.

He covered his eyes with his hand and dragged it down his face with a heavy sigh. He slitted his eyes open to look at her. "I see."

"Why didn't you say anything?" Jade couldn't help the fresh tears that flooded her vision as she stared up at Zak. "How long have you known?"

He didn't meet her eyes. "I've known you since you were born." Zak's words were pained. His gaze flicked away from her, and his brows knit together. "I was with Garnet when we had to flee the palace." His hands fisted. "I knew when they changed your name, when they created the cover story. I promised to keep that secret safe."

She gaped. *He was there? With me? When the royal family fell in Doldra?*

"And you didn't think to mention to me, 'Hey, Jade, you're not who you think you are'? Or, 'Hey, Jade, you don't need to lay flowers at your own grave'?" Hurt leaked out with every word, and she clutched his arm until his gaze met hers. "Aren't we friends?"

"Of course we're friends." His voice was low, strained, and his broad shoulders hunched over. "I couldn't say anything. It wasn't my place."

"Your place?" Jade scoffed, her body tense, itching to fight. Too much emotion, too much hurt, too many lies. "Is it my place? Is this," she gestured to herself, unable to think of what word could describe her newfound status, "why you can barely look at me these days? Because you have this opinion on who I'm supposed to be?" She whirled away, fighting the tears that sprung to her eyes. She turned and marched back, poking Zak's chest with her index finger. "Your place is as my friend. My friend who doesn't lie to me my entire life!"

Zak's eyes narrowed and he straightened, looming over her. "You are my princess, first and foremost. My place is behind you, to watch your back and protect you. I'm your Guardian."

"I thought you were supposed to be a Guardian of the Barrier." *Like your brother.*

He shook his head. A muscle worked in his jaw, and his adam's apple bobbed as he swallowed. "I'm your Guardian."

Tears slipped down Jade's cheeks and she fisted her hands. "I don't want you to guard me. I want you, as my friend, beside me." She looked down and watched the wood blur. "I want to know I can trust you with…everything. With me."

"Jade." Zak's calloused hand lifted her chin toward him.

She scrubbed at her eyes while trying to even out her breathing. Her lungs ached.

"You can always trust me," he whispered. Regret and sorrow and countless other emotions she couldn't name swam in his eyes. "I'm sorry I couldn't say anything before. Truly."

"Is this what you meant last summer? When you said I was so much more?" Jade tried to hold back her sniffle and failed. A fresh thought occurred to her, and she rocked back on her heels. "Is that why you defended me from Weston? Because I'm a princess?"

Zak's lips had turned up at the edges during her first question, but his shoulders drooped at the accusation in her tone. He pulled an inky blue handkerchief from his pocket and pressed it into her hand, then stepped back with a sigh as she wiped at her eyes and blew her nose. He watched her askance, and enough light spilled from the med-bay that she could see his cheeks color.

"Partially." Zak closed his eyes and ran his hands through his hair, leaving long dark strands askew as he crossed his arms. "I stopped him because you're my princess. I also stopped him because you're my friend. But it's not my place, so—"

"What's not your place?" Jade interrupted. "Don't give me any of that steam about what's anyone's place or not. I've been hearing too much of that excuse." She scuffed her boot against the floor and settled her hands on her hips. She was desperate for answers, desperate to hear him explain, desperate to understand what he was thinking behind those curtained eyes. "Please, if you haven't ever done it before, just this once, look at me and treat me as the person *I* am. Not the title I was born as. Not some princess of a country that I've never called home. Me. Jade. The mechanic. Your friend." Her shoulders sagged, and she dipped her head down, squeezing her eyes shut. This day had dragged on long enough, draining her of all emotional energy. "Please."

Warm arms wrapped around Jade, and her eyes flew open. She returned the hug and rested her cheek against his strong shoulder.

"Forgive me." Zak's words were low, husky. "But you asked. And

I can't refuse."

"Refuse what?" Jade clung to him, unwilling to risk him stepping away. "What I said? That I want you to treat me as me? Whales, Zak, it wasn't an order. It was a request." She leaned back to look up at him, fisted his shirt in her hand, and let the fingers of her other hand skim up his arm.

His eyes softened, and his lips quirked in a half grin that hinted at the mixed emotions hiding within him.

Her tears threatened to overflow for the umpteenth time that evening. Why, oh why, did her heart ache at the simple sweetness of the smile that he aimed at her? It filled her soul to the point of overflowing, and she wasn't strong enough to contain it all.

He tilted his head down, brushing his forehead against hers, his touch soft, hesitant. Then he pressed his lips against hers.

Jade's world flipped upside down. Chemical reactions in the boiler room had nothing on this. Molten energy flowed through her body, leaving her tingling from head to toe, and she gasped against his lips. Then she clutched the back of his head, and pulled him closer.

Zak's hand slid under her loose braids as he crushed her body against his and deepened the kiss. His arm wrapped around her, preventing her from sliding to the floor while her muscles liquefied under the heat of his passion.

Jade's heart hammered, threatening to break out of her ribcage, as they broke apart for air. She tilted her head back to regard him. His eyes blazed even as he offered her a heartbreakingly bittersweet smile.

Zak released her from his hold and gently ran his hand from her neck down to her fingers. She shivered under his touch. He lifted her hand and kissed the back of it, still holding her gaze. "You deserve so much more than me." Zak shook his head with a glance at the captain's quarters and med-bay. "And you deserve better timing for all this." He bowed low and stepped back, regret etched around his eyes. "I'm sorry."

CHAPTER FORTY-TWO

BEN

Ben hugged Sara as they watched the double-wide casket sink into the earth. She turned away, burying her face in his chest, her tears dampening his suit jacket. Tears burned behind his eyes, and he swiped at them with his free hand. The terrorists would pay. Too many funerals were happening this week. Too many families, too many kids, too many parents mourning their loved ones.

No one should fear going to a café for breakfast.

One of the gravediggers approached them. "Do you want to be the first?" He gestured awkwardly with a shovel at the mound of dirt.

Ben shook his head, and the man bowed his head and turned to his partner by the edge of the burial. No, Ben knew what would happen once he let go of his sister. They were both underage and would be separated into different homes.

Sara rubbed her face against his jacket and stepped back, her hands clinging to his. Her smile had dimmed, but the fire in her eyes remained. She squeezed his fingers. "It's only for a few years. We'll find each other. That's what family does."

Ben groaned and shook his head. He reclined on Elinora's couch in her sitting room. A clock ticked on the far wall, and floral and wood scents soothed little of his growing headache. Even though it'd been a week since he'd worn Jaxton's circlet, Ben's head hurt. He blinked his eyes open and wasn't surprised to find Finn sitting in a chair next to him, hand supporting his bearded chin as he watched Ben.

Finn didn't say anything as he leaned back and crossed his arms. Ben struggled to find his words as he processed what he'd seen in his mind. What he remembered. He stared at the white molded ceiling.

"She...she's my sister."

Finn shifted. "Sara?"

"Yes." Ben shifted his gaze to a wood table with a flickering gas lamp. "She's younger than me. Our parents died." His head throbbed as he wrestled with memories that returned in their own time—never in the order that he needed. "From a bomb."

"Good progress, Ben." Finn laid his hand on Ben's shoulder. "It can be difficult suddenly recalling your past, but you're doing well."

"Thanks." Ben clenched his fists and released them slowly. "Have you dealt with memory-loss patients before?"

Finn started plunking lids on metal tins of ointments. "They aren't too rare. How are you handling the change of location?"

Ben closed his eyes again and took a deep breath. He'd agreed with Captain Stohner's reasoning for leaving him in Lucrum for recuperation, but he still felt a pang of loss, even as his memories filled in his past. He missed his bunk on the airship. His friends. It was quiet here at Ellie's. No hissing from the engine room, no rumble of the turbines, no swaying from the wind.

It had scared the entire crew when Ben slept for two solid days after Jaxton's murder. Even Geist, for all his cutting words and snark, seemed concerned. And it didn't make Ben feel any better when his brain started releasing memory after memory, rendering him useless under the onslaught. So when the Sapphire landed in Lucrum, the captain had found Raine's grandfather and asked him to help care for Ben, now that the Sapphire had no doctor and the crew had to finish another mission.

Finn, it turned out, knew something of memory loss.

And now Ben knew he wasn't married. He didn't have to worry about having a wife or kids frantic for him back home. *The ring. It's Mom's. Sara has Dad's.*

But his sister. He could remember her words when he shipped out. *"You'll come home, right?"* He promised he'd return. He couldn't leave her alone. He had to get back. Somehow.

Ben groaned as he dropped his wrist over his eyes. "My head is killing me again."

"I brought water for tea," Raine announced from the doorway, her voice soft.

Ben lifted his arm and twisted his head to watch her. Today mustn't have been a practice day, as she wore an ankle-length dress of swirled blues and greens accented with silver. A delicate bracelet dangled from her toned copper wrist. Her smile held a hint of compassion.

But was she nicer because he had been so out of it, or because she was truly warming up to him?

She set the metal tray on the table by Ben's couch with a quiet *clink*, then she looked up at her grandfather. "Same as before?"

"Yes, please," Finn replied. "And the same dose as before, too." He spoke to Ben, "We'll continue with the same until your headaches ease up."

Ben pulled himself to sit up on the couch with a groan. He squeezed his eyes shut against the light that suddenly seemed too bright for the room. "Sounds great."

Warm fingers wrapped around his as Raine placed the teacup in his hands. She didn't remove her supporting pressure until he gripped the mug securely himself.

"I added a bit of honey this time," Raine said when he opened his eyes. "I know how the medicine can be bitter."

Ben's tongue twisted as the taste of the underlying herbs hit it, but the honey she added did seem to help mask the worst of the flavor. "Thanks."

Finn stood and brushed his hands against the knees of his pants. "I leave you in her care for now, if you don't mind." Humor sparkled in his eyes, and Ben purposefully looked away from the woman sitting next to him. "I found something interesting in the Doctor's notes that Slate left for me, and I need to research it further."

"We'll be fine," Raine replied with a sunny smile at her grandfather. "Madame Stohner said dinner will be ready soon, so I'll follow you home shortly."

Ben stared at his hands after Finn left. He really couldn't deny that Raine had warmed up to him over the last two days, and he didn't want to ruin their tentative friendship by saying something wrong.

"You seem to be improving," Raine observed after a spell of silence.

Ben nodded and swallowed. "I am. Better. Much better. Yes." He sighed and closed his eyes again, frustrated. What was it about this woman that made him so tongue-tied now? He'd shamelessly flirted with her the first time he saw her. Somehow insulted her the second time. And now that his memory was returning, he could barely speak to her in coherent sentences or look her in the eye.

Raine leaned back into the golden couch and carefully pulled a leg up under her skirt to rest her chin on her knee. She smoothed the draped fabric as she looked at him out of the corner of her eye. "You've changed," she said. "Is it because of your memories?"

Ben shrugged halfheartedly. "I suppose."

Raine dropped her leg and twisted on the couch to fully face him. Her black eyes glittered as she frowned at him. "I can't believe I'm asking this, but do you want to talk about it?"

He snorted and raised a hand to belay the affront building in her face. "I'm sorry. But considering how I've managed to muck up the last two conversations I've had with you, I doubt I could."

She said nothing, and Ben hastened to explain. "It's not that I don't want to talk about it. I just don't know how." He set the empty porcelain cup on the tray and sank back against the couch. He stared at his hands and rubbed his fingers together, remembering the gritty feel of dust on them. "It's weird. The memories, I mean. Some of them make sense. Some of them don't, and it feels as if I'm missing a key that explains what it all means. Everything seems so different, and it almost feels like I've gone crazy. Like, what I'm remembering has to be some fever dream, or what I'm experiencing now is a dream."

Raine pressed her lips together as she absorbed his words. She nodded finally, and cleaned up the small tray before standing. She looked down at him, effortlessly balancing the platter on one hand. "I think it was very wise of your captain to leave you here in Papa's care."

"Probably." Ben wrinkled his brow. "I feel like there's something I was supposed to warn the crew about—something bad—and it's driving me crazy."

"Do you remember anything of Jaxton's death yet?"

"Just blood and screaming." Ben shook his head with a groan. "Last thing I really remember is not being able to move, then my mind goes blank, with just hazy memory of sensation and sound."

Raine propped her fist on her hip and offered a gentle half smile. "You'll remember soon enough. Don't worry."

"Right." Ben allowed himself to slouch over on the couch, his legs claiming where she'd sat just moments before. He dropped his hand over his eyes again, blocking out her sympathetic eyes and the still-too-bright room. "Hopefully I'll start remembering without it being triggered by someone's death this time."

CHAPTER FORTY-THREE

BLADE

Blade paced on the deck of his airship, ignoring the wind that whipped the tail of his hair to and fro. He looked back at his helmsman and the man nodded fervently.

"We're still following them, sir." The freckled man motioned to his glass-encased map and shining bronze compass. "They're on a direct course to High Doldra. I'd wager that's their destination."

The speck on the horizon was almost impossible to see without his monocle, but he was content to trust Tanin for now. Maybe Slate believed he could do something with the barrier there. Again. Blade snorted.

For now, there was nothing else to do while they waited to catch up to the mighty Slate Stohner's airship. And once they caught up . . .

Blade breathed deeply and loosened his fingers from their grip on his sword handle. If only he hadn't dispatched Jaxton as quickly as he had. Maybe then his bloodlust would be satiated. But no, he'd had to kill that vile excuse for a doctor quickly, and now he regretted that mercifully fast ending.

Before he boarded Slate's airship to scout, he'd spent the morning finding more mercenaries to fill out his crew. The few men under

Blade's leadership from Kadar's group grumbled and complained that he had gone aboard the *Sapphire* without them, but that wasn't Blade's problem. Coupled with the chaos that unfolded after Jaxton's body was found—and the warning that Blade had given the young man in Jaxton's clutches—Blade had declared that they wait. And that time of waiting drew near the end.

Soon, very soon, they'd have what they wanted, and Blade would have the revenge he craved. And, as luck would have it, it would be where it all began. In Doldra.

CHAPTER FORTY-FOUR

JADE

So that's why it's been making that sound lately, Jade thought as she stared up under the dash of the skiff she hid in. She reached up into the mess of wires and tugged on the loose coil. *I'll have to fix that later.*

Everyone onboard the *Sapphire* carried on through their traveling with a grim, dolorous air. Despite the guys' best efforts to clean the med-room, they ended up opening the tiny outside window and locking the door, as the overpowering stench of the blood-soaked wood worsened with the heat of each day. They would need to gut and replace the room as soon as possible. In the meantime, all the medical supplies had been relocated to the mess, which forced everyone to eat meals on the main deck.

Eating outside wasn't a problem to Jade, but the reason for the necessity of it was. Losing Doctor Taylor in such a brutal fashion hurt. And having to leave Ben behind to recuperate from his trauma only worsened the ache.

Her heart still stung with betrayal. Her whole family. Zak. How could they not tell her? How could they sit on that secret for so long, lying to her face? Jade swiped angrily at a tear that trickled from her eye. Even if what they said was true, and her parents were Brandon and

Sapphire Doldras, it didn't matter. Not really. Slate and Samantha were the ones who'd raised her, encouraged her, corrected her, and loved on her. They were her parents—even if she wanted to throttle them both for keeping such a secret.

"I found you." Krista peered over the edge of the skiff. "You're done hiding, missy." Krista swung her legs over the edge and clambered onto the bench seat, wiggling onto her side to look down at Jade, who was wedged in the footwell. "It's time you vent all the steam you've got stored up in that head of yours. Something is up, and you can't deny it anymore."

Jade licked her lips and looked away, shaking her head. "I can't."

"Yes, you can." Krista sighed. "Whatever is going on is eating you alive. And I know it isn't just…Jaxton." Krista's voice dropped, and her fingers skimmed over Jade's hair. "Zak has been brooding worse than when Weston kissed you, your father and aunt can barely eat, and I swear you've lost at least five pounds. What's going on?"

Void take the persistence that Krista had. Jade brushed away another tear and squirmed out of the cramped spot to sit next to her friend. "Nothing. Everything." Jade dropped her head to Krista's shoulder and groaned. "I'm so confused."

Krista offered a coy smile. "Good news is that Briar has Zak up in the galley, so I know we won't be disturbed."

Jade's stomach shuddered. "He's not letting Zak spice the food tonight, is he?"

"Whales, no!" Krista laughed. "Zak's helping with the dishes. That's all. Briar knows better than to let Zak do anything with food that the rest of us will be eating."

"Oh, good." Jade settled back against the hard cushion and

perched her boots on the dash. She tapped the pointed toes together, fidgeting. "Slate's not my father."

A full three heartbeats passed before Krista exploded. "What? What do you mean? Vent everything. Now."

Once Jade started, she couldn't stop. Words tumbling over themselves, Jade shared the conversation between her and Slate and Garnet, then her encounter with Zak. She paused and lifted her fingers to her lips that tingled at the memory. "He kissed me."

Krista whooped. "It's about time!"

Jade shook her head, and another tear fell. "He kept saying that it wasn't his place." She wrapped a loose thread from the knee of her pant leg around her finger. "He apologized for kissing me. He said that even if we want to be together, we can't."

"Why? Because you're a princess?" Krista's eyes blazed. "The Void with that! I know that there are heaps of responsibilities if you take on the crown, but you haven't been raised in the palace. You're a mechanic. You belong here. On the *Sapphire*." Krista paused, and her eyes widened. "Oh, that's awkward. The ship is named after your mother, isn't it?"

"My mother is Samantha!" Jade snapped. She buried her face in her hands. "Maybe I'll come to think of Sapphire as my mother someday, but she wasn't the one who fought for me to be allowed to wear mechanic pants, showed me how to make flower crowns, or taught me what it means to be a woman."

"Fair enough," Krista murmured. She pulled a strand of her black hair out, and then let go, letting it bounce by her face. Her fingers roamed the hem of her azure shirt. "Have you talked to Zak since then?"

"No," Jade moaned. "I can't. What am I going to say?"

"That as his princess, you order him to set aside all perceived proprietary and treat you as you want." Krista replied promptly. She shook her head with a small frown. "Honestly, I don't know. But you need to talk to him before we get to Doldra."

Jade glared at the control board of the skiff and tucked her hands under her legs. "I know. But it's not like I'll be going to the citadel with them or anything. I can talk to Zak while we wait for everyone to get back. I don't have to be on speaking terms with him right now."

Krista shifted, and the skiff rocked with her movement. "And if something bad happens? What if Zak has to deal with Mister Tight Gears and it puts him in an even worse funk? Do you want to risk not having things cleared between you two, and the tensions being even higher?" Krista played with a loose curl as she speculated. "You should also talk with your father." She paused and frowned. "Your uncle. Captain Slate. What are you going to call him now, anyway?"

"Father." Jade sighed as her eyes traced the scratched coloration of the skiff. "It's all he's been to me, and I'm not changing that now."

Krista nodded slowly. "Well, you should talk to him, too." She cocked her head. "How does this affect our plans?"

"I don't know." Jade moaned. She pulled her legs up and set her chin on her knee. "I want to get away from here even more now." Her lips tingled, and she brushed them against her wrist as heat rose in her cheeks. "I...I also want to stay and try to convince Zak that me being a princess means nothing. And I want to see Father succeed with the keystone."

"Sounds like we have our plan then," Krista replied easily. She waved her hand about airily. "First, we'll go to Doldra as planned, wait for Slate to finish his mission there. If you've successfully convinced Zak that you're not some princess wrapped in gauze, we'll stay longer. Otherwise we'll bail in Doldra and look for another airship." She shrugged. "Simple."

"Hm." Jade mulled on Krista's words for a few minutes. "I guess that works."

"But," Krista held out a finger and waggled it by Jade's face. "This means you need to talk to Zak sooner than Doldra. And not just about your princessness. To use Briar's word, *communicate*. And make sure that things are good between you and your father. Especially if we do end up leaving."

Jade fell silent. After all that had happened recently, her father would likely drink himself sick if she left. But what choice did she have now? She couldn't stay and become a princess.

"He's going to hate me for leaving."

"Who? Zak? Your father?" Krista wrapped an arm around Jade and tugged her over for a hug. "No, they won't. They may be mad or hurt, but they'll get over it. They both love you, each in their own way. And they'll only be perturbed if we leave. Who knows? Maybe Zak will have a change of heart, and your father will lighten up."

Jade snorted. "Unlikely."

Krista bobbed her head side to side with a crooked grin. "Stranger things have happened." She shifted and rubbed her thumb over a stain on the dash. "I'm just worried something's going to go wrong once we go to fix the keystone."

"What could go wrong?" Jade raised her eyebrows, skeptical. "All they're going to do is go in and stabilize the barrier. We even have Lord Everett's approval and everything."

Krista shot her an odd look. "I don't know if you've had a sudden change of heart or something, but I don't trust Lord Everett."

Jade fell silent as she recalled Everett watching Zak's flogging, satisfaction in his cold eyes. "Good point."

"Of course it is," Krista smirked. "I made it, didn't I?"

Jade's heart lifted at Krista's snark. What would she do without Krista? She was as close as a sister—a sassy, crazy, spunky sister, who gave solid advice when needed, and knew how to push all Jade's buttons for good or bad. Jade nudged her friend with a laugh. "Are you ready to be back in Doldra, regardless?"

Krista wrapped her bare arms around her legs with a smile. "As ready as can be. It'll be good to get off this ship for a few days."

Her words reminded Jade of a fear that had been lurking since they left Lucrum. "What if whoever killed Jaxton is following us? What if he kills again?"

"Zak won't let anything happen to you."

The image of Zak's bloody back melded with the memory of Jaxton's hacked corpse, and Jade choked on the bile in her throat. "What if he gets Zak? Or you? Or Briar?" She pressed her hands against her head, pushing her red hair flat. "What if he prevents us from fixing the keystone? What if he wants to take it down or something? What if—"

Krista pressed a hand against Jade's mouth and shook her head, eyes fierce. "No more what ifs. We don't know the future, and you worrying about it isn't going to help anything. You'll make yourself sick."

"I already can't sleep," Jade confessed. "Every time I close my eyes, I see Jaxton and blood and Ben."

Concern clouded Krista's brown eyes. "Talk to Zak. He's lived through bad stuff, and he *sleeps*." She dipped her head to the side and frowned, studying Jade. "I'm sure he can help you."

Jade shot her friend a mild glare. "You just want me to talk to Zak."

Krista shrugged. "Guilty as charged. It's for the betterment of both of you. Seriously." She rested a hand on Jade's shoulder. "And being a princess? That's up to you. They can't force you to be someone you don't want to be."

Jade hugged Krista. "Thanks." She scrubbed her face with her sleeve. "What do you say we go see what trouble Zak has caused in the galley?"

"Sounds like a great start." Krista grinned and climbed out of the skiff, then bowed dramatically. "After you, your mechanic-ness."

CHAPTER FORTY-FIVE

BEN

Blood sprayed in time with Laurent's pulse despite the pressure Ben had on his friend's leg. Ben pressed down with one hand and gripped Laurent's chin with the other, leaving bloody streaks across Laurent's rapidly paling face. "Don't close your eyes, soldier. You stay with me, you hear? You can't get married if you're sleeping on the job."

A faint smile twitched Laurent's lips as he stared at the crumbling cement ceiling overhead. "Tell her I'm sorry."

Frustration clouded Ben's vision while grief punched him in the gut, and he shook his head. "You tell her yourself. You're gonna have one hell of a scar for your honeymoon."

Sous-lieutenant Pelletier skidded into the room and thrust a wadded-up jacket at Ben. Pelletier's head bandage covered one of his eyes, and his toss missed. He scrambled after it and handed it to Ben with a muttered apology. "We've radioed for reinforcements, but—"

A boom shook the building they were sequestered in, and concrete dust floated through the air, choking both of them. The sound of steady gunfire from their sergeant's rifle reverberated through the room, and Ben clenched his teeth. There was no way they'd be able to move Laurent from here. He glanced down at his quiet patient and swore.

Laurent's glassy eyes stared into nothing.

Pelletier braced a hand against Ben's shoulder and cursed. "They're picking us off like flies."

Ben pushed away from the improvised medical table and hobbled out to where the rest of his section sheltered from the onslaught of the terrorists. Only eight of their original twelve survived, and all of them were wounded. He crouched, as best as he could with his injured leg, next to Sergeant Thomas and waited for him to pause and reload. "Reinforcements?"

Their leader shook his head with a blistering oath. "Not close enough. We have to hold out on our own." He looked back at the side room. "Laurent?"

"Gone, sir."

The blond man swore again and raised his rifle. "They're going to regret that."

"Grenade!"

Ben reacted first. He threw himself at the orb arcing through the air and prayed he'd be in time to save his brothers-in-arms.

Blood sprayed into his face at the same time as curses and shouts from his section abruptly cut off. Then purple. Wavering wisps of purple, black, and green danced through his mind. Finally, black swallowed him.

A different blond man, splattered with blood, stood before him. "Leave, or you risk death." The stranger yanked on the circlet enslaving Ben. "Anyone left on this ship will meet a similar fate as him. I'll give you a day to recover."

"…a day to recover."

Ben woke with a yell and fell out of bed. Landing on his hands and knees. He untangled himself from the sweat-soaked sheets and leaned against the bedframe, his muscles trembling. His hands were clean, utterly devoid of the stain of blood. He tugged his pants leg, revealing a small pink scar—no bleeding bullet wound. He staggered to his feet and stumbled to the washbasin in his borrowed bedroom. He looked into the mirror. Wild blue eyes stared at him from beneath his unkempt hair. And his scruffy red beard begged to be trimmed.

He sank his head against the mirror with a shaky sigh. It was a dream. He frowned and shook his head. No, that was a memory.

Sorrow bowed his shoulders. Now he knew what had happened to Laurent.

"Leave, or you risk death. Anyone left on this airship will meet a similar fate as him."

Bitter bile rose in Ben's throat at the memory of what happened to Jaxton, and he swallowed hard. He turned away and snatched a sky blue shirt from a hanger and shoved his arms through the sleeves. His hands trembled as he buttoned it, his head whirling with gory memories. He yanked on his boots. Then he combed through his hair with his fingers as he clattered down the wood stairs into Elinora's dining room.

Elinora looked up with a welcoming smile. "Good morning." She set aside the newspaper she'd been reading and gracefully stood, keeping her fingers on the sunshine-yellow tablecloth. "What can I get you for breakfast?"

"Uh." He spied the slice of bread and link of sausage on her plate. "Whatever you're having is fine. Thank you." He sat at the table and worked to calm his racing heart while she gathered the simple meal together in the adjoining kitchen.

It wasn't just a dream. It had been a memory. Or was it a memory and a dream combined? Should he be panicking right now?

She slid a plate piled with twice as much food as hers in front of him and rested her hand on his arm. Her forehead wrinkled as she looked down at him. "Your head hurting again? Finn said he'd be by this morning, and we can get you more of that medicinal tea."

Ben took a ragged breath and tried to banish the visions that his mind supplied him with: blood, disembodied limbs, and the screams of his dying friends. "Thank you," he rasped.

She hummed in reply and returned to her seat, only to get up a moment later when the doorbell whistled. Ellie straightened the tiny hat nestled in her silvery-brown curls and left the elegant room.

Ben slouched and stared at the steaming food in front of him. Appetizing though the smell was, the idea of eating caused his stomach to churn in rebellion. How had he survived that grenade? How did he get *here*?

"Madame Stohner says you need more tea," Raine spoke as she passed through the dining room and into the kitchen. She had yet to ever greet him with a simple "hello." Raine flicked her long hair over her shoulder, lit a fire on the stove, and set a tea kettle over the grate. She turned to face him, and her eyebrows shot up. "Rough night?"

Ben nodded and bit into his bread. It tasted of sawdust and ash. The second bite reminded him of MREs, and the third tasted like sweet bread with melted butter.

Finn entered, talking to Ellie in serious tones, and squeezed Ben's shoulder in silent greeting as he walked around the table to sit. Dark puffy circles under his eyes and a wrinkled tan shirt from the previous day indicated that Finn had had a difficult start to his day as well.

"Elinora, do you have any jav? I could really use some right now."
Finn tapped his hand against the sheath of papers he'd brought in. "I've
been looking over the notes, scrolls, and documents salvaged from
Doctor Taylor's office, and, to be perfectly honest, I'm concerned."

Ellie pulled a metal jar down from a cupboard and set it by the tea
pot, then looked over her shoulder. "How so?" She grabbed a teacup
and leaned her forearms against the counter to look under the ceiling-
mounted cupboards into the dining room. "What did you find?"

Raine set a mug of tea in front of Ben, slid a jar of honey over,
then settled into a chair next to her grandfather.

Finn shuffled the papers and pulled one out. "Did you know
Jaxton was looking into the barrier and Void magic?"

"Oh, that?" Ellie smiled and moved away to fix Finn's drink. She
returned to the table a moment later with a mug of something that
smelled even more bitter than Ben's tea. The chair made no sound as
she pulled it out and sat down. "Slate has been searching for a way
to restore the Doldran keystone to full functionality, and Jaxton had
helped with the research. They found the artifact they needed on a
recent mission."

Lines creased Finn's brow like a freshly plowed field. "What
artifact?"

Elinora shrugged. "A stone."

"A black-and-red stone?" Ben spoke into his mug of tea. He lifted
his face to look at Finn. "That's the mission that they're on while I'm
here with you."

Tea sloshed out of Finn's trembling cup. He hastily set the drink
down and patted a napkin on the damp tablecloth. Color drained
from his face until it matched his shirt. "A bloodstone?" He pressed

a hand against his papers. "They can't! Why would they think that would *help*?" Panic imbued his voice, and Raine put her hand on his arm with a disquieted frown.

Ellie settled her fork on her plate and wiped her fingers on a linen napkin. "Doctor Taylor and the royal manipulators assured Slate and the crew that it would work."

Finn gaped. "How could that be?" He gestured at a flattened scroll. "This here very clearly describes that a bloodstone would take down a keystone. Not restore it!"

"That's not the scroll Jaxton sent to the palace with the captain. It—" Ben stopped as Finn slid the scroll to him across the table. Ben traced the lettering, and his voice grew quiet. "It looked exactly like this."

"A forgery." Finn rubbed his forehead. "Jaxton gave the palace a forgery? This is an original." His lips pursed. "I know for a fact that this is the real scroll. Please, don't ask how I know."

Ben looked up from the letter. "Why would he give the palace a forgery?" The memory of Jaxton asking inane questions about the Void rose to the forefront of Ben's mind. There had been something off about the doctor for the last few weeks. But would he have really lied about something so important?

"Your guess is as good as mine."

Ben studied Finn. The older man hadn't changed his posture, but his expression had smoothed to be purposefully bland, and he met Ben's gaze with a steady eye. Finn leaned back and drummed his fingers against the table.

Ellie wove her fingers together and settled her chin on them. "What about the stone they have?"

"We need to know if it was a bloodstone or not." Finn pulled a clean piece of paper from his pile and pulled a pen out of his pocket. He scrawled a message and folded it twice, then he handed it to Elinora. "Please deliver this to the palace as quickly as possible. I need an answer from them immediately to know how to proceed. And arrange the fastest possible passage to Doldra for me. I need to run home and prepare a few things—in case this is what I fear."

Ellie tossed the letter on the table in front of Ben. "I'll take care of the travel arrangements. Samantha should be arriving within the hour, and I can rearrange her schedule for this. Ben has been to the palace before; he can take the letter."

Ben stood and slipped the paper into his pocket, his head feeling remarkably clearer. "I'll go right away."

"Not dressed like that, you're not!" Raine exclaimed. She pushed away from the table and marched past him. "If you're going to the palace, you need to be presentable. We need them to take you seriously." She tucked a strand of raven hair behind her ear as she eyed what Ben wore. "I'll be right back. Stay here." She paused, her boot on the first step, and turned. "Either trim your beard or go shave it while I find something suitable."

Finn nodded. "Go to the palace and find the queen or someone who can answer this." Fire burned in Finn's eyes. "And do not dawdle."

Ben straightened the jacket Raine had thrown over his shirt and skimmed his fingers over the watch chain that she'd tucked into his pocket before he'd rushed out the door. She'd warned him to not lose her watch and that she'd personally end him if he did. His small smile of amusement slipped away as the guards pulled open the massive doors on silent hinges. His boots echoed eerily in the grand hall.

He couldn't afford to mess this up. Not if everything he understood of this world was true. He clenched his jaw as he looked around the stark entryway. The guard had told him that someone would be with him soon, but who?

"What are you doing here?"

Ben turned to the voice to the side of him and had to remember to bow. *Good thing Jade isn't here.* "Prince Weston. Good morning."

Weston frowned and crossed his arms over his silver-embroidered black jacket. He raised a black eyebrow and exaggerated looking around Ben. "Here by yourself?" His eyes narrowed. "What do you want?"

Ben set his shoulders and clasped his hands behind his back. "I need to speak with the queen on behalf of Madame Elinora Stohner."

"Mother just left for a trip to Perennia."

Taken aback, Ben quickly thought over his options. What he'd heard of Lord Everett suggested that the man would be even less helpful than his son. Ben eyed Weston. "I need to talk to Andre, then. It's urgent."

Weston tapped his foot against the tile while he studied Ben. He nodded once. "Andre's likely in his chambers right now." He crossed the vast entry and paused in a hallway. "Are you coming?"

Ben followed the prince through the palace's twists and turns with long strides. Silence stretched between them, despite the side glances that Ben could feel from Weston.

Finally, Weston spoke. "How is Jade?"

"She's fine."

Weston brushed a short, dark curl off his jacket shoulder. "What did she think of the steam-pistol?"

"She gave it to me."

Weston's shoulders sagged, and Ben decided to give the man a crumb. "We discovered I have more skill at it than her."

"I'll have to design something that fits her better." Weston stopped at a closed door that matched all the other white doors in the hallway. He rapped his knuckles against it, and they waited.

Andre opened the door, and only the slight twitch in his brow showed his surprise. He bowed at the waist and pressed his palms against his regal, deep blue coat. "Your Highness." He nodded to Ben. "What can I do for you?"

Weston gestured to Ben. "He wanted to speak with my mother."

Ben nodded. "I have an urgent request from Madame Stohner and a friend." He stepped forward. "If I may speak with you in private?"

Weston cocked his head with a severe frown. "What can't you say in front of me?"

Ben floundered for words for a long heartbeat. He shrugged. "I don't want to betray the confidence of Madame Stohner. That's all."

Andre motioned for Ben to enter the spacious two-chamber room, and he bowed again at the prince. "I'm sure this won't take long, Your Highness."

Ben walked into the room and stood in the center of a plush burgundy carpet with golden-yellow designs woven in.

Andre closed and locked the door, then faced Ben, his eyes sharp. "What happened?"

Ben pulled the note from his jacket pocket, handed it to Andre, and started explaining as Andre's eyes skimmed over the message.

"If it's a bloodstone, as Finn fears, apparently it could take down the entire barrier. Do you know of it, by any chance?"

Alarm flashed in Andre's blue eyes as he crumpled the note in his hand with an oath. "They have a bloodstone. I'm sure of it." He looked at Ben. "You have to get a message to them as quickly as possible, before it's too late. The Quee—"

Andre's door reverberated with the pounding of fists. "Andre Catalina! Open this door, in the name of Lord Everett!"

Ben stumbled as Andre shoved him toward the four-poster bed. "Hide under there. Stay down and don't say anything, no matter what."

Ben scrambled under the bed as best as his stocky frame would allow and held his breath as Andre adjusted the burgundy bed skirt.

Andre opened the door. Ben could just barely see through the fabric. At least six guards clattered in and surrounded Andre, followed by a shining pair of black boots that stood nearly toe-to-toe with him.

"Do you know why I'm here?" A voice asked with icy anger.

Andre's voice was calm, betraying no hint of his earlier agitation from Ben's news. "No, Your Majesty."

"You are under arrest for treason against the crown of Aerugo."

"On what charges?" Concern colored Andre's tone, but he didn't sound surprised—more resigned.

Ben took in shallow sips of air, unable to breathe deeply, wedged between the cold tile and the sharp wood bed frame. He inched forward, trying to see better.

"On account of hiding that you knew the Doldran princess, Adeline, was alive." The shiny boots stalked away from Andre, pivoted, and then returned. "How dare you hide that threat against the throne? My throne?"

Andre didn't answer. After a moment of silence, he said, "How did you find out?"

"I had an inside source on the *Sapphire*. I can't believe you, parading her through my palace, under my nose, calling her your family." A wad of spit landed on the floor near Ben's hiding spot. "I'm done with your mockery."

"Jade doesn't even know who she is."

Shock rippled through Ben at Andre's words. Jade? A princess? He tried to imagine the fiery mechanic in an elegant dress and tiara, but he couldn't.

Lord Everett spoke again. "Whether she knows or not is not my concern."

"What are you going to do about her?" Andre asked, a dangerous edge to his voice.

The malice in Lord Everett's tone sent a chill down Ben's spine. "As far as I'm concerned, Adeline Doldras has been dead for the last nineteen years. I see no reason for that to change." Ben jerked up, and his head bumped the wood slats. *No!* Someone snapped their finger, covering the sound. "Take him away."

Ben waited for a full two minutes after the group left the room to settle his breathing and crawl out from under Andre's bed. He stared at the closed door and wracked his brain. What should he do now? Jade—*a princess!*—was in danger. There was a traitor on the *Sapphire*. And the crew that had taken him in was about to inadvertently take *down* the barrier! That couldn't happen.

He had to escape Aerugo and get to Doldra. He paced on the rug. How was he going to get out now? If Lord Everett discovered that

Ben had overheard everything, it wouldn't go well. And the timing of Andre's arrest. Did Weston have something to do with it?

Ben dismissed the thought as quickly as it came. If Weston had been involved, they would have searched the room for him as well. Nothing in the conversation hinted that the guards or Everett knew Ben was there.

"Ben."

Ben whirled and dropped to a fighting crouch at the unexpected voice. A bookshelf swung open, revealing a dark hallway and Weston leaning against the framework. Weston's warm brown skin tone had faded to an ashen hue, and he swallowed hard. He pressed his hand against his stomach.

"I…I was angry, and I eavesdropped on you and Andre, and—" Weston gulped in a lungful of air and shook his head. "I wasn't expecting that." His gaze dropped to the floor, and he closed his eyes. "She's the princess. He was protecting the *princess*."

"I need to get out of here," Ben interrupted. The prince could have his meltdown of revelations later. Ben had to get back to Ellie's.

The *Sapphire* crew had a bloodstone.

Weston pulled himself upright with a weak nod. His jaw set and he nodded again, firmly, eyes hard. "I'll get you out."

CHAPTER FORTY-SIX

SLATE

Slate peered over the railing as Victor steered the *Sapphire* to her assigned berth on the edge of Doldra. They were here. After years of searching, years of haunted memories, and years of regret, he finally had a chance to redeem some of his actions. He wouldn't be able to bring back any of those who had died, but he'd be able to honor the memory of one who gave his life in defense of the barrier.

And now that Jade knew her own past, maybe he could honor Brandon and Sapphire's legacy by bringing his niece to the throne she deserved. Let a Doldran rule, not a sniveling governor sent by Aerugo.

A flash of red hair caught his eye, and he turned to see Jade approaching, the set in her jaw so similar to the way his little sister—her mother—had looked when she was about to battle. The similarities ended there, however. Today Jade must have searched for her grungiest pair of mechanic pants, and she'd donned a loose Vodan blouse paired with a leather waist-cincher. She couldn't have looked further from a proper princess if she tried.

"Interesting outfit," he finally commented.

Jade shrugged with a disinterested air. "Thanks." She joined him at the railing and gripped it, her eyes slowly welling with tears.

"This land is beautiful, but it isn't my home. My home is here, on the *Sapphire* with you, or on the *Phoenix* with my *mother*."

Her emphasis wasn't lost on Slate, and he hugged her as his heart cracked for what had to be the third time that morning. "As much as I appreciate that sentiment, your place isn't here, dearest." She stiffened and pulled back, and Slate gestured over the rail, to the barely visible palace in the distance. "You deserve to be there. Leading our people, enjoying the luxuries that you were born into." He swiped his thumb against the grease on her jaw and met her pained gaze. "Doldra needs her own strong ruler. Queen Violet will step aside when you're ready."

Jade's jaw dropped. "Sh-she knows?"

Slate offered a small, sad smile. "She's a very astute woman. If she doesn't already know, she suspects it. And I know for a fact that she's not fond of how Everett has taken over as ruler of Doldra."

"But I don't want to be a queen." Jade turned away and pointed to Victor's back. "I want to work my way up and be a first mate, eventually a captain. I want to be free of politics, free of entitled rulers, free of impractical dresses and stupid formal events."

"I know." Slate rested his hands lightly on her shoulders. "Once this is all over, and the keystone is fully restored, we'll talk. I want to honor your desires, and I also want to honor what your parents would have wanted. I promise I'll do my best to find a balance of some sort for you."

Jade lurched forward and squeezed his middle, using the palm of her hand to wipe at her eyes. "Go, do your protecting-the-world mission."

Slate dropped a kiss on the crown of her head. "I love you."

Jade stretched to her toes to kiss his cheek. "I love you, too, Father."

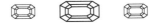

Slate billowed his shirt and used his hat to fan his face. He stopped in the shade of a tree, and Victor sighed next to him. Summer humidity had a wonderful way of taking away the pleasure of such beautiful, lush vegetation. Slate settled his hands on his hips as he surveyed the Doldran palace. White-washed walls towered above a new wrought iron gate, and though Slate couldn't see the garden around the side, he smelled the sweet fragrance of flowers. His nose twitched.

"Let's get the unpleasantries over with." Slate nudged his first mate, and they walked abreast of each other into the main entry of the palace. Gold embroidery shimmered in the red-and-gray Doldran tapestries that hung side by side with the Aerugan black and blue, and the gleaming white tile had to be new, but the foyer itself was the same. Slate's steps stuttered and he halted, overwhelmed with memories: digging through the dead piled in here, finding remnants of Clara, returning to Sapphire's body upstairs.

Victor looked over his shoulder, a black eyebrow raised. "You feeling ill, Captain?"

Slate took in a shallow sip of air and shook his head, willing away the bloody images haunting him. *I'm here to right my wrongs.* "I'll be fine. Let's see how quickly they can announce us."

More Aerugan tapestries hung in the narrow hallway leading to the throne, and Slate's lip curled in distaste. Aerugan governor or not, the Doldran palace should have only the Doldran colors—not some other kingdom's. They met Bentley's right-hand man, Nevin, outside the main chamber's doors and waited to be announced.

Slate had to fight the urge to pace. Nervous energy bled off him.

The memories, the mission, the changes—it was proving to be too much. He distracted himself as best he could with watching Victor talk to Nevin. The two chatted briefly, and Victor pulled something from his coat and handed it to the overseer. Nevin peered at it through his monocle and tapped it against his hand before nodding to Victor, then he slipped into the throne room.

Just as Victor returned within speaking distance of Slate, a guard pushed open the double doors, and Slate swallowed his question. He opted instead to give Victor a quizzical glance as they strode through the long, spacious room. Time hadn't dimmed the luminary crystals embedded in the floor, and the gleaming white marble pillars appeared just as majestic as Slate remembered. It wasn't until his gaze fell on the black-and-blue tapestry hanging over the solo throne that his mind snapped back to the current time.

Governor Ethan Bentley perched in the burnished chair like a dactyl sensing fresh prey. His cobalt blue suit made his shining blue eyes appear even more piercing. He drummed his fingers against the arm of the throne as he cocked his head at Slate. "It's been a long time, Captain Stohner." He looked to Victor. "And you are?"

Slate dipped his chin in a deferential nod. "This is my first mate, Victor Kalende. We bring tidings from Lord Everett in regards to the keystone and barrier."

"Oh?" Bentley stilled his hand, and his shoulders raised. "Tell me."

"First, I have this letter from Lord Everett." Slate waited until Bentley gestured, and then Slate handed the letter to Victor, who ascended the three steps to the dais to hand the missive over. "Then I need to discuss the details and logistics of such news."

A guard handed Bentley a small blade to break the blue wax seal on the letter. He skimmed the contents quickly and hummed lightly at the end. He set the letter on a small table next to him and leaned back, steepling his fingers. "Fascinating. So you believe this stone will answer our problems, do you?"

"Our mani-med studied all that we found, and Lord Everett's mani-meds agree, so yes. Yes, I do believe this stone will solve our problems." Slate pressed his lips together as he studied Bentley's impassive face. *Why doesn't he seem surprised, or excited at the prospect of strengthening the barrier?*

Bentley settled his ankle over his knee and returned to tapping the arm rest. "Well then, you'll want to go when the keystone is most stable." He waited for Slate and Victor to nod before continuing. "We've discovered that the time flux at the citadel worsens at night. Theoretically, because of the time that the initial damage occurred. If you were to just waltz over, you may just lose an hour or more in a bubble of time." He raised his eyebrows. "Thus, tomorrow morning will be your soonest opportunity to go. I'll look into the guards' schedules and arrange an escort for your team." He tapped his fingers against the arm of his chair, while waving a hand at the letter from Lord Everett. "I assume that you'll have your own team going in?"

"Yes, sir." Fierce hope rose in Slate's chest. Bentley was being even more cooperative than he'd dared to dream. "What time should we be back in the morning?"

Bentley quirked his lips and stroked his thin moustache. "The keystone is at its most peaceful state and time flows most normally around seven in the morning. Come to the palace here by five-thirty, and you'll be escorted to the citadel."

Slate and Victor both offered shallow bows. "Thank you, sir," Slate said.

They spent the walk back to the *Sapphire* in silence. Slate remained absorbed in his own thoughts and memories: playing with Garnet and Sapphire in the City Circle, long before it had grown into a bustling location for shops and markets. Staggering to the Crimson Hawk, covered in blood after the fall of the Doldras family. Strolling through the streets with Samantha and Jade, caught up in the lie of being a real family. And tomorrow he would return to the citadel and keystone, and repair the damage he'd done.

Victor was just as quiet, his dark eyes hooded and pensive, focused on the road ahead of them. The red rays of the setting sun glinted off his shaved head as they entered the Stohner Shipping Yard.

First things first. Slate searched the grounds until he finally found Zak, who was blending in with the shadows where he perched on the cross beams of one of Ellie's storage sheds. A small smirk crossed Slate's lips. *Zane always preferred being on the ground, but Zak was always as high as he could be.* "Zak, I need to talk to you."

Zak slipped away the blade he'd been idly twirling in his hands. He gripped a beam and swung to a narrow ledge, paused there a heartbeat, then jumped toward the brick wall, kicked off it, and landed before Slate. A hint of the little boy that Slate once knew shone through when Zak grinned. He dusted off his pants as he looked up at Slate. "What can I do for you, sir?"

"I need to borrow that ring that Zane had me give you."

Humor faded from Zak's green eyes, and he wiggled an inky-black ring out from under his fingerless sable gloves. He clenched it in his fist before holding his hand open for Slate to take it. "I'm sorry I can't go with you for this."

"I am, too." Slate sighed and shook his head. There were moments that talking to Zak felt eerily like talking to Zane. His stance and his words hauntingly familiar. "But your priority is to protect Jade. And she's staying here. I'm not letting her go anywhere near the barrier."

"I know." A muscle in Zak's jaw twitched, and he looked past Slate, eyes narrowed. "And she knows now, though she's not too thrilled about it." He shifted his glare to Slate. "I know I said it before, but, sir, your timing on that really grinds my gears."

Shame warred with defensiveness, and Slate propped his hands on his hips. "She needed to know after everything that happened with Jaxton. And what's done is done. Keep her out of trouble tomorrow, and we should be back by evening." He paused. "Where is she, anyway?"

Zak blew out a breath and nodded. "Yes, sir. She's with everyone else, letting my family know we're in town and what's going on. I sent Geist as an escort for her. And I expect the crew will be back soon, and my family will show up whenever they show up." He shrugged. "For all I know, they're going to be here bright and early, wanting to go with you."

"Oh. Very good. I'd welcome them to come along, if Bentley wouldn't get too steamed over that idea." Slate nodded his thanks and flashed a quick grin. "If not, I'll see them when I get back."

"Sounds reasonable." Zak's lips twisted as he crossed his arms. "When do you leave?"

"Before the sun is up, unfortunately." Slate scratched at the evening stubble on his jaw. "I'm going to get what rest I can before then. Update them when they return, please?"

Zak tossed Slate a lazy salute. "No problem." His eyes burned into Slate, so very reminiscent of Zane's serious gaze. "And don't let us down tomorrow."

CHAPTER FORTY-SEVEN

JADE

For once, Jade wasn't griping about being left behind and out of an adventure. Even for a mission as important and exciting as strengthening the magic of the keystone and thus the barrier that protected all of Terrene, getting up before the sun even peeked over the horizon did not fit into her idea of excitement. She, Krista, and Briar had talked it over last night after Geist offered some half-baked excuse before leaving them to visit a friend. They'd wait for her father to return from the keystone mission before leaving. For now, though, after all the emotional turmoil from the last week, she was content to stay right where she was and sleep some more while she could. She waved goodbye to her father and his small group before slipping inside the open door with a yawn.

Firelight danced behind a metal grate on the far wall, and a form that blended with the shadows sprawled across one of the several couches and tables scattered throughout the room. A door on either side of the hearth led to sleeping quarters that her grandmother kept for traveling crews that wanted somewhere homey and close to their airships to crash.

Jade walked as quietly as she could, but Zak's eyes opened before she could pass him.

He released his crossed arms with a cat-like stretch and offered her a lopsided grin. "And just like that, they're off and away," he observed quietly.

"Just like that," she echoed. Despite Krista's urging, they hadn't had time to talk just the two of them since they kissed—every time they saw each other, someone was with them.

Heat rose to her cheeks as she fidgeted. What to do with her hands? Setting them on her hips might make her look like she was about to lecture him—which she wouldn't mind doing, but now wasn't the time. Crossing her arms would make her look angry. Holding her hands in front of her would look like she was going to make a request. Holding her arms behind her back—*Krista makes this look so easy!*

Zak sat up and patted the cushion next to him. The fire cast shadows across his face and highlighted his strong jaw, but did nothing to hide that he swallowed as he studied her. "We need to talk."

She didn't return his gaze as she sank onto the couch. Jade plucked at her loose lounge pants and mentally thanked her lucky stones that she'd had the foresight to change out of her sleeping smallclothes and into something a bit more decent. She stared down at Zak's scuffed charcoal boots. "I don't know what there is to talk about." *Liar.* She shrugged with one shoulder. "I meant what I said. I don't want weird formalities that mean nothing to me to come between us. I'm a mechanic." She lifted a hand and dropped it with a sigh. "Not someone I've never been."

The couch shifted as Zak leaned forward, his green eyes intent on her, even as she strove to not look at him. He reached forward and took the hand she'd just gestured with, his grip firm, yet gentle.

"I disagree." He kept his voice low, kind. "You are much more than a mechanic. And I don't mean just about your heritage." His lips quirked in a small smile that reached his eyes. "You're a loyal friend. A challenge when it comes to archery competitions. You work hard to make sure everyone is comfortable." She scoffed and he narrowed his eyes. "You did with Ben," he reminded her. "And—"

"And what am I seeing?" A feminine voice interrupted. "Is this a touching moment that I should walk away from?"

Zak propelled himself farther back on the couch, dropping Jade's hand as if it were scalding him. Jade whirled to look behind them and saw his sister Zaborah leaning against the doorframe, a single eyebrow pointedly raised at Zak. Zaborah walked around the couch and tilted the sword on her hip before deliberately sitting between them.

She turned to face Jade. "The rest of our family will be here after breakfast. I came early with two who are joining your current guards. It seems prudent to be on the alert after everything that happened in Lasim." Zaborah flicked her blonde hair over her shoulder with a sympathetic smile. "We're not taking any risks today, not with part of the crew out with your father."

Jade had to test the waters. "You mean, my uncle, whom I still consider my father."

Zaborah's smile faltered and she dipped her head in a silent nod as Zak stood and paced to a nearby window. "So you know now." She clapped her hands and rubbed them together briskly. "I suppose that makes some things easier. You missed Ensign Brigley when he came by late last night. Ever since Slate told Bentley the news, the garrison has been on edge, and James is concerned about some patrol changes for today."

Jade smiled briefly at the memory of her friend's excitement over his promotion, then Zaborah's words registered. "Why in Terrene would the garrison be on edge?" Jade asked, wrinkling her brow. "It's not like they're involved at all. They just get the benefit of a stabilized barrier."

Zaborah shrugged. "We don't know. That's part of the reason we three are here early. Something felt…off."

Zak stepped away from the clear glass pane, and Jade tensed at his expression. "What's wrong?"

He shook his head as he strode across the room, his fingers on his hilt. He looked out the window next to the door and turned to Zaborah. "Who came with you?"

"Zabir and Joseph." Zaborah sat up straighter.

Jade leaned forward, catching on to Zak's subtle anxiety. "I think Erynn and Owen were the guards that my grandmother had on duty to begin with." She moved from the couch to touch the pane where Zak had first gone. The dark of the night was fading under the onslaught of the coming sun, and she shaded her eyes as sunshine peeked over the brick Doldran wall. "Where are they? I don't see anyone."

The door banged open, and Jade slammed into the wall. Zaborah had her back to Jade, blade pointed at the door. Erynn silhouetted the doorframe. Blood gushed from his side and splattered on the hardwood floor. His eyes fixated on Zak, who stood at the ready a sword's length away. Erynn stumbled, and Zak dropped his sword to catch him.

"What happened to you?" Zak demanded as he flicked open a

pouch on his sable pants and pulled out a large square of thick fabric. His eyes flicked toward the door. "And where are the others?"

"Bandits," Erynn gasped and his legs thrashed against the ground as Zak shoved his hands onto Erynn's side with the pad in an attempt to slow the bleeding.

Zak's eyes hardened, and he exchanged looks with Zaborah and Jade. "Stay with me, Jade. I need an extra set of hands."

Zaborah ran down the closest hall, yelling for all swords to wake up. Zak helped Erynn to a couch where he could lie down. Zak pointed at Jade. "I need you to get my med-pack, it's in my room."

Jade dashed from the window and scooped up Zak's sword, her fingers grasping the familiar black-and-silver twisted hilt. She ran. A quick search in Zak's room yielded the location of his black leather bag. She tossed it over her shoulder and stopped to pound on Krista's door before returning to Zak.

Jade caught a glimpse of Ash as he slammed the door shut behind him. Zak held out a bloody hand for his bag, thought better of it, and pointed instead. "I need gauze."

She set his sword between them, where they could both reach it, and dove her hands into his bag. Gauze squished under her fingers, and she held it out to him, then shrank back against the couch as someone bellowed and the wall to the outside thudded. "Why does battle always find us?" she moaned as she held out the scissors for when he'd be ready.

Zak grunted as he took the offered tool, leaving bloody streaks across her palm. "That's another reason why you're trained with a sword."

Jade ignored the double meaning of his words and dug out his suture kit before he could ask for it. "Who's out there now?"

"My sister, Tamon, William, and Ash." Zak didn't look up from Erynn's side.

"Briar," Krista added as she jogged in and joined them, a sword strapped to her waist. She held out Jade's inherited sapphire-blue sword and sheath. "You may need this."

Jade tied it to her belt and looked over at Zak. "I'm going out."

"Like the bleeding Void you are!" Zak exclaimed, his eyes wide. He glared at her as he grabbed a threaded needle from his kit. "Absolutely not. We don't know what they want, and you'll be a target."

"Argue all you two want; I'm not leaving my boyfriend to do the fighting alone," Krista shot over her shoulder as she left the room.

Jade shook her head at Zak as she jogged to the door. "And I can't leave my best friend to face whatever is out there without me at her side."

"Jade!"

The fear and frustration in Zak's voice halted her hand before she could twist the knob. She hesitated and looked back.

Erynn groaned as Zak stitched his side. Zak shook his head at her, dark hair falling into his eyes. He cursed and shook the strands out of his face. "Please, wait for me. Don't go where I can't follow."

Jade pressed her lips together. His plea hammered at the walls that she'd built around her heart. She couldn't let them crack or she'd give in and stay—forever a damsel in distress in his eyes. She had to prove her point. She could hold her own. She was more than the title he thought of her as. "A princess needs a bodyguard. A mechanic doesn't." She stepped out into chaos and clicked the door shut behind her, blocking out his shouts and curses.

CHAPTER FORTY-EIGHT

BEN

Ben's hands shook with nervous energy, and he gave up on standing still, opting to pace instead. Captain Samantha stood at the railing, her jaw clenched as she looked over the edge. The Doldran brick wall loomed closer as the *Phoenix* drew near, and Ben had to bite back the urge to ask Samantha how much longer until they docked.

Samantha and her crew had been ready the moment Ben returned to Elinora's, and he boarded with Ellie, Finn, and Raine within a half-hour of his return. He'd explained all that had occurred in the palace while on the main deck. The members of their party had listened while Samantha steered them out, bent on not wasting a single minute. But the *Sapphire* had a full two—almost three—days' head start, and anything could have happened by now.

Though it was dangerous, due to low visibility, Samantha and her sister, Rebecca, took turns flying the ship through the night in an effort to catch up.

"We're not too late for the keystone." Relief colored Samantha's words, and she shot Ben a tired smile as she handed him her monocular. "The barrier is still intact."

He lifted the spyglass and sighed in relief to see that the

shimmering purple in the mountains hadn't changed or disappeared. He handed the lens back to Samantha and checked his safety line before leaning over the edge of the rail as Rebecca steered them into the airship dock. *So close...*

The sound of metal jangling distracted Ben from the blessed sight of the wooden dock, and he turned to see Raine and Finn standing amongst several others of Samantha's crew.

Raine buckled her sword over her tunic and fixed Ben with a stare. "I'll help you rescue your princess."

"She's not *my* princess." Ben snorted. "If she's anyone's, she's Zak's. Just don't let either of them hear you say that."

Raine shrugged and started braiding her black hair. "Nonetheless. We'll assess the situation, and I'll help with her if needed. Papa will help with the keystone."

Finn settled his hand on her shoulder, his eyes drooping with an ancient quality of concern and sorrow. "I may need your help, dearest. Time will tell."

The *Phoenix* came to a smooth stop, and Samantha kicked down the gangplank while Rebecca called out orders to the remaining crewmembers. Ben followed Jade's adoptive mother as she led the group to the Stohner Shipping Yards. He cocked his head, listening. Shouts and the clanging of metal echoed in the air of the quiet morning. His chest tightened, and he burst forward, the crew hot on his heels.

They were too late. *Jade!*

They skidded around a brick pillar, and Ben gaped. Beyond the fence that surrounded Ellie's house—among other buildings—a battle raged. At least twenty shabbily dressed men fought against Slate's crew and a mix of people that Ben could only assume were Ellie's men. A flash of red hair back by the lodging drew his eye. Ben pointed with a shout, fear lodging in his throat. Splashes of crimson wavered around the edges of his vision.

Blood. So much blood.

Ben could barely see Jade through the hazy memory that threatened to pull him under. She kicked at the knee of the man towering over her. Her opponent stumbled back and lifted his blade.

Raine squeezed Ben's arm, and his attention snapped back. He pulled out his steam-pistol, aimed, and fired. Steam puffed out the side of the gun and rolled over his gloved hands. Jade's opponent dropped in a spray of red. She collapsed against the wall, chest heaving.

Someone rushed past Ben on the right. A man dropped, blood spouting from his neck. One of Samantha's crewmembers, Serena, stood over his body, dagger in hand. She pointed to Jade. He couldn't hear her over the din, but he could read her lips: *Hurry.*

The arrival of the *Phoenix* crew bolstered the beleaguered defendants of Ellie's yard. Ben and Raine worked their way through the yard with a grim resolve. Raine covered him with her sword while he pumped and reloaded his gun. A bandit with a well-trimmed moustache veered their way. Raine glided forward from Ben's side to meet the challenger. Confident in her skill, Ben left her. He had to get Jade to safety.

Sweat was rolling down Ben's forehead by the time he joined Jade. "What the blazes are you doing out here?" He exclaimed, his eyes roving over the sprawling fight. "What was Zak thinking? Where *is* Zak?"

Jade glared at him with watering eyes, gripping her sword with trembling arms. "I came out on my own. I'm not going to hide behind my friends and do nothing."

Ben groaned. "You can hold your own, and you know how to fight, but it isn't for this purpose." He lifted his gun and tracked a bandit with shiny boots that stalked behind Finn. The man paused, and Ben shot him. The man collapsed. Ben yanked ammo from his belt and reloaded. "Who are these guys?"

She shook her head, her eyes following Krista and William as they teamed up against a man hovering over a crumpled form that looked like Briar.

Ben grit his teeth. His purpose here was to get Jade to safety first. He couldn't leave her side to go defend his other friend.

A stray tear rolled down Jade's cheek. "No idea. Zak will likely have an idea."

"Where is he?"

Jade stared down with dull eyes, and Ben noticed then the blood that covered her hands and sword. She pressed her thumb and forefinger together absently, pulling them apart with a sticking sound. "He's inside."

Ben scanned the crowd until he found Samantha. She kicked at her opponent's knee, and Ben immediately knew where Jade had learned that trick. Samantha met Ben's eyes as Serena finished off the bandit. Even across the yard, Ben could see the tell-tale glimmer of tears in Samantha's eyes when she saw Jade. The soft look disappeared quickly, and Samantha pointed to Jade, then to the nearby house, her meaning clear enough.

Ben nodded and tried to not let his frustration at Jade be apparent in his grip as he pulled on her arm. "Come on. We gotta get you out of here."

She followed without protest while he led her into the crew quarters. Ben's short tirade against her foolishness died behind his lips when his eyes adjusted to the darker room. Zak knelt by a blood-smeared couch, his hands on a man's crimson-stained side. Relief flared in his eyes when he saw Jade and he turned back, snipping off the end of a row of stitches.

"Zak, I—" Jade started and Ben held out his hand, stopping her.

"Before we discuss what's going on out there, or what you did," Ben shot her a reproving look, and Jade's gaze dropped to the ground, "you two need to know what happened in Aerugo." Ben crossed his arms and nodded to Zak.

Zak raised a dark brow as he wiped blood away from the long stretch of stitches. "Tell us."

Ben looked at Jade, sympathy overriding his vexation and softening his tone despite his concern over the battle raging out the front door. "Your uncle Andre is in prison for treason." She paled, and he continued, "Lord Everett knows who you are, and he wants you dead."

A strangled sound emitted from Zak, and Ben whipped his head around to the Monomi. "Ellie told me everything. I'm no threat. You know that."

Zak's grip on his sword hilt eased, but the tension remained in his shoulders as he studied Ben like he'd never seen him before. "I need you to tell me everything for me to judge that."

"I will. Later. But know that Everett said Adeline Doldras has been assumed dead for this long, and he sees no reason for that to change. That's as solid a threat as I've heard." Ben turned back to Jade. "Where is the captain?"

Color had returned to her cheeks, and Jade bit her lip. "He left for the citadel about two hours ago."

Ben's adrenaline surged and he knocked into a chair in his haste.

He swore and flung open the door. "Finn! Raine!"

"What's going on?" Zak demanded, his powerful fingers digging into Ben's shoulder. "Why is this a problem?"

Ben didn't look back, focused on flagging down Finn and Raine. "Who went with him?" Zak and Jade glanced at each other, and Ben drew his shoulders back. "Tell me! Did anyone from the crew go with him?"

"Geist, Victor, and Kerlee," Zak answered. His eyes narrowed. "Ben. What's going on?"

Ben dropped his arm when Raine veered toward him. Blood pounded through his veins, thundering in his ears. He clenched his jaw. "There was a traitor on board the *Sapphire*. And you were all lied to." Ben forced himself to look into Jade's wide eyes.

"That bloodstone won't do what you think it will. Slate's about to take down the entire barrier."

CHAPTER FORTY-NINE

SLATE

Ghosts of the past tugged on Slate's memory as he followed Bentley and his honor guard from the palace. With each clop of his horse's hooves, another image presented itself to Slate.

When at the palace waiting for Bentley, it had been Clara, guarding the huge double doors. Sapphire, nowhere in sight, but her presence haunted the back of his mind like an unreachable itch. As they passed the overgrown practice discus field, a broken image of his friend, the traitor, flickered behind Geist. Kerlee and Geist talked in hushed voices as they neared the citadel, and Slate shook his head to dispel the memories of himself walking with his brother-in-law on the same road.

At this rate, Slate feared and wanted nothing more than to get to the citadel. He knew exactly what memory his mind would haunt him with. It was the same that he'd seen in his dreams every night immediately after the fall of the royal family. They had faded in intensity with time, but for the last week, they'd returned with increased ferocity and vividness. But he was here to face their accusations. To keep his promise. To fix his wrongs. Slate tightened his grip on the stone in his pocket. It would all be over soon.

He watched Victor as he rode alongside Nevin in the dappled sunshine up ahead. Since when did they become so buddy-buddy? Slate shook his head with a slight snort. And what were they thinking, both of them wearing suit jackets? The keystone affected time—not temperature.

Slate took a deep breath and tugged a finger under his collar. Despite the cool of the predawn morning, the lack of a breeze made the humidity even more stifling than he remembered. Everyone else in their group wore their typical attire: button-up long-sleeve shirts with vests, or, in Geist's case, a sleeveless shirt and vest.

Nevin reined his horse back to draw even with Slate. "When we get there, we'll know right away if the time is fluctuating or not." He held himself aloof as he peered down his nose at Slate—despite Slate sitting taller on horseback.

"Oh?" Slate forced himself to focus on the conversation and not the foreboding that lurked in the back of his mind. He cleared his throat of the emotion that thickened his voice. "How's that?"

"We'll toss in a pebble and watch if it floats or falls. It's the safest way."

Slate nodded. "Sounds like a good plan." He glanced at the guards that rode ahead and behind them. "Is everyone going in?"

Nevin sniffed. "Of course not." He splayed his fat fingers across his chest and raised his brow at Slate. "I will escort you in. There's no reason for the illustrious Governor Bentley to get close to the keystone."

"No?" Slate frowned. "Then why'd he come?"

"To be seen, of course." Nevin shook his head at Slate and *tsked*. "Leadership is clearly not your strong suit. He will remain outside with the guards."

Slate bit back a sarcastic reply and dipped his head silently. Nevin rode forward again, and Geist nudged his horse closer to Slate.

"Annoying little prick, isn't he?" Geist flicked a hand at Nevin. "I'd give you a hundred-to-one odds that he's never even set foot in the keystone chamber."

Slate snorted through his nose. "No need to mince your thoughts. I won't tell on you." Geist's choice of words suddenly registered, and Slate adjusted the reins in his hands as he narrowed his eyes at Geist. "After this is over, we need to talk about your gambling, man. Don't think I haven't noticed."

Geist coughed and looked away, scratching at his cheek. "I'd wondered."

"Kind of hard not to, with you disappearing left and right." Slate raised an eyebrow. "And your last request for an advance on your pay was the final clue."

A grimace crossed Geist's face and he nodded to himself, but Slate wasn't going to let him out of the dragon trap just yet. Slate sighed. "Geist, I'm not upset at your gambling."

"Sir?" Geist looked up from his horse.

"I mean, the gambling is a problem, yes, but that's *your* problem." Slate bounced his fist against his thigh. Like he was one to talk about personal problems. His adrenaline-loving crew member watched him with a quizzical expression. "The problem is when you leave without saying anything," Slate elaborated. "If I can't trust you to be where you say you are, how can I count on you for important missions?" He nodded to the citadel in the distance. "Missions like this one."

Geist's cheek twitched as he dropped his gaze. "Sorry, sir." He swallowed hard. "I'll work on it." He glanced sideways at Slate.

"Think this will go smoothly?"

"Who knows?" Slate sighed, then took a deep breath, and tried not to choke on the pollen in the air. "But it would probably be best to have you guys stay out here with Mister Tight Gears. Victor has already volunteered to go in with me."

Geist grimaced. "Sounds like fun."

Tall evergreens broke away from the path to reveal the sturdy stone of the citadel, and Slate swallowed hard at the sight. Almost there. The keystone would be stronger, his family and southern Terrene protected, and he could finally lay his ghosts to rest. He dipped his head back to enjoy the last bit of sunlight he'd get for the next few hours. After this, he'd take a break. Ride with Sam for a bit on the *Phoenix*. Let Victor captain the *Sapphire* for a while.

Slate pressed his lips together when they reached the gate of the citadel. Two guards opened the heavy wooden door. It creaked open and Bentley cantered through, immediately pulling up short and leading his horse to the side furthest from the keystone tower. Slate glanced over at Geist, breakfast leaden in his gut. "The sooner this is over, the better."

Gravel crunched as Kerlee approached. Slate dismounted and handed his reins to a nearby guard, then turned to his crewman. "I'm sorry, but I do need you to stay out here." Slate lowered his voice and nodded meaningfully toward Bentley's back. "Keep an eye on the pompous one, will you?"

Disappointment flashed across Kerlee's face, but he nodded and struck his fist across his heart. Pride shone in his eyes. "Thank you, sir, for letting me come along this far." Kerlee shoved his hands in his pockets and looked up at the tall building. "It's strange, knowing that a crystal in there is the reason my town got wiped out." He sighed before sticking a hand out to Slate. "For the sake of our people."

Slate swallowed the lump in his throat as he shook Kerlee's hand. "And for the safety of our families."

Kerlee stepped back, chin high. "Go on, sir. Strike a blow against those Void-cursed Elph, and fix that barrier."

"Gladly." Slate motioned to Nevin and Victor. "Let's go."

CHAPTER FIFTY

BLADE

Blade chopped with his sword, severing the palace guard's arm at the shoulder. It fell free and hit the formerly white marble floor. The man dropped his spear and grasped at his stump with a guttural yell. Blood squeaked underfoot, and the sound only fueled Blade's fury.

His mind was his again, and he refused to let memories slow him down now.

The entire foyer of the Doldran palace had been cleaned of the Aerugan guards that sullied it. Their blood would wash away the taint.

Sneaking into the city had been pitifully easy for Blade's small company. When they'd arrived, they discovered that the palace had a reduced guard, and one of Bentley's men had been overheard talking about an undercover mission that morning—something about eliminating a political threat. Whatever the reason, it made Blade's goal laughably simple to accomplish.

There had been too many guards around Slate that morning when they saw him leaving the palace, talking with Bentley's men about the keystone. Blade had decided to lead his men to the now under-guarded palace and through the secret passage that led straight to the citadel. He didn't know, nor care, what Slate's business was there. All that mattered was revenge. His mind was his again, but he still suffered the aftereffects of the control bracelet: remnants of Kadar's hate swirled through his brain, mixing with his own hatred and desire for revenge. But as long as the lingering emotions and desires didn't interfere with his own revenge, Blade couldn't care less.

As for those who hindered them here in the palace, they could be eradicated without guilt. These were Bentley's men. Everett's governor stooge, who had no right to sit on the throne of Doldra.

One of Blade's men shouted and followed a screaming maid down the hall. Blade's lip curled and disgust stirred in his stomach at the fate of the innocent woman. He turned away and pointed up the stairs. "We need to get to the library."

His remaining five men followed as he charged up the familiar steps. Sunlight streamed in from the main doors, and Blade paused to see who entered. His breath caught, and he lowered his sword to stare in confusion.

Of the five that stood in the doorway, only two looked familiar. One looked eerily similar to Blade's best friend from a previous life. From the dark hair, black clothes, and the multitude of weapons strapped over his body—he had to be a Monomi. Maybe even Zane's younger brother. How unfortunate that he would be here, now. If he tried to interfere, Blade would stop him. As for the other...

The other could have been Sapphire twenty years ago. Red hair, delicate facial structure, the same brilliant blue eyes. This had to be Slate's daughter. She looked up at him, and her eyes widened as her jaw dropped. She tore her gaze away and spoke to a man next to her.

Blade turned away to see a new group of guards run out from a side hall. He started up the stairs again and flicked a free hand toward the entryway as he passed his second-in-command. "Take them out."

Stannin hefted a metal orb with a gap-toothed grin and raised his eyebrows. "Boom?"

"Boom."

CHAPTER FIFTY-ONE

JADE

Horror stiffened Jade's spine while guilt threatened to melt her knees as she stood in the Doldran palace—technically *her* palace—and stared at the carnage surrounding them. Blood glimmered on the white and black tiles, and the smells of adrenaline, sweat, and human waste burned her sinuses. Her mind still reeled from Ben's explanation on their hard ride here. Her father had no idea what he was about to do. Her heart squeezed again.

Jade stepped closer to Zak and swallowed back tears as she thought of Krista. Krista, crying over Briar's prone body as Schultz, the *Phoenix* doctor, tried desperately to stop Briar's bleeding. Jade hadn't wanted to leave her best friend's side, but she had to help. She couldn't *not* help.

How could so much go so wrong so quickly?

"It's him." Ben breathed.

Jade looked up to see a blond swordsman on the balcony across the foyer. The crew had described him well enough after their mission-gone-awry for her to recognize him. "I think I saw him outside a store in Vodan once, while with Krista," she realized aloud.

"More than that." Ben gripped his steam-pistol. The bandit

turned away as Ben lifted his weapon. "He killed Jaxton!"

Zak and Jade inhaled sharply, and Jade glared up at the man. His blond ponytail bounced as he nodded to a man next to him. The bandit continued up the steps without looking back as his goon launched an orb over the balcony at them.

"Move!" Ben shouted as he pushed Raine to the right. "Everyone, down!"

Pain screamed up Jade's knees as she fell to the hard floor. Ben's fear infected her, though she didn't know why he was so scared of what looked like a potion bottle. Zak's weight pinned half of her down. Out of the corner of her eye, she saw Finn drop. The floor rumbled. Her teeth rattled and she bit her tongue. Fire rolled over them. The flames swirled away as quickly as they came, and Jade gasped.

Finn had rolled on his back, both hands upstretched, his eyes narrowed and focused. He flicked his fingertips, and the remnant of smoke dissipated. His gaze met hers and a smile glimmered over his lips before he rocked upright and looked around the empty room. "I don't see Slate anywhere."

Jade wiggled out from under Zak. What in Terrene had Finn just done? She shot him a glance from the corner of her eye. He must be a sage, to some degree. She wanted to ask him, but her tongue ached and blood coated the inside of her mouth. Zak stirred under her. She looked down at him and grabbed his pale, clammy face in her hands, terror pounding a harsh drumbeat in her ears.

He trembled without blinking. "Zak? Zak! What's wrong?" She slid a hand over his arms and back to confirm that he wasn't injured. His black shirt had no rips or tears that she could find.

He blinked and took a shuddering breath. "Bombs. Here." He

squeezed his green eyes shut with a grimace. "Bad memories. Not here, not again," he whispered, his voice small.

Jade rubbed his back as she looked around and confirmed that the rest of their party was unhurt. Ben knelt and inspected the shattered water tank of his steam-pistol with a scowl. A puddle of water and glass below his knee proved that Ben's weapon was now useless. Raine shook sharp fragments off her tunic.

Jade glared up the stairs to where the blond bandit had left. So he had been the one to kill Jaxton? She ran her fingers gently through Zak's hair. Then she stood, testing her knees for any unexpected aches. "Finn. Find my fath—" she shook her head. "Slate. Find Slate. Do what you need to do."

Finn turned to her, his hand out, as if to constrain her. "What are you going to do?"

"What needs to be done," she growled. She dashed across the entryway, jumping over prone bodies and striving to not dwell on the severed fingers and limbs that she passed. Her sword rattled in its sheath as she pounded up the stairs, ignoring Ben's shout for her to come back. She ran through the open door, catching a glimpse of Raine down below, running up the stairs, chasing after her.

Luminary crystals lit the warm amber-colored walls in what should have been a peaceful palace hallway. But bloody shoeprints marred the illusion, and Jade followed the blatant trail, determination surging through her veins. She pulled out her blade as she came close to a corner. She held it defensively as she passed the open space. A tiny trickle of relief eased her tight shoulders when no one jumped out at her.

Let me find you. I need to prove I'm not some helpless little princess.

Let me avenge our friends. You loathsome Void Born.

Sweat beaded on her forehead, and Jade swiped at it with the back of her wrist. She pulled up short when the blond stepped out of a doorway. Books lined the shelves behind him. She raised her sword, and his eyes flared wide, fixated on the shiny blue metal.

"You killed Doctor Jaxton." Jade's voice held steady. She clenched her jaw. "You had no right—"

"I had every right." The bandit unsheathed his sword, but held it loosely as he regarded her, hatred burning in his eyes. "How dare he give you *her* sword?"

Terrified as she was, Jade blinked at his odd question. Were they even talking about the same person? She consciously kept the blade up and between them. "Jaxton didn't give me this. This was my aunt's sword." *Although, I guess it was actually my mother's sword. Weird.*

"Give my regards to your father when I send him after you." The blond leapt forward, his crimson blade sweeping down at her. She blocked the strike, barely, but the impact vibrated up her arms and shoulders in a wave of pain. She stumbled back and tripped over a rug as he slashed again.

His blade bit into her, and something crunched in her shoulder. Agony flared blindingly bright. She couldn't recall letting go of her sword, but when she collapsed, it already lay on the ground by her feet. Voices behind her shouted, and she watched through tear-blurred eyes as the blond man escaped. Light and sound dimmed, then faded to black.

CHAPTER FIFTY-TWO

BLADE

Blade stalked to where his men waited at the back of the library. Though a part of his heart ached after cutting down the young woman who so resembled Sapphire, his hatred armored him. If she wasn't dead, she would be soon enough.

It was Slate's fault that Blade's wife and daughter were dead. It was only fair for Slate to experience the same pain that Blade felt. The same loss. The same mind-numbing sorrow.

Nothing would stop him.

He flicked the gem under the lamp and waited patiently for the bookcase to slide back, revealing the secret passageway. Voices rose in a panic outside the library door, but no one came in after them. Blade entered the dark doorway, and his men followed.

No one would stand in his way.

CHAPTER FIFTY-THREE

BEN

Ben skidded around a corner and nearly slipped in a crimson puddle that slowly soaked into an amber-and-burgundy rug. Blood poured from Jade's shoulder and chest. Raine bent over her, trying to hold severed skin together.

"Son of a—" Ben dropped to his knees on the other side of Jade and ripped off his button-up over-shirt, all but throwing it at Raine. "Use this."

Raine pressed it to Jade's chest. The sky-blue fabric soaked up blood, which stained the shirt an odd shade of purple. Raine glanced up at Ben, her face tense. "Where's Papa? Zak?"

"Coming." Ben grabbed Jade's flailing hand as she gasped to breathe. "Some Monomi arrived just as I was following." He used a free hand to push a tendril of hair out of Jade's mouth. The memory of losing Laurent flashed through Ben's mind, and the air whooshed out of his lungs. He rocked forward on his knees and gently grasped her jaw. "Stay with me. You hear? Focus. Slow breaths."

Footsteps echoed from the hall, and Ben let go to grab his steam pistol. Glass tinkled and he swore as he let go of it. Short of bludgeoning anyone, the weapon was useless for now. He pressed against the wall and peeked around, then moved out and waved at Zak and Finn. "We need a medic!"

Zak barreled around the corner, and stopped short. His eyes widened and he flung himself toward Jade with an oath. He lifted the soaked shirt to look at the wound and swore again.

"Finn!" Zak rotated his black belt around his hips and unlatched a vial holster. He yanked out a little glass bottle.

Finn came around the corner as Zak pulled the stopper from the vial and started to pour a clear liquid over her wound. "Help her, please."

Ben stepped aside to let the older man kneel beside Jade. Ben swallowed hard as he watched Jade struggle for each shallow breath. Finn inspected the gash. Shattered bone poked out of her shoulder, and the jagged gash cut through her flesh down to her visibly cracked breastbone. Whatever Zak put on it helped to slow the gushing blood. Ben knelt, woozy, when he counted at least two broken ribs sticking out of her skin.

During war with one of his brothers-in-arms was bad enough. But this? A friend on a mission like this? He closed his eyes and tried to control the shaking in his hands as another memory tried to breach his awareness.

"Her lung is collapsing," Finn muttered aloud, and Ben's gaze shot to the old man. Finn's eyes were closed as he ran his splayed hand over her chest, concentration pinching his brows. His eyes fluttered open, and he pulled a speckled green stone out of his pocket, holding it over her ribcage. The wrinkles around his lips deepened as he frowned.

Raine frantically motioned to Ben and Zak. "Hold her down. We don't have any nullification stones, so this is going to be—"

Jade jerked under Finn's hands, and her chest arched as she

screamed. Zak flung his leg over hers and grabbed her closest hand while Raine braced Jade's head from thrashing side to side. Ben rushed to flank Jade and grab her other hand before she could smack at Finn.

Ben stared in horrified astonishment as the ribs he could see slipped back under her skin. His stomach turned. Her clammy hand nearly tore from his grasp, and he gripped her slender fingers with one hand while pressing his other against her stomach to prevent her from twisting so much. A quick glance showed that Zak's tan face had paled to the color of sand as he fought with Jade's jerking, fighting, and blood-curling screams. Tears leaked from her eyes, and her hoarse shriek fell silent as she mercifully lapsed into unconsciousness. Her collarbone merged together with discernible seams in the bone. A second later, her breastbone knit together.

Sweat beaded on Finn's forehead, and he slipped the stone back into his pocket. He took deep breaths as he carefully arranged the loose skin back to its proper location on Jade's chest and shoulder. He looked at Zak's shell-shocked face before turning to Ben. "I've managed to repair her ribs, but she's lost so much blood." Finn tugged her blouse to keep her decent as he worked. "Her lung is too delicate for her to be moved much, and I can't do any more mani-med healing without risk of killing her. The next few minutes will be crucial. No one has seen Slate?"

Ben shook his head and met Finn's gaze with awe. "No, sir."

"We still need to find him, or her life won't be the only one endangered." Finn frowned as he gently smoothed a bubble in her skin on her shoulder. He glanced at Raine. "I need to stay with her for now. Zak can remain. The Monomi are clearing out the palace below, so we should be safe enough here."

Raine pressed her lips together, her eyes dark with an emotion that Ben couldn't identify as she nodded. She looked up at Ben. "I'll need you to come, too, in case we run into trouble that I can't handle alone."

Surprise rocked Ben. "Really? My pistol is busted. I—"

Raine dipped her head, her eyes tight, and Ben loosened his grip on Jade's slack hand.

He directed his words to Zak. "Okay, then. If you're sure you'll be fine without us?"

A muscle in Zak's jaw twitched, and his eyes didn't leave Jade's frighteningly pale face. "Go." His eyes flicked to the open doorway on their right. "There's a secret passageway in there. Back wall. Quickest way to the citadel. Crystal under the lamp."

Ben touched Jade's face. She looked so small, so frail, so *broken*. He leaned over her and whispered in her ear, "Fight to live. Zak needs you. *I* need you. Who will I tease if you're gone, sister?"

He tucked her hair behind her ear and didn't fight the protective urge that welled up in him. Somehow, she'd filled the role of Sara, and had proven to be just as precious to him, even in the short time he'd known her. The idea of losing her now rocked him to the core.

Ben nodded grimly to Finn. "Protect her." He scrambled to his feet. Raine did, too, staring at Jade, still as death on the marble floor. "We'll be back as soon as we can," he promised.

Finn grabbed Raine's hand before she could step away. He peered up at her, his eyes shining with sorrow and pride. "You know what you need to do."

Raine patted his hand, her own eyes reflecting resolve and a trace of fear. "I won't fail you." She turned, gripped her sword hilt, grabbed

Ben's blood-coated hand, and pulled him into the library.

Books passed by in a blur as Ben followed Raine through the quiet room. A dark opening yawned before them, between shelves of books, and she paused there, hand on the wall. She stepped in.

Darkness greeted Ben's eyes as he fought to see the steps under his feet. A cool breeze blew through the thin fabric of his undershirt, reminding him that his thicker over-shirt was being used to mop up blood in the other room. He stifled a shiver. "What is it that you need to do when we get there?"

Raine's voice echoed back to him, barely audible over the scuff of their boots on the dirt-covered ground, "Whatever I must to succeed."

CHAPTER FIFTY-FOUR

SLATE

The hair on Slate's arms rose as he approached the wavering purple barrier. Everyone said that the barrier didn't react to people, but he most vehemently disagreed with those folks right now. Blue rippled into lavender, followed by green as he stepped closer to the shimmering black keystone.

Does it remember me? Slate glanced down at his palm and the faint scar that his gloves hid. *Does it remember my blood?* He didn't dare look at the back wall, where he could feel Zane's ghost watching him. *Our blood.*

Victor stayed at the edge of the circular room, close to the single doorway where Nevin and two of his guards also stood. Victor glared over Slate's shoulder at the keystone. "It doesn't look like it's happy that we're here."

Nevin sniffed and wiped his pince-nez against his sleeve before settling it back on his face. "Impossible. It's a rock. Even if it's magical, rocks don't have feelings."

Staying near the edge of the room, Victor edged toward the closest of the large stained-glass windows where the morning sunlight threw colorful patterns on the floor. He rapped his knuckles against it and looked at Slate. "Either way, Captain, you should get started. Who knows how much time we have before it gets unstable again?"

"True." Slate walked back to Victor and slipped Zak's—Zane's—black ring off his hand and into his pocket. *I'm not going to risk mixing magic.* He accepted the stone from his first mate and stared at the dappled surface for an eternity of a heartbeat. It weighed heavy in Slate's hand, and it was too easy to imagine it being pulled down with the burden of secrets, promises, and the blood spilled nearly two decades prior. He gripped it and approached the barrier, excitement and nervousness coursing through his bloodstream as the purple and black rippled before him.

Ironic, that to protect the barrier from collapse in case of emergency required the lodestone and blood, but to restore it completely, he only needed a bloodstone.

Slate lifted the bloodstone up to the barrier, as the scroll illustrated. He stopped a sword's length away from the keystone and stared as orange blossomed from its center, a starburst of red following a moment later. His skin prickled as ice crept down his spine. *This isn't how it's supposed to look.* He twisted to look behind at Victor and Nevin, but one of the guards stood directly behind Slate, sword drawn. Nevin stood in front of the open door, buffing his nails against his sleeve.

"What's going on?" Panic shot through Slate's veins as orange and pink lightning ripped along the wall of the barrier, casting color on the guard's stony face. "This isn't how it's supposed to react!"

The man said nothing and lunged forward. Slate dropped the stone and pulled out his sword, but not fast enough. The jab sliced through Slate's bicep, and scarlet anguish lanced up his arm. He fumbled with his blade as he sidestepped and tripped over the bloodstone, kicking it toward the edge of the room. He looked at Victor and Nevin with wide eyes. "What are you waiting for? Do something!"

Nevin pressed his lips together and looked away. Victor flicked his hand toward Slate, then kneeled and picked up the bloodstone. He inspected it casually. The second guard drew his blade with the ring of steel and advanced toward Slate.

Bloated whales. What was going on?

Slate threw a desperate glance over his shoulder to make sure he wasn't going to back into the barrier. He looked over in time to see Nevin collapse on the ground. A moment later, the closest guard dropped, too, a crimson sword protruding from his chest.

The guard crumpled, revealing the blond bearded bandit from Vodan. Fury danced in his eyes as he glared at Slate. His blue gaze switched to the second guard, and he stalked toward him. The man swung at the bandit, but the blond blocked and pushed against him.

Horror swept over Slate as the guard screeched and slipped into the barrier. His skin withered. Muscles sagged. Everything melted and collapsed, revealing bone—and then he was gone. Evaporated. Nothing.

The bandit returned his glare to Slate. "No one has the right to kill you, but me." He flicked his wrist, and droplets of blood flew off his blade. He drew himself up. "Sapphire is dead because of you."

Slate's body turned numb from shock, and he squinted at the man. The blond hair was far too long, his skin weathered, and he'd never had a beard before. It was impossible, but Slate knew he wasn't mistaken. The familiar eyes, the bump in his nose so like his daughter's, the misery when he spoke of Sapphire…

"Brandon?"

Who else could it be?

How had he survived? Where had he been?

Victor swore and banged his hand against the window. It exploded inward with a burst of blue, red, and green glass. A man dressed in casual pants and a green vest swung in and landed next to Slate's first mate. Victor held the bloodstone out. The newcomer yanked his goggles from his eyes, grabbed the bloodstone, and rushed forward. He pulled a short sword from a sheath on his hip and swung at Brandon—*it has to be Brandon*—but Brandon blocked and pushed against the stranger.

The bloodstone fell from the green-vested man's grasp, and he stumbled backward over the body of a guard, the barrier just behind him. He teetered on his heel, then fell back. Red and orange rippled around his body as he disappeared from sight.

Slate swallowed hard, staring at the sword that Brandon pointed at him.

"I—" Color drained from Brandon's face, leaving him ghost-white. He stepped back, his eyes dilated as he stared at the barrier. "What the bleeding Void is *that*?"

Slate looked over his shoulder. Brilliant tongues of crimson swirled and pulsed into orange and yellow as the stranger stepped out of the barrier.

He looked at Victor and shrugged while he straightened his green vest. "It looks like it'll be down within minutes."

Slate dropped his sword and scrambled back.

Void Born.

CHAPTER FIFTY-FIVE

BLADE

Blade ignored the clatter of Slate's dropped blade and stepped back, giving the Void Born a wide berth. The abomination stooped to leisurely scoop up his short sword. He looked up, eyes narrowed.

"Chris." Slate's first mate spoke from the corner. "Change of plans. We're going."

Blade's eyes widened. The rising sun shone bright through the open window, making it difficult to discern his features. But he recognized the man. The sharp nose. The high cheekbones. The cruel eyes. Hatred surged through Blade, and he trembled at the memory that wavered behind his eyelids.

It's him.

Chris's eyes darted to the bald man, and he nodded. "Yes, sir." He picked up the black-and-red-flecked stone and slipped it in his pocket.

"No." Blade pointed at the bald male, his voice rough with rage. "You killed Zane."

"What?" Disbelief colored Slate's choked gasp. He took a short step toward the window. "Victor, you killed Zane? And you were riding with us. My first mate—pretending to be on our side? Why?"

Victor shucked off his sleek brown jacket to reveal a harness and metal gauntlet similar to what Blade's crew had on their airship for emergency escapes. The traitor grinned as Chris jogged over to his side. "You failed, Captain. The barrier will fall soon, and it will be all your fault. Then we shall claim what is rightfully ours in this miserable land." He pivoted on his heel, and gears whirred as the grappling hooks shot out.

Chris tested his line and jumped out the window. Victor saluted mockingly with his free hand, then rode the line out to freedom.

Stunned shock left Blade reeling. Zane's murderer had been right here. With a Void Born.

A Void Born. They're real. And one's here.

"What just happened?" Slate's ragged voice cut through Blade's internal panic. He turned to regard his former brother-in-law. He'd worry about the Void Born later. He had to deal with this situation first.

Slate visibly swallowed as he leaned over, hands on his knees as he trembled. "Victor killed Zane." He looked up at Brandon. "How did you survive?" A flare of orange and yellow burst from the barrier, and Slate flinched. "Where did you go?"

Blade lifted the blade in his hand to point at Slate. Slate's eyes focused on the tip. "Doctor Taylor took me in." Blade let the rage and venom in his voice seep out. "And I was his mindless slave until you happened to stroll through our camp not too long ago." He offered a mocking bow. "I thank you for freeing me. And now I shall free you of your life, you vile traitor."

Blade lunged forward, and Slate scrambled for his sword. A silent tremor surged from the keystone, shaking the tower. Alarm spiked through Blade. If the barrier fell, too many innocents would die. Those of his own kingdom, even if he wasn't a prince anymore, as well as all over southern Terrene. What had happened to it? A quick glance showed Slate's white-faced alarm. *Was it something Slate had done, or the Void Born?*

Slate used Blade's moment of distraction to grab his own sword and slip to the side. He glanced toward the door, and Blade stabbed, gashing Slate's arm. Slate howled as a chunk of his arm ripped free.

Almost there. I'll avenge all of you. Air rattled in Blade's lungs as he moved in toward Slate again. "I'll send you after your daughter to shehalla."

Slate stumbled to his knees, sweat beading on his forehead as he tried to block Blade's sword. "What did you do to Jade?"

"You raised a stupid girl. She chased me, and I cut her down."

Tears slipped down Slate's cheeks, and glee rose in Blade's chest at the devastation in Slate's eyes.

"You killed…that was Adeline, Brandon," Slate whispered. He curled forward as he bowed, palms up, tears falling down his face. "Your daughter. I raised her, protected her. I wanted her to reclaim the throne, to make you and Sapphire proud."

The broken expression along with Slate's words filled Blade's body with horror. He didn't have to torture Slate to hear the truth of his words. He'd seen the truth himself when he first saw her. She didn't take after her father's side of the family with the red hair and delicate features. She took after her *mother's* side of the family.

She had been alive. And now she was surely dead. By his own hand.

What have I done?

"But you," Blade raised the sword again. "You killed Sapphire!"

"No." Slate's face twisted in pain as he shook his head. "No. That was an accident. I swear. I never meant for her to die. For you to disappear." He looked over his shoulder at the barrier as it rippled yellow. "I never meant for any of this to happen," he breathed. "I'm so sorry."

Fury coursed through Blade's blood, and he stood over Slate. "It's too late to be sorry."

CHAPTER FIFTYSIX

BEN

Dust rained down from the ceiling as the shaft shook. Ben added another burst of speed while he ran behind Raine, his toes squelching uncomfortably in his boots. Zak had failed to mention that there was an underground river. And no lights to see by. And though they managed to get across the water, and figured out which of the three tunnels to take, it hadn't been an easy endeavor for Ben.

Of course, Raine had made it across the stepping stones perfectly. And she'd even managed to hold back a bark of laughter when Ben slipped on the last stone and fell in, spluttering and howling in the cold water. But now neither of them were smiling as another tremor rocked their underground tunnel.

The darkness provided the perfect backdrop to the nightmarish images that kept playing in his mind. Jade, pale as death, crimson blood splashed over her face, her chest, and the floor. Laurent, his face ashen under the dust and dirt, bleeding out from the artery in his leg. One of them was dead. One of them may yet die.

Ben gritted his teeth as he followed the sound of Raine's strides. Jade had to live.

"Stairs," Raine panted, and Ben paused long enough to place

where the steps were before he followed her up.

Too many stairs later, they stumbled out of the tunnel and into a deathly silent library. She kept her hand on her sword as she led him through the maze of bookshelves and out into a corridor. Ben stumbled into Raine's back when she stopped abruptly. He peered over her head.

Five men blocked their path, all of them leering at Raine in her sweat-stained, form-hugging tunic. Her sword rang free of its scabbard as she settled into her fighting stance.

Ben didn't want to hide behind her like a useless damsel in distress. His hand dropped to his steam-pistol before he remembered the glass tank had shattered in the foyer. He swore.

The lead bandit scoffed. "You're outnumbered."

"Let us through, and you'll live." Raine's voice reverberated in the hall. She dropped into a low crouch. "Hinder our cause and die."

The men hooted and drew their swords. "Don't hurt her face, lads," one of them called out. "I'd like to have a go at her—"

Raine didn't wait for him to finish his sentence. She surged forward, and the men backpedaled at her scream of fury.

Ben cast about for a sword, a stick, anything, that would help Raine now that he didn't have the steam-pistol. He had to beat that guy. Had to make him pay for even *thinking* such vile things toward her. *Scum.*

But the woman was a master. She ebbed and flowed around the bandit men like an ocean wave. Relentless. Untouchable. And yet everywhere. Her blade sliced through the men with frightening ease. And there was nothing Ben could do to help. Raine didn't stop moving until the last man fell, his fingers twitching. She stabbed his back, and his digits stilled.

She looked back at Ben and raised her eyebrows at him. "We're in a hurry."

He shook off his daze and jogged over to grab one of the fallen bandits' swords. He had to help her. Not be a deadweight. Ben glanced up at Raine as he shook off the severed hand that gripped the handle. "Why did you need me to come again?"

Raine glanced over her shoulder. "Because I may need help getting through obstacles."

Ben focused on the stone tiles on the floor instead of trying to maintain eye contact while running. "Either you overestimate my usefulness, or you underestimate your skill. I need you to teach me, someday."

Raine twitched her head in a small shake as the floor rumbled beneath them. "If we survive this, I'll teach you whatever you want to know."

CHAPTER FIFTYSEVEN

JADE

Finn doubled into two figures as Jade watched him work on the throbbing line of torn flesh on her chest. Just over his shoulder, there were two Zebediahs watching the corridor. She blinked twice, and both men converged into a single image. Finn shook his head while he dabbed white cream on her shoulder, the pain receding as his fingers continued.

"I don't have what I need for the keystone. I sent her in without the very tool that we need." He ground his teeth and dipped his finger into the little jar that Zak held out. "I'd given it to your brother, you know, and I haven't seen it since the fall."

Jade caught Zebediah's grimace at the mention of Zane. She still didn't know when they'd come, but the Monomi were in the palace, and now their hallway had at least four of the Guardians posted at each end.

The jar nearly slipped from Zak's grip, and he shifted by Jade's side, his knees brushing her hip. "What did you give him?"

Finn sighed and dabbed down to the edge of the cut that ended just above Jade's left breast. He wiped his hand on the hem of his shirt while Zak screwed the lid back on the bottle. "A black ring—a lodestone—that if used in tandem with a bloodstone can restore stability to the keystone."

He compressed his lips and sorrow haunted his eyes. "It requires a willing sacrifice of blood or life, depending on the criticalness of the situation, and the strength of the one wielding them."

Zak's eyes widened as Finn talked. He set the jar down next to her arm. "Finn, I had that ring. I gave it to Slate last night."

Finn rocked back on his heels. "That ring can save all of southern Terrene." His voice dropped. "And, I'm sure he doesn't know it, but it can also be the death of him." Finn reached into his pouch and pulled out a large roll of gauze. He tossed it to Zak and nodded at Jade. "Take care of her. I need to get to him." Finn looked down at Jade and brushed a sweaty strand of hair off her forehead with a gentle smile. "Rest, and don't move on your own. I'll do my best to look after him."

"All of them." Jade rasped, her throat burning from screaming earlier. Finn raised an eyebrow, and she elaborated, "Father, Victor, Ben, all the crew. Bring them all back."

"I'll do my best. Don't move or talk much, you're still in a very fragile state." Finn stood and looked to where Zebediah watched over them, a large sentinel in black.

Zebediah nodded at the unspoken question. "I'll escort you and leave a group here for them."

"Excellent." Finn didn't wait a moment longer and hustled into the library, Zebediah behind him.

Despite the sticky blood coating Jade's shirt, the edges of her blouse started to slowly slide without Finn's hand to keep them in place. She tried to lift her hand to tug the fabric closer together, but all she could manage was to twitch her fingers. She strained, and her vision swam from the effort.

Zak didn't seem to notice her growing concern for modesty as he focused intently on laying gauze over the stitched skin. He pursed his lips and pressed his warm fingers into her cool arm. "I'll be right back." He clambered to his feet and disappeared around the corner, returning a long minute later with his elder sister, Zandra.

The siblings settled on opposite sides of Jade, and Zandra offered a small smile. "How are you feeling?"

Jade blinked back tears as Zak lightly pressed the gauze into the cream on her shoulder. "I've been better."

"I bet." Zandra tucked a chocolate brown strand of hair behind her ear, and reached out to delicately tug Jade's top back in place, leaving space for Zak to work without compromising Jade's decency. "I'm going to help you sit up while Zak bandages you." She held Jade's gaze. "I'll help keep things proper."

Relief and embarrassment rolled through Jade as she managed a tiny nod. "Thanks."

Zak's ears had a pink tinge to them, and Jade smiled internally. At least she wasn't the only one who'd been wordlessly embarrassed by the situation.

He leaned into Jade's field of vision, concern bright in his eyes. "I need to have you sit up now. Let us hold your weight as much as possible. Save what strength you have—let us do the rest of the work. Tap your hand if you can't breathe."

Jade took a shallow breath and braced for the pain, but it wasn't enough. Even with Zak's steady arm around her shoulders, her muscles screamed in agony after so long against the hard floor. Her torn flesh shifted, stretching tissue in ways that it shouldn't. Spots danced in her vision, and her stomach threatened to rebel. Zandra straddled her legs, a hand keeping Jade's shirt closed while bolstering her torso. The sutures in Jade's chest pulled as she moved, and she whimpered into Zandra's shoulder.

Zak reached around Jade to hand Zandra the starting end of the gauze, which she nestled at the lowest point of Jade's injury. Zak paused. "I, uh, shouldn't wrap over your shirt."

Breathing hurt, sitting upright hurt, being so weak and vulnerable in front of Zak hurt. Jade rested her forehead on Zandra as she sucked in tiny sips of air. "I give up," she whispered.

Zandra squeezed Jade's arm. "No, you don't." Jade felt Zandra tilt her head back to look at Zak. "Close your eyes." A moment passed, and Zandra moved slightly. "Try to stay still, I'm going to re-position your shirt."

It took a solid two minutes of agony, but Zandra finally got Jade's ruined shirt peeled off and strategically layered Ben's bloodied shirt over Jade's chest. "She's decent, Zak. Just, wrap her up quick."

Jade could hear Zak gulp behind her, and she shivered in response. Never in her wildest of worst nightmares had she ever considered the possibility of being essentially shirtless in a palace hall with blood and rags to cover herself while her oldest friend bandaged her. It didn't help that her heart stuttered every time his fingers brushed her skin. *Let this day be done already.*

She closed her eyes to avoid seeing Zandra blur and spin before her. Drums pounded out a rhythm of pain in Jade's head as she took in shallow sips of air. Zandra re-positioned the starter bit of gauze and used one hand to wrap the front of Jade until the lowest part of the gash was covered in the soft material. The firm pressure helped to soothe the angry ache in Jade's skin, and once her chest was covered she sighed softly. At least she felt less exposed now.

Zandra held Jade up as her strength flagged, and Jade focused on the chore of breathing. Every inhale felt like a thousand knives impaling her lungs, and every exhale left her dizzy. Her mind replayed all the events of the morning, and tears slipped down her cheeks again. She'd run out to fight alongside Krista, ignoring Zak's warning, and she hadn't even reached her friend before Ben escorted her inside. At the time, she'd been simmering with impatience to prove that she could hold her own, that she wasn't some delicate princess who needed protecting.

And now here she was: she'd chased after someone who deserved justice and retribution. She'd left the safety of her team. And she'd been wounded to the point where she couldn't move on her own. Humiliation blurred with the burning pain in her chest, and she sniffled as tears splashed onto Zandra's neck.

Zandra rubbed Jade's arm with quiet shushing noises while Zak continued his ministrations. It wasn't until he smoothed his fingers against her arm that Jade realized how much time had passed.

"Finished." Zak pronounced. "Think her shirt will fit over the bandage?"

Jade twitched her nose as a strand of Zandra's hair brushed against it.

"That had been my thought. Let's try it," Zandra said.

This time, it was easier for Jade. Having both Zandra and Zak support her weight while guiding her arms into the sleeves of her blouse helped immensely, and though the shirt was blood-stained in the front and ruined to the point that only the bandages provided modesty, it felt as good as armor.

Zak braced her arms as he moved around her. "How are you

feeling? Dizzy? Cold?"

"Yes." Jade smiled her thanks as Zandra wiped Jade's tears away. "Cold. Seeing double." She bit her lip. "I can't decide who I'm more concerned about right now," she confessed. She stared down the warm amber hall devoid of the palace guard, black-clad Monomi patrolling in their stead. Exhaustion weighed heavy on her, and she fought against the drowsiness. "My father? Briar? Ben and Raine?" Jade trembled as pain radiated from her lungs. "Where'd that swordsman go? What about—"

Zandra touched a finger to Jade's lips and shook her head. The steady determination in her eyes soothed some of Jade's panic. "Don't borrow trouble. We have Monomi at Ellie's to help with cleanup and protection." Her eyebrows knit as she frowned. "And don't you worry about us breaking the treaty. That's our choice. As for Briar, I don't know how he's doing right now, but he is being cared for. The swordsman is nowhere near you, and I'm accepting that as good enough for the moment. Father and Finn will be with Slate soon. He'll be fine. For now, your job is to rest."

"Exactly." Zak scooted behind Jade and pulled her back from Zandra's balancing support. He took Jade's weight fully and held her against his chest. She stiffened, then melted against him. She could feel his heartbeat on her back, and she blinked back fresh tears at the warm feeling of safety that washed over her.

Zandra squeezed Jade's knee. "Seriously. Rest." She rocked to her heels. "I'm going to look for a couch or a bed we can move her to." Zandra shot Zak a burning look. "You're dangerously close to the line, brother." She didn't wait for him to reply, but turned on her heel and started walking down the hall, pausing to look into each open doorway.

Absurdly, the thought occurred to Jade that she was being held by Zak—truly, cradled—and she was covered in blood. She could feel that her hair had become a rat's nest of frizz and sticky knots, and her face was covered in sweat, grime, and tears. She closed her swollen eyes and tried to focus on steady breathing. Dwelling on where her pride had let her down wasn't going to help the situation any. Why, oh, why did she find this just as stressful as worrying over Briar and Father and the barrier?

"I can't lose you."

Jade's heart fluttered at Zak's whispered words. He brushed his nose against her head, and his arms tightened just enough for her to feel the pressure. She couldn't see his face, and it frustrated her, but he didn't move to shift her or anything.

"This was too close," he said. She could feel him shake his head. "Far too close. Days like this make me wonder if I should find a safe haven to hide you away in."

Jade groaned and closed her eyes against her pounding headache. "No."

A strand of hair tickled Jade's neck from Zak's whispered sigh. "No matter. Zandra was right. Rest. We'll wait here for news from Slate and Finn."

Distant shouts echoed from down the hall, and two of their Monomi guards left, their boots pounding and clacking on the tile floor. Jade struggled to sit up, and Zak kept the palm of his hand firmly pressed on her good shoulder.

"Rest."

Another yell, and this time several voices replied.

Panic surged through Jade, then dimmed. Even her body was too exhausted to keep up with the fear and worry. "But—"

Zak pressed a tense finger against her lips as he leaned forward, his hair hiding his eyes. She could imagine them being narrowed in concentration. He shook his head after several heartbeats passed. "We stay here. Where we're safe. And you get some sleep." He flashed her a quick, strained smile as the clamor escalated. "I'll let you know if something changes."

CHAPTER FIFTY-EIGHT

SLATE

Every heartbeat thundered in Slate's ears as his world fell to pieces around him. Shock numbed his legs, and he stood there, struck dumb, trying desperately to understand just how he'd reached this point. How had he failed so spectacularly?

Victor had killed Zane.

Victor was the one whom Slate had been searching for.

Victor and a *Void Born* now had the bloodstone.

Victor had been there when Brandon disappeared and was assumed dead.

Brandon was alive—by some form of miracle or magic, Slate didn't yet know. His words stuck in his throat as Blade—*Brandon*—glared at him from the other end of a crimson sword. The hard eyes cut into Slate, eviscerating him without sound or blood. What had happened to his brother-in-law? Where did the soft-hearted, friendly, young, hopeful prince go? The man whom Sapphire had loved so dearly?

Brandon had killed Jade.

His own daughter.

Grief punched a hole in Slate's chest. Jade may be Brandon and Sapphire's child, but it was he, Slate, who'd raised her. Cheered on her first steps. Taught her the wonder of skyfaring. Encouraged her to love life and live it to the fullest.

How could such a vibrant ray of hope be gone?

Was everything Slate ever did in life doomed to fail?

Slate had done everything he could to find a way to stabilize and save the barrier. And now it was collapsing from his own hand.

I failed. In everything.

Red flared iridescent and shot out from the keystone. The curtain of purple rippled, then waves of the magic splashed out toward Slate and Brandon as the ground rumbled.

Slate stumbled back from the tongue of purple and green and stared, horror twisting his gut. He fell to his knees and shivered despite the sticky heat in the room. If anyone remembered his name after this, it would be to curse him as the one who'd doomed the world.

"What did you do?" Brandon reached Slate's side, the tip of his sword poking Slate's throat. "Reverse it."

"I…" Slate tried to swallow and couldn't. The keystone flared orange. Wisps of pink and blue pulsated in time with the shuddering ground. He blinked and looked down at his hand. "I don't know if I can."

The sword point dug into Slate's neck, and warmth dribbled down his collarbone. Brandon leaned forward, his blue eyes promising murder. "Try."

Slate twitched his head in a tiny nod. "I need to stand."

Brandon backed up, his sword still drawn. Now that Slate recognized him, it was easy to match some of the old prince Brandon to this new Blade. They both took small sips of air when upset. Beneath the weathered skin and patchy beard, Slate could make out the tiny scar on Blade's chin that Sapphire had scratched there during sparring practice.

What would Sapphire have thought of all this?

Slate stood shakily. Tears slipped down his cheeks, and he bowed to Brandon. "I formally apologize to the rightful King of Doldra for my actions that resulted in the death of your family and for my actions this day."

"Just get on with it," Brandon growled.

Slate pulled out the black ring of woven stone he'd borrowed from Zak. The ring Zane had used nearly two decades ago to prevent the barrier from collapsing. He fingered the smooth edge. Zane had been injured at the time, but he gave his life over to the magic. Did Slate need to sacrifice himself, too?

Memories flitted through his mind: Jade's laughter, Garnet's teasing smirk, Samantha's loving eyes.

He'd failed Jade. But he could still protect his twin and his wife.

But would it work a second time? There was only one way to know. He tugged off his gloves and slid the artifact over his finger. Slate pulled his knife out of its sheath and laid the blade across his scarred palm. He took a deep breath, pressed the metal down, and yanked.

Blood welled up, running over his ring, his fingers, and dripping off his hand. Slate clenched his fist, and pain sent a shudder down his spine.

I'm sorry, everyone. I failed you, Zane. I love you, Samantha. The barrier blurred into a kaleidoscope of yellow and green as he stepped up to it. Bittersweet peace flooded his heart. In his death, he could be redeemed. What would Jade have thought of all this? *Goodbye, Garnet. I'm sorry to leave you alone.*

The barrier pulsated again, and Slate held his bloody hand out toward it. He stepped as close as he dared to the keystone, just out of reach of the barrier's ripples. "I give my life to defend them." A wisp of purple flared out and brushed his leg.

Icy cold flared in his shin. Weakness spread up through his leg, and he locked his knees so he wouldn't stumble into the barrier. *Finish the job. Atone.* Slate groaned as his hips started aching. His shoulders hunched of their own accord. He closed his eyes and tipped his head back.

"I offer all of me," he whispered as arthritis withered his hands. "My life for all of theirs."

Blackness swallowed Slate.

CHAPTER FIFTY-NINE

BEN

Ben gasped for air, and his legs wobbled as he ran after Raine into the citadel tower. Despite being in excellent physical condition, he'd clearly lost some of his endurance after several days recuperating from Jaxton's murder. Too focused on watching his feet, he smacked into Raine's back, and they both stumbled.

He grimaced. "Sorry, I—" Ben looked up from Raine, and his words died in his mouth. Bodies littered the keystone chamber. Three of them. The blond swordsman from Vodan knelt next to an old man crumpled close to the keystone. A breeze blew across the room from a shattered stained glass window.

He killed Jaxton. He hurt Jade—nearly killed her. Ben pushed himself off of Raine and grabbed his borrowed sword. She scrambled up with a grunt, gripping her sword while he bit back on his anger to focus on the mission at hand. Protect the world first. Revenge second.

The barrier itself shone a crimson purple, and it wavered sedately, like a rodless curtain in a room. Orange spiked from the black stone on a pedestal, and a ripple shot out from the center, but other than that, all appeared peaceful. Too peaceful.

"Where's the captain?" Ben stepped cautiously around the blood puddles to look at the first man. Overseer Nevin's glassy eyes stared at the ceiling, crimson staining his chest.

Raine approached a body on her side of the room, her sword staying between her and the swordsman. She shook her head. "Not this one." They both looked at where the swordsman knelt, his head bowed.

"He's here." The voice sounded so quiet, so broken, that Ben wasn't sure he really heard the words.

"Excuse me?" Raine asked as she approached the gray-haired dead man and the kneeling blond.

Ben shifted his grip on his blade as he approached the swordsman's side. His crimson sword lay on the floor just a stretch of the arm away. Ben toed it and kicked it farther from the blond.

The man watched his sword slide out of reach, then sighed shakily and rolled the frail man over. Raine gasped, and Ben gawked.

It was Captain Slate. Aged by several decades, but him nonetheless. Leathery wrinkles lined his face, and his arms now looked thin and reedy, with sagging skin instead of the toned, strong muscles that Ben remembered. Slate's eyes were closed, and his brows were pulled together in a grimace despite the peaceful smile on his lips.

Ben's sword slipped in his grasp as he stared. "How?"

The man nodded sideways at the barrier. "It touched him." He lifted his red-rimmed blue eyes to look at Ben. "The girl that had been with you. Is she—"

"She may yet live," Raine interrupted with a snarl. She stalked forward and held the edge of her blade to the man's throat. "No thanks to you, scum."

Please, let her live. Ben's shoulders sagged as he glanced at her father's body. How would he break the news to her?

A clatter in the hallway announced the arrival of Finn, Zak's father, and two black-clad Monomi, whom Ben didn't know. Color faded from Finn's face when he looked down at Slate's body. He shook his head, took a deep breath, then muttered and moved closer to inspect the barrier. His fisted hands trembled. Zak's father strode between Raine and Ben and stopped abruptly when the swordsman raised his face.

"Who are you?" Zak's father's strong voice came out in a pained gasp. His eyes traveled from Slate's aged body back to the blond.

The blond lifted his hand slowly. He hunched forward, his spine curving fully as he sighed. "Zebediah…it's me." His eyes flicked up, then squeezed shut. "Brandon."

Ben watched, feeling as if he was missing some important piece of the puzzle when Zebediah dropped to his knees, staring over Slate's body at Brandon. The elder Monomi worked his mouth for a moment, before spreading his fingers over his knees and fisting them there.

"How are you alive? Where have you been?" Zebediah's eyes narrowed on the crimson blade beyond Brandon. "Is that sword yours?"

Brandon bowed his head. "It's mine, yes." His hoarse voice shook with emotion. "Take me into custody. I tried to kill…my own daughter without knowing who she was."

Zebediah rocked back and ran his hand through his hair with an oath. "You're the one who struck Jade." He lumbered to his feet and motioned for the other two Monomi who came in with him and Finn. They hauled Brandon up. "We'll sort this out later, Highness. But no, you didn't kill her." He glanced at Finn. "She's gravely wounded, but she'll live. For now, we have more pressing business to attend to."

Raine joined Finn in his inspection of the barrier. She stood barely a hand's breadth away from it, whereas Finn stayed farther back, both of them peering through the purple veil. Finn frowned as he studied the keystone, straddling Slate's feet.

"Raine, come here." Finn motioned and pointed toward the rock. "I can't tell, is there yellow in the center, or orange?"

Raine leaned over, her face far closer to the wavering energy. "Yellow."

Finn carefully stepped back and around Slate's body. He knelt on one knee next to Slate, lifting one limp hand, then the other. Slate's hands looked ancient in Finn's strong grip. "Slate must have prevented it from fully collapsing." Finn gently tugged a black ring off Slate's blood-coated hand. He folded the fingers into a fist and rested it over Slate's breastbone. White hair brushed over Finn's forehead as he dropped his chin. "Go, rest in peace in Areilia, my son."

Finn stood and slipped the ring on his smallest finger, then looked at Ben. "Raine and I will need to stay for a while to finish the restoration of the barrier." He shot Ben a tired look. "Before you ask, the 'how' is something for another day. Please return to the palace and check on Jade's recovery." His eyes drooped. "And give her news of her father."

Brandon twisted between the two Monomi to look back at Finn. "You. You're—" His eyes widened and he pulled against the guards, his pupils dilated. "My daughter, Adeline, she's injured. A grievous sword injury. Please—"

Zebediah pressed his hand between Brandon's shoulder blades and pushed him toward the door. "She's been taken care of. And we'll settle everything later." Zebediah looked back at Ben. "Let's leave them to it."

Ben glanced at Raine and Finn and nodded, following the strange procession out. He'd done barely anything helpful on the way. He was always just a moment too late. Weariness sank into his bones, and he shook his head with a sigh.

He had to get stronger. He had to finish piecing together his past. He knew he didn't belong here—that his sister was waiting for him back home. How to get home, how he'd gotten here, who he could trust with that information...all that would need to be discovered still. For now, he had to accept that this would be his new normal. He'd have to regain his strength here, do what he could to help—and find a way home.

And that meant getting back to Jade and Zak. And the rest of the *Sapphire* crew.

Blood stuck to the bottom of Ben's shoes as he paused in the doorway, glancing back at Raine and Finn. Finn held his hands up to the barrier, head bowed. Raine waited close to the keystone, watching Ben. She offered a quick, tight smile, and motioned for him to leave.

Ben nodded and turned away. Whatever the future held, he wanted to be strong enough to face it.

CHAPTER SIXTY

JADE

Jade woke silently, her body tingling as she tried to place what was wrong. A quick inhale reminded her of the jagged cut across her chest. Her lungs ached with a sharpness that she'd never felt before this day. Her eyes popped open. They were in Doldra. The keystone. Her father!

She tried to sit up but red-hot fire raced through her body, and she dropped her head back against the pillow.

This wasn't the open, golden hallway in which she had fought that swordsman. She was in a room now, stretched out on a plush couch. Luminary crystals in sconces shone dimly, illuminating an elegantly carved and gilded door frame and a center table with a crystalline sculpture. Jade craned her neck to look back, and she could barely make out what looked to be a wet bar. Her breath hitched.

Zak sat in a chair by her head, his bare sword across his knees as he watched her, his green eyes glimmering, dark and inscrutable. His fingers twitched, but he didn't move toward her. "How are you feeling?"

Jade leaned her head back, attempting to keep him in her line of sight without pulling the skin on her chest. The tender skin on her shoulder stretched, and agony lanced through her, so she forced herself to relax into the couch, letting her head loll to the side. *It's awkward to talk to someone I can't even make eye contact with.* "I'm alive. What have I missed?"

She heard his quiet snort, and she jumped when his knuckles brushed against her matted hair. He moved to the couch across from her, allowing her to see him without straining herself.

"Alive is good." Zak glanced at the open doorway as someone hustled by, their shadow momentarily darkening the square of light that illuminated the rug. "We've taken over the palace."

Exhaustion and pain fogged Jade's mind, and she blinked at Zak. "We?"

"We Monomi." He smiled grimly, and a minute shrug lifted his frame. "Now we're all guilty of breaking the Monomi Treaty. Either some major reform will happen since Bentley has just been kicked out, or they'll all be banished like me."

Zak's words didn't make sense to her, and she licked her dry lips as she struggled to make sense of it all. "Bentley is gone?"

"He fled." Zak leaned against the couch, and the dim light did little to hide his muscles as he folded his arms behind his head. "Coward left as soon as Brigley showed up and announced that he'd been to the shipping yards, witnessed the cleanup there, and that you—our crown princess—are alive and had been attacked by Bentley's men dressed as bandits." His lips quirked. "I guess Ellie decided it was time to let the secret free."

Jade struggled to sit up and grimaced when Zak sprang from his seat to help her. No matter how injured she was, there was just some news she wasn't going to be lying on her back for. Sweat beaded her forehead, and she tried to blink back the tears that sprang to her eyes as pain radiated through her chest.

He brushed a wayward tear from her cheek.

She searched his eyes. "Zak, I don't want to be a princess."

"I know." He rubbed his thumb against his forehead. "I don't know what to tell you. You are who you are."

The doorway darkened, and someone rapped lightly against the frame. Samantha and Ben walked in, and Krista pushed past them and rushed to Jade's side.

Tears shimmered in Krista's eyes as she knelt by Jade, her hands over her mouth. "Oh, Jade, what *happened*?"

Samantha nudged Krista, and Krista scooted over to make space. Sam's belt tools clattered as she sat next to Jade. Samantha's hands trembled while she gently un-braided Jade's hair.

"Hey," Ben greeted softly. He tweaked the toe of Jade's boot as he sat with his back to the door, keeping himself in her line of sight. "How are you feeling?"

She was going to be hearing that question often. Jade's lungs ached, but she smiled tremulously regardless. "I'll survive." She closed her eyes against the dizziness that threatened to overwhelm her. So many questions to ask, where should she start? She strained to reach out and brush her hand against Krista's cornrow braids. "Briar?"

Krista grasped Jade's trembling fingers and pressed them between her brown hands. Her smile quivered. "He'll live." She took a deep breath and rubbed the back of Jade's hand. "When you're up to it, we'll need to design a prosthetic for him."

Some of the pressure in Jade's chest eased. "That'll give me something to do while I lay about, I guess." She studied Ben's drooping brow and slumped posture. "How about you?"

Ben sighed and shifted his gaze to the sculpture on the table. He glanced at Samantha.

She looked sideways at the woman she considered her mother and read the story of pain and loss in the lines around Samantha's eyes. "What happened? Was there another attack at the shipyard?"

Samantha shook her head, and loose strands of brown hair brushed her cheek. "No, love, the yards are safe again. Aunt Garnet and Aunt Rebecca are overseeing the cleanup." A small smile lightened her eyes before they dimmed with sorrow again.

Another stone of worry off her chest. "That's good news." Jade's smile slipped away as she surveyed her mother. "There's more, though. Where's Father?" She hesitated, and added, her voice almost inaudible to her own ears, "Slate."

Samantha closed her eyes, and two tears trailed over her cheekbones. She swallowed and thumbed away the proof of sorrow before she blinked open her eyes and looked at Jade's lap. "Garnet told me that they finally told you. I'm sorry I wasn't there for that."

Zak shifted on the couch across from Jade.

She shot him a look to prevent him from jumping in with his opinion on her uncle and aunt's poor timing. "It is what it is. Nothing between us has changed; you're still my mother. Family is a choice." She tried to suppress her shiver of trepidation. "What aren't you saying?"

Jade played with the fringe of a pillow just within reach of her fingers and tried to swallow the lump of fear in her throat when no one answered.

Zak's gaze found hers, and she could see her quiet dread reflected there. *Where is Father if Mother is here?*

Ben gripped the wooden arms of his chair and crossed his ankle over his knee, then dropped both feet to the floor. He leaned forward, pressing his palms together, shooting Samantha a look that Jade couldn't decipher. Krista's eyes dropped.

Samantha sniffled in the silence.

Zak sheathed his sword and settled it across his knees. He crossed his arms. "Out with it."

Samantha motioned to Krista and turned her face away.

Krista's brown eyes filled with slow tears. "He's gone."

Jade heard wrong. She let go of the fringe and struggled to pull in a deep enough breath to banish her dizziness. "Say again?"

Ben stood and paced away from her, and she finally noticed the blood splatters on his pant legs and the grime that dirtied his hands. He turned and settled his hands on the back of the couch that Zak sat on. "A vapor of the barrier touched him." Ben's voice gentled, and he shook his head. "I'm sorry, but Captain Slate is dead."

Black spots swam in her vision, and she couldn't make out what Zak said over the rushing in her ears. Her eyes fluttered shut as she wordlessly mouthed her denial, tears brimming. Samantha leaned into Jade, her arm gently winding across Jade's back, tugging her into a side-hug. Krista gripped Jade's hand.

"When I left, Finn and Raine were working to stabilize the keystone," Ben answered Zak, his voice distant. "Sounded like the captain had prevented its collapse, and they were going to use a ring or something to finish the job." Ben knelt before Jade. Compassion softened his face as he squeezed her ankle. "I'm truly sorry that we're the bearers of such bad news."

Jade swallowed thickly as tears streamed down her cheeks. "He did it though? He helped with the barrier? Protecting us?"

Samantha nodded, her voice hoarse with tears. "As best we understand, yes."

Heartache curled Jade over until her chest felt like thousands of knives were being stabbed into it, and she straightened as best she could. Breathing felt impossible now. How could he be gone? Dead?

Jade shook her head, desperate to reject the ring of truth in Ben's voice, the tears of sorrow on Krista's cheeks, and the sound of honest grief coming from Samantha. *I want to wake up from this nightmare.*

A muscle in Ben's jaw twitched as he pressed his shoulders back. "There's more. Victor stole the bloodstone and escaped." Ben pressed his lips together. "And he apparently had a hand in killing Zane."

Jade watched Zak's face pale to ashen gray. Then he wore broken, naked sorrow. Finally, his eyes burned. His knuckles cracked as he squeezed his hands into fists. "Victor?"

"Victor," Ben confirmed.

Jade's body ached as she rubbed at her eyes, but she couldn't halt the flow of grief any more than she could stop the burning pain across her chest and lungs. *Gone. Father is gone. We had a traitor onboard.* "But he was our friend," Jade whispered.

Zak rubbed his face in his hands.

The light pressure of Samantha's comforting arm pressed into Jade as her mother began sobbing quietly. Jade held her breath while she shifted forward just enough to relieve the strain on her back. Krista jumped up and slid a pillow behind Jade, and Jade smiled her thanks up at her childhood friend. Then she clutched Samantha's slender fingers, trying not to break down herself.

"We'll give you ladies some privacy." Ben glanced at Zak, and his expression hardened. "I need to talk to you."

CHAPTER SIXTY-ONE

BEN

Ben stepped into the brightly lit hallway with Zak. They moved across the wide hall, keeping in sight the room where the ladies mourned together.

Reflexively, Ben settled into a wide stance, hands clasped behind the small of his back. *Parade rest,* his mind supplied. He pressed his lips together. When he'd started thinking of Zak as a superior officer, he didn't know, but the role fit the Guardian well enough, and Ben didn't mind giving respect where it was due.

And it was another thing that distanced him from the situation. He wasn't from here. He had a flesh-and-blood sister waiting for him back home. An image of a magnificent metal-wrought tower, lit up for Christmas, flashed through his mind. *Paris. My home is in Paris.* How he'd traveled from Earth to Terrene, he had no idea. But it'd happened. Somehow.

Ben's eyes followed Zak as the Monomi paced, his stride sharp and jerky—not his usual smooth, prowling saunter.

Zak finally stopped in the center of the burgundy carpet and exhaled deeply. "What more is there?" Loss radiated from Zak's eyes. "How do you know Victor killed my brother?"

Ben centered his weight and lifted his chin, ignoring Zak's questions. "This is all hypothetical, but I'm guessing that Victor is the one who somehow figured out who Jade is, told Everett, and got Andre arrested. He must have also helped to orchestrate that attack on the shipping yards. Probably told Bentley of our recent trouble with bandits. Apparently those 'bandits' at the yards were actually Bentley's men." He smirked. "Their military-issue boots would have given them away, even if Geist hadn't overheard Bentley talking about the attack and put the pieces together. Irony is, the real bandits attacked the palace here while the guards were at the yards."

Zak crossed his arms and rubbed his jaw, his gaze distant. "Victor stole the bloodstone, you say?" He dropped his hand and tucked it under his arm. "Why? What was his motive?"

"From what I was told, I'm guessing bring it down." Ben relaxed and shoved his hands in his pockets, studying the intricate whorls woven in the rug. "It sounds like he didn't do anything to help the barrier today." He looked up to see Zak staring at him with knit brows. "And a Void Born joined him."

Zak blinked several times and raised a hand to his forehead. "What do you mean, a *Void Born* joined him? How do you know all this?"

"I'll get to the 'how' in a minute." Ben lifted his hands in a shrug. "A man joined Victor in the citadel, got knocked into the barrier during a fight, and walked out, unscathed."

Color drained from Zak's face. "That's impossible."

"I'm just repeating what I've heard." Ben paced away, then back. "And this is a guess of mine, but I think Jaxton had been working with Victor to take down the barrier."

"Lord Everett's mani-meds agreed with Jaxton, though." Zak scowled. He settled his hand on his sword hilt and tapped his fingers against it. "Unless he's in on it and they lied, too. Does Everett want the barrier down? Why would he risk his power and control against the north?"

Ben shrugged. "Your guess is as good as mine. But apparently Jaxton altered the scrolls we sent to Lord Everett's mani-meds."

"Who's this source you know so much from?"

Spine straightening as he sighed, Ben clasped his forearms behind him, and he led Zak to the portrait that had caught his eye when he'd come in with Samantha earlier. He stopped and silently took in the young couple sitting for the portrait. Though dignified, humor sparkled in the red-headed woman's blue eyes, and, even in the painting, Ben could see the dusting of freckles across the woman's creamy cheeks. The man next to her held himself with a regal air, a simple crown resting on his blond hair. Though somber, his lips had a slight curve to them, as if he was about to laugh or smile.

"You know these two, right?" Ben asked Zak.

Zak raised a dark eyebrow and nodded. "Jade's parents. Prince Brandon and Lady Sapphire." He swallowed convulsively as he stared up at Sapphire. "I made a promise to her, on the day she died, that I would protect her daughter. I failed today."

"Jade's alive—and her injury isn't your fault." A lead ball settled in Ben's gut. What a twisted web this was. He inclined his head to the painting.

Zak sighed. "What's your point?"

"You won't like this. And Samantha hasn't heard this yet, so be forewarned." Ben gestured. "Blade is Brandon. He's my source. He was there when the barrier was first disrupted, he saw Victor kill Zane, and he was enslaved by Jaxton."

Ben ignored Zak's jaw drop and continued to look up at the portrait. Now that he could really look at it, he could see the similarities between the young, happy prince and the broken, toughened swordsman. From what he'd overheard between Blade—Brandon—and Zebediah, the prince had been through hell and back. No wonder he hadn't recognized his own daughter. He hadn't even known she'd survived the attack against the palace as a baby.

Zak blanched, and he widened his stance, presumably to stay steady on his feet. "This is confirmed? How do you know?"

"He's under arrest and was talking to your father with familiarity."

"Whales of the bleeding Void," Zak swore, pushing both hands through his dark hair as he stared at Ben. "That's why he looked familiar." He lapsed into silence, hands still in his hair, while he processed the information. "I knew I recognized him in Vodan, but I thought it was impossible. But it was him. And he hurt his own daughter." He clenched his fists. "He's not getting near her again. Ever."

"Agreed." Ben scratched at his beard and shrugged. "But how do we explain all this to Jade? Samantha?" He leaned against the cool wall and looked down to the dark doorway. "They're already processing so much. And I don't know how Jade would take it, losing her adopted father and nearly being killed by her biological father all in one day. Let alone Briar's injury."

Zak pinched the bridge of his nose and breathed deeply. "I'll tell her myself in a bit. She needs some time for Slate first." He shook his head, and Ben noticed the glimmer of tears in Zak's eyes. "The man who murdered my brother…I've dreamt of killing this faceless man for so long, and now I find that I trained, worked, lived alongside him. Unbelievable."

Ben crossed his arms and waited for a few minutes to let Zak mull over everything. "What are you going to do now?"

"I don't know." Zak stared at the floor, his brow wrinkled. "I'm not leaving Jade's side." He closed his eyes and pressed his lips together, fists clenched. "And I don't want Zane's killer to walk free. I'll need to think about it."

Ben stared down the elegant hall, taking in the sweeping portraits, the gilded doorways, the carved luminary crystals. This was supposed to be Jade's home. "Here's to hoping we have time to think. Lord Everett won't waste a second when he finds out that Jade's still alive. He wants her dead."

Zak pivoted and slammed his fist against the wall. Plaster dented under his knuckles. His shoulders pressed back as he shook his head, his voice deep, nearly a growl. "Over my dead body."

CHAPTER SIXTY-TWO

JADE

Grass rippled across Jade's ankles, and she closed her eyes against the feeling on her hyper-sensitive skin. She clutched Aunt Garnet's hand while Samantha walked through the crowd. Her mother's freshly cut hair rippled along her jaw in the breeze. Samantha kept her head high, though her hands trembled as she presented the long lock of brown braided hair to Finn, the officiator of Slate's funeral.

Finn accepted the offering, his own eyes moist, and Samantha sank into the seat next to Jade as Finn lifted Samantha's hair in the Piovant custom of widow-rites.

"Today we mourn the changing season of life." Finn spoke, his voice clear and loud enough to ring through the cemetery field filled with Slate's family members, friends, and business associates.

Jade held her breath as Finn continued, hoping desperately that he would remember his promise to her.

"Captain Slate Stohner gave his all in defense of Doldra and southern Terrene, leaving behind his mother, Madame Elinora Stohner, his elder sister, Garnet Stohner, his wife, Captain Samantha Stohner, and his daughter, Jade Stohner."

Samantha's hand slipped over Jade's and squeezed as Jade

let out a sigh of relief. *Thank you, Finn.* Her fingers crept up her high neckline and she touched the somber burgundy ruffle that lined her throat, hiding her healing chest. It didn't matter what her grandmother, Mister Monomi, Zak, Ben, or anyone else said. She was not a princess. Her father was Slate Stohner. Not the man who'd slaughtered so many and nearly killed her.

Jade glanced over to where Zak stood amongst his family, his square jaw set while his eyes roved over where she sat with the women in her family. The Monomi had insisted on providing security for Slate's memorial, and so they lined the gathering, the sun reflecting off their formal, white clothes, nearly blinding anyone who looked directly at them. *They look like avenging angels.*

Somewhere in the back, Zebediah and his brother guarded Prince Brandon, who had insisted on coming today. She wove her fingers with her mother's and refused to even glance over her shoulder. Jade's family was *here*. And in the crew of the *Sapphire*.

She tilted her head to see the two somber rows of airship hands. Kerlee caught her eye, and a corner of his lip tilted up before he looked away. These were her people. Not those who would put her on a throne.

And definitely not the one in the back—whose blade had brought the death of so many. The *Sapphire* crew had lost four in the attack on the yards, the Monomi had lost one, and her grandmother had lost six of her men.

Blade and his bandits had murdered at least twenty-six in the palace.

Finn's voice pulled Jade from her dark musings, "We declare him a hero. May his legacy live on in those who knew him." Finn lit the two shallow bronze bowls of incense and stepped back as the smoke drifted across the grass. He lifted his hands, signaling to those gathered that they could approach and say goodbye to the aged body in the simple casket.

Jade rose and followed the scarlet hem of Samantha's long skirt. Doldran custom dictated that surviving family wear red as a symbol of the bond between family, and Jade hated it. She'd seen too much blood in the last three days. The moment the ceremony was over, she planned to change into something less nausea-inducing.

Smooth wood met Jade's unsteady fingers as she looked down on the lined face of the man she called father. Slate's closed eyes looked relaxed, almost peaceful. Samantha's long braid had been tied around his folded hands in Piovantian tradition. Tears blurred Jade's sight, and she brushed a kiss against his cool forehead before hastening away for Garnet and Ellie to say goodbye.

Jade took a shaky breath, and, for once, didn't jump when Ben's hand steadied her elbow. "Where to?" He had been her shadow whenever Zak wasn't readily available. No matter what time of day or night it was, she was guaranteed one of them. She pointed and he nodded.

People parted to let Ben lead Jade to where Krista sat with Briar in his wheelchair. Briar offered a tiny smile as he gingerly rubbed his knee, just above the empty pants leg.

"I'm waiting for everyone else to go through," Briar said as he waved a hand at his mobile contraption. "Navigating grass and crowds with this isn't a great idea."

"Are you sure you should even be out of bed?" Jade asked, regretting the question even as she spoke.

Briar nodded firmly, a fire burning in his brown eyes. "I can't not say goodbye. Not when I was lucky enough to survive."

Jade hugged herself awkwardly, her healing skin protesting the movement. What could she say to that? He was right, of course.

Krista wove her fingers between Briar's and lifted her face to Jade. "Our plan is postponed for the time being, obviously."

Jade huffed a small laugh, then winced. "No kidding." She fluttered a hand between the palace and herself, and then gestured to the people gathered. "Three days, and I still don't know what to think about all this, let alone what to do."

"For now, rest, Jade." Briar's grin looked more like a grimace. "You have the same problem that Krista does: you think better on your feet. You need to learn how to take it easy, let your body heal, *and* process it all." The lines of pain around his eyes eased, and he offered a soft smile. "I know you can do it."

She nodded her silent thanks to her friends and turned to look for Zak, quickly spotting him despite the sea of white. His gaze met hers, and his eyes widened.

"Adeline."

Jade lifted her hem so as not to snag it on a particularly tall lump of grass and started moving toward Zak, not recognizing the voice behind her. Ben swore loudly, and she turned to scold him, then stumbled when she saw who stood behind her, flanked by two white-clad Monomi.

Zak gripped her arm to steady her as he stepped in front of her, his broad shoulders shielding her from Brandon. Ben moved to Zak's side, the two of them facing down the shorter blond man.

He'd cleaned up well, for being a lost prince of ruthless bandits. His long ponytail had disappeared in favor of a shorter one that curled just below his shoulders, and his scruffy beard was shaved.

Shadows danced in his blue eyes as he tried to peer around Ben and Zak. "Adeline."

"My name is Jade."

A flash of irritation darkened Brandon's eyes, and he flattened his lips. "I'm sorry. We named you Adeline, and it's hard for me to think of you as anyone different."

Zak shifted, blocking Brandon from her sight. "What do you want?" Anger burned in Zak's voice, and he touched his sword hilt.

Jade slid her fingers under Zak's elbow and pressed her hand against Ben's shoulder, gently moving them apart just enough that she could see.

Brandon's head snapped up, and he stared at her, his eyes searching hers. "I'm sorry," he said, his voice cracking. "I didn't know. I...I thought you were dead. And—"

"And you nearly killed her," Zak muttered.

Jade squeezed his elbow in silent warning.

Breathe. Jade focused on shallow breaths, trying to avoid hyperventilating or pulling at more of her stitches with deep inhales. She blinked back tears of frustration and fear, opting to look at the shiny buttons that lined Brandon's dark blue jacket. *Why did they let him talk to me?*

"Jade," Brandon spoke her name hesitantly, trying it out. "Your name suits you."

"Thank you."

Silence stretched between them. Ben shifted his weight from foot to foot, and Zebediah coughed.

"What—" Brandon cleared his throat. "–what will you be doing now?"

Jade resisted the urge to shrug and shook her head instead. "For the immediate future, healing. I was recently maimed, you see."

Pain shadowed Brandon's eyes. *Good. Let him hurt.* He deserved so much worse.

Now it was Zak's hand on her elbow, offering silent support. She recognized the slight tremor in his shoulders as a suppressed snort. She raised her eyes to stare into Brandon's unfamiliar gaze. "Whatever I do, it will be what I want to do. I'm a mechanic, daughter of Slate Stohner."

Brandon's eyes flashed, and he lifted his eyebrows with a derisive laugh. "That may be how you see yourself, but that's not how others view you. Like it or not, you're my daughter. And once news of you spreads to the nobles here, let alone the other kingdoms, your life will never be how you want it. Accept that."

Curiosity warred with the desire to spin on her heel and walk away. What was with him and his constantly shifting attitude? She leaned into Zak, seeking stability from the exhaustion that rolled over her. "What do you mean?" Jade shivered at Brandon's look of pity.

"Politics are a battlefield you are woefully unprepared for." He looked to the Doldran palace gleaming in the distance. "And Lord Everett will not be pleased to know that either of us is alive."

Ben coughed deep in his throat while Zak's body tensed.

"Actually, he does know about me," Jade said finally. "And he's already arrested my uncle for hiding the truth."

Confusion crossed Brandon's face as he mouthed *uncle* to himself. "Then you know the danger you're in."

Zak tucked Jade's hand over his arm and steered her away, looking over his shoulder at Brandon. "She knows, as do we. We will keep her safe, unlike her father."

Jade allowed Zak to guide her away, Ben trailing after them. The people mingling parted to let them through while Jade's mind tumbled over itself in consternation.

What if he was right? Her life wouldn't be what she wanted. *Am I going to lose all my freedom?*

She blinked at the green directly in her face and realized that Zak had leaned down to be at her eye level. Tiny lines furrowed his brow as he gently gripped her upper arms.

"Don't think of what he said. Not today. We'll figure out how to protect you, no matter what you choose." He nodded to Samantha as she walked toward them. Ellie and Garnet stood in a tearful discussion just beyond. "For now, you need to focus on the moment. Here and now. Be with your family. We'll deal with tomorrow when tomorrow comes. Not before."

"And you'll be there tomorrow?"

Surprise flickered across Zak's face, and a fresh line creased his forehead. "Of course. Why wouldn't I be?"

"Because you think you're not right for me. Because you think you failed, that I got injured when you were supposed to protect me. Because you think it's not your place to be with me." Tears welled in Jade's eyes, and she fluttered her eyelids in an attempt to hold the evidence of her distress back. She stared down at her shoes and the blade of grass that waved in the breeze between her feet. "I'm afraid you're going to leave."

"I'm not going anywhere."

Jade didn't look up. She released a shuddering sigh and raised her gaze enough to see his chest rise and fall as he breathed. "What do you think I should do?"

"Right now, I think you should focus on getting better, taking it easy, and spending time with your family. If you get bored, help Krista design the prosthetic for Briar." Zak ducked into her line of sight and pinned her with his brilliant gaze. "The challenges that you'll face won't be for you to deal with alone. I'll be with you, every step of the way, and that's that."

"Why?"

At last his confidence wavered, and he shifted back and rubbed the back of his neck, looking at her out of the corner of his eye. He sucked in his cheek for a moment before replying. "I already told you why: you are my princess." A faint blush rose in his face, and he swallowed, breaking eye contact. "And, I care about you." His gaze darted toward her and then away. "'Care' may be too soft a word. Regardless, I will follow where you go, and do all within my power to protect you."

Something in Jade's belly warmed at his words, and the sight of his flushed cheeks made her smile. She carefully tucked her hands behind her back to resist the urge to touch his jaw. "If I choose to not be a princess, can we be together?"

"Jade." Pain flashed in Zak's eyes, and he closed them, taking a deep breath. "I can't make promises. There's no guarantee that you won't be forced to take up leadership. I know you don't want to," he added hurriedly as she narrowed her eyes, "and I support whatever you choose. But we need to take things one day at a time. Let's see what tomorrow brings. And I'll be here for whatever that is."

Jade nodded and leaned into Zak, hugging him as best as her wounds would allow, unwilling to even contemplate what tomorrow would bring.

CHAPTER SIXTY-THREE

BEN

Ben ran his fingers down his mug, rubbing off all the condensation. He wiped his wet hand on his pants leg, then set his elbows on the table and leaned forward to better hear Finn.

Finn sat at the far end of the sturdy table with Raine to his right, and Garnet next to her. Zebediah and Zak sat across from the ladies, flanking Brandon.

Why Brandon had to be there, Ben wasn't sure.

Ben hadn't been too surprised to learn that Garnet owned a pub that the Monomi ran in her absence. She managed all the financial and managerial aspects on the *Sapphire*, so somehow her having another business endeavor on the side just made sense. This morning it was open just for their group—the kitchen silent, the drinks and food provided by Garnet and Zandra, Zak's elder sister.

A long oak bar gleamed in the luminary light. Sparkling glasses and polished mugs sat on a rack behind it. Sunlight streamed through the fogged glass panes, casting a crimson hawk on each table from the center of each window. Though the place was empty but for their group, it was easy to imagine the bustle, the laughter, the noise of the pub when it was open. Scuffs and scratches marred the floor by the door, and the tables bore the inevitable dents of time and wear. The entire place had a feel to it that Ben could only think of as "homey," if such a word could be used for an eating establishment and inn.

Finn pulled a thick stack of discolored papers from a worn leather satchel and set them reverently on the polished wood. He braced his hands on the edge of the table and looked around at the small group.

"For those of you who didn't know, Raine was orphaned by thugs looking for me, and right before that dark time, several of my important documents were stolen." Finn tapped a finger against the papers before him. "These are Doctor Taylor's notes." He shuffled the papers and drew out a stack that was half the size of the original. "These are *my* notes from twenty years ago."

Ben's eyebrows shot up as he digested Finn's words. Finn hadn't mentioned any of those details when they were on the *Phoenix* together. Ben glanced at Raine's smooth face, her calm eyes. She hadn't mentioned why she was with her grandfather either, so hearing that she, too, was an orphan interested Ben. How had she lost her parents? Did she remember them? Ben blinked away a hazy memory of his own parents dancing in the kitchen, and he honed in on the conversation before he could miss something important.

Zandra pulled out the remaining chair at the table and sat at Ben's right. She tucked a strand of dark hair behind her ear as she nodded to Finn.

Finn continued. "As you know, we were able to determine through these notes that the keystone was in danger of being brought down—due to Jaxton lying about the bloodstone and its intended uses. What you don't know is that Jaxton was sharing his findings with someone, and I suspect this person could make Jaxton's motives look sweet and cuddly in comparison."

"Lucio." Brandon kept his palms flat against the table while he spoke, his eyes wild with hatred. His nostrils flared as he fisted his hands. He looked around the table, the fire in his gaze almost searing to the soul when he reached Ben. "Jaxton talked about him on occasion."

That's why he's here. Intel. Ben racked his brain, but couldn't think of meeting anyone named Lucio.

"He spoke freely to you about his activities?" Garnet asked softly.

Brandon's lip curled. "I was his obedient puppet, his dog. You don't mince your words or your activities around your pets, do you? That's all I was to Jaxton. He didn't think of me as someone with a mind anymore, and so I learned more than he ever intended."

Garnet shrank into her high-backed chair with a pained sigh. Ben studied Brandon's loose blond hair that tried to hide his clenched jaw. It had been wise to leave Jade at the shipping yards with Samantha and the rest of the group to recover. Physical health aside, she would not have handled this meeting well.

Finn nodded. "It looks like Jaxton was working alongside Victor to at least some degree, though there's not much of a paper trail to prove that."

"And now Victor has the bloodstone. *And* a Void Born." Zak hunched over the scarred table on his elbows, his fists white-knuckled.

"Yes." Finn rubbed at the line creasing his forehead with a grimace. He looked to Garnet. "Do we have any idea where he would go with it?"

Garnet shook her head and unwrapped her fingers from her clay mug with a helpless shrug. "Your guess is as good as mine. If he was working with Everett at all, maybe he went to Aerugo? But I can't imagine why Everett would want the barrier to fall." She fiddled with the lace on her sleeve. "Does Everett know about the Void Born? What's his endgame?"

"I'm guessing that Everett teamed up with Victor only because he wanted the Doldras family gone, or for some reason we haven't figured out yet," Zebediah stated. His posture remained perfect as he sat, arms crossed, dark eyes thoughtful. "We need to get teams out to each of the locations to make sure he can't access any other keystones."

Ben leaned in toward Garnet and whispered, "There are seven keystones, right?"

She turned, a red curl falling over her cheek as she murmured, "Right. Scattered all over southern Terrene. They're all connected, so if one fails, they all go down. And the barrier that rings around southern Terrene will be gone."

Ben shook his head in quiet awe. Victor could go anywhere, and they'd be scrambling to figure out which location. This would be beyond challenging.

"Victor is a phantom." Brandon warned. "When I first saw him in the citadel, twenty years ago, he had a ponytail, a suit, and looked like a respectable shopkeeper. Now he's bald with an earring and worn clothing. Even his gait changed, though that may be because of time. The only real way to know it's him is in the eyes."

Ben hummed in agreement before clearing his throat to speak up. "It's true. I was on a mission with Victor earlier this year, and he had some solid tips for blending in with the crowd. He's going to be hard to find." Ben fell silent, resentment at being fooled by Victor burning in his blood.

Finn shrugged. "Maybe so, but we need to find him before he

can do anything else."

"Do you think he would try anything against the royal family?" Garnet raised her eyes to look at Brandon. She swallowed hard, and her fingers traced her neck. "Would he attempt to finish off the Doldras line?"

Zebediah sighed heavily and leaned back, his chair creaking under him in protest. "Who knows?"

Brandon took a sip from his mug and set it down with a quiet tap. "Rumors are already abounding about Ade—about Jade being alive. I'm not going to take up the crown." He crossed his arms and tilted his head. "I'll acknowledge Jade as my heir, when the nobles and people demand action, but the leader they're going to want isn't me."

"She makes her own choices," Zak all but growled, his eyes glowing with green ire. He leaned into Brandon's space and stabbed the table with a finger. "If she's to be heir, that's something she decides, not anyone else for her. And she doesn't want anything to do with *you*."

"And if neither of us holds the throne, what then for you Monomi?" Brandon returned, his tone as harsh as his eyes. "If Everett stays in power, the lives of all the Monomi are forfeit. You raised weapons against the governor. You didn't just break the treaty—you completely shattered it. Do you want all your family and people to die?" He gestured to Zandra, whose face had paled, though her eyes remained sharp and focused. "Aren't you an uncle, by now? What about your nieces and nephews, your cousins, your brethren?"

Garnet held her hands out over the table, as if she could keep the two men separated. "Let's not get ahead of ourselves."

"What's the condition of the keystone?" Ben called out. He took a quick swig of his ale before it could warm too much, and shot

Garnet a small grin when she mouthed "thank you."

The stiffness in Zak's spine softened just a smidge, and Brandon's glare eased.

Finn's lips twitched as he inclined his head to Ben. "It has been fully restored." Finn paused for the quiet sighs of relief to die down. He held out a hand to squeeze Garnet's fingers. "We wouldn't have been able to do so, if it wasn't for Slate's help. We needed both the lodestone ring and the bloodstone to accomplish the work."

"It's fully restored?" Zak echoed, wonderment erasing his face of all traces of bitterness. "How?"

Finn sat back and wove his fingers together. "The keystone needed to be weakened for us to accurately restore it." He thumped his hands against the stack of papers. "Think of it like this: if a bone is broken, and it is allowed to heal without being set, it can work, but it won't work properly, won't be as strong as it could be. It needs to be re-broken and set in place for it to heal as it should. Still using that analogy, the bloodstone allowed us to re-break the keystone, and the ring allowed us to set and heal it."

Brandon picked at his nails and shot Finn a sharp look. "I've been wondering about something. How do you know all this—how to do it? You're more than just an herbalist. You're a remarkable healer and mani-med. I know this, personally, when…" his voice trailed off and he coughed, then continued, "You know so much about the keystone and barrier. How? Who are you?"

Finn's gaze traveled from the table to the unlit hearth in the corner of the room, and he was silent for so long that Ben wondered if Finn intended to answer the question.

Finn sighed. "I was the apprentice of Sage Randall Silvers. He had been apprenticed to—"

"Sage Flint." Zebediah nodded in what looked like sudden understanding. "He was one of the sages who disappeared after they erected the barrier." Respect shone in his eyes. "It makes perfect sense now."

"Ah, yes. Exactly." A small smile crossed Finn's lips and he looked at Raine, then around the table. "The question is what we will each do now." He thumbed through the papers before him, and unbuttoned his cuffs to roll his sleeves to his forearms. "Raine and I need to find Victor. The bloodstone will need to be recharged before he can use it again." Finn drummed his fingertips against the table. "I suspect that Lucio will be able to do this for him. And if that happens, they'd be able to take down the barrier from any of the keystones. We can't allow that to happen."

Zebediah folded his arms. "We will stay and see how the political climate here changes. Assuming our lives aren't immediately forfeit for standing against Bentley, we will remain to guard the citadel." He looked past Brandon to Zak. "We will send Zak to go wherever Jade goes, of course."

Zandra coughed.

Garnet nodded from next to Ben. "As will I. She has a long road of physical recovery ahead of her, along with whatever life decisions she will be called on to make." Garnet cleared her throat and turned her face away as she lifted a hand to her eyes. "And we should stay together while we grieve my brother."

Zebediah slipped Garnet a deep purple handkerchief that she accepted with a barely audible "thanks."

Brandon closed his eyes and leaned back in his chair. "Assuming

I get released from Monomi custody—which will likely be dependent on the people's good graces of how much authority the Monomi keep—I think I'd like to join you on your search, Finn. There's nothing for me here right now." Brandon sighed and looked to the ceiling. Something in his haunted gaze hinted at the man of nobility that he used to be. He dipped his head down, letting his chopped hair cover his eyes. "Jaxton did something to my mind, and I suspect you're the only one with the skill needed to help heal me."

Finn rubbed a hand against his chin as he studied Brandon with narrowed eyes. "I suspect you could be right." He nodded once. "You'd be welcome to join us."

"Thank you." Brandon swallowed hard. "I need to find myself before I hurt my daughter again."

Heads turned toward Ben, and he rapped his knuckles against the table as he stared at the polished wood, weighing his options. He had no idea where Earth was, but that's where Sara was, and he had to find a way to return to her. He hadn't broken any promises to his sister yet, and he wasn't going to start now.

But what could he say to the group right now? The guy in the store that he and Briar had first stopped at ages ago had panicked at just the sight of Ben's dog tags. He clearly knew something, and had practically begged Ben to leave. Thus far, Ben had no idea what made someone a Void Born, but knowing how much hate and fear they got, it probably wasn't wise for Ben to suddenly announce, *"Hey guys, I'm pretty sure I lived in another world and probably died there because of a grenade, and now I'm here and want to go back. Does that make me a Void Born or something?"* Who knew what they'd do to a flesh-and-blood ghost?

Ben rubbed the shiny wood of the tabletop as he thought. He needed to find answers, and without giving himself away as someone, or even some*thing*, that didn't belong here. He leaned back in the chair and looked around the table. These people had taken him in, gotten him on his feet, and proved to be friends when he had none. How could he abandon them, now that they were hurting and in such desperate straits? He touched the dog tags and ring hidden under his shirt. He couldn't abandon Sara.

"Ben?" Garnet prompted. "What do you think you're going to do at this point? Continue traveling, even if the Sapphire isn't flying?"

Unbidden, the memory of Victor teaching him how to properly use the grappling hook gauntlet floated to the surface of his mind: *Victor cocked the spring in the wrist of the gauntlet and aimed it across the deck to a board they'd set up. "You should never have to ask for loyalty out of a man." He shot, and wood splintered as the hook embedded itself. Victor turned to face Ben with an odd half smile. "Either they're with you, or they aren't."*

Victor proved that he hadn't been with them at all, and Captain Slate had been the one to pay the price.

A plan clicked in Ben's mind. There was a way to help the *Sapphire* crew and the Monomi, as well as let him search for answers to get home.

"I'll travel with Finn and Raine." Ben clasped his hands and leaned over the table. "I want to hunt down Victor."

EPILOGUE

EVERETT

High Lord Everett Windsor smiled as the brunette beauty sashayed to him across his private chambers. Her sheer dressing gown left little to the imagination, and he stirred when she knelt before him.

It was beyond pleasurable to be the most powerful ruler.

A knock sounded from the door, and she stopped, looking up at him with a question in her eyes. He flicked his hand and she stood, backing away with a bow.

The interruption sounded again, and Everett trembled as anger replaced the satisfaction that had been pounding through his veins. He snatched his robe from the sandalwood-scented bed and shoved his hands through the sleeves, yanking it shut and tying it before flinging the door open.

"I told you I was not to be disturbed," Everett snapped at his guards. "What is it?" Motion caught his eye, and he frowned as Bentley slunk forward, head bent and palms up.

Bentley bowed deeply, his blond hair swinging forward and covering his ears. "My lord, I need to speak with you, immediately."

Curiosity allowed Everett to nod, but irritation made him slam the door as Bentley entered his chamber.

"You may stand right there," Everett ordered, pointing to the large tile by the door. He strode to his bed and pulled back part of the velvet curtain, revealing the bare legs of his current mistress. "Go to my bathing room. We're not finished."

She slipped out of the bed, clutching a sheet around her shoulders and curvaceous body while she scurried to the adjoining bathing chamber. Everett snapped his fingers to draw Bentley's eyes back to himself and away from his mistress.

Bentley cleared his throat and bowed again, freezing halfway down, and staying low. "My apologies for interrupting your—"

"Just tell me what news you have that's so urgent."

Bentley rose. Fear and anger blended in his eyes. "Princess Adeline survived."

Icy rage slid through Everett, and he gripped the sash of his bathrobe. "Did she, now? Tell me how that mistake was made. Is the barrier fixed?"

Bentley fiddled with the hem of his gray jacket and pressed his lips together. "She was critically injured, but survived." Bentley's tongue flicked out to lick his lips. "Many in the city have remained loyal to the Doldras family, and came to her aide. The Monomi included." He dipped his head. "I'm not sure about the keystone. The barrier had colors in it that I've never seen before, and the ground shook frequently. I left immediately after to inform you as quickly as possible."

Incompetent fool.

"I want that keystone fixed!" Everett raged, his hands fisted. He turned on his heel and marched across the soft rug before turning back, rubbing his temples. He needed a massage after this. "If that barrier goes down, my power is severely threatened. Fix. It. And that Doldran princess is a lingering plague. Eradicate it. I won't tolerate another failure."

Bentley's face paled while he nodded and bowed. "Yes, my lord."

Everett snapped his fingers as a new thought occurred to him. Bentley froze again. Everett stroked his chin as he considered, turning the idea over in his mind before speaking. "Return to Doldra. Do whatever you need to convince the plague to come here. I will greet her as the royalty she is, and I'll deal with her myself. I can use this to my political advantage."

"And if she refuses, sire?"

Everett rolled his eyes. "Then—oh, well. Do what you must to either get her to agree and come here, or finish her off yourself. And deal with the Monomi problem, while you're at it. We can't have a whole clan going back on their word, now, can we?"

"No, sir."

"I'm glad we have this understanding." Everett twitched his hand to the door and waited for Bentley to leave before he ground his teeth. *Expendable fool has lost his worth to me.* Everett paced in his chamber. He would need to contact his spy to learn more about Bentley's failure and what exactly had happened in Doldra. If the barrier had been weakened instead of strengthened, he'd have to marshal his forces, and before the other nobles of Aerugo scented blood. Marrying Doldra's queen had been politically advantageous, but if the true heir to Doldra's throne was to suddenly appear, those advantages would all crumble away. Unless there was a way to guarantee his family's ties to the Doldras bloodline. War always brought about uncertainty, and Everett wouldn't risk some ill-conceived and ill-timed threat against his throne while facing an inevitable invasion.

And if the nobles were to hear about this Doldran princess first? *She'll be married into our family or dead before they hear her name.* The Monomi would be a pain to eradicate, but threats had to be eliminated. Business was business, after all.

Everett growled and stomped toward the bathing chamber. He needed a diversion from this frustrating development.

As long as the keystone was fixed, the Monomi taken care of, Bentley's incompetence replaced, and the Doldran princess brought to heel before the leaders' summit, Everett had nothing to fear.

TO BE CONTINUED IN

VOID BORN

AUTUMN 2018

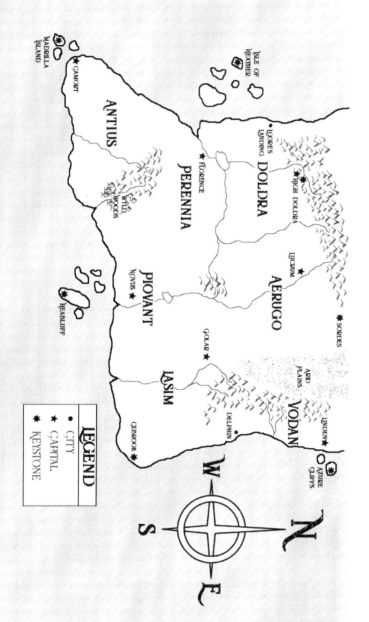

RENEGADE SKYFARER REGISTER

ADELINE DOLDRAS – Princess of Doldra, deceased

ANDRE CATALINA – Bodyguard and advisor to Prince Weston

ASH – Dragon hunter on the *Sapphire*

BRANDON DOLDRAS – Prince of Doldra, deceased

BRIAR SASPERIL – Chef on the *Sapphire*

ELINORA STOHNER – Head of Stohner Shipping Yards, Garnet and Slate's mother

ESTHER MONOMI – Wife to Zebediah

ETHAN BENTLEY – Governor over Doldra in Everett's stead

EVERETT WINDSOR – Ruler of Aerugo and Proxy Ruler of Doldra

GARNET STOHNER – Chief Liaison/Communications, Slate's twin sister

JADE STOHNER – Mechanic on the *Sapphire*

JAMES BRIGLEY – Family friend of the Stohners, ensign in the Doldra military police

JAXTON TAYLOR – Doctor on the *Sapphire*

KEENE – Navigator on the *Phoenix*

KERLEE – Dragon hunter on the *Sapphire*

KRISTA CEDRUS – Mechanic on the *Sapphire*

MICHAEL WORTHINGTON – Mechanic on the *Phoenix,* husband

to Rebecca Worthington

NEVIN – Bentley's right-hand man

REBECCA WORTHINGTON – First mate on the *Phoenix,* sister to Samantha Stohner

SAMANTHA STOHNER – Captain of the *Phoenix,* wife to Slate, mother to Jade

SAMUEL THISTLE – Advisor and uncle to Queen Violet

SAPPHIRE DOLDRAS – Wife to Brandon, deceased

SCHULTZ – Doctor on the *Phoenix*

SLATE STOHNER – Captain of the *Sapphire,* husband to Samantha, father to Jade

STEBAN – Shipwright of the *Phoenix*

VICTOR KALENDE – First mate on the *Sapphire*

VIOLET WINDSOR – Queen of Doldra and Aerugo WILLIAM CEDRUS – Shipwright of the *Sapphire,* father to Krista

WESTON WINDSOR – Prince of Doldra and Aerugo

ZABORAH MONOMI – Third eldest of Zak's siblings

ZANDRA MONOMI – Second eldest of Zak's siblings

ZANE MONOMI – Eldest of Zak's siblings, deceased

ZAK MONOMI – Combat Medic and Security Officer on the *Sapphire*

ZEBEDIAH MONOMI – Leader of the Monomi Clan

About RJ

During the day, Becky is a stay at home mom of two active little boys. When she has 'free time', she enjoys reading, writing, baking and sewing.

After many years of creative writing classes, writing fanfiction drabbles and daydreaming, it was high time to start writing her husband Mike's story. She dove into the world of Terrene and hasn't looked back—except for when she runs out of dark chocolate.

Any free time not spent in Terrene is typically expended on hosting dinner and game nights, running amok with the two little monkeys or watching nerdy movies with Mike.

For updates,
behind-the-scenes posts,
giveaways, and new releases,
visit RJMetcalf.com

More thrilling fantasy from FAYETTE

——— THE SENTINEL TRILOGY ———

Blood-bonds with angels. Surreal mental abilities. Elemental gods.

 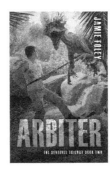 

The meteor storm wasn't such a big deal until a comet landed in the middle of the road. Now Darien's car is wrecked, his sister is bleeding out, and the only medical aid is at the reclusive Serran Academy.

Jet sees Darien for what he is: a lost teen who doesn't deserve to know about the aether gifts. And his sister's rare future-seeing ability is exactly what the enemy is after.

As fractured governments and shadow organizations vie for control of a dying world, the Serran Academy students—and their angelic secrets—are targeted for harvesting.

Made in the USA
Columbia, SC
30 July 2018